A Gathering

of

Angels

Also by Katherine Valentine

A Miracle for St. Cecilia's

A Gathering

of

Angels

Katherine Valentine

VIKING

F
Val

VIKING
Published by the Penguin Group
Penguin Putnam Inc., 375 Hudson Street, New York, New York 10014, U.S.A.
Penguin Books Ltd, 80 Strand, London WC2R 0RL, England
Penguin Books Australia Ltd, 250 Camberwell Road, Camberwell, Victoria 3124, Australia
Penguin Books Canada Ltd, 10 Alcorn Avenue, Toronto, Ontario, Canada M4V 3B2
Penguin Books India (P) Ltd, 11 Community Centre, Panchsheel Park, New Delhi –
110 017, India
Penguin Books (N.Z.) Ltd, Cnr Rosedale and Airborne Roads, Albany, Auckland,
New Zealand
Penguin Books (South Africa) (Pty) Ltd, 24 Sturdee Avenue, Rosebank, Johannesburg
2196, South Africa

Penguin Books Ltd, Registered Offices: Harmondsworth, Middlesex, England

First published in 2003 by Viking Penguin, a member of Penguin Putnam Inc.

10 9 8 7 6 5 4 3 2 1

PUBLISHER'S NOTE: This is a work of fiction. Names, characters, places, and incidents either
are the product of the author's imagination or are used fictitiously, and any resemblance to
actual persons, living or dead, business establishments, events, or locales is entirely coinci-
dental.

LIBRARY OF CONGRESS CATALOGING-IN-PUBLICATION DATA
Valentine, Katherine.
    A gathering of angels / Katherine Valentine.
      p. cm.
    ISBN 0-670-03229-8 (alk. paper)
    1. Catholic women—Fiction. 2. Connecticut—Fiction. 3. Churches—Fiction.
4. Miracles—Fiction. 5. Clergy—Fiction. I. Title.
PS3622.A44 R67 2003
813'.6—dc21   2002035935

This book is printed on acid-free paper. ∞

Printed in the United States of America

9-23-05
6040
23.95

To my dearest friend, my daughter, Heather, who has grown into an exceptional woman of grace, intelligence, and faith. If we are judged by the gifts our children present to the world then I will be judged well indeed.

Acknowledgments

Rosaries and the stories they evoke have intrigued me since I was a child. There was Louis Pasteur, who credited much of his discoveries to help he received while praying the rosary. Photos taken after Robert Kennedy was shot show him clutching a rosary as he lay dying on the floor of the Ambassador Hotel. On a personal note, a rosary from Medjugorje given me by a dear friend suddenly began to glow on the anniversary of my granddaughter's death.

These and countless other stories abound, which is why I was so delighted to highlight this special form of devotion to the Blessed Virgin Mary in this newest chapter in the Dorsetville series.

I wish to offer special thanks to Fire Chief Dan Jones of the North Chapel Hill Fire Department in North Carolina, who patiently walked me through the various fire-fighting procedures; and to Sergeant Paul Vance, the Public Information Officer for the Connecticut State Police Department, for his help in understanding the intricacies of a hit-and-run investigation.

A heartfelt thanks to all the St. John of the Cross quilters, who act as both prayer partners and sounding boards. They include: Shirley DeRito, Laurie Chisholm, Barbara Haggi, Mary Kaukas, Nancy Stroh, Evelyn Poremba, and Betty Cipriano. Thanks bunches! (Girls, I'm free again to quilt on Wednesday mornings.)

Once again a special thank you to all the wonderful priests who continue to intercede on my behalf, such as Father Daniel Francis and

Acknowledgments

Father Bill McCarthy. To all my readers who cheer me on with their letters and e-mails; and always to my dear *Saint Paul*, whose prayers continue to lift me above life's storms.

My main purpose in writing is never just to tell a good story, but to showcase God's faithfulness in the hopes it might stir readers' hearts and encourage them to seek a deeper relationship with Jesus Christ. My heartfelt good wishes go out to you all with the prayer fashioned by Saint Paul (no . . . not *my* Paul . . . the *real* Saint Paul) in the Ephesians:

"May the God of our Lord Jesus Christ, the Father of glory, give to you the spirit of wisdom and revelation in the knowledge of Him, the eyes of your understanding being enlightened; that you may know what is the hope of His calling, what are the riches of the glory of His inheritance in the saints and what is the exceeding greatness of His power toward us."

A Gathering

of

Angels

Medjugorje, Yugoslavia

The Apparitions

I t was August, and in the small Bosnian village of Medjugorje it was the worst heat wave any of the local peasants could remember. For nearly three weeks, temperatures of 100 degrees locked humid moisture in the valley like the lid on a pressure cooker. Under this great dome of liquid heat were packed thousands of pilgrims who had come from all points of the globe to experience the town where the Blessed Virgin Mary was reported to have been appearing daily for nearly two decades.

By eight o'clock in the morning the sky had disappeared under a white blanket of haze that slowly drifted downward, obscuring most of the farmland below. Acres of Herzegovenian tobacco to the south and the famous Zilavka and Blatina vineyards to the north baked as waves of heat rose off the plants. By ten o'clock the valley had seemingly begun to melt under the relentless heat, filling the air with the smell of over-ripened fruit cooking under the sun's searing flames and rendering limp the leaves of thousands of cherry, plum, pear, peach, apple, apricot and marasca trees, which now pointed downward as though in surrender.

The village peasants had hoped the oppressive heat might stem the tidal wave of people that ebbed and flowed, like an ocean tide, into the town—powered by their need to touch, to feel, to be part of the extraordinary happenings that had turned this obscure village into a holy shrine.

For it was here, on June 24, 1981, that the Blessed Virgin Mary first

1

appeared to six children on a small mountain now called Apparition Hill. This hundred-meter circular plain of ground, once filled with brambles and wildflowers, was now bare of all vegetation, trodden under the footfalls of the millions of pilgrims who walked this pathway each year, searching for miracles of their own.

Nothing, it seemed, could keep the pilgrims away, not even the soaring temperatures that filled the crude hospital on the outskirts of the town with victims of heatstroke, severe sunburn and dehydration. For the last three weeks, pilgrims had lined the hallways in various stages of physical discomfort. Those whose symptoms were more severe—cardiac patients and the elderly—were sent by ambulance (a rusted-out 1952 Oldsmobile station wagon that also served as the town's hearse) to the larger facility in Mostar.

The medical personnel—local people who had grown accustomed to the daily apparitions and the religious zeal they produced—just shook their heads, privately stating that the pilgrims would be better served if they had also packed their suitcases with some common sense.

Medjugorje was comprised of thirty-five hundred citizens whose numbers swelled to the tens of thousands as pilgrims flooded in, overrunning every available space, seeping into every home, until the hamlet swelled like a soaked sponge unable to absorb any more. In an effort to accommodate this ever-rising tide, hotels and hostels were hastily erected by local businessmen, inciting some to dub the Blessed Virgin Mary as "The Lady of Foreign Currency."

Tour groups came from India, Iran, Australia, Brazil, Ukraine, the United States, Canada, Finland; from cosmopolitan cities, farmlands, suburbia, deserts and plains. Christians, Muslims, Jews, Hindus and Buddhists alike came to this obscure place. Some came in search of their lost selves. Some came for redemption. Forgiveness. Renewal. But almost everyone, if questioned, would admit that he or she came hoping to witness a miracle.

Since the beginning, miracles had been associated with the apparitions, first witnessed as a bright light that illuminated the mountainside when Mary first appeared to the children. Later, thousands would watch spellbound as the sun spun on its axis, as it had done at Fatima.

And, more recently, photographs taken of the outside of St. James Church during the apparitions, when developed, revealed an overlayed image of the Madonna and Child. Stories of miraculous healings also abounded. Collectively, they helped to swell the daily surge of pilgrims in search of confirmation of the Divine.

Most agreed, however, that the stories about the rosaries that miraculously appeared during apparitions were the most intriguing.

It was another hot, sultry evening, as the pilgrims—as wilted as the landscape that surrounded them—began to merge around St. James Church. It was nearing 6:40 P.M., time of the daily apparition.

Positioned upstairs, to the right of the sanctuary, was a ten-by-twelve-foot alcove where a small group of men and women were seated on the bare wooden floor, having been chosen either by special influence or by Divine Providence to witness that evening's apparition. Seventy-two-year-old Sister Regina Francis sat among them. It was the last evening of her weeklong visit to Medjugorje, a place that she had yearned to visit for nearly twenty years and which now—much too soon—she must leave.

Tomorrow, Sister Regina Francis would begin her journey back to Dorsetville, a small New England town along the Connecticut River where her order, the Daughters of the Immaculate Conception of the Blessed Virgin Mary, had just finished renovating an old mansion that was to be used as a retirement home for the religious. As soon as she returned, there was to be an elaborate dedication ceremony for the facility, which was being named in her honor in recognition of her years of service to the elderly and the poor. A Mass was to be celebrated by the bishop. But even the excitement of that event paled in comparison to what she was experiencing now.

The air in the small alcove was heavy with the smell of sweat, stale perfume and garlic, the latter used most generously in cooking by the host families who opened their homes to pilgrims. Sister Regina Francis and her traveling companion, Sister Claire, were staying in one of these homes owned by a Mrs. Zolvoč. It was Mrs. Zolvoč who had slipped the highly prized invitation to St. James Church into the nun's hand just before dinner.

"I am sorry that I could not get another one for your companion," Mrs. Zolvoč said in her thick Croatian accent.

"Don't worry about Sister Claire," said Sister Regina Francis, with tears of deep gratitude in her eyes. "She will only feel joy for me." She searched the deep pockets of her habit for a handkerchief. "I have prayed against all hope that I would be allowed to be present during an apparition and now it's come to pass. I can hardly believe it."

"The Lord answers all our prayers in His time and in His own way," said Mrs. Zolvoč with the authority of someone who had come to trust the Lord for all of her needs. "Now come. Eat some dinner before it's time to leave."

But Sister Regina Francis barely touched her food. She was too excited, eager to begin the twenty-minute walk back to the church. Sister Claire eyed her anxiously, having been sent by their Mother Superior to watch over the older nun who had recently recovered from a heart attack. Sister Regina Francis ignored her concern.

As it neared six o'clock, Sister Regina Francis began to grow impatient with Sister Claire, who had mislaid her prayer book and was rummaging through their room. Unable to contain herself one second longer, Sister Regina Francis gathered her things and headed out into the oppressive heat.

"I'll meet you later after the Mass," she said, shutting the door on Sister Claire's protests.

Feeling free at last, Sister Regina Francis indulged her growing sense of excitement and rushed across the fields like a schoolchild, hiking her heavy blue habit up above her knees, heedless of the sharp, arthritic pain in her hip joints. She arrived at the church in just under ten minutes.

Ignoring the heaviness in her chest and an increasingly rapid heartbeat, she took the steps leading to the church alcove two at a clip. By the time she had reached the landing at the top, her breath was coming in short, labored spurts, and a wave of dizziness made her feel lightheaded and nauseous. She reached out for the wall to steady herself.

If only she could sit down and rest, but there were no chairs, only a small, makeshift altar and bare floors. Unable to stand any longer, and fearful that she might faint, she carefully slid down onto the floor and modestly covered her legs with her skirts.

By the time the others began to arrive, however, she was feeling better. The dizziness had passed. Her breathing had returned to normal. Once again, she was filled with a sense of great excitement. She even managed to smile brightly as the others in the room, like her, sought a modicum of comfort. Some leaned against the walls. Others made little cushions out of sweaters and backpacks, and it seemed everyone was dabbing their foreheads with wadded tissues as the temperature in the tiny space soared. Someone passed around a bottle of water as they all began to speak excitedly about the apparitions.

The heavy wooden door being drawn fully open sounded below and a wedge of sunlight shone at the top of the stairs. Sister Regina Francis looked up expectantly, as did the others, their attention riveted on the muffled footsteps that brushed against the wooden stairs. The three visionaries had arrived.

Ivan Dragicevic, Vicka Ivankovic and Marija Pavlovic quickly walked into the room. They had been children when the Blessed Virgin Mary had first appeared. Now in their thirties, they were still possessed of the shyness of youth. All three avoided eye contact as they hurriedly took their places in front of the two-foot-high altar that was covered with purple embroidered cloth depicting religious themes. Fresh flowers had been placed in an earthenware jar in the center of the cloth. Several votive candles completed the embellishments.

Ivan reached inside his pants pocket for his rosary. Vicka and Marija already held theirs in their hands. Together, they made the sign of the cross, then joined in the Our Father from the sanctuary below—a prayer that now filled the church with its cadence, coursing like an electrical current that charged the air with a sense of expectancy.

Sister Regina Francis prayed along, her attention, like those of the other pilgrims, riveted on the faces of the visionaries. Moments later, the three's eyes were drawn upward, locked on a space about five feet above the altar. They were instantly transformed: their eyes illuminated with an unearthly glow, beatific smiles exploded across their faces. Many in the room would later recount how circular rays seemed to emanate from the crowns of their heads.

In union, the three visionaries fell to their knees. Everyone in the room followed suit. The Blessed Virgin Mary had arrived.

Sister Regina Francis watched in rapt fascination as the three moved their lips in silent conversations, often nodding as though they had received some instruction. Although no one in the room could hear what was being said between the visionaries and the apparition, nor see the Blessed Mother, the nun had no doubt that what was transpiring was real.

Then the truly unexpected happened.

A rosary of cerulean blue glass beads appeared from out of nowhere. One second, the space had been empty. The next, there it was, hovering in the air just inches above the visionaries' heads. Someone gasped. A man fainted.

The rosary remained suspended for several seconds, then gently slipped through space as though released from some invisible hand. Marija caught the beads just inches before they fell to the floor, then nodded toward the apparition as though receiving further instructions.

A woman beside Sister Regina Francis began to tremble. Several others began to recite the Magnificat. Then, as quickly as it had begun, the apparition was over and the three visionaries' faces dimmed like snuffed candles. They sat quietly for several moments, their eyes closed in prayer, then leaned back onto the soles of their shoes, made the sign of the cross and got up to leave. Only Marija lagged behind, scanning the pilgrims' faces as though looking for someone in particular. The rosary was draped in her right hand. Finally her gaze settled on Sister Regina Francis and she headed her way. A middle-aged man, a translator, trailed closely behind.

"Our Lady said this is for your village," Marija said in Croatian, offering the rosary. The interpreter quickly translated.

Sister Regina Francis, who had remained kneeling, tilted her head back to look up into Marija's face.

"Our Blessed Mother wishes this to be brought to your village,"

Marija explained. "She knows the special devotion the people of your parish have shown for your church and she is very pleased. She wants you to know that she continues to intercede on their behalf to her Son."

Sister Regina Francis reached out a tentative hand, tears flowing copiously down her weathered checks. "Our Lady has entrusted it to me?" she whispered.

Marija nodded as though she understood the nun's confusion, then smiled sweetly before turning to speak to the translator.

"She wants to know if she might pray for you?" he asked.

"I'd . . . I'd be honored," the nun stammered.

Marija stepped closer, raising her hands to place them on top of the nun's veil. As she prayed, the rosary vibrated with a strange soft hum. Sister Regina Francis clutched it tighter to her breast. When Marija finished her prayer, the nun found she was too drained to rise. Instead, she weakly squeezed Marija's hand. The visionary smiled shyly; then, with a wave to the others, who had sat spellbound by the exchange, she hurried out of the room and back down the steep wooden steps. As soon as the downstairs door opened, the crowds outside began to call out Marija's name.

Slowly, one by one, the others in the upper room rose and quietly filed past, some reaching out a hand to touch Sister Regina Francis's habit as though to draw forth a special blessing.

At last the alcove was empty and Sister Regina Francis was left with a plethora of emotions. She rose painfully to her feet and adjusted her habit, which had adhered itself to her back like wallpaper to a wall. Suddenly she felt as though every morsel of energy had been drained from her body. Just standing was an effort. She glanced in the direction of the stairs. Could she make it down unaided? But what choice did she have? There was no one left to help her, and she was too proud to call for help. She gathered her resolve and took a tentative step. Immediately, a sharp pain tightened around her chest like a tourniquet. She stood absolutely still, willing it to go way, and drew in a slow, labored breath. The pain only grew more unbearable as she fought against a rising sense of panic.

A bright light flashed directly above the altar, then flashed again. Was the pain inducing hallucinations, she wondered? The light came a third time, only now it had expanded, and from its center a shape began to form. Sister Regina Francis clutched her chest as a voice sounded: *"Fear not, Sister Regina."*

Sister Regina Francis watched as the image came into sharp focus. It was the Blessed Virgin Mary suspended on a small white cloud. She was dressed in a gray robe with a long white veil, from which wisps of chestnut hair had escaped. Stationed at her feet was a ring of roses whose sweet-perfumed fragrance filled the sanctuary.

"I'm not afraid, Blessed Mother," Sister Regina Francis finally managed to reply.

"Come, my child," the Blessed Virgin Mary said, stretching out a hand. *"My Son has sent me to bring you home."*

Sister Regina Francis hurried toward the vision like a child into the outstretched arms of a mother. No longer could she feel the floor beneath her feet or the sharp pain in her chest. The rosary she was holding slipped onto the floor.

And, as naturally as the smoke of incense rising during a High Mass, her spirit rose as her mortal body fell away like a discarded garment. Only once did the nun look back over her shoulder to view her lifeless body lying crumpled on the floor. Yet she felt no sense of alarm. She was pure spirit now, as she rose to meet the Queen of Peace. She gazed into Mary's gentle face and stretched out her hand, which Mary took into hers.

"Come, my child," the Blessed Virgin Mary said, as they began to ascend into the heavens. *"Come and see what my Son has fashioned for you since the beginning of time."*

Sister Claire prayed that Sister Regina Francis's coffin—held in place with only lengths of threadbare twine that had been strung together as a sort of makeshift rope—would not fall off the roof of the bus as the rickety vehicle made its steep descent along the narrow twisting roads that led from Medjugorje to the Adriatic Sea. The crude wooden coffin had shifted twice since they started out, scraping across the top of the metal roof, sounding as though it would fly off at any minute, plunging Sister Regina Francis's remains into the sea five hundred feet below.

Although it had been less than twelve hours since the nun had died, her body had already been embalmed and the small earth brown pine casket hermetically sealed with plastic, like a deli sandwich from a Subway shop. A small window on the front of the coffin had been cut out to expose her face, for under no circumstances was the plastic to be removed. The Yugoslavian health officer who had handed Sister Claire the death certificate, along with several other forms attesting that the nun had died of noncontagious, natural causes, had been most adamant about this. It appeared that Sister Regina Francis would have to be buried sealed like a time capsule.

Sister Claire reached inside the deep pockets of her habit and pulled out the rosary that had been found near Sister Regina Francis's body. She examined the strand more closely: cerulean blue glass beads and an intricately carved silver crucifix. It was beautiful but not unlike the dozens of rosaries she had seen throughout her life; yet there was something different about it, something comforting. She turned it over in her hands. Funny, she didn't remember Sister Regina Francis owning a set like this.

"They found this next to Sister Regina Francis's body," Mrs. Zolvoč had said, slipping the rosary into Sister Claire's hand.

What would she have done if it weren't for the help of this formidable woman who had completely taken charge? She had arranged for a local doctor to sign the death certificate and the town's mortician to ready the body for transport. Sister Claire was insistent that she would not leave Sister Regina Francis behind.

The only thing that Mrs. Zolvoč couldn't seem to do was help Sister Claire send a telegram back home to Mother Superior.

"Lines are down all over the country," she had said. "The heat wave has caused massive power outages."

Although that conversation had taken place just twelve hours before, it felt much, much longer. She was tired, so very tired, and she longed for the comfort of her own bed back home, the other sisters' friendly faces, the familiar landscape. Besides that, she longed for a good old-fashioned cry, something she hadn't felt free to do under the circumstances. She rubbed her temples, wondering how much longer it would be before they reached the airport.

Oh, why had she allowed Mother Mary Veronica to talk her into accompanying Sister Regina Francis to Medjugorje, even though both of them knew this trip was a foolhardy venture for an old woman with a bad heart? But Mother Superior had been adamant, and she was, after all, her prioress. Sister Regina Francis was going to Medjugorje and Sister Claire was to be her chaperone.

"Me?" Sister Claire had asked incredulously when Mother Mary Veronica announced her decision. "Why me? Can't Sister Theresa or Sister Bernadette go instead?"

Mother Mary Veronica had overseen the renovations on the home and handled the various state and local permits. Sister Claire was in charge of setting up the interior, which had been a relatively easy task until it came to the home's commercial kitchen. It seemed no matter what she did, how hard she tried, someone from either the local or state health or building department found fault. The kitchen had yet to meet everyone's regulations and she had only a few weeks before the residents were scheduled to arrive. Sister Claire had taken to long novenas to Saint Joseph and a nip of sherry every evening before bed.

"Dozens of things still have to be done before our official opening. Furniture deliveries have to be scheduled and there's another inspection from the health department."

"What's it this time?"

"They want to test the temperatures on all the ovens and refrigerator units." Sister Claire cast her eyes heavenward. "Please, Lord, let it pass this time." She took a breath, then rattled on, fueled by nervous energy. "Room assignments must be completed: Like Sister Joanna, who snores. Deviated septum, her medical papers say. Now, she will need a roommate who is basically deaf . . . and who may or may not snore . . .

so neither is disturbed at night. Then there's the ongoing problem with the appliance store over the dent in our new clothes washer . . ."

Mother Mary Veronica threw up a hand. "I know, I know. I was counting on your capable administrative talents, but this can't be helped. We'll just have to delegate some of these things to the other sisters."

Sister Claire met this suggestion with an eye roll.

"Like who? Sister Theresa . . . bless her soul, a kind and gentle spirit . . . but she couldn't organize a spelling bee let alone all the things that need to be done. And Sister Bernadette is a disaster anytime you put her in charge of something in the house. Remember when you put her in charge of menu planning and she ordered twenty cases of lima beans? I still gag every time I see one of those things."

"You're right, I know. Your talents would obviously be better served here," Mother Superior said. "But I need someone I can trust to accompany Sister Regina Francis and you're it. Medjugorje is thousands of miles away. Should something happen, I want to know that Sister Regina Francis is in capable hands."

"But Mother Mary Veronica," Claire implored. "Why not convince her to take her trip *after* the opening ceremonies? When things calm down? Besides that, there's Sister Regina's health to consider. It's only been a few months since her heart attack. What if we were to ask her doctors to advise her not to travel?"

Sister Claire looked hopeful even though Mother Superior had already begun to shake her head. "I've talked to the doctors and they *have* advised Sister Regina Francis not to travel. But Sister won't hear of delaying this trip. You know how she is when she's set her mind on something. There's little anyone can do to dissuade her."

That was true enough. Sister Regina Francis could be more stubborn than a farmer's mule. Sister Claire tried another approach. "What if you ordered her to stay?"

Mother Superior laughed. "Order Sister Regina to stay? It's not very likely she'd listen even if I had the courage to do it."

"I suppose you're right."

Sister Regina had been their prioress before taking ill and had ruled with an iron hand. Both Sister Claire and Mother Mary Veronica were still more accustomed to taking orders from this indomitable woman than issuing them.

Sister Claire heaved a ponderous sigh. "Are you certain that there is no one else you could send?"

"No one I trust with this type of responsibility."

"Then I suppose I'm going."

"I suppose you are." Mother Superior couldn't help smiling. "And don't worry about things back here. This is God's ministry, not ours. He'll make certain that everything gets done in time for the opening."

"I hope you're right. I'd hate to return to find our residents sleeping out in the streets."

"'O ye of little faith,'" Mother Superior reprimanded. "God has brought us this far. What makes you think He would abandon us now?"

And so, reluctantly, Sister Claire had accompanied the elderly nun to Medjugorje . . . and now Sister Regina Francis was dead. Oh, how was she going to break the news to Mother Superior?

Bob Peterson also watched the Bosnian countryside slip past the bus windows. He, too, had been on a pilgrimage to Medjugorje in thanksgiving to the Blessed Mother, whose intercession he had invoked throughout his illness and petitions to whom he was certain had helped bring about his healing.

It still was somewhat hard to believe. Less than a few months ago, he had been dying of leukemia. His only hope had been a bone marrow transplant. But for nearly a year a match could not be found. There wasn't anyone he knew who hadn't been tested. Even his little seven-year-old daughter, Sarah, had bravely allowed the doctors to insert a large needle into the base of her spine and extract a bone marrow sample. It hadn't been a match.

Finally, as the months waned on, Bob resigned himself to his fate. The frequent blood transfusions were no longer able to stem the disease, nor were his veins able to sustain the damage from constant abuse. Finally a shunt had been inserted into his left forearm. Bob was self-conscious of the scar and wore long-sleeve shirts even in this heat to hide the deep purple area that ran six inches long on the inside of his lower arm and looked as though someone had scooped out a section of his flesh with a melon baller. Worse was the constant pain due to the damage done to the nerve endings around the site. But Bob didn't complain. He felt it a fair trade-off, especially when he remembered that less than five months ago the oncologists had given him only six, maybe eight months tops, to live.

Funny, now that he looked back on that time, how he had never felt any fear. His Catholic faith had steaded him well, and he knew, with as much certainty as anyone this side of heaven can know, that this life was but a foretaste of things to come.

No, he hadn't been afraid to die. It was the thought of leaving his wife, Lori, and their daughter behind that had grieved him.

Bob pulled out a recent photograph he kept in his shirt pocket that was badly dog-eared. It had been taken on the front steps of Mercy Hospital the day he had been released and declared cancer free. He wondered if there had ever been a happier family portrait.

A bone marrow donor had been finally found. A perfect match, the doctors said. The procedure went better than expected. A month followed in isolation, by the end of which the doctors gave him a clean bill of health. The transplant had been a success. And, although none of the doctors would dare say the world "healed," his white blood cell count remained normal. All cancer cells had disappeared.

Bob studied the photo, etching the outline of his wife and daughter with his index finger. Sarah stood with her arms wrapped around his leg as though saying, You're never going to leave without me again. Lori stood to his right, her dark brown hair falling slightly into her face, looking very much like the high school sweetheart who had stolen his heart during his senior year. He studied her eyes. Something about them was different. There was an inner strength there that had not been there before he'd taken sick. Part of it came from her job at the Country Kettle. Lori had been forced to take over the role of bread-winner several months into his illness.

Although she had never worked outside the home before, Lori stoically set out to find a job. Bob had watched her put on a brave front but was not fooled: he knew she was scared. It nearly ate him up knowing that there was nothing he could do to alleviate those fears. Instead, he prayed and prayed and prayed as he had never prayed before. He prayed one large circular prayer beginning with *Lord, please let me live,* and ending with *Lord, give Lori the confidence needed to take care of herself and our daughter if I don't make it.*

God had answered part of that prayer through a help wanted sign in the window at the Country Kettle. Owner Harry Clifford had taken Lori on as a waitress even though she had no experience. But then, that was just like Harry, whose heart was bigger than the whole eastern seaboard. He had patiently showed her the ropes—how to greet customers, take orders (mistakes were good-naturedly fed to Ethel Johnson's golden retriever), the proper way to make coffee (Harry's coffee was known for miles around as the best in the valley), bus tables, set up for lunch, how to run the antiquated cash register. Harry became like a big brother to Lori and a good friend to Bob, loaning the Petersons his van, so Bob could lie down for the thirty-minute ride to and from the hospital, and baby-sitting Sarah.

The sun streamed in the side window and caught Bob in the eye. He shifted over toward the center aisle.

He thought of all the people in his hometown of Dorsetville who had helped throughout his illness. Of course, there was Father James, the parish priest at St. Cecilia's Catholic Church and who was also a dear family friend. Father James had continued to encourage him not to give up hope.

"None of us know the mind of God," Father James had assured him. "And I believe with all of my heart that the age of miracles is not past. Besides, you have a whole town praying for your recovery. That's a lot of prayer power."

One of those praying was Harriet Bedford. Harriet owned a small nursery on the north side of their small valley and was also known as St. Cecilia's mightiest prayer warrior. Harriet kept a small journal filled with prayer requests of those in need of heavenly assistance. Most everyone in town had a story of how their needs were met after being listed in Harriet's journal. Now Bob was one of them.

Besides prayers, the people in Dorsetville also lent an outstretched hand. Sheriff Bromley, often referred to as "The Rottweiler" for the way he could intimidate even the most hardened criminal with just one sober look, patrolled by their home twice a day, checking in to see if Bob needed anything while Lori was at work. Later, the sheriff had sent Matthew Metcalf over to shovel the Petersons' driveway when it snowed and later to mow the lawn.

"Judge Peale has leveled some community service on the boy," the sheriff explained. "Your home is a good place for him to begin."

Matthew had been given one hundred hours of community service for his part in a hoax that had turned Dorsetville upside down. The sixteen-year-old had "borrowed" some expensive lasers from the nearby university, which he used to create a holographic image of the Blessed Virgin Mary that was beamed into an empty nave inside St. Cecilia's Church.

The idea had come to him when his grandfather and friends were lamenting the loss of a statue of the Blessed Virgin Mary that had been broken during a small repair project. The men were concerned that the recent announcement that St. Cecilia's was to be closed after the Easter service had less to do with the building's state of disrepair than the fact that the missing statue had somehow "jinxed" the church. Knowing that the beleaguered church could ill afford to replace the expensive statue, Matthew lit upon a plan to create a hologram instead. But while testing the image inside the church, it was mistaken for a real Marian apparition and within days hundreds of pilgrims had descended on the town.

Bob always smiled when he recounted it. And some people think life in a small New England town is dull!

No, Bob couldn't think of living anywhere else. He took strength from the rolling countryside, the rushing streams and the smell of fresh country air. But mostly he felt that there was no better place to raise a family than in a small town. Apparently, God felt the same way. He chose a small village, after all, to raise His only Son. As far as Bob was concerned, there were no finer people in the entire world than in Dorsetville.

Take George Benson, for instance. George was the town's fire marshal and heating and air-conditioning specialist. Oh, he had a way of irritating just about everyone with his outlandish opinions issued freely in a voice normally used to address the hearing impaired, but he had kept the Petersons' furnace running smoothly throughout Bob's illness and always managed to somehow "forget" to leave a bill.

Chester Platt was the same way. Chester ran his own construction company, and when the Petersons' gutters rotted away, and the resulting runoff of water turned to ice on their driveway, he showed up with his crew.

"We can't have you falling down on the ice and breaking something," Chester said.

Bob tried to protest. There was no money in their budget for home repairs. Chester waved aside his concerns.

"Listen, you'd do the same for me, wouldn't you? Besides, it's no big deal. I just finished putting some gutters up on a house over in Woodstock and have a lot of material left over. Take my guys half a day to install that section over the kitchen."

But when Chester's men pointed out later that most of the gutters around the Petersons' Victorian home were either rotted or in peril of falling down, Chester called in another order of aluminum and had his crew refit the entire house.

Bob had gone to see him a couple of weeks after getting out of the hospital.

"I still haven't gotten that bill," he reminded Chester.

Chester looked up from the plans he was studying and gave Bob a crooked smile.

"I hear Doc Hammon gave you a clean bill of health, is that right?"

"Yep, I'm cancer free and fit as a fiddle," Bob said proudly.

"I suppose you'll be looking for a job."

"Yes, as a matter of fact, I thought I'd start searching for something today. Heard there were some openings over at the Home Depot in Waterbury."

"How about working for me instead?"

"For you?"

Chester rolled up the plans he had been studying and handed them across his desk to Bob.

"I know you did some estimating for the mill when it was opened. Assistant project manager, weren't you?"

Bob nodded.

"Then how would you like to help me manage some of my projects? I could really use someone with your cost-estimating background." Chester watched Bob hesitate. "I've got steady work and I could use the help. And besides, didn't you say you wanted to pay me back? Well, this sure would be a good beginning."

"You've hired yourself a project manager," Bob said and shook his hand. He started that same day.

Raised voices outside the bus drew Bob back from his thoughts. A small group of children had gathered alongside the dirt road and were now shouting and waving energetically as the bus passed by. Bob waved back. Locals on the bus shook handkerchiefs, shouting greetings in their native Slavic tongue.

Farther along the road stood a small girl with big, luminous brown eyes and a wide grin in a dress that was several sizes too small. On her head she wore a babushka. His Sarah often wore a babushka when she helped Lori in the kitchen. The little girl waved shyly as the bus drove past. Bob leaned out the window and tossed her a handful of coins. She quickly scrambled to scoop them up, yelling foreign words that Bob had no problem interpreting as being filled with thanks.

He leaned his head against the seat and closed his eyes. Medjugorje had been a wonderful experience and he had savored every moment of his visit. But suddenly he was overcome with a sense of homesickness, a dull ache that had settled around his heart. He missed his family. His home. Harry's coffee. He smiled. He could hardly wait to get back to Dorsetville.

The bus slowed and then stopped. A sharp bend in the road required the driver to back up to the edge of a dangerous precipice, then inch the twenty-four-foot vehicle back and forth in an effort to negotiate the turn. Several of the passengers began to murmur. Suddenly the right wheel slipped over the edge and the bus listed slightly to one side. Voices merged into a unified scream, followed by a deadly silence. Dozens of rosaries suddenly appeared.

Women seated at the back of the bus, which was perched over a five-hundred-foot drop to the sea below, began to cry. The bus driver spoke rapidly in Croatian, smiling into the rearview mirror as though to assure everyone that there was no need for alarm. Two more hair-raising maneuvers and the bus was once again safely ambling down the narrow mountain road. The atmosphere inside the bus lightened considerably.

Sister Claire remained lost in a montage of images recorded during the last few days and barely noticed the man seated near the front of the bus get up and pat the driver on the back until she heard him speak.

"Great job!" the man said enthusiastically. "For a minute there, I thought you weren't going to make it."

The bus driver nodded, then smiled as though he understood, his face flushed with pride.

"You're American!" Sister Claire shouted spontaneously from the back of the bus.

"Why yes, Sister, I am," answered the personable young man, his face lighting up like travelers' faces do when meeting fellow country-men abroad. "My name's Bob Peterson." He walked back to greet her, extending a hand.

"Nice to meet you, Mr. Peterson. I'm Sister Claire."

"What part of the States are you from?" she asked.

"A little New England town along the Connecticut River called Dorsetville."

"Dorsetville? What an incredible coincidence."

"Do you know it?" Bob asked.

"Know it? Why, I'm headed back there myself."

"You are? To Dorsetville? What a small world."

The bus hit a huge bump. People bounced several inches off their seats. Bob had no choice but to grab onto the overhead luggage rack with his bad arm to keep from falling on Sister Claire. The bus came down hard against the packed-dirt road, sending a wrenching pain up the length of his arm whose epicenter was the area where the shunt had been removed. Quickly following, the bus lumbered through a succession of deep potholes, tossing passengers to the left and right. A woman, seated toward the front, cried out as her head slammed hard against a side window. Bob clung to the rack more tightly and winced with pain.

"Oh, dear, my rosary," Sister Claire cried. It had flown out of her hand, landing underneath a seat toward the rear of the bus.

"You sit right there. I'll get it," Bob offered.

He carefully threaded his way along the aisle, steadying himself by holding the backs of the seats with his good arm. The other arm felt as though it were on fire. Had he torn something, he wondered, with that last jolt? He'd better have Doc Hammon look at it when he got back home. The pain had gotten worse throughout this trip. Maybe there was something Doc could do, perhaps some kind of surgery to repair the nerve.

Bob gripped the metal side of a seat with his good hand and worked through the pain as he extended his injured hand to grasp the rosary. His fingers were closing around the beads when suddenly he felt something like an electrical current shoot up his arm. He yelled out with surprise.

"Are you all right, Mr. Peterson?" Sister Claire called in alarm as she started to rise.

He waved her back. "Yes, I'm fine. See, I've got it." He stood and held out the rosary.

Bob had taken two steps back toward Sister Claire when the bus hit another succession of bumps. The force made his teeth rattle. He grabbed ahold of the luggage rack again and held on for dear life.

Several passengers screamed something at the driver in their local dialect. The driver yelled back, then threw up his hands as though to say, What can I do?

Finally, Bob made it back to Sister Claire and handed her the rosary.

"Thank you, Mr. Peterson."

"Please call me Bob."

"Bob, then, it is. This belonged to Sister Regina Francis." She quickly explained about the nun's sudden death. "I wouldn't want to lose this." She shoved the rosary into her deep skirt pocket.

They made arrangements to meet when they arrived at the airport and Bob offered to help Sister Claire negotiate the transportation of Sister Regina Francis's body back to the States.

"I'm afraid that I don't know much about these kinds of things, but I'd be more than happy to offer any assistance I can."

Sister Claire thanked him profusely.

That settled, he made his way back toward the front of the bus. It wasn't until he had reclaimed his empty seat and was reshuffling his bags that he realized the constant pain in his arm was completely gone.

"That's strange."

He rotated his arm this way, then that way. Nothing. The pain had completely vanished.

"Well, if that isn't the darnedest thing," he said out loud.

Later, Bob Peterson would discover that more than the pain had disappeared. The thick purple scar that had once covered his lower arm had also vanished.

Chapter 1

It seemed the town green had been filled with the sound of hammers, diesel trucks, rock music and hordes of construction workers in various modes of undress for months. In fact, it had been eighteen months since both the Sister Regina Francis Retirement Home and St. Cecilia's renovations had begun. Although the retirement home had been completed right on schedule, due exclusively to Mother Superior's vigilance, the repairs on the church and the rectory had barely begun, due to Father James's constant indecision and unwillingness to hold anyone accountable to a timetable.

"Sometimes things take longer than we think they should," he had told Mrs. Norris, the housekeeper, whose expression showed she wasn't buying it.

The rectory kitchen and most of the rooms downstairs had remained in a type of renovation limbo since the project had begun, suspended somewhere between being ripped apart and being put back together. The refrigerator stood on the back porch, where it had been moved last fall so the tile man could examine the kitchen's subflooring. Since that time only the plywood flooring had been replaced but new linoleum had yet to be laid. Father James couldn't decide between a brown brick pattern, which didn't come in no-wax finish but was a heavier grade, versus the gray slate pattern that was no-wax but was much thinner. Mrs. Norris had watched Father James, slumped over the tile samples for weeks, looking as though the decision might be eternal and therefore never subject to recall.

"If we get the no-wax, that will certainly cut down on your work-load," he told her. "But the other will last longer and be more beneficial to the church's long-range budget. I don't know, Mrs. Norris, what do you think?"

She had told him repeatedly it didn't matter to her in the least what he chose. Pick whatever one you want, she said. She wouldn't be around long enough to care one way or the other.

Mrs. Norris had decided that she was dying ever since embarking on a family genealogy the previous fall that uncovered the gruesome fact that none of the women on her father's side of the family had ever lived past the age of sixty. Mrs. Norris was sixty-two, which could only mean that her death was already two years overdue. Although Doc Hammon had been unable to diagnose what she was in peril of dying from, Mrs. Norris held firm to her belief.

"Genes don't lie," she said, tight-lipped.

And it was a good thing she was dying, she told Father James, be-cause if she wasn't she would have quit as soon as the first construction worker laid siege in her kitchen. But, since she was dying, she had de-cided to conserve her energy for things that really mattered—like find-ing the four-quart bowl of ambrosia that she had made yesterday afternoon before going home and which was now missing. It was meant for the luncheon this afternoon after the retirement home's dedication ceremony. The entire town had been invited. Even the bishop was to attend.

"Well, it just didn't get up and walk out of here." Mrs. Norris was bent at the waist, her head deep inside the refrigerator, as she moved items back and forth as if a four-quart bowl could be hidden easily. "No, it's just not in here."

Father James could hear the refrigerator door slam shut, then Mrs. Norris's heavy footsteps march back into the kitchen. He also noticed that Father Dennis, seated beside him at the kitchen table, seemed in-ordinately engrossed in the Lifestyle section of the morning's paper.

Hands on hips, right foot slightly extended, tapping out a malevolent code on the plywood flooring, Mrs. Norris asked in her most testy voice, "Which one of you took it? Fess up."

She looked straight at Father James, who, through habit, involuntarily slid guiltily down in his chair.

"I doubt that it was you, Father James."

He sat up higher.

"Not that you wouldn't be above taking a taste here and there. You didn't get that pouch by eating just celery. But since the doctors put you on that restricted diet, you've been pretty good about staying away from the things that might tie your intestines up in a knot again."

Father James wondered how long his intimate bodily functions would be up for discussion. Since the discovery of his severe case of diverticulitis, coupled with a cholesterol reading of 280, Father James's diet had been greatly curtailed. Even his beloved coffee had been denied him. Worse yet, everyone in Dorsetville seemed to know about it, which gave him precious little opportunity to cheat.

"No, Mrs. Norris, I didn't take your dessert," he said mournfully.

"That's what I thought," she said, turning to stare at Father Dennis, who appeared oblivious, completely engrossed with the newspaper. She tapped his sleeve.

"Did you say something to me?" asked Father Dennis, as though surfacing from the depths of some great tranquil ocean. "I'm sorry. I wasn't listening. This is such an interesting article."

The housekeeper leaned over Father Dennis's shoulder and read, "'How to Create Crochet Antimacassars of the Depression Era.' You really expect me to believe that you've taken an interest in chair coverings?"

In response, Father Dennis meekly lowered his head and awaited further blows.

"So it *was* you! How could you? You knew it was for this afternoon's luncheon."

Father Dennis bowed his head even farther toward the table. "Forgive me, Mrs. Norris, for I have sinned."

23

Father James repressed a smile while asking, "Who did you feed this time?"

"The construction workers next door," he said meekly.

Father James looked at Mrs. Norris. She appeared as though she were about to explode. Father Dennis was in for it now. If only the young prelate had listened to his warning. "Take anything you want from the rectory but never invade Mrs. Norris's kitchen," he had said. Apparently his words had landed on deaf ears.

Last week the young priest had snatched a chocolate sheet cake to surprise his fifth grade catechism class. He was under the mistaken assumption that Mrs. Norris had baked the cake for the two priests. Unfortunately, it had been promised to the seniors' Wednesday night Bingo game. Mrs. Norris had rained down fire and brimstone over that one. The seniors hadn't been too happy either.

Father James commended Father Dennis for his big heart and his acts of charity, but Mrs. Norris's kitchen was a place that he feared even the Lord Himself wouldn't tread without permission.

Father Dennis hastened to explain. "They worked so hard putting in that last piece of marble behind the altar. I thought a little celebration was called for." He quickly added: "You might as well know that I used up all the ice tea, too."

Mrs. Norris pulled out a kitchen chair and sat down with a plunk. "Father Dennis, you are hastening my demise. I don't know how much longer I can hang on with this type of constant aggravation."

Neither man argued or tried to convince her otherwise nor stated what they knew to be fact—Mrs. Norris was healthier than the Platt family's stable of Morgan horses. Both men had watched her clean the rectory from top to bottom in less than three hours without getting winded. Was that the profile of someone near death's door?

They had tried reasoning with her in the beginning of June when she had first concluded her fate. Their arguments hadn't made the slightest impression. Nothing could convince Mrs. Norris that she was not soon for the grave. By July they had given up trying and learned to simply ignore her histrionics.

"I might not even make it to the dedication ceremony this afternoon." She began to fan herself with the ends of her apron. "I certainly don't have the strength to go to the market, buy more ingredients and make a new batch of ambrosia. And what will I tell Mother Superior and the sisters, who are counting on my dessert?"

The mention of Mother Superior gave Father Dennis cause for deeper remorse. The woman scared him half to death. Reminded him of his mother's sister, his Aunt Ethel, to whose farm he was sent each summer to take in the fresh country air and lose some of his "baby fat." The only thing he had taken in, however, was his Aunt Ethel's continual displeasure, and all he had lost was his self-respect.

Nothing that he did could please her, although he had tried his hardest. He'd gotten up at four o'clock in the morning with Uncle Artie to milk the cows, but somehow he'd always manage to fall asleep and fall off the milking stool just as his aunt walked into the barn to tell them that breakfast was ready. He had even nailed rusted wire fencing back on fence posts until his hands bled, but his aunt never saw this. Instead, she always seemed to appear on the rare occasions that he would slip into the pond to float on his back, stare longingly into the heavens and wish that summer was over so he could go back home.

He was "listless and lazy," according to his Aunt Ethel, and his mother was much too soft on him.

"If you don't practice more self-discipline, you're going to grow up to be as fat as one of my prize heifers," his aunt had concluded, a prophecy that seemed to be closer to coming true with each passing year. Last time he had stepped on a scale it had registered three hundred and fifty pounds. Father Dennis was barely five feet five inches tall.

Beads of sweat now formed around Father Dennis's upper lip. "I'm truly sorry, Mrs. Norris. I am."

"Um! Fat good you're being sorry is going to do. What am I going to tell the bishop? He loves my ambrosia. Looks forward to it each time he visits. And not just *any* ambrosia, may I remind you. It won a blue ribbon at the Goshen fair three years in a row. Well, you're going to have to go right next door and tell Mother Superior the dessert that she was counting on for the luncheon has disappeared."

Father Dennis looked pleadingly over toward Father James, who hunched his shoulders as though to say, You're on your own.

The thought of confessing to Mother Superior brought on an immediate case of hiccups, a nervous tic he had developed in childhood.

Dealing with Mother Superior often gave him the hiccups, which was why last October Father Dennis offered to conduct the Blessings of the Animals on Saint Francis of Assisi's feast day if Father James would take his place, working with Mother Superior on the Pumpkin Harvest, even though Father Dennis was allergic to every animal known to man. He also knew that blessings would have to be bestowed on the Galligan twins' boa constrictor and little Jennifer Crawford's two ferrets—savage little beasts that literally bit the hand that fed them—and a plethora of dogs and cats.

Father Dennis had stoically performed the ceremony, willingly enduring days of red welts, itchy eyes and nasal congestion. In fact, he would have walked on nails . . . anything rather than have to work side by side with Mother Superior.

"What if I run to the store and buy some more ingredients . . . *hiccup?*" Father Dennis asked hopefully. "Couldn't you make a new batch without letting on what had happened to the . . . er . . . *hiccup* . . . last bowl?"

"If I live that long," Mrs. Norris said listlessly.

"You can't leave," Father James reminded him. "You're saying Mass this morning. Besides that, you offered to pick up Bishop Ruskin at the train station. I'm without a car, remember?"

Father James's Jeep had blown a tire rod yesterday morning as he traveled the back roads from Woodstock returning from visiting patients at Mercy Hospital. Triple A had towed it to the Fergusons' garage, Tri Town Auto. He had meant to call there this morning and find out how long he would be without wheels.

"Can you go to the store and pick up what Mrs. Norris needs?" asked Father Dennis with somewhat of a desperate twinge to his voice.

"No problem," Father James assured him. He hated to see his young assistant squirm. "I planned to walk down to Main Street and pay a visit to Lori Peterson at the Country Kettle. I could easily swing by the Grand Union on the way back." He turned to Mrs. Norris. "I shouldn't be gone more than an hour or so. Will that give you enough time to make another bowl of ambrosia?"

"I suppose. That is, if the good Lord hasn't called me home by the time you get back."

Father James stood up, pushed his chair in under the table and began to brush crumbs off his black shirt. "Well, in case that should happen, why don't you leave out the recipe card so Father Dennis and I can whip up a new batch while we wait for the undertaker."

Shades of the old Mrs. Norris rushed to the surface. "Go ahead. Make all the fun you want. A person knows when their time is up. I don't care what those doctors say. I'll be going home to my glory any day now. You'll see." She looked over to Father Dennis. "And if you don't keep out of my refrigerator and cupboards, you'll be coming right alone with me!"

The humidity had dropped and a slight cool breeze blew in off the river. Puffs of cumulus clouds floated on a perfect blue sky that the mountains surrounding the valley seemed to hold aloft with tall, pointed spears of the pine trees to the north and the spindly oaks to the south.

Father James stepped out of the rectory's side door and felt his spirits lighten, a combination of the fine summer day and the excitement of that afternoon's ceremonies. Even the rectory and church swathed in scaffolding—a stark reminder of his inadequacies as a building supervisor—couldn't depress him. In fact, it seemed to heighten his mood when he remembered that only two years ago the church was in such disrepair that it had been scheduled to be closed. But God had miraculously intervened by way of Mother Superior, Sister Mary Veronica, and her order, the Daughters of the Immaculate Conception of the Blessed Virgin Mary, who had decided to open a retirement home across the street and insisted that St. Cecilia's former pastor, Father Keene, become the home's first official resident. This forceful woman had also convinced the archdiocese that both the nuns and the home's residents would be in need of a church and a priest, ensuring St. Cecilia's survival. She had even managed to finagle the archdiocese into renovating St. Cecilia's from top to bottom, which meant that, for the first time in nearly thirty years, the buildings finally met with town codes.

Yes, it was a fine day for celebrating, Father James thought, as he heard the inner words of the Apostle Paul: *Now thanks be unto God, which always causeth us to triumph in Christ.* He bound down the rectory's four wooden steps and did a slight jog along the stone pathway that lead to the sidewalk, being certain to rein in his stride before rounding the church's façade. Lord help him should anyone think he'd taken up jogging! Lately it seemed that no matter where he went someone was giving him unsolicited advice about adopting a healthier lifestyle, most of which had to do with exercise.

"Kickboxing," Jeff Hayden, his recently married best friend and one of Dorsetville's newest residents, had suggested. "It's perfect for your busy schedule. It's an aerobic exercise and cardiovascular workout all in one. Make you feel lean and mean."

Retiree Timothy McGree, who was St. Cecilia's head usher, had suggested a stationary bike. "It's just the thing you need. Thirty minutes a day. That will lower your cholesterol." As an afterthought he added, "And eat lots of oatmeal."

Father James hated oatmeal.

Ben Metcalf, Timothy's best friend for over seventy years, had been privy to this exchange. Shaking his head, Ben countered, "Those bikes are only good for the legs. What Father needs is a treadmill with a hand glider. Works both the upper and lower portion of your body all at one time. I have one in my bedroom. Why don't you drop on over and give it a try?"

There had also been suggestions for hiking, rock climbing, horseback riding, swimming, yoga and aerobics classes, none of which sounded the least bit interesting to Father James, who had steadfastly ignored any form of exercise for over forty years and didn't see why he should take it up now.

Father James arrived at the Country Kettle and pushed open the front door. Aromatic smells filled the air—Harry's famous rich coffee, bacon smoked and cured right up the road in Goshen and home fries seasoned only as Harry could. Father James breathed in deeply, savoring the smells. It was like coming home.

In fact, everything about the County Kettle made you feel right at home, from the faded curtains on the front windows to the worn wooden floors. Mismatched plates and mugs made the customers feel more like they were visiting a favorite relative's house than a restaurant. In fact, since Harry bought most of his dishes at local tag sales, practically everyone could point to some plate, saucer, cup or mug that had once graced their own kitchen tables.

The windowsills were filled with live potted flowers. The walls were covered with various needlework designs donated by the town's women. A carved bear, made by one of Chester Platt's men with a chain saw one day as he waited for a shipment of lumber, stood guard right outside the door. It wore a brightly colored scarf that changed with the seasons.

Father James headed toward the front counter just as Harry Clifford began to clean the grill after the breakfast rush. Several waitresses scurried about, clearing off the tables and booths filled with stacks of dirty dishes and empty coffee cups. Among them was Harry's newest waitress, Wendy Davis.

Wendy had arrived in Dorsetville four months ago. She and her husband, Harold, had bought the Cape Cod on the edge of town that had once belonged to Arlene Campbell's Aunt Cybil, who died two years ago. The house was situated on the northern portion of Main Street right before the turn-off onto Route 7. It had once been a cute little place with a white picket fence and a small orchard of apple trees in the back. But since Cybil's husband's death, the place had been allowed to run down.

Wendy's husband, Harold, a top-notch machine mechanic, had been transferred in early May from New York to a tool-and-die plant over in Gaylordsville. They had been in their new home for less than three months when Wendy went in search of a job. Their house needed a host of repairs, including a new wood-shingled roof. If they didn't want water pouring in through the ceiling this winter, Wendy knew she had better find work, a premise that didn't bother her a bit. She had never been a stay-at-home kind of gal.

Wendy, just shy of her thirty-eighth birthday, had waitressed since she was sixteen. Unlike other women who considered waiting tables a route to another career, waitressing *was* a career for Wendy and she took pride in it. Her white rubber-soled shoes were polished every night after supper; her crisp white uniforms were spotless; and her apron pockets carried her favorite twenty-five-dollar pen and a package of Life Savers breath mints. She wore her red hair (Clairol's Nice 'n Easy, Natural Copper Red #109) tied at the nape of the neck in a neat pony-tail and neutral-colored polish on her neatly trimmed nails.

When Wendy spied Harry's ad for a waitress in the *Dorsetville Gazette* she had wasted no time in applying. The résumé that she had handed Harry stated that she was a "Professional Waitress." Harry had never met a professional waitress before, but he could see at a glance that Wendy had a great deal of experience. Listed were several diners in and around New York City, the ones that had menus that stretched on for six or seven pages and offered everything from hamburgers and fries to sole amandine. He had hired her on the spot.

The next day, Wendy arrived promptly at 6 A.M. She asked a few questions: Where did they keep the extra bags of coffee? What did he charge for two eggs, bacon and toast? Then she dove right into the morning melee. Both Harry and Lori had watched with amazement as Wendy sailed through the morning rush, working both the front tables and the entire counter. By eight o'clock, she had taken on the takeout orders as well.

"You call that a rush?" she had asked when it was over, looking just as fresh as when she had arrived, every hair in place, her uniform spotless.

"More like a trickle back from where I come," she said, refilling the salt and pepper shakers. Everyone else looked as though they were about to collapse.

There was, however, one thing about Wendy that worried Harry. Her thick New York accent and "Don't mess with me" attitude scared most of his locals, including the St. Cecilia's regular morning crowd. Ethel Johnson had taken Harry aside and requested that Lori wait on them.

"Fred Campbell can't understand a word she says and my sweet Honey (Ethel's beloved golden retriever) won't come out from underneath the table when she's near."

Wendy even scared Father James, who was relieved to see her taking her morning break as he strolled in. He headed toward the front counter and sat down on a red vinyl-covered stool.

"Any coffee left?" Father James asked hopefully, directing this query to Harry, who was working hard cleaning the grill. Just *one* cup shouldn't bother his intestines *that* much.

"Sure, help yourself," Harry said from behind the grill. "I think Lori just finished making a new pot."

"Nice try, Father James," Lori Peterson said before he had even risen off his stool. "You know the doctor said that caffeine's out. How about a cup of herbal tea? You like the Lemon Balm I gave you last time?"

Hopes dashed, he lied and said he'd love a cup.

Lori placed Father James's tea on the counter. He stared at the mug, which bore a picture of the Golden Gate Bridge. Who in Dorsetville had vacationed there? he wondered.

The phone rang as Wendy was walking back toward the kitchen. "Hello, Country Kettle Restaurant."

The greeting seemed a little off in Wendy's New York accent, Father James thought.

"Hey, Harry. It's Nellie Anderson. Says she's at school. She can only talk a minute."

"I'll take it in the back," Harry said, wiping his hands on his apron, then practically running down Pedro, the dishwasher, as he charged through the kitchen door.

"I'd say someone is in love," Wendy mused, replacing the receiver, then heading outside for her midmorning cigarette.

Father James glanced over at Lori. Both smiled. Harry and Nellie had been dating since early spring and, by the looks of things, it was getting serious. This love affair had become the main topic of conversation in Dorsetville.

"Hello, Father James," Lori's daughter Sarah said, walking by. She had a dishcloth in her hand, a towel tied around her waist and her curly blond hair was tied back behind a pink polka-dot babushka. She looked like a miniature serving wench.

"Did you finish wiping off those side tables, Sarah?" her mother asked.

"Yes. Can I go in the back and color now? I'm bored." Coloring was Sarah's favorite pastime. The Peterson house had her pictures hung everywhere. Even Uncle Harry had several tacked up around the restaurant.

"Wouldn't you rather stay out here and visit with me and Father James?"

Sarah looked down at the floor and shook her head no.

"All right. You can go in the back but stay out of Pedro's way."

Lori watched her daughter head toward the kitchen with deep concern, then poured herself a cup of coffee and settled alongside Father James.

"I feel so guilty at having to drag Sarah to work each morning while school's out for summer vacation," Lori lamented. "There's not an awful lot for a seven-year-old to do around here."

The coffee's intoxicating aroma wafted up from Lori's Baseball's Hall of Fame mug. My kingdom for a cup of coffee, Father James silently lamented. Life wasn't fair. The priest watched, like a dog fixed on a bone, as Lori blew on the steam rising from her cup.

Lori continued. "But there isn't much that I can do. Bob's illness last year drained all of our savings, so summer camp's out. And now with this new bakery business. I can't just pick up and leave whenever I feel like it."

A few months ago, Harry had expanded the restaurant, knocking down a wall into the adjacent store and creating a bakery that showcased Lori's famous muffins and cakes, recipes all gleaned from her grandmother's files.

"Several of us working moms have approached Mother Superior

about starting a daycare at the retirement home. It certainly would be a wonderful addition to our town."

"And what did she say?"

"She wants to wait until all of their residents are settled in before the nuns can seriously consider it."

"Maybe things will be a little better when Bob gets back," Father James said. "And how is his doing?"

"Not a trace of cancer," Lori said joyfully. "Doc Hammon said the oncologists have never seen such a perfect bone marrow match."

"'Great is the Lord, and greatly to be praised,'" he fairly sang. The entire town had prayed fervently for Bob's recovery. "And I take it the bakery is still doing well."

"Too well, if you can imagine such a thing," Lori said. "We're sold out most mornings by ten o'clock. I keep coming in earlier and earlier in hopes I can bake enough to satisfy the demand, but unfortunately there are always a few disgruntled customers who arrive after everything is gone."

"Well, that's a nice problem to have."

"Oh, I don't mean to sound ungrateful," she said, "but all this success means I have a lot less time to spend with Sarah. I'm beginning to wonder if Harry shouldn't find someone else to run the bakery. I could always go back to just waitressing. Less hours."

"What? And deprive the town of those delicious confections? Why, I've yet to get a taste of your Haddam Hall Gingerbread. Every time I come in they're sold out."

Lori laughed, "I'll save you one next time I bake a batch."

Father James took a swig of his Lemon Balm and tried not to grimace. Replacing the mug, he suggested, "Why don't you enroll Sarah in the Bible camp? Father Dennis and Reverend Curtis are starting one up next week. It's free to parishioners. Classes are going to be held in the basement of the Congregational church. Arts and crafts, story time—you know, things like that. They're using the town green for outdoor games and activities. Barry Hornibrook has even offered the kids the use of the beach by his new hotel complex. Sarah would have a great time, and it would free up some of that guilt you're carrying around," he teased.

"That sounds like a wonderful idea."

Sarah peeked out from around the corner. "Mommy, it's too hot in the kitchen. Can I color over there on a table?"

"Sure. Pick any one you want."

"Let's see what you've been coloring," Father James said as she started to pass by.

Sarah shyly handed him her picture.

Father James pretended to study it with great earnestness, then looked up and smiled. "Why, Sarah, this picture is supercalifragilistic-expialidocious!"

Sarah giggled. Father James felt as though he had won the Lotto.

"How would you like to go to summer Bible camp?" her mother asked, suddenly feeling not quite so desperate. "There will be games to play and trips to the beach and lots of fun things to do. It's got to be more fun than hanging around here or with Daddy when he gets home. What do you say?"

Sarah looked up and frowned. "Will Jamie be there?" Jamie Rupert was her very best friend.

"I don't know," Father James said, "but if your mom will come around to the rectory after work, I'll give her a brochure and she can deliver it to Jamie's mom and maybe she will be allowed to come, too." He patted the top of Sarah's head. "How's that sound?"

"Will I be allowed to color?"

Nellie kept an anxious eye on the clock in the teacher's lounge. She and her coworkers had only a few minutes left before the principal expected them back into the auditorium to resume their pre-school-year briefing. Classes were to begin in just a few weeks, and several changes in the state's educational policies and their ramifications needed to be discussed.

But before she allowed ideas about possible new placement tests and curricula to invade her thoughts, she deliberately closed her eyes, blocking out everything except the memory of Harry's gentle voice, which still rang in her ears. She turned toward the window and closed her eyes, sealing in its sound, committing every morsel of their conversation to memory. She would replay snatches of it intermittently throughout the rest of the day.

Just look at me, she thought, like some moonstruck teenager. Nellie Anderson, the town spinster, acting like an adolescent. It made her giggle. Two teachers seated in reading chairs by the large paneled bookcase looked at her quizzically, but she didn't care. How glorious it felt to be loved and adored by a man. Harry had helped to refashion her quiet, lonely world, filling her lackluster days with bright, hope-filled moments. Suddenly, she believed that anything was possible, even the miracle for which she so fervently prayed—the means to save her family home.

No one except Father James knew that Nellie was in peril of losing her home, a property that had been in her family for hundreds of years. Her mother had heavily mortgaged it when her father had gotten ill, then she herself had taken sick, which greatly added to the expenses.

The family lawyer had suggested that Nellie make her mother a ward of the state, place her in a nursing home, declare bankruptcy. Nellie refused. Instead, she worked more hours, even through the summer months, stopped taking vacations and personally attended to her mother's needs. When her mother died, Nellie was left with a mountain of bills that included a balloon mortgage payment due in a few weeks' time. She had no way of paying it.

"Coffee break's over," one of the teachers announced, rising from his chair. "Time to get back."

There was a brief scuffling of feet and folding of newspapers and closing of books. Nellie gathered a stack of papers bearing the state's seal that she had intended to review but, instead, had called Harry. Her movements were slow, deliberate. She lingered behind, watching the others file out of the room.

She could still hear Harry's deep, baritone voice, and the way it sounded when he called her "Honey." She loved him so much and hated keeping her financial problems to herself. But if he knew he'd want to help. Nellie couldn't allow that. She was much too proud.

No, she would work it out alone somehow. She had been thinking about taking on a second job. The *Dorsetville Gazette* had advertised that office cleaners were needed over in Woodstock. She had circled the ad. She planned to drive there after today's meeting. Another reason for her call to Harry. She needed to break their date. They had plans to meet after the retirement home luncheon today.

Finally, Nellie could procrastinate no longer. She slowly made her way out into the hall.

Chapter 2

B arry Hornibrook stood on the balcony with his back to the ballroom of the Old Mill Hotel and Conference Center as he looked across the Connecticut River, feeling the same depth of gratitude that he had felt since a youth at being able to call Dorsetville his home.

The air was bright and pure; the leaves on the trees glistened and the river flowed softly, lapping against the shore with a gentle rhythm. He closed his eyes as though to contain the landscape and the deep sense of peace it evoked; a panacea to the fear that made it hard to swallow and his hands so sweaty that they kept sliding off the balcony railing.

In a few minutes, two New York mobsters would arrive to demand the money his partner, Clyde Hessler, had borrowed. Barry didn't know anything about the money, nor did he know where to find Clyde Hessler.

He focused more intensely on the gentle rolling hills across the river, stemming the tide of unwanted thoughts that rose like flotsam. For a moment, he succeeded and savored the landscape's beauty. The slant to the August sun's rays spotlighted the periwinkle blue chicory that grew around the mountain range like a garland. His eyes continued to travel until they came to rest on a cluster of red ash trees. Their seven-leaf patterns reflected off the gently rolling river below and provided shelter from the hot summer sun for a family of mallard ducks and a cool haven for the smallmouth bass. How many summer days had he sat with his back up against one of those trees, a fishing rod in his hand?

This summer, however, there had been precious little time to fish. In fact, there had been little time for anything except worry. Would the town inspectors allow for the creative management of electrical and plumbing issues, items that could not be changed due to the original structure of the buildings? Would the wetland commission give him permission to finish construction on the marina, now that it had been discovered that a rare species of fauna grew in that area alongside the riverbank?

Barry had pushed and prodded, working feverishly to get the hotel complex opened by Thanksgiving. But all of his hard work had been in vain. Right now it looked as though the hotel would never open.

The conference room behind where Barry stood was one of only a handful of rooms in the five-million-dollar conference center that was completed. He was fourteen months into the project, several million dollars in debt and not at all close to opening on the projected target date in three months.

Carpet was missing around the dais area. The industrial-size kitchen needed a fifteen-thousand-dollar exhaust fan above the stove, per order of the fire marshal George Benson. Half of the other sixty-three rooms needed trim. Light fixtures in the two smaller conference rooms were still in boxes. The electricians had walked off the job three weeks ago in protest against unpaid back wages; Barry owed them several thousand dollars. The carpet layers, painters and landscapers, also unpaid, had packed up their tools and left two days later. Even George Benson, a longtime family friend, had suddenly become "too busy with other folks" to finish installing the heating and air-conditioning units. Barry couldn't blame any of them. Having run his own roofing and siding company in Dorsetville for twenty-five years, he would have done the same thing.

A slight breeze blew in off the river, lifting the remaining portion of his rapidly thinning hair, now heavily sprayed and shaped like an electric stovetop coil. Barry was too vain to lop it off and concede baldness at fifty-two.

He reached inside his coat pocket for his pack of Marlboros, then remembered that he and his best friend, Chester Platt, had quit two months ago. Chester had developed an ugly smoker's cough that had only grown worse over the summer. Barry was concerned and had come up with a plan.

"We learned to smoke together in the sixth grade. We might as well quit together," Barry had told him in a gesture of solidarity.

Besides, it seemed that Chester was the only friend he had left in Dorsetville. Few others in town were talking to him. He couldn't blame them. He owed just about everybody. Even his wife, Cheryl, had taken to replying in monosyllables and then only when necessary. Most of her friends' husbands were the ones to whom he owed money.

Barry continued to scan the horizon. Pockets of deep lavender ironweed grew along the marshland on the north side of the complex, which he had insisted be preserved even though the blacktop guys had wanted to fill it in to extend the parking lot. Barry loved the country-side, the wildlife. This morning he had watched a blue heron wade into the marsh he had saved and felt a deep feeling of satisfaction at having stood his ground.

No place on earth was as dear to him as Dorsetville. He couldn't imagine living anywhere else and often told people that he didn't have to go to heaven when he died. He already lived there.

Unlike others who felt the need to travel to foreign ports or make plans to move to warmer climates when they retired, Barry felt no such need. Everything he wanted was already here in this small town he so dearly loved—good friends, great neighbors and the rich New England landscape filled with soft rolling hills, gentle streams and rivers. Living here was one of the many blessings he made certain to thank God for each morning upon rising. It was Barry's deep love for his hometown that had been the reason he had dared to take on this project.

The breeze grew stronger, lifting Barry's hair again like a manhole cover. Barry patted it down more firmly and backed up against the building, wondering how much longer it would be before the mobsters arrived. He assumed they'd be carrying guns. His stomach hurt.

Why had he risked everything to save these old mills? He guessed he would never be able to explain it. Maybe it had something to do with his feelings of patriotism. Hadn't these mills supplied American soldiers' cloth for uniforms and blankets throughout two world wars? It had saddened him to the core when foreign markets had come in with cheap woolen products forcing the mills to finally close. It was as if an important part of Americana had ended.

Then, one day, he had overheard John Moran on the town council say the mills were scheduled to be auctioned off for back taxes. At that moment, Barry knew he had to buy them. He became even more determined when Moran added that if there were no buyers, the town would level the mills and sell off the land.

"I want to buy the old mill property," he had told Cheryl that night as they got ready for bed. "I think it would make a great investment. A little nest egg for our retirement years." Cheryl wasn't responding, so he quickly added, "We could take out a second mortgage on our home."

She had paused while lathering cold cream onto her face. "You're kidding, right?"

"No, I'm perfectly serious."

She looked away with long-suffering languor.

Barry tried to explain his need to save the old mills. She glanced back at him through the mirror as though he lost his mind. He changed tactics. It would be a great investment, he told her. He'd renovate them. Lease them out to some corporation.

"What corporation is going to want to move up here? This is Dorsetville, not Hartford." Cheryl scooped another handful of cold cream out of the economy-size Pond's jar. "Really, Barry, who do you think you are? Donald Trump?"

Chester Platt wasn't any more enthusiastic. "Buy the old mills? Sounds like you're losing more than just your hair, old buddy. It would probably cost a half a million just to bring it up to code."

Barry knew they were right. Knew he should abandon this crazy idea. But something inside him urged him on. It was as if he just couldn't stop. He simply *had* to save the mills. So, without Cheryl's knowledge, he took a second mortgage out on their home and went to the auction feeling like a kid who had just stolen from the collection box. There was going to be quite a row when Cheryl found out.

The auction was held in the lunchroom at the back of the town hall. Only three people showed up and much to Barry's great surprise, no one bid higher than his opening bid of sixty-five thousand dollars.

"Sold to Barry Hornibrook for sixty-five thousand dollars," Tom Pastronostra, the town's building inspector and professional auctioneer, said without enthusiasm. Where was the sport in having just one person bid?

Barry could hardly contain his joy. He had just bought two brick buildings with over two hundred and seventy thousand square feet of space on ten prime riverfront acres all for a mere sixty-five thousand? Even Cheryl, after she got through swearing, would have to admit it was quite a steal, which she eventually did . . . although she was unclear what he was going to do with it now that they owned it. They certainly didn't have the money to fix it up. Barry had no idea either until he met Clyde Hessler.

The night they met, Barry was celebrating with the Dorsetville Firemen's Bowling League. Even though he wasn't a fireman, Chester (who was) had waggled him a place on the team. The Dorsetville league had lost two consecutive years to the Woodstock unit in the fire marshal's state finals. They were not about to lose again and were hoping that Barry might give them a decisive edge. Barry had maintained the highest bowling score throughout the county during his high school years.

This night, Barry had bowled a perfect 300 and had gone with the rest of the league over to Kelly's Bar to celebrate. It meant that this year they were certain to win the state trophy. Clyde was standing alongside the bar as teammates offered Barry their congratulations.

"It's not every day that a guy makes a score like that," Clyde said, sliding over to offer a celebratory handshake. "Let me buy you a drink."

Clyde Hessler, otherwise known by those who knew him well as Clyde "the Hustler," was an average-looking guy—medium build, five feet eight inches tall, with neatly trimmed reddish brown hair and light amber-colored eyes. Although Clyde's features might never distinguish him in a crowd, his walk was a dead giveaway. He suffered with a chronic ear condition that played havoc with his balance. Most days, the man was incapable of walking a straight line.

The two men talked "guy talk" for several minutes: bowling, football, baseball stats. Clyde appeared to Barry as an upstanding kind of guy; but then Barry had never been a good judge of character. In fact, he thought the men on the WANTED posters at the post office looked like decent Joes, too.

After a couple of drinks, Barry happened to tell Clyde about the old mill property and how the town council wanted to tear it down. How he had bought it at auction and still didn't know what he was going to do with it. Clyde listened quietly, occasionally asking a question here and there.

"They're great buildings, solid. All brick. And the architecture is classic Greek Revival. Built in 1886. Then there's the historical significance. How many places like this still exist in New England? But does the town care? *Nooooo.* Instead, they want me to run a wrecking ball through the whole lot."

"What would you do with them if money were no object," Clyde asked.

Barry studied the foam on his beer. "I'd turn it into a hotel and conference center."

"You think something like could make money in a small town like Dorsetville?" Clyde asked.

"Why sure it would!" Barry said with fervor. "The university is always looking for extra conference space, and God knows we need a hotel around here." Two beers had greatly loosened Barry's inhibitions. He was normally shy around strangers.

"And do you know how many times Cheryl and I have had to put up someone's relatives because the closest hotel was twenty miles away over in Waterbury? I've lost count. Even Woodstock doesn't have a decent place to stay."

"Then why not do it?"

"Do what?"

"Turn the mills into a hotel complex."

"Oh, sure," Barry laughed. "Right after I move my yacht up from Fort Lauderdale."

"I'm serious," Clyde said, moving in closer like a bird of prey.

"Well, there's just one little problem: where do I get that kind of cash?"

"*You* don't need cash."

"Oh, really? So what do I use?"

"*Other* people's cash."

"And you think they're going to loan me money just like that?" Barry snapped his fingers.

"You've got collateral. Prime riverfront property plus two great buildings. You said so yourself."

"That's true," Barry said. He had never thought about it like that. He took another sip of beer, then asked, "So were do I find these investors?"

"They're around. I know at least a handful myself. Guys who are always looking for a way to make a good return on their money. They'd be happy to co-sign a construction loan on a project like this." Clyde ran his thumb around the lip of the beer bottle. "How long would the complex take to complete? Three . . . four years?"

"Heck no. I could have it up and running in less than eighteen months." Barry reached for some peanuts.

"You're kidding!"

"No. I've had time to study it for several months. It wouldn't take long to renovate. I'd maximize the old structure. Just a matter of studding out the rooms and putting up some Sheetrock. The big cost would come in revamping the heating and electrical systems. Fire sprinklers. Things like that."

"And the asbestos and lead paint? You said the place was loaded with it."

"I know a couple of guys over at DEP. They'd move it along."

Clyde looked down into his beer, like a Gypsy studying a crystal ball. "I'm telling you, Barry, you're sitting on a gold mine. Once word gets out that you're looking for cash, investors will be lining up."

"Maybe you're right," Barry conceded. "But I sure wouldn't know where to find them."

"Another round, doll." Clyde nodded to the waitress as she passed. "That's why you and I would make great partners. You know about the construction end of things, and I know about financing. Together we'd be a dynamic team. We'd make a killing."

In hindsight, Barry should have paid the bar tab and run. He had never wanted to make a killing. He'd only wanted to preserve the riverfront and save the old mills. Instead, he had let Clyde talk him into a fifty-fifty partnership, several sizable construction loans and over a million dollars' worth of fixtures, carpeting and appliances on credit, not to mention the two-hundred-seventy-five-thousand-dollar Dale Chihuly glass chandelier in the front lobby. The bill had just come in from the art gallery the other day. Who was Dale Chihuly, anyway?

If only he had access to the seven hundred and fifty thousand Clyde had stolen, he could have finished the project, completed the landscaping, outfitted the restaurant and finished up the boat slips. Several German investors had already made inquiries about buying the complex when it was completed, but they would never want it now with all the liens, banknotes and soon-to-be lawsuits pending.

Other men less honorable than Barry would have simply walked away from the project. Called the bank and let them know that his partner had stolen what was left of their construction loan. Filed a report with Sheriff Bromley. Had him issue a warrant for Hessler's arrest. But Barry wouldn't do that, and for a very good reason. If he abandoned the project now, the bank would foreclose, sell the property at whatever price it could get to pay back the loan, and Barry's subcontractors would never see a dime of the money that was owed them. Nope, he just wouldn't do that to his friends like Pete Carlson, the excavator. He and Pete had played basketball together in high school. He'd even dated his sister, Janet. Barry owed him thirty-five thousand.

Sirius Gaithwait had done all the masonry work. Barry had known Sirius since the third grade. They'd fished together off the river down by Judge Peale's place every summer. He'd managed to pay Sirius everything except about eight hundred dollars. It had meant selling his great-great-grandfather's Civil War rifle and powder horn. He hated to part with it, but what could he do? Sirius's wife was expecting. They needed the cash.

Then there was Mark Stone from the hardware store, and Jason Phelps at the lumberyard, not to mention his old friend Chester who had done all the interior work.

"Don't worry about what you owe me. I still have plenty of work at the retirement home and at St. Cecilia's to keep me in ready cash. I can hang on," Chester said when Barry explained about Clyde's disappearance. "But I think you're making a big mistake if you don't let the sheriff know."

"I can't. If I told the sheriff about Clyde, the bank will get wind of it and they'd call in the loan. Where am I going to get three-quarters of a million dollars in cash? Which means the bank would be forced to sell the property at bargain basement prices to cover their costs and there goes any chance I might have of paying back my subs. I'll just have to think of something else."

And if these debts weren't sizable enough, Barry had just learned that Clyde had also borrowed another quarter of a million dollars from a bunch of guys from Long Island. Two men, Tony Forlano and Vinnie Costello, had called earlier this morning asking for Clyde. Barry told them that Clyde had disappeared. That's when they told Barry that his partner had borrowed money against the project and that "the boss" was sending them to collect.

A sleek, black Lincoln Navigator slid in front of the complex. Barry leaned over the railing and watched as two men got out. They stood on either side of the vehicle, stretching their legs, running a hand through their slicked-back hair. Then, slowly, they started toward the front of the hotel, casually pointing to this and that as they walked, just as though they owned the place and were planning changes.

What did Father James always say? When you come to a place where there's no way out, just stand and trust God to lead you through. Barry sure hoped that God wasn't busy elsewhere because he wasn't sure how long he could stand with his knees shaking this badly.

"I can't have it for you until late next week," said Nancy Ferguson, Dorsetville's ace lady mechanic. "Hey! Pete!" she yelled to a gangly, acne-faced kid who pumped gas. "Go in the back and get me a case of 40-weight oil, will you? And while you're back there, see if we have any oil filters for this 1972 Plymouth."

She bent back over the engine and tightened the fan belt. "I've got four small jobs before yours and a valve job. Both promised for this week. Sorry, Father, but it looks like you're going to have to wait a while on your Jeep."

Nancy and her husband, Don, ran the Tri Town Auto repair shop on the corner of Bank Street and Main. They had been fixing Dorsetville's automobiles for over twenty years and were considered one of the town's greatest assets. Everyone had a story of how Nancy or Don had found *this* or *that* and fixed it for under a hundred dollars, while the dealerships over in Woodstock had wanted to replace an expensive *this* and *that* and charge forty-five dollars an hour for labor to boot!

Recently, Dorsetville's most famous radio personality had listed Tri Town Auto as one of his picks for reliable auto repair and turned Father James's dependable hometown mechanics into near celebrities. Customers now poured into the shop from surrounding towns, increasing the wait on repairs from a few days to a week or sometimes more.

"I suppose there's no chance of a cancellation?" he asked hopefully.

Nancy pushed a stray hair out of her eyes. Later she would discover a large grease smudge across the right side of her forehead. "I'd say you'd have a better chance of turning water into wine."

Nancy saw Father James's crestfallen face and threw up her hands. "All right . . . all right. I can't stand to see a grown priest cry. I'll see what I can do. Maybe I can talk John Moran into waiting on his tune-up."

"God bless you, Nancy."

"If He blesses me much more, I'll have to open another shop." She wiped her hands on one of her husband's old T-shirts. "Instead, I wish that He'd send me another good mechanic."

Feeling he had to say something, Father James replied rather lamely, "I suppose you've advertised."

"Yeah, we've run an ad in the *Dorsetville Gazette* for over a month now."

"No luck?"

She shook her head. "Not yet. So far we've had kids whose only experience is working on their own cars, or guys who are tired of working for a dealership but only know one make of car."

"I'll add it to my prayer list."

"I'd appreciate that, Father."

"Hi, Nancy," Sam Rosenberg said. "Don told me that you were still working on my Duster."

"Hi, Sam," Father James said brightly. Sam was one of his favorite people and the volunteer driver for Dorsetville's Meals-on-Wheels program.

"Good morning, Father James. What, no Mass this morning?"

"Father Dennis has it covered."

"Then I'd say your congregation will be greatly blessed. I like that young priest of yours. He's filled with great enthusiasm and has a generous heart."

Too generous, he thought, when it comes to giving away contents from Mrs. Norris's cupboards. Which reminded him, he'd better not dawdle: Mrs. Norris was expecting her ambrosia ingredients.

"Will my car be much longer, Nancy?" Sam asked.

"I'm just about done. That noise you heard was a loose fan belt. I've tightened it up and, if you'll give me about fifteen more minutes, I'll do an oil change. I noticed the sticker. You're due for one in about fifty miles, so I might as well do it while it's here."

"I appreciate you taking it in on such short notice," Sam said, explaining to Father James that the noise had started yesterday while delivering meals. "I couldn't risk breaking down."

"No, of course you couldn't," Father James agreed.

Sam's 1972 Plymouth Duster was a familiar sight plying the back country roads on his daily route to deliver hot meals to shut-ins. For many, Sam was their only contact with the outside world. Several elderly people literally owed their lives to him; he kept a keen eye on both their health—making certain that they had taken their medication or renewed it when it was near empty—and their living conditions.

Twice last winter, Sam had arrived at homes only to discover them without heat. One man had forgotten to pay his heating bill; Sam helped him make out a check, then ran it right over to Pearson's Fuel Oil. Another man simply couldn't afford the fuel. Sam called the Dorsetville emergency fuel program and the town's social director, then waited around making pots of hot tea until both the director and the fuel truck showed up. Father James always said that if he were Catholic, instead of Jewish, the Church would have to canonize him as a saint.

"You need a ride?" Sam asked. He had noticed the priest's Jeep parked in the back lot.

"I was headed up toward Grand Union."

"If you'd like, I could swing over that way en route to pick up something for Harriet. She and Allison are in charge of the flowers for the dedication ceremonies over at the retirement home this afternoon."

"How is their business going?"

Harriet's granddaughter, Allison, owned a shop in New York City that sold exotic flowers and now was using her grandmother's Dorsetville nursery greenhouses to grow many of her plants.

"Fine. In fact, they've just launched a new Web site. Now they're getting orders from all over the country. Harriet says she never thought she'd be a mogul at her age."

Father James couldn't be more pleased for Harriet, not only for her business success, but also for this new relationship with her granddaughter. Twenty-five years ago, Allison had lost her two-year-old sister and mother in a tragic car accident. Harriet's son, Peter, was inconsolable, blaming God for his terrible loss. He had given Harriet an ultimatum. She could either abandon her faith or never see him and her granddaughter again. When Harriet refused, Peter had taken Allison and disappeared.

Then eighteen months ago, Father James had been invited into New York by his best friend, Jeff Hayden, to meet Jeff's new fiancée. In a wonderful stroke of good fortune, the fiancée had turned out to be the missing granddaughter. Father James still got all choked up every time he thought about the mysterious and wonderful workings of the Lord under the heading of "Coincidences."

Father James checked his Timex watch, the one with the large, readable numbers. His eyesight wasn't what it used to be. It was nearing eleven o'clock.

"I'd better not wait for your car, Sam. Besides shopping for Mrs. Norris, I still have to welcome the bishop and review this afternoon's proceedings."

Pete returned from the storeroom and handed Nancy an oil filter. "You can borrow my bike, Father."

Bike? Father James hadn't ridden a bike since high school, and, as much as he hated to admit it, he doubted he had the stamina to make it up Main Street's hill.

"Thanks, but I think I'll walk."

"All right with me." Walking away, Pete added, "But my motor scooter could have gotten you there a whole lot faster."

A motor scooter?! Who said anything about a motor scooter? Now, that was something he had always wanted to try.

Chapter 3

T he Sister Regina Francis Retirement Home had been charged with activity since dawn as last-minute details were made for the afternoon's ceremonies. Delivery trucks pulled in and out of the driveway, the first of which was Harry Clifford's van. Harry delivered a sheet cake and twelve dozen rolls—all made by Lori at five o'clock that morning, while Sarah had slept on a cot in the back of the restaurant, and baked in the new Country Kettle's ovens. Harry deliberately forgot to include the bill.

Next, Lenny Miller from Marcus Dairy arrived to deliver two cases of milk in glass bottles with paper lids, five pounds of butter and three quarts of cream, making certain to place them directly into the industrial-size refrigerator (the refrigerator that the Health Department had finally declared working in accordance to the state code yesterday afternoon at four). Not until the winter had firmly settled in would Lenny again use the tin milk box outside the back door.

While Lenny was pulling his white truck out of the driveway, Harriet Bedford and Allison arrived with their full-size van, shelves packed tightly with floral arrangements. The women had spent two days combing the countryside in search of wildflowers, which they had assembled into old-fashioned posies. One would grace each place setting and make for charming keepsakes. In addition, two four-foot-high arrangements of calla lilies, designed to flank each side of the outdoor altar, rode on the floor. There were also sixty centerpieces, four banquet table arrangements and a twenty-foot garland for the front dais woven from bougainvillea. Their work would be the talk of the Dorsetville Garden Club for months to come.

On the south side of the building, the home's first official resident, Father Keene, had risen early to trim the front hedge, a chore he had promised Sister Bernadette to complete well before the bishop's arrival at noon. Sister Bernadette, a large boxy woman who wore steel-reinforced construction boots and a tool belt, was in charge of the retirement home's maintenance and grounds, having proven herself inept at all indoor chores. This fact made it even more implausible that Mother Superior had ordered her to help out in the kitchen this morning because Father Keene would be left unsupervised, which deeply worried Sister Bernadette.

Father Keene didn't mind. Not at all. In fact, he enjoyed working outside and was happy to oblige. Sister Bernadette gave him a firm set of instructions on the best way to tackle the project, going so far as to run a nylon fishing line the length of the hedge as a level.

"Just keep the shears even with this line and you'll get a nice straight edge." Then she added forcefully, "And be careful to keep the cord out of the way of the shears or you'll get knocked right on your fanny."

Father Keene found the job quite soothing. First run the shears up and then down . . . then back and forth, careful to keep the plumb line in view as Sister Bernadette had instructed. The first ten feet of hedges went smoothly and looked just as accomplished as any professional gardener could have achieved. He was quite proud. But a few feet farther along, the priest's thoughts began to wander under the monotonous motion of the hedge clippers and the hypnotic buzz of the electric motor. A deep reverie with images of the Irish glades of his youth and the gardens back home overshadowed the task at hand and soon he left the gardens in Dorsetville to meander down lanes filled with old memories of other gardens until finally his mind had become completely detached from the chore at hand.

Father Keene was hidden from the view of Matthew Metcalf and a group of his friends, all of whom looked as though they had just tumbled out of bed. It was the boys' job to set up the fifty-seven folding tables and three hundred forty-two chairs. Sister Bernadette had furnished a diagram. But the boys quickly abandoned the form as it was soon discovered that table placement would mainly be determined by the clean areas which Sister Bernadette's German shepherd, Harley, had not favored during one of his nightly unsupervised runs.

Ben Metcalf, who was supervising his grandson and friends, cupped his hands around his mouth and shouted, "Matthew, move that table to the right. Otherwise, people will be staring into the sun."

He wished he could be out there with his grandson, working hand and hand, but he knew neither his heart nor his back could take the strain. Pity. He missed the moments they used to spend together. In fact, this morning was the first time in weeks that he and his grandson had even been in close proximity to each other.

Up until a few months ago they did everything together—fished down by the old mills, played checkers before supper, watched reruns of the old *Andy Griffith Show*. But lately Matthew was too busy with his new friends and had little time to spend with his grandfather. Ben understood how it was. Matthew wasn't a kid anymore; still, it was a hard adjustment for the doting grandfather to make.

Worse was the feeling that Ben was no longer needed . . . by anyone. His lifelong friend, Timothy McGree, kept telling him to get a hobby. But what kind of hobby? Stamp collecting? Model building? Maybe he should make a hobby out of dressing Tim. Lord knows the man could use some help. Today Tim was dressed in one of his signature outfits—purple-and-orange-striped shorts, a green polo shirt with a collar that had been repaired with duct tape, black dress socks and leather moccasins. Those who knew him well enough to tease always said that he gave the appearance of someone who had gotten the day's outfit out of a Goodwill dumpster while blindfolded.

"A little more to the right . . . a little more," Ben hollered, "Hey, kids . . . I said a little more to the *right*."

The boys looked down. To their right sat another one of Harley's dinosaur-size droppings.

"To the right!" Ben shouted. "You boys deaf?"

"We can't," Matthew hollered back.

"Why not?"

"Because Harley . . ."

Matthew was suddenly interrupted by the ten-year-old Galligan twins, Rodney and Dexter, who raced past, toppling over several chairs that had been leaning up against a tree.

"Hey!" Matthew and his friends yelled in unison.

The twins increased their speed, tromping through a bed of hostas, crushing several fronds for which the German shepherd would later be blamed.

"Rodney!" Ben shouted after him. Or was it Dexter? "Behave yourself or I'll have your father take you both back home."

Mike Galligan was on the east side of the property with his order of the Knights of Columbus setting up the tents under which today's Mass would be celebrated.

A horn honked and the group turned just as an older model Honda Accord pulled alongside the front gate. The sedan, which had once been a delivery car for a pharmacy over in Woodstock, still bore a rectangular roof sign; only, the original lettering that had advertised FRED'S FRIENDLY FAMILY PHARMACY . . . WE DELIVER DRUGS NIGHT AND DAY had been prudently painted over by order of Dominic Costello's parents.

Before the cherry red, two-door sedan, pockmarked with rust, had come to a complete stop, fourteen-year-old Stephanie Costello jumped out of the passenger side dressed in her newest Britney Spears outfit— lime green *very short* shorts and a neon yellow tube top that stopped several inches short of her waist.

"Hi, Matt!" she shouted. "Look what my brother and I picked up." She dangled a large McDonald's bag over the wrought-iron fence. "Anyone hungry?"

"Hi, Matt," her brother Dominic called, stepping around the car. Dominic was a university student and several years older than Matthew, yet both boys were good friends. Especially after the previous year's hologram fiasco. "Sorry we're late, but Stephanie wanted to stop off and get you guys something to eat."

The twins reappeared, and, like noisome flies, began to circle around, snatching at the bag. "Hey, neat! We'll take some of those."

Stephanie held the bag up over their heads. "You'll have to wait until Matthew and his friends are finished." And when she said Matthew's name she purred.

"There goes our work team," Timothy lamented, but quickly added, "Think they bought any extras?"

"Stuff gives me gas," Ben said. Nodding toward the house, he added, "Someone inside could have at least offered us a cup of coffee, don't you think? We've been out here since eight o'clock. I told you we should have stopped off at the Country Kettle on the way over."

"The women probably forgot all about us," Timothy offered. "You know how they get when the bishop visits."

"Maybe we should knock on the back door and remind them."

Timothy rose stiffly. "I think it's safer if we just see what the kids brought and risk a case of gas."

Mrs. Norris glanced up at the kitchen clock. Ten forty-five and they still hadn't finished the finger sandwiches *and* there were all those strawberries needing to be washed and hulled. She could feel her pulse quicken. Was something wrong with her heart? she wondered. Don't panic. Breathe deeply. She couldn't die. Not today. Who would take care of the luncheon?

But it was no wonder that her heart was racing. She had been on her feet since six o'clock this morning. First she had made breakfast for the priests, then cleaned up the rectory's kitchen, threw a load of dish towels into the washing machine downstairs, made the beds upstairs, then gone back downstairs to toss the towels into the dryer. By eight o'clock she had begun to supervise things over here.

She should sit down, take a few minutes' rest. After all, she was no spring chicken anymore. She was sixty-two, which brought her back to the fact that no woman on her father's side of the family had ever made it past her sixtieth birthday. Her death was already two years overdue. Well, be that as it may, she had work to do. And if it hastened her demise, so be it. What better way to go out than in the service of the Lord?

A cursory look down the long kitchen table confirmed that thoughts about resting were most definitely out. The women of St. Cecilia's were holding their own, but the nuns at the other end of the table were absolutely useless. Heaven only knew how they were going to manage to feed themselves and an entire retirement home of residents due later today. Not one of them seemed to know the difference between a paring knife and a melon baller.

"Sisters, we've only a few hours left before the bishop arrives, so you'd better put a move on it." She walked over to inspect more closely.

"Sister Bernadette, remember to double-wrap those sandwich trays with plastic wrap before putting them in the refrigerator. Otherwise, the bread will dry out."

"What does she want *hung out?*" asked ninety-two-year-old Sister Joanna, a new resident of the home who had arrived last night and had been plied into service.

"Nothing, Sister Joanna. Turn up your hearing aid," Sister Theresa suggested.

"Don't have my hearing aid in this morning," Sister Joanna said. "I think I left it next to my eyeglasses."

"Well, where are your glasses?" Sister Theresa asked.

"Don't know. Can't find them either."

Sister Theresa smiled one of her ethereal smiles. Nothing ever troubled Sister Theresa. She went back to garnishing a tray of luncheon meats.

"I hope we have enough food," Mrs. Norris worried out loud.

"Enough food?" Sister Theresa laughed. "Why, Mrs. Norris, we have enough food here to feed the entire town."

"I hope you're right, since the *entire* town will probably show up," Mrs. Norris countered.

"One thing's for certain," Arlene Campbell said, deftly cutting the crust off from a loaf of freshly baked whole wheat bread, "most of St. Cecilia's parishioners will be here with bells on. None of us will ever forget that this retirement home helped to save our dear church."

Eighteen months ago, the archbishop had ordered St. Cecilia's closed due to a dwindling membership and a building in dire need of repairs. But the people had prayed without ceasing and God had sent a miracle by way of the Daughters of Mary of the Immaculate Conception of the Blessed Virgin, who offered to open a retirement home for the religious right across the street from the church. Through Mother Superior's intercession, the archbishop agreed to keep the church open to help minister to the residents' spiritual needs.

"'Saved'? What do you want saved?" asked Sister Joanna, wrapping yet another one of Sister Theresa's gherkin pickles, instead of a cocktail frank, in a wedge of Pillsbury Crescent Rolls.

"No, no, Ethel!" Mrs. Norris yelled as though someone was about to be robbed. "I told you to place the chicken salad on the flowered plate, not on the silver platter."

"If you had told me I would have remembered," Ethel snapped. Margaret was really getting on her nerves. Who did she think she was anyway, Julia Child? Ethel heaped another mound of chicken salad onto the silver tray in defiance.

Mrs. Norris had already moved on, inspecting the napkins that had been folded earlier by Sister Joanna. No two were folded the same way. She shook them out and began all over again. If only there was time to press them with a hot iron. Several were a mass of wrinkles.

"I wonder what happened to Father James?" Mrs. Norris asked no one in particular, trying to press a crease out with the palm of her hand. "If he doesn't get here soon, my ambrosia will never be chilled in time, and there's nothing worse than warm ambrosia."

Darn! The wrinkles were holding fast. She glanced down the table.

"Sister Theresa, are you out of pickles again?" She threw down the napkins and headed toward the pantry door. "I'll try and find another jar."

Ethel leaned over and whispered to Arlene. "I know Margaret says she's suffering from some kind of mysterious illness, and that it's fatal, but apparently it has nothing to do with her tongue." She slipped a portion of chicken salad to her golden retriever Honey, lying underneath the table.

Arlene laughed softly, then whispered, "To borrow a line from Mark Twain, 'I think *her* imminent death is greatly exaggerated.'"

Both women giggled like schoolgirls.

"Personally," Arlene continued, "I think it's all a lot of baloney."

Ethel agreed.

Ruth Henderson, resting heavily on her walker, called from the other side of the room. "We're almost finished with the nectar punch, Mrs. Norris. Are you sure you don't want us to help with the desserts?"

"Oh, do let us help," her sister, June, implored, clapping her hands like a small child. "On our walk over this morning, we spied some lovely yellow daisies growing alongside the back of the church that would look just darling on top of that Lady Baltimore cake."

Arlene and Ethel both gasped. They looked beseechingly over at Mrs. Norris. The Henderson sisters' wildflower cake decorating always resulted in insects emerging just as it was being served. The parish women would die of shame if the bishop got an ant along with his spoonful of cake. The two women held their breath.

But they needn't have worried. Mrs. Norris took charge. "Thank you, Ruth, but we have the desserts covered. How about refolding some of these napkins? They seemed to have come undone."

"Well . . . if you would prefer; however, don't you think a few daisies would add just the right touch of color to that cake?"

"Thank you, June, for the suggestion, but I think we'll go with what we had originally planned."

Ethel and Arlene sighed with relief.

Mrs. Norris plunked a jar of pickles in front of Sister Theresa just as Sister Bernadette, seated across the table, began to spread the orange marmalade and Dijon mustard mix on a slice of chicken.

"No! No!" Mrs. Norris shrieked with horror. "The mustard goes with the maple ham. The herb mayonnaise is for the chicken."

Sister Bernadette smiled weakly, not at all certain why Mrs. Norris was so upset. A sandwich was a sandwich. Mustard or mayo . . . did it really matter?

"I'll be more careful" she placated, then carefully spread a smear of mayonnaise on the next piece of chicken. Mrs. Norris nodded her approval before moving along.

Sister Bernadette didn't mean to be impudent. She was just greatly distracted. Hidden in her room upstairs was the hundred-pound German shepherd Harley, who desperately needed to go out. Sister Bernadette was supposed to have found him a home before today's ceremonies. Mother Superior's orders had been explicit. Sister Bernadette had fervently tried to do as she had been ordered, but all efforts had met with defeat.

First she had contacted every animal rescue organization within a hundred-mile radius; but either they were already filled with long waiting lists or didn't take in German shepherds. (After living with the breed for several months, Sister Bernadette knew why—it was like living with a loaded cannon.)

She had approached dozens of people in town, pleading with anyone who hadn't cowered in fear at the dog's size to consider adoption. Last Tuesday, she had thought Ethel Johnson might give him a home as sort of playmate for her golden retriever. The nun had washed and brushed Harley until his coat shone, then stuffed him into her car, lifting his hindquarters off the ground with a grunt and a shove. No doubt her back would never be the same.

Of course all of this nonsense with the car could have been avoided if only they had walked to Ethel's. It was only two miles outside of town. But Harley had treed several cats in the past few weeks and their owners had called Mother Superior with complaints. Sister Bernadette had been summoned once again into the prioress's office, where she had tried to explain that Harley hadn't meant to hurt the cats. He merely thought them playthings. Like Frisbees.

Sister Bernadette and Harley arrived at Ethel's right on time. Things went along nicely until Ethel suggested that the two dogs be allowed to play out in back in the fenced-in yard. But Harley, ecstatically happy to be allowed to run free, had charged right into Honey and pummeled her to the ground, nearly knocking her unconscious. Sister Bernadette was greatly shocked to learn the number of curse words Ethel Johnson knew.

Last Sunday, Sister Bernadette had placed a display ad in the paper, complete with a cute photograph of Harley with a red bandana tied jauntily around his neck, lying next to a statue of Saint Francis of Assisi. Sister Bernadette had labored fiercely over the ad's wording for days, convinced that the truth would frighten off most prospective owners. Instead, she settled on some highly ambiguous copy.

"Lovable, large dog. [To those he knew. Everyone else he tried to tackle.] Well trained. [Harley knew how to sit and lie down, but the word "Come" seemed an enigma.] Loves to ride in the car. [The driver's seat, that is, about which Harley and she continually argued.] Extremely curious about small dogs. [Probably sizing them up as an alternate food group, she suspected.]"

She waited near the phone most of Sunday and all day Monday. No one called. Like it or not, Harley was still hers.

Sister Bernadette had never wanted to own a dog, especially such a large one, but Providence had intervened with other plans.

Harley had been her Uncle Ed's dog up until two months ago. Uncle Ed had keeled over one morning of a heart attack, right into his bowl of Special K. Her uncle had been a police sergeant and Harley was a trained police dog. Both had recently retired from the force.

Since Sister Bernadette was the only living relative, she had inherited her uncle's small Cape Cod home in New Jersey and the dog. The house had been easy to get rid of. It sold in less than a week. The dog had not.

In the beginning, she had no intention of keeping Harley. She had picked him up at the kennel where he had been boarded since her uncle's death, then drove directly to the dog pound. Harley had sat in the passenger's seat, staring out the windshield at the concrete-block building with mournful brown eyes, looking like a prisoner about to go on death row. She had tried to ignore his sad, downcast face, the way he placed a large paw on her lap as though to say, No hard feelings. I understand.

But when she walked around to his side of the car and he looked up into her eyes and gently licked her cheek, she folded. She got back in the car and drove home to Dorsetville, then smuggled Harley up the back stairs to her room. How hard would it be to hide the dog until she could figure out what she would tell Mother Superior?

The next morning, someone walked past her door and Harley began to bark as though the entire town needed to be alerted. Nothing she said could make him stop: "Quiet, down! Bad dog! Shut up, you stupid mutt!!!" She had even rolled up an old newspaper and threatened him with it. Harley quickly pulled it out of her hand, shredding the paper within seconds, then resumed his attack of the bedroom door.

Finally, she threw her hands up in surrender. There was no way that Mother Superior was not going to discover she had the dog hidden in her room. Having come to terms with this, she went about doing what she always did during times of duress. She walked over to her closet and pulled out a new package of double-stuffed Oreos. That got Harley's attention. Two cookies later, he had completely forgotten about his tirade. She was summoned to Mother Superior's office shortly after.

"What is that?" Mother Superior asked, gazing over her half-moon glasses.

"A dog," Sister Bernadette replied.

"I *know* it's a dog, Sister Bernadette. What I don't know is what it is doing here."

Sister Bernadette explained about Uncle Ed and his former canine partner. "I didn't feel as though I had any an alternative. The pound would have kept him for only one week, then he would have been put down."

Mother Superior walked out from behind her desk and examined Harley more closely. "Good Lord, Sister Bernadette. He's *huge!*"

Harley wagged his tail and lunged forward. Sister Bernadette watched helplessly as he placed his mammoth-size paws on Mother Superior's shoulders, then tackled her to the ground. As Mother Superior crashed to the carpet, her habit flew up over her shoulders and exposed her sensible white cotton Hanes briefs. Harley covered her face with wet kisses.

Sister Bernadette screamed and yanked furiously at his leash. "Get off, you brute! Off! Do you want to kill her?"

Mother Superior tried to push him away, but the dog's feet were firmly planted on the voluminous sleeves of her habit. She was drowning in a pool of dog saliva.

"Get him off me, Sister Bernadette!"

"I'm trying but he won't budge." Sister Bernadette pulled on the dog's choker until she thought he was certain to faint from lack of oxygen. Harley continued to shower the nun with affection.

"Get off of her, you beast!" She took her leather work gloves and began to beat him across the head. The dog didn't flinch.

Mother Superior's voice rose out from the dog's underbelly in an authoritative boom: "Off!"

It was as if someone had thrown a switch. Harley stopped, backed off and sat on Sister Bernadette's foot.

"Oh, Mother Superior . . . are you all right?" Sister Bernadette pushed Harley off, then reached down to help Mother Superior to her feet. "I'm so sorry. I don't know what came over him."

Sister Bernadette tried to straighten Mother Superior's habit. She slapped away Sister Bernadette's hand.

"That dog is a menace."

"Not a 'menace,' Mother. He's just . . . overly exuberant at times."

Mother Superior's veil hung low on one side but Bernadette resisted the urge to help right it.

"Imagine if he did that to one of our residents? He'd break every bone in their body." She wagged her finger at Sister Bernadette, "That dog has to go, do you understand?"

"I'll try to find him a home, Mother."

"Try harder," Mother Superior ordered, seeking safety behind her desk. "I'll give you one month . . . until the opening ceremonies. But if you haven't found him a home by that time, I'm afraid he goes to the pound, and it will be no concern of mine what becomes of him. Meanwhile, I'm holding you completely responsible for this . . . 'Cujo.' Keep him under control or I might put him down myself."

Darn! Sister Bernadette had put dill mayonnaise on the maple ham again. She quickly slapped another bread triangle on top and placed it on the platter, hoping it would go unnoticed. Fortunately, Mrs. Norris had gone to answer the phone on the other side of the room.

"A collect call for Mother Superior from Sister Claire?" Mrs. Norris was saying. "I'll have to go and find her. Just a minute, please." Mrs. Norris disappeared through the kitchen door.

This was her chance. Sister Bernadette quickly ripped off her apron and whispered to Sister Theresa, "If Mrs. Norris asks where I've gone, tell her that I had a small errand to run. I'll be right back."

"Why does she need to get a gun?" Sister Joanna asked Sister Theresa, placing another carefully wrapped gherkin pickle on the baking sheet.

Sister Bernadette left Sister Theresa to explain, as she took the back stairs two steps at a time. If she hurried, she could sneak Harley outside and across the road to the park while Mother Superior was busy on the phone.

Mother Superior replaced the phone, Sister Claire's words still ringing fresh in her head.

"I'm so sorry to have to break this to you, Mary Veronica, but Sister Regina Francis is dead. She died from a heart attack two days ago in Medjugorje. I'm at JFK now waiting for Customs to release her body. We should be home by midafternoon."

From some distant place, Mary Veronica could hear herself say, "I think it's best if we keep Sister Regina Francis's death a secret until after the ceremony. This is supposed to be a celebratory occasion and we have hundreds of guests arriving. I don't want to turn this afternoon into a wake. They'll be plenty of time for people to mourn tomorrow. Find a way to stay away until this evening, say around seven o'clock. I'll tell the other sisters after all our guests have left."

She sat quietly for several minutes. She was too stunned to cry.

Mary Veronica had lost more than a fellow sister, she had lost a treasured friend. They had worked together all of her adult life. In fact, she couldn't remember a time when the older nun wasn't there, encouraging, offering support, acting as a mentor and spiritual adviser. That wasn't to say that Sister Regina Francis couldn't be firm when needed. In fact, at times, she could be as tough as nails. But she had been fair and Mary Veronica had always found working with her quite stimulating. Later, when Sister Regina Francis had been chosen as their Mother Superior, she had asked Mary Veronica to act as her assistant.

The women had worked together for over two decades, guiding their order through several financial crises, the declining interest in religious vocations and their shifting roles in today's society. It was Sister Regina Francis who had seen the need for retirement homes for the religious and it was under her leadership that their order had worked, planned and prayed to make this new retirement home a reality. It was the reason why Mary Veronica had insisted that it be named in her honor.

Mary Veronica rubbed her temples. Why had she been so timid in not insisting that Regina Francis postpone her trip until she had completely recovered her strength? It had been less than six months since her last heart attack. The question, however, was rhetorical. She already knew the answer. With or without Mary Veronica's permission, Sister Regina Francis was going to Medjugorje. To visit Medjugorje had been the nun's long-held dream.

Mother Superior rose and walked over to the pair of French doors that opened out onto a small flagstone patio. She paused just inside the archway to watch the volunteer workers. At least, she thought, Sister Regina Francis died in a place that meant so very much to her. She had never seen anyone so obsessed as Regina Francis was with Medjugorje. She had eagerly followed every story involving the town ever since the first apparition twenty years ago. Mother Superior knew that upstairs in Sister Regina Francis's dresser drawer she would find dozens of scrapbooks filled with clippings on the six visionaries and the messages Our Lady had given them over the years to share with the world.

Mother Superior tried to divert her grief by turning her attention to Matthew Metcalf and his friends, who were seated in a circle sipping from large red paper cups. There was laughter and jostling for the attention of the nearly naked girl seated alongside. The dress codes had certainly loosened up since she was a teenager. She still was uncertain about all this new freedom. Surely the lack of stronger parental restrictions helped lead young people into making decisions they were ill equipped to make.

She stepped out farther into the patio. Fred Campbell was fast asleep under a tree, snoring so loudly that it sent the teenagers into gales of laughter. Ben and Timothy were trying to rewind the water hose which someone had left undone.

CRASH!!!

Swearing filled the air. She leaned over the small row of hedges that walled in the patio. Several Knights lay on the ground tangled in tent poles and canvas.

Mike Galligan looked up and caught her eye. "Sorry, Mother."

She nodded, hiding a smile, then turned to walk back inside. A movement in the branches of the old elm tree caught her attention. The Galligan twins were straddling a lower branch just a few feet above Fred Campbell's head, poised with a water balloon readied to be launched.

"Dexter! Rodney! Get down from there this minute!" she shouted, then turned to summon their father. "Michael, come get your boys."

He looked up and she pointed toward the tree. The twins were frantically trying to shinny down. He threw down the tent poles and rushed over.

"Didn't I tell you two to behave or I'd send you home? Well, that does it! I'm calling your mother to come and get you."

"Ah . . . c'mon, Dad. *Please* . . . we'll be good! We promise."

Fred Campbell slept on.

Mother Superior watched it all and thought, Sister Regina Francis is dead yet the world continues. A part of her rebelled and, for just a second, her self-control began to crumple. She wanted the world to mourn, not to go on as though nothing had changed. The vile taste of grief rose in her throat and she struggled to force it back down. Where was her faith? Didn't the Bible teach us that to be absent from the body was to be present with the Lord? If she truly believed, she wouldn't mourn for her friend, she would rejoice. Sister Regina Francis had joined the host of other saints, saints whom the Book of Hebrews stated were "cheering us on." She could use a little cheering right about now, she conceded.

Looking up toward the heavens, she prayed. "Sister Regina Francis, if you're listening, I could use a little help getting through all of this . . . the ceremonies, your funeral. I need strength."

And then the strangest thing happened. It was if her dear friend was standing right beside her. So strong was this sensation that Mother Superior reached out a hand fully expecting someone to grasp it. In fact, she wouldn't have been at all alarmed if Sister Regina Francis materialized right there before her eyes. The feeling lasted for several seconds and then it was gone. A new peace stole over her soul.

She turned to look out into the side gardens and was brought sharply back to the reality of the present. Father Keene was poised with electric shears over what was once a lovely row of front hedges and he was about to take another swipe off bushes that had been reduced to bonsai.

"Good grief!" she exclaimed, then yelled, "Father Keene! Turn off the shears!" But he couldn't hear her above the noise. "Where in blazes is Sister Bernadette?" she murmured, rushing over to unplug the cord. She was supposed to be supervising him.

Chapter 4

"Oh, no, Harley, not there!" Sister Bernadette yanked hard on the heavily woven leash connected to the shepherd, trying to edge him closer to the woods just to the right of St. Cecilia's, but his paws were firmly planted, his ears pinned back and he had a look of enormous relief. She looked down at what Harley was creating, then at the pint-size Ziploc bag in her hand. She should have brought a five-gallon garbage bag.

Sister Bernadette hoped that none of the parishioners from the neighboring Congregational church had seen. Everyone knew how the Congregationalists deeply disapproved of anything or anyone connected with St. Cecilia's, a discourse that had begun with the Catholic church's design—or, rather, lack of it—over a hundred years ago and continued between the two congregations today.

The Congregational church and St. Cecilia's sat on opposite sides of the town green. The Congregational represented New England church architecture at its finest—white clapboard siding, perfectly aligned Doric columns, twelve-over-twelve windows and a picture-perfect garden. St. Cecilia's represented the worst, with its misshapen European Gothic, pseudo-cathedral façade. Irish mill owners originally had commissioned a church to be built fashioned after the great edifices of Europe, and they had succeeded, to a degree, by stuffing tons of stone and marble onto a half-acre parcel of land. The effect was one of dough left to rise over the rim of a bowl.

In truth, St. Cecilia's parishioners felt their church an eyesore, as did the Congregationalists, but their immutable Yankee pride refused to allow them to voice their accord.

Harley finished his business, brushed his hind legs against the grass and looked out toward the road. He froze as still as a piece of marble, his complete attention riveted on the man walking up the pathway toward the front of St. Cecilia's. He began to growl.

"Hush up. That's Chester Platt, you fool. Remember the man who worked on our retirement home's renovations? He's the one who gave you that lovely ham bone that you scarfed down in minutes and then threw up all over Sister Theresa's shoes."

The nun waved to Chester, but he looked right past her. Oh, well. She didn't have time to stop and chat anyway. The hands on the large wrought-iron clock in the center of the park were nearing eleven.

"Dear Lord! Look at the time. The bishop will be here before you know it and I still haven't checked on Father Keene. Come on, Harley. It's back in my room for you."

"Room" was a word that Harley had come to know since living with the nun. She said it a lot. But he had absolutely no desire to go back there just now. The sun felt too good on his coat. The air was filled with a dozen tantalizing smells. He decided to ignore her, firmly planting his grizzly-size paws and sniffing the grass as though it was the most interesting patch of earth he had ever encountered.

"Come on, you brute! You're going to make me late." She tugged on the leash, but it was like trying to move concrete. Why did dog owners wax poetic over these creatures? It was a mystery to her.

Part of the nun's inability to make Harley obey was that the dog had learned that he could ignore her without consequence, unlike his previous owner who had taken none of his nonsense. Harley took a leisurely look around the park, first this way, then that, as the woman continued to pull on his lead and shout. He gave her no mind. Then, much to his delight, he spied Reverend Curtis's charcoal-colored cat, Pewter, dashing into the woods. He lunged forward, barking frantically.

"Stop that!" Sister Bernadette shouted.

Harley pulled harder. The nun leaned back with all of her weight, trying to contain the beast.

"Sit! Stay! Lie down!" Some command should work. This was supposed to be a highly trained police dog. He had always obeyed her uncle instantly.

Harley no longer heard Sister Bernadette's voice or felt the tug on his lead. All he knew was that a cat had disappeared into the woods and he must give chase. With one powerful lunge, Harley broke free, propelling the nun face first onto the grass.

"Come back here, you ungrateful flea bag!" she yelled, spitting out clumps of freshly cut grass as Harley disappeared into the woods.

Of all the days for this brute to break free! She scrambled to her feet, invoking a litany of saints, then plunged into the woods in hot pursuit.

Chester Platt entered the church doors under an archway of metal rod scaffolding and wooden planks. After several months, the building was still under heavy renovation, mostly because Father James kept changing his mind. At this rate, the church's renovations would take another three years to complete.

The sanctuary was quiet. "Sanctified stillness," his former high school sweetheart, Mother Mary Veronica, called it. It was still hard for him to come to grips with her as the head of a religious order. They had grown up together here in Dorsetville, attended church picnics, football games, movies at the Palace Theater, shared hamburgers and fries at the Country Kettle. When he thought about those days, the images were still as crisp as a new dollar bill. Where had the years gone?

In some ways it was great to have Mary Veronica back in town, in others, disconcerting. First of all, what was he supposed to call her? "Mother Superior" sounded heavy, unnatural to his ears, yet "Mary Veronica" seemed too familiar. Since landing the renovation job on the Sister Regina Francis Retirement Home, he had taken to calling her "Sister" as though he were addressing one of his female siblings.

Even after all of these years, Mary Veronica's decision to become a nun still confounded him. The teenage girl he knew didn't seem like "nun" material. Even St. Cecilia's former pastor, Father Fanny, had had his doubts. He called her a "live wire." That was right after she had gotten caught skinny-dipping in Judge Peale's swimming pool. Mary Veronica had thought the family wasn't home.

But something had happened to change her during their senior year in high school. It happened right after her father died. Suddenly the vivacious Mary Veronica became quiet, reflective, finding excuses not to join classmates and friends in their usual lighthearted romps. Instead, she began to volunteer at the soup kitchen over in Waterbury and to champion a plethora of social causes. Her special interest was in helping the poor. The energy that had once fueled her pranks was now channeled into making certain that the downtrodden received their fair share. When Mary Veronica discovered, quite by accident, that Chester's uncle's clinic secretly excluded welfare recipients even though it received state funding, she launched a rigorous campaign to expose this injustice. Her efforts led to a full-scale investigation by the state's attorney. Charges were leveled and his uncle was jailed.

Chester's family had been completely ignorant of the clinic's policies; yet they still felt mortified. Even today, family members studied the ground when someone mentioned it.

The heavy doors closed behind him, blocking out the sunlight as he headed toward the marble basin filled with holy water. He dipped his finger, made the sign of the cross and began the long trek down the center aisle. This was his second visit today. Earlier, he had attended Mass with Barry Hornibrook. If only he could convince Barry to let the sheriff know that Clyde had skipped town with seven hundred fifty thousand in construction loans.

"So, then, what do you plan to do?" he had asked Barry.

"I don't know. Just pray, I guess," Barry said. "Isn't that what Father James always says to do when you've haven't any other option?"

"No, Father James always says to pray *first* and you'll never run out of options," Chester reminded him.

It was late morning, the sanctuary was empty. He was the only person here, yet he didn't feel alone. There was something that seemed to resonate within this space, as though the many prayers uttered within these walls never ceased to resound.

Outside, a ridge of clouds slipped across the morning sun, casting the church's interior into shadow. The candlelight beside the tabernacle that held the host was the only source of light, and he used it to guide his way toward the altar, his heavy work boots pounding against the marble floors in time with the fear that tolled inside his head like some ominous bell. He had tried to keep the fear in check as he had driven over from Doc Hammon's. But now it began to unravel, first one strand . . . "Cancer." Then the next . . . "Maybe four months." Faster and faster, each strand revealing yet another, more powerful fear.

A steady stream of people, conversations, articles, news stories . . . anything and everything that he had ever heard about the horrors of cancer came tumbling forth—women without breasts; children without hair; shrunken, shriveled bodies washed of all color, curled in fetal positions waiting for death to alleviate their constant pain. Suddenly, like a computer unable to process another bit of information, his mind seized. He felt powerless, weak, alone, without hope. He wanted to die now, this moment, circumvent that which lay before him. If only life was a game of Candy Land and he could just skip over the square marked "Suffering," perhaps dying wouldn't be so fearsome.

Chester genuflected facing the host then slid into the pew, reached for the riser and lowered it to the floor, all in one fluid motion through decades of practice. He knelt, closed his eyes and tried to form a prayer.

Where should he begin? He figured he'd start with the Hail Mary but, halfway through the recitation, found the words wouldn't come. He switched over to the Our Father, got as far as "hallowed be Thy name" before his mind went completely blank. What came after that? The Apostles' Creed didn't fare any better. It was as if the prayers, recited since childhood, had suddenly vanished like vapor.

Cancer. His thoughts were moored to this word.

"The tests are in and the results are conclusive," Doc Hammon had said with tears in his eyes. "I'm afraid it's as I suspected, Chester. You have an advanced stage of lung cancer." The doctor laid a hand across his shoulders. It was the only comfort he could offer him.

Chester's first thought was of his Uncle Al, who had died of colon cancer in May of 1991. Before the disease, his uncle had been a strong, strapping man—six foot two, weighing nearly three hundred pounds. By the time he died, he weighed less than a hundred pounds and looked as though his body had been hollowed out with an apple corer, left to shrivel and decay. To this day whenever anyone spoke of Uncle Al, they would preface all statements with a "before" the cancer and "after" the cancer, as if the disease had severed his life in two, a giant black marker drawn down the center of his life.

He thought about Bob Peterson. Hiring him as his company's estimator was the smartest thing he had ever done. Bob had already saved him several thousand dollars.

He wondered how Bob had survived the news that he had cancer and, later, that the odds of him making it through were slim to none. Toward the end, right before a bone marrow match had been found, everyone had braced themselves for his death.

Chester remembered the haunted look Lori wore those last few weeks. He often dropped in at the Country Kettle for a cup of coffee on the way out to a job. He had stopped asking Lori how Bob was. Chester couldn't bear to see the pain the question seemed to inflict.

Everyone in the town had prayed for Bob's healing and God did come through. The thought gave him a modicum of hope.

Chester felt cold and looked up at the air vents. Had George Benson reset the temperature? The streamers tied to the vents to test the airflow were only blowing softly, same as before. Then he realized that the chill he was feeling had nothing to do with the temperature inside the building.

He was scared. Death no longer was an abstract idea, something that would occur at some distant time in the future. It was coming for him now, had earmarked a page to which he was about to turn. His stomach did a flip. For a moment, he thought he might vomit.

Like most people, he had always assumed that he would live into his late seventies or eighties, not die at fifty-three. But he supposed everyone felt the same way, that there was supposed to be more time, that death would come later and that the marker which defined "later" would continue to move forward as one grew older. He looked up at the crucifix and remembered that even Jesus had hoped there would be more time . . . "If this cup can be taken from me . . ."

Chester had brought this upon himself. He took full responsibility. He had smoked two packs of cigarettes a day since he was twelve years old. Everyone—his wife, parents, kids, grandkids—had tried to get him to quit. Truth was, he enjoyed his smokes. Chester looked down at his right index finger, The skin was as tough as shoe leather and stained a deep brown.

About six months ago, he had developed a persistent cough. He had tried Robitussin, lozenges, honey and tea. Nothing worked. In fact, it got worse.

His wife, Patricia, nagged him relentlessly to see Doc Hammon. "Get it checked out, Chester," she continued to plead. "Something's wrong."

He knew she was right, which only made him further delay the checkup. What he didn't know couldn't hurt him, right?

Then he had come down with what he thought was a case of the flu. He felt washed-out. Had no energy. Low-grade fever. Finally, his wife took matters into her own hands and made an appointment with Doc Hammon.

The Doc had taken an X ray, which revealed a shadow on his left lung. A CAT scan and later a biopsy followed. Chester had gotten the results this morning. Stage IV small cell lung cancer, the most deadly and untreatable form of cancer. Apparently it had already metastasized into his bones and liver.

"How much time do I have left?" he'd asked Doc Hammon.

The Doc's eyes filled with tears. "I won't quote numbers. No one knows how long any of us have. Only God."

But when Chester pushed, Doc Hammon conceded that few patients with Chester's advanced form of cancer lived more than three or four months.

Chester broke out in a cold sweat.

"I'll call Patricia to come and get you," the Doc offered.

"No, please. Let's keep this between you and me for now."

Chester looked up into the face of the crucified Lord and studied His wounds. When he was a kid, St. Cecilia's pastor, Father Fanny, once gave a detailed sermon depicting the sufferings of Christ. Four-inch Jerusalem thorns were pushed, savagely, into His head. He was beaten forty times with a whip studded with metal tips and broken pieces of sheep bone. A portion of His beard had been ripped from His face, flesh and all. The nails that the Roman guards had nailed into His feet and wrists had shattered the bones. Father Fanny then went on to describe the horrific hours Christ spent hanging on the cross, the weight from His own body crushing His lungs until He slowly suffocated to death.

For most of his entire adult life, Chester had managed to push that image aside. Like others, he preferred to station his thoughts around the miracles and happy moments of Jesus' ministry, not on His ghastly death. But now, it was the death of suffering and pain that brought him closer to Jesus than he had ever felt before. Through His suffering, Jesus personally knew as a man—not as God—the fear that had now taken possession of Chester's soul.

Lord . . .

Chester looked up with tears in his eyes; his voice broke. He swiped at his nose with the back of his hand.

Lord, I'm scared. I'm really scared. In fact, I've never been so scared in my life. Not even when I was in 'Nam. Over there, we knew the 'Congs could kill us. Sometime. Someplace. But then everyone knows that someday they're going to die. It's different when you know for certain that your time's about up.

I'm ashamed to say that I don't have the kind of faith that's needed to get through this, Lord. Not like Bob Peterson had. I remember once talking to him about dying. He said it was like blowing out a candle because morning had come.

I wish that I could retain that image, Lord, but that's not what I see when I think of death. I see darkness, uncertainty. Like I'm about to walk through a door that will forever close behind me, not at all certain what I will encounter on the other side.

I need Your help. I'm filled with doubts. It's one thing to believe in heaven and salvation when you know that death is some-where . . . out there . . . in the future. It's quite another to believe when you're staring it right in the face.

I want to believe with all my heart that what the Church has taught me is true. That there is a God and there is a heaven. I want to believe, but, instead, all I can feel is terror . . . fear. I kept hear-ing, "What if this is it? What if there is nothing after this life? What if everything I've believed in is a lie?"

Chester looked up at the crucifix and heard the words of John: "For God so loved the world He gave His only Son so that all that believeth on Him shall not perish, but should have everlasting life."

Chester covered his face with his hands and cried out:

Jesus,

Are You real or myth? And if You are real, show me. Please show me because I want to believe. With all my heart, I want to believe that You are real and that You love me and that if—when—I die, You'll be there to greet me. Jesus, You're called the "Great Physi-cian." I want to believe that You have a healing somewhere up there for me.

I once heard Father James say that "death is the ultimate healing" because it reunites us with You. He said that when we really under-stand this, we realize that all prayers for healing are always an-swered. I wish that gave me comfort, but it doesn't. I'm still afraid to die.

I know You must hear this from every dying person, but . . . I have so much I still want to do down here. I've promised my wife for nearly thirty years that I'd take her on that trip down the Mississippi on a steamboat. I'd really like to see the renovations on St. Cecilia's completed. I love this church and it would make me real happy to see that I had a hand in bringing it back.

I've also got two new grandsons. As you know, that now makes four. I'd love to be the grandparent to them that my grandfather was to me. When I was a kid, I could hardly wait for summer vacation so I could spend an entire month at my granddad's. He taught me how to tie a lure, build a blind to hunt ducks, how to track deer through the woods. I remember the magic of those moments with my grandfather. O Lord . . . I want to do the same for my grandsons.

He looked up at the cross, his face streaked with tears and whispered:

But if You decide that it's my time . . . I accept it. I just ask that You help me through this like a man. No whimpering or looking for pity.

Either way, I'm in Your hands. I'll try to believe in Your mercy. Only, please . . . help me with my unbelief.

Father James had just rounded the intersection of Main Street and Harbor Avenue on Pete Jansen's scooter. He leaned slightly into the turn as he rounded the corner, filled with fantasies of trading his Jeep Wagoneer in for a "hog."

Then, from out of nowhere, a cat flew out in front of him immediately followed by a black-and-tan dog the size of a small pony. Father James pulled the handlebars sharply to the left into the oncoming lane and somehow managed to get the scooter back under control. He had just begun to breathe again when suddenly a huge black vehicle loomed up in front, heading straight for him.

He swerved again, this time sharply to the right, but there was not enough time to maneuver. The black vehicle's front fender caught the back end of the scooter, spun it around, hurling the priest into the air like an arrow shot from a bow.

Father James landed twenty feet across the road in a cluster of mountain laurel at the edge of the woods. Thankfully, he lost consciousness as the pain in his leg—now tucked underneath him at an unnatural angle—began to bear down on him with meteoric speed. Just before he blacked out, he saw two men, dressed all in black, rush over and peer down from somewhere outside a rim of darkness. For some reason, they reminded him of the movie *The Godfather*.

Tony Forlano nosed the Lincoln Navigator out of the Conference Center, thinking that the meeting with Barry Hornibrook had gone much better than he and his partner had expected. The look of terror etched on Barry's face when they told him that "the boss" wanted his money back in full, *NOW*, was priceless.

"I don't have it," Barry said, turning a sickly gray. "I told you, Clyde took off with everything. I don't even have enough to pay the contractors to finish this place. If I did, I could open up and eventually pay you back what Clyde stole. You've got to believe me."

"And so Clyde stole your money and that's somehow *our* problem?" Vinnie Costello asked.

Tony grabbed Barry by the collar, pulling him out of his chair. "This is how it is. Your partner took our money to invest. Now we want it back, with the interest we were promised. *Capisce?*"

"But how?" Barry wanted to know. "I don't have the money you guys loaned him."

"Apparently you weren't listening. This isn't our problem. It's yours." Tony pushed Barry back into the chair.

"You want me to take him outside, Tony?" Vinnie asked. "I could show him what we do with welchers?"

"I'll find the money," Barry pleaded, his voice raising an octave. "I'll get it somehow . . . I don't know how . . . but I'll find a way. I just need a little time."

"What do you think?" Tony asked Vinnie. "Should we give him a break?"

"I dunno." Vinnie looked as though he was thinking it over. "What will the boss say?"

Tony rubbed his chin. "Yeah . . . the boss. He might think we were too soft. You know how he feels about us guys getting soft."

"Let me have a couple of months," Barry pleaded, looking from one man to the other. "I know I can figure something out."

"Months?" Tony laughed. "You're kidding, right? What months? A couple of days, maybe. A few weeks, tops."

"All right, all right, a few weeks, then. I'm sure I can work it out in a few weeks."

"Oh . . . let him have a little more time," Vinnie said. Tony frowned. Vinnie threw open his arms. "It's my birthday tomorrow. I'm feeling kinda generous. Can I help it if I'm a sucker for a sob story?"

"All right . . . all right . . . if you want to give him some more time, I'll go along with it. But he's got two weeks . . . tops . . . to come up with the cash, then we'll be back."

Tony bent down and pretended to straighten Barry's tie. He tightened the knot. "And when we come back, you'd better have *all* of it or else . . ." He drew up hard on the tie, cutting off Barry's air supply. "You get my drift?"

Tony's thoughts were still on the meeting as he rounded a sharp corner at the exact moment a German shepherd dashed out of the woods in chase of a gray cat. He swerved hard to the left, missing the dog by a hairsbreadth.

"You see that?" Tony said, giving a nervous laugh. "I nearly hit that mutt."

"WATCH OUT!!!!" Vinnie screamed.

A priest riding a motor scooter had just rounded the bend and was headed directly for them.

"Is he . . . dead?" Vinnie asked.

"I dunno."

Tony leaned down and felt the priest's pulse.

Father James moaned, opened his eyes for just a second, then sank back into unconsciousness.

"He's alive."

"Thank you, Mother of God," Vinnie shouted. But with the relief came a flash flood of anger. "You idiot! You stupid idiot. You hit a priest!"

"You think I did it on purpose?" Tony snapped. "You saw the dog. I swerved to avoid hitting the dog and then this guy shows up heading right for me. There wasn't anything I could do."

"I know. I saw it too, but Jesus . . . you hit a priest," Vinnie stared at Father James's crumpled body. "We'd better call an ambulance."

"Wait a minute." Tony grabbed his wrist. "You're not calling anyone."

"You can't be serious. The guy's hurt. He needs medical attention."

Tony stood up and looked anxiously around. "Listen, *paisan*, if you call an ambulance the police will get involved."

Father James moaned.

Tony shoved Vinnie toward the Lincoln, which was still idling by the side of the road. "Let's get out of here before he wakes up."

"You're talking about hit-and-run?"

"No one's seen the accident so we're still in the clear."

Vinnie hesitated.

He pushed Vinnie inside the SUV. "We'll make an anonymous call to 911 when we hit the interstate. The priest will be okay until then. Trust me."

"Trust you?" Vinnie sneered. "Trusting you is what got me into this mess to begin with."

Neither of the two men noticed the bag lady hidden under a clump of mountain laurel. Her name was Molly and she had just arrived in town an hour ago. She had seen the whole thing.

She waited until the Navigator had disappeared around the bend before stepping out from her hiding place and heading toward the injured priest.

"You'd think the good Lord would let a body get settled in and rested before putting her to work," she mumbled, bending over the fallen priest. The temperature was already past ninety and she pined for a nice lie down after several hours spent riding in a stuffy bus.

Father James tried to open his eyes, but they felt as though they were being weighted down. With seemingly Herculean effort he was finally able to open them just a slit, but found he couldn't focus. There was a bright light and it was blinding.

His eyelids began to grow heavy again. He relinquished his hold, allowing himself to be dragged down, down like an anchor thrown from the side of a ship, into the depths of unconsciousness.

Molly bowed her head and prayed. When she was finished, she walked to the center of the road to wait.

Sam Rosenberg had just delivered the last of the noontime meals to ninety-two-year-old Mrs. Hemmings on the north side of town and wouldn't have been running late if Mrs. Hemmings hadn't forgotten where she had left the medicine that she was supposed to take with each meal. It was especially taxing since he had wanted to return home after the meal deliveries so he could take a shower before the afternoon's ceremonies. Sam had searched every kitchen and bathroom cabinet before spying the bottle of pills tucked into Mrs. Hemmings's sweater pocket.

Harriet had called Sam just as he was leaving Mrs. Hemmings's.

"I'm afraid that Allison and I need an extra foot of garland for the front dais and we're running out of time. Would you be a dear and stop by my greenhouse on the way back and grab some more bougainvillea? It's on the worktable just as you walk in."

Sam said he wouldn't mind at all. He'd just change his shirt instead of taking a shower. He loved being needed by Harriet.

Normally, Sam would have taken the back way to Harriet's, turning off of Harbor Road by Judge Peale's place and making a left onto Sherman Hill. He liked to avoid Main Street when Deputy Hill was directing traffic. The young officer had a habit of stopping people as they drove by for a little chat, which created something of a traffic jam. Last time it had taken Sam nearly twenty minutes just to go a half a mile.

But as Sam neared the turnoff, his mind was less on driving and more on whether he should search for a large box to transport the bougainvillea or put it directly into the trunk of his car; consequently, he went sailing right past Judge Peale's place. By the time he realized what he'd done, it just seemed easier to take the route through town than to turn and go all the way back. Maybe the sheriff had given Deputy Hill the day off, he told himself, hopefully.

Sam's Plymouth Duster had begun the slight incline past the new Conference Center when he spied a scruffy old woman in the middle of the road. She motioned for him to stop. Suddenly images of the film Sam had recently seen at the senior center warning of just such situations used to hijack cars from unsuspecting motorists flashed through his mind. Still, she seemed as though she needed help. He certainly couldn't just pass by and ignore someone in trouble. His conscience got the better of him. He slowed down, making certain his doors were locked, pulled over and lowered his window only an inch.

"Hello. Do you need help?"

"Yes. I'm afraid I do. You see a man's just been hit by a car. He's lying over there." Molly pointed toward a body sprawled by the side of the road.

"A man . . . ?" Sam jumped out of the car. "Dear God of Abraham! It's Father James."

Chapter 5

Sarah Peterson was hidden behind the low branches of a weeping willow. It provided the perfect place to watch without detection as her classmates ran around the Congregational churchyard ready for Bible camp to begin. A few frazzled mothers still continued to hop out of minivans and station wagons with rumpled children in tow, issuing orders:

"Don't forget to give Mrs. Phillips your milk money."

"Stay away from peanuts, you know you're allergic."

"Have Father Dennis deliver this get well card to Father James."

Intermittently, an explosive scream would pierce the quiet morning air like a popped balloon.

Sarah liked Bible camp. There were lots of fun things to do. Normally, Sarah would have been part of the gaggle of girls who were now racing around the park, but today was special. She was waiting for her best friend, Jamie, to arrive and didn't want to play. Sarah had been invited to Jamie's for a sleepover tonight and her little heart was aflutter with joyous anticipation. It was her very first overnight stay.

Mommy had splurged and bought her a new pink nightgown (her favorite color) and slippers to match just for the occasion, now carefully packed inside her nylon backpack. Several times, Sarah unzipped it to run her hand over the soft, brushed-cotton nightgown and bury her face in the cloth. Sarah loved the smell of new things.

On top of her nightgown lay Daddy's pretty blue rosary, which had been lent to Sarah for this very special event.

Sister Claire had given it to Daddy because he had helped get Sister Regina Francis back home to Dorsetville. Sister Regina Francis had died. They had gone to her funeral. Sarah felt sad for the nuns, many of whom were crying. But the Mass was very long and boring and all she wanted to do was to go home and play with her Barbie dolls. Her mother had told her to stop fidgeting.

But she did get a chance to peek through the glass opening in the casket and look at the dead nun's face when she accompanied her father up to the front of the church to receive communion. They had had to file past the coffin. Sister Regina Francis looked as though she were sleeping.

Sarah held the rosary up to the dabbed sunlight that softly filtered through the branches. The beads sparkled like glitter. They were such a pretty blue and they felt smooth, like the sea glass she and Mommy had found last June on the beach when they had visited Martha's Vineyard. She wished she could put the beads on around her neck and wear them like a necklace, but Mommy had said they were not jewelry. Each bead was a prayer and must be treated with reverence. She had asked what reverence meant. Mommy said it meant treating something special because it belonged to God.

Sarah would tell Jamie not to wear them either. Jamie wouldn't know anything about rosaries. She was Baptist.

Sarah was startled by the loud warlike cries of the Galligan twins and nearly dropped the strand of beads. She quickly slipped it into her pants pocket just in case the twins discovered her hiding place and tried to snatch it away from her. Last week they had taken her favorite book, *Goodnight, Fish*, and wouldn't give it back. In tears, she had gone to Father Dennis. He had made the twins stand in the corner.

"Tattletale," Rodney taunted later at playtime.

"Baby," Dexter added.

Sarah waited until the twins' voices had faded before peeking out from her hiding place.

"Why, there you are," said Mrs. Phillips, parting the willow's lower tendrils. "I was just about to give up trying to find you when I remembered that this was your favorite hiding place. It's time to go in."

Mrs. Phillips was the director of the Congregational church's Sunday school and oversaw the morning portion of the Bible camp. Sarah liked Mrs. Phillips. She gave them lots of pictures to color.

Sometimes Father Dennis helped out, too, and Mother Superior taught in the afternoon. She had taken over for Father James. Father James had gotten run over by a car and had a broken leg and couldn't teach. He had been in the hospital, but now he was back at the rectory. She and Mommy had gone to see him yesterday.

Mrs. Phillips helped Sarah with her backpack. "We're just about to go in and say our morning prayers."

"Can't I wait out here until Jamie comes?" Sarah asked. "I'm having a sleepover at Jamie's tonight."

Mrs. Phillips looked down at the young child with compassion, hating to be the bearer of ill news.

"I'm afraid that Jamie's mother has just called. She has the mumps and won't be coming for the rest of the week. I assume that means your sleepover will have to be postponed."

Sarah looked as though she would burst into tears. Mrs. Phillips patted her golden curls.

"I'm so sorry, dear. It is a great disappointment, I'm sure. But maybe you can arrange another sleepover at Jamie's when she's better. Now, you'd better hurry inside." She handed Sarah her backpack.

"Yes, Mrs. Phillips," Sarah said, dragging the nylon bag behind her as she made her way across the lawn to the basement entrance.

Mrs. Phillips watched her leave. Poor dear, she thought. Maybe she could find something special for her to do today.

Mrs. Phillips took another look around the grassy area, making certain that all the children were inside, when she spied the Galligan twins standing by the edge of the woods. They were shoving something inside one of their backpacks.

"Rodney! Dexter! Come here. You'll be late for class."

The twins looked up nervously and quickly zippered up the bag. What were these two up to this time? she wondered. Last week it had been a paint gun smuggled into class. The men's downstairs bathroom still bore fluorescent lime green paint spots. Well, one thing was for certain: next year Bible camp would be held at St. Cecilia's.

"Hand it over," she demanded, stretching out her hand as the twins tried to speed pass.

"Hand *what* over?" Rodney asked with practiced innocence.

"What part of me looks stupid, Rodney Galligan?"

Mrs. Phillips had taught Sunday school at the Congregational church for more years than she'd like to remember and she knew trouble when she saw it. She grabbed for his bag and opened it. "I saw you stuff something inside."

Dexter stood off to one side and shifted his backpack behind him. Something moved inside it.

"We're not hiding anything," Dexter said, then added boldly: "Go on. Look all you want." His brother threw him a deadly glare.

Mrs. Phillips pulled out a handful of blank magazine subscription cards. *Cooking Light, National Geographic, Audubon, Writer's Digest, Good Housekeeping.* She frowned.

"We collect them," Rodney offered.

"Whatever for?" Mrs. Phillips asked.

"Er . . . we . . . we're trying to set a Guinness world's record for the most subscription cards," lied Dexter, truly amazed at his innate ability to conjure up a tale on the spot. It was a gift.

"I see," Mrs. Phillips said, stuffing the cards back inside Rodney's backpack. "I didn't know that the Guinness people gave out awards for subscription card collections."

"Oh, yeah," the twins lied in unison. Rodney added, "It's a new category."

"Well, be that as it may, you had better leave your collecting until later and hurry along. Class is about to begin." She handed the backpack to Rodney.

"Do you have any magazines with subscription cards we could have?" Dexter asked. Rodney punched him in the arm.

"Ouch!"

"I suppose I might. I'll take a look when I get home. But right now, you two had better hurry on downstairs. Father Dennis wants to do a head count on how many chocolate cupcakes will be needed for dessert at lunchtime. You don't want to miss out, now, do you?"

"Chocolate cupcakes?" Dexter yelled, racing toward the entrance-way.

"We're allergic to chocolate, remember?" Rodney whispered to his brother as he caught up with him by the back door.

"What's a few little bumps?" Dexter said, electing to forget the last time chocolate had led to a body covered with hives.

By early afternoon, the town park had grown quiet, except for the muted sounds of hammers and saws still emanating from St. Cecilia's. Inside the Congregational church the children had returned from re-cess. The small ones were taking naps; older children were reading qui-etly or writing in their journals. Father Dennis watched over this portion of the school day until one-thirty, when Mother Mary Veron-ica usually arrived. But for now, she was luxuriating in an hour of unin-terrupted time, quite a rarity on any given day. She sat in the gazebo with a canvas bag of unopened mail at her side, enjoying the soft, cool breeze that caressed her cheeks. It was one of those halcyon August days when temperatures dropped into the lower eighties and an occa-sional puffy white cloud sailed across a flawless sky. The air was filled with birdsong and the subtle scent of wild phlox and gardenia. How easy it would have been just to lose herself in the beauty of the day. But being a person of great discipline, she opened the bag. With any luck, she would have most of this mail sorted through before it was time to take over the camp. She had assumed Father James's role while he was recuperating.

Mother Superior still marveled that the priest hadn't been killed. She had seen the scooter, or, more accurately, what had once been a scooter. Now it was an unrecognizable mass of twisted metal stashed behind Tri Town Auto. She shuddered to think what would have hap-pened if Father James hadn't been thrown clear upon impact.

She reached in her deep pockets for her reading glasses, then began shifting through the pile of unopened envelopes that arrived in varying colors, shapes and sizes. Sorting through the mail was such a simple thing, yet she had been unable to manage it for more than a week. Lately it seemed as though there were more tasks than hours in which to perform them.

Overseeing the running of a retirement home was a twenty-four-hour, seven-day-a-week job. There were the elderly residents and their myriad needs, an order of nuns with varying temperaments and the home's complex administrative duties. If only Sister Regina Francis were alive. How many times had Mother Superior wished this since her death? Each time, the thought evoked a deep ache in her chest more painful than a physical wound. The older nun had been both a mentor and a close friend. But more important, she had been a pillar of faith. Mother Superior could certainly use some of her spiritual strength right about now.

She glanced down at the mail lying on her lap. How many envelopes contained requests from retired clergy for admission into the home? Half? Some would have to be turned away, others added to the waiting list that already exceeded eighty-five. And the home had been open less than a month.

If only there were something else she could do, but what? Most of the order's resources had been invested in the home. What was left had been reinvested to provide the capital needed to keep it financially solvent.

Sister Regina Francis's voice rang in her ears. "When God is present, He asks us to dream big. We offer up our hands and a willing heart to do His work, confident that He will provide a way."

As doughy as this philosophy might have sounded, it seemed to have served Regina Francis well throughout her tenure as Mother Superior. How many times had Mary Veronica watched with awe as the older nun's prayers were miraculously answered? She was reminded of the new station wagon donated the day after their old car had been declared not repairable. The repeated gifts of unsolicited money that had shown up whenever they had a financial need, including the initial funding for the retirement home. Someone had anonymously sent them a check for what turned out to be the exact amount they had needed. And how many times had she watched Regina Francis place her hands over a meager box of food provisions for the soup kitchen their order had overseen in Burlington and pray that there would be enough to go around. Each time there had been plenty, with some left over.

"Dear Lord," Mother Mary Veronica prayed, "if the burden I feel placed upon my heart is truly from You, I trust that You will find a way."

She looked out into the town green and noticed Dorsetville's newest resident, a bag lady named Molly, plopped down on a bench and reading the *Dorsetville Gazette*. Since her arrival a few weeks ago, Molly had become a familiar sight in town, wandering down tree-lined avenues with her shopping bags in tow, occasionally stopping in to chat with business owners along Main Street.

Dorsetville folks were by nature very curious and many had tried to get Molly to open up about her past. But she remained quiet on the subject, preferring, it seemed, to retain an air of mystery. Eventually folks stopped asking. Most assumed that like many in her position she had fallen on hard times and simply didn't want to talk about it. They respected that.

And, of course, everyone in town was so grateful that Molly had been around to help Father James after the accident. It made people even more insistent that she be given a decent place to stay. Both Father James and Reverend Curtis, the Congregationalists' pastor, had each offered Molly a room at their rectories. Molly said no. She preferred the fresh air and the park bench. The Salvation Army had fixed up a room just off their meeting hall and said it was hers in exchange for sweeping the floors after meetings. Molly showed up each morning to sweep their hall clean but steadfastly refused the lodging. Even Mother Superior and Sister Claire had offered her shelter at the retirement home, and Sister Bernadette personally invited her to share her room. Molly had declined both these offers as well.

Eventually people resigned themselves to Molly's choice of residence on the town green. Several stopped by Molly's bench each morning on their way to work to drop off coffee or a muffin. Others visited throughout the day for a little chat. Nellie Anderson dropped off a sandwich and chocolate shake from the Country Kettle each afternoon en route to her office-cleaning job over in Woodstock. (She still hadn't told Harry about the job, instead making excuses as to why she was not available certain nights.)

Molly thanked them all for their kindness but said they shouldn't worry themselves on her account. She was fine. Used to fending for herself. Liked her independence. People honored that, but it was still hard for the compassionate souls of Dorsetville not to worry when the skies grew dark with rain clouds or when a fierce wind roared down from the mountains.

Mother Superior watched Molly settle down for her afternoon nap and wished she could join her. Instead, she glanced up at the clock. It read one-fifteen. Where had the time flown? She quickly stuffed the letters back inside the bag and hurried down the gazebo stairs. Her Bible story class was about to begin.

"Mother Superior, can I have a tissue?" Dexter asked.

"*May* I have a tissue," the nun corrected, reaching down to open the lower desk drawer where the box of Kleenex was kept.

She was just about to reach her hand in when a large, gray snake raised its head. Its tongue brushed against the tips of her fingers. The nun recoiled in horror and screamed as the five-foot boa constrictor edged its way up the side of the drawer and spilled out onto the floor.

Five-year-old Ebony Clark was the first to spy the cause of the nun's alarm. "It's a snake! A snake is loose!" she screamed.

The classroom erupted. Children bolted out of their seats. Some joined in screaming. Others began to cry. Three boys started to climb up the bookshelves at the back of the room.

"Children, get down from there this minute. You're going to fall and hurt yourself!" Mother Superior shouted above the melee.

Two boys came down, but seven-year-old Sean Michaels ignored her warning and, as predicted, fell and hurt his arm. More cries.

"It's coming this way!" shouted a small, curly redheaded girl whose freckles had all but disappeared under the high color of fright.

The children swarmed like a nest of bees to the other side of the room, tipping over chairs and desks, scraping knees and hands. It seemed the entire room was in a state of panic. Sarah Peterson slipped unnoticed inside a cubbyhole and closed herself in. She was certain the snake couldn't get her in there.

"Calm down, children. Just make your way toward the door and head outside," the nun commanded, cradling the injured child in her arms. The snake had disappeared behind a tower of brightly colored plastic cubes on the opposite side of the room.

"Kevin, run next door and see if you can find the janitor. Rodney and Dexter Galligan, I want to see you as soon as we get outside. This has your handiwork written all over it."

A stampede of screaming children raced out of the classroom door, up the stairwell, and exploded into the churchyard. Several mothers, who had gathered on the lawn to wait for the school dismissal bell, and who had been discussing the new Japanese restaurant scheduled to open in town, stopped midsentence.

"A snake . . . a snake is loose downstairs," cried one breathless little boy.

"A snake? Are you sure?" asked his frantic mother. "What kind of a snake? Did it bite you?" She snagged him in midflight. "What's this?"

"A mosquito bite," the child whimpered.

"Are you sure? I don't know. It looks suspicious to me. Maybe we'd better have Doc Hammon take a look just to be on the safe side."

The child was immediately rushed off under Mother Superior's protests.

"Please, you must let me know who you're picking up," she shouted.

No one paid any attention. Instead, parents whisked children away into an assortment of minivans, SUVs and station wagons, leaving the nun with absolutely no idea who had been picked up and by whom.

She had carried Sean Michaels up from the classroom and now set him down on the grass, but he refused to let go of her neck. She tried to pry his hands loose.

"Hush now, Sean. It's only a little cut. We'll walk across the street to the home and have Sister Claire put a Band-Aid on it."

"Does Sister Claire have Harry Potter Band-Aids that glow in the dark?" Sean sniffed.

"Harry Potter . . . ? No."

He resumed his wailing. Good grief!

"But Sister Bernadette does keep a box of Oreo cookies in the back of her closet."

"Double-stuffed?" he queried.

"Yes, I'm sure," she fibbed.

Chapter 6

F ather James was seated in bed with his leg propped up against a stack of feather pillows, enjoying the landscape from his makeshift bedroom window. From here he had an unobstructed view of the town green and a portion of the Congregational church and, if he leaned hard to the left, he could catch a glimpse of Molly's park bench. He especially liked to watch the children at Bible camp during recess; the boys raced around the green while the girls sat in the shade making dandelion necklaces. Oh, to be a kid again.

Mrs. Norris had commandeered several of Chester Platt's workers who had been plastering the church sanctuary's walls to move Father James's mahogany bed down from the rectory's upstairs and into the dining room.

"You can't expect a woman in my condition to be running up and down stairs all days. Carrying heavy trays of food and whatever else you might need," she explained to Father James when he had first arrived home from the hospital. "Besides that, my arthritis has been acting up. My big toes pain me something terrible. It's going to be a wet August."

Although many doubted Mrs. Norris's insistence that she was on the brink of death, no one in Dorsetville would think to question her weather predictions. Her arthritis hasn't been wrong in forty years.

Father James was fine with the new arrangement. In fact, it seemed to be less intimidating to many of his parishioners. There was something unnerving, the Henderson sisters had told him, about speaking of spiritual matters while seated in a priest's bedroom.

"Somehow seems downright indecent," Ruth Henderson said. Her sister June emphatically agreed. Ruth added, "But here, in the rectory's dining room is like visiting the Pope at Wendy's."

Father James had just smiled without comment. Ruth's train of thought perplexed everybody.

Since Father James couldn't serve Mass while tethering on a set of crutches, or visit parishioners, these duties had been delegated to Father Dennis and Father Keene. That left him with confessions. Every Wednesday and Saturday afternoon, his makeshift bedroom/dining room also served as a confessional.

"Forgive me, Father, for I have sinned. It's been one week since my last confession," Father Dennis intoned, then paused. "I confess I've done it again. I took the tuna casserole that Mrs. Norris had made us for supper.

"You see, Sam Rosenberg was short a few meals for Meals-on-Wheels. Seems there was some sort of mix-up over in Woodstock. They forgot to add the two new seniors that signed up last week. Anyway, I offered our supper. I thought you wouldn't mind. How about a hamburger from the Country Kettle? My treat."

"Forgive me, Father, for I have sinned," said Mrs. Norris. "It's been one hour since my last confession. Now, before you get your cassock all in a twist, I know you just heard my confession, but that was before I went into the kitchen and discovered the tuna casserole I had made for supper was missing. And we both know who took it, now, don't we? It's times like these that I understand how some people take to plotting murder."

"Bless me, Father, for I have sinned. It's been one week since my last confession," intoned Sister Claire. "I'm afraid that I've been lying to people who call, inquiring if we have any vacancies at the retirement home. Instead of saying that we're completely booked up and the likelihood of something opening in the near future is slim to none, I tell them that I would be happy to put them on our waiting list, implying that they might shortly receive a call. I know this is deceptive, but I just can't bear to hear the disappointment in their voices when they find out we haven't any more room."

"Bless me, Father, for I have sinned. It's been about six weeks since my last confession," said Timothy McGree, wearing a pair of Christmas red, polyester bell-bottom trousers and a black T-shirt bearing a photo of The Rock, the wrestler, a recent cast-off from one of his nephews.

"I swore. Twice. Got my finger caught in Sam's car door. We went for a ride over to the Kmart. Thought I might help cheer up Ben. He's been a little depressed lately ever since his grandson started hanging around with his own gang of friends. Not that that's a bad thing. Fact is, I think it'll do the kid a world of good. About time he made some friends his own age instead of hanging around with us old coots. But Ben feels left out. You know how close those two are. And now that Matthew has a girlfriend—her name's Stephanie Costello—you know who she is, right, Father? Used to live in Uniondale. Has a brother, Dominic. The boy who helped Matthew with that hologram last year. Maybe we'd better not go into that.

"Anyway, the family moved to Dorsetville a few months ago. Now, because of this girl Stephanie, and Matthew's other new friends, Ben hardly ever sees him anymore." Timothy paused a moment, then concluded: "Ben needs to find something else to occupy his mind, but I'll be darned if any of us can think of what that might be. Would you pray on that, Father?"

"Bless me, Father, for I have sinned," Matthew said. "It's been a couple of months since my last confession." The teenager grew quiet. "It's about my grandfather. I haven't been spending a lot of time with him lately. You see, I have a lot of schoolwork and things to do." He paused. "No . . . that's not exactly true. I guess I could find the time." Another pause. "It's just that I have these really neat new friends and, well, if they see me hanging out with Granddad they'll think I'm a geek.

"I know I shouldn't care what my friends say, but the truth is I do. I guess that's wrong, right, Father?" Matthew sat back in the chair and studied his hands. "You see, I've never been very popular. But now, since the hologram last year and everything—I know I said it before but I *really* am sorry for all the trouble it made for the church—the kids think I'm sort of . . . cool. I don't want to mess that up by having them see me hanging out with Granddad."

Matthew paused again. "And since I'm confessing and everything, I might as well tell you it all. You see . . . there's this girl. And, well, I . . . sometimes . . . have . . . these . . . impure thoughts . . ."

The air over Long Island was hot and humid, draped like an iron curtain across the fish-shaped landmass. For days, not a single breeze drifted in off the Atlantic near Fire Island or from the sound along the north shore. Suddenly the air seemed as motionless as the Long Island Expressway on a Friday night.

People with asthma or emphysema were warned not to venture outdoors. Stay inside with the air conditioner, News Channel 4 weatherman Chris Cimino cautioned. It was advice most heeded until the Long Island Lighting Company was unable to meet all the demand. Brownouts popped up first in Nassau County, then worked their way out to Suffolk County. In desperation, people flocked to the shopping malls. There were generators there.

Larry Pulaski's clinic had gone dark at the precise moment his receptionist alerted him that a Vinnie Costello was holding on line 4.

"I'll be right back, Jeanie," he told his young patient, then walked out into the hall, making certain to close the door tightly behind him. He picked up the phone anything but pleased.

"I told you *never* to use the name Vinnie Costello around here. What if one of my girls remembers it?"

"So then they'd know you got a mobster friend named Vinnie Costello."

"Cut that out, Ernie, it's not funny."

"Do I sound like I'm laughing? You're the one who came up with this harebrained scheme." He mimicked Larry's voice. "'Let's pretend we're mobsters so Hornibrook would get scared into getting us back the money we loaned his deadbeat partner, Clyde Hessler.' Isn't that what you said . . . 'Tony Forlano'?"

"Cut it out, Ernie," Larry looked anxiously over toward the front desk. Fortunately, none of his girls were on the phone. He couldn't risk anyone overhearing this conversation. "So, what do you want and make it quick. I'm in the middle of taking an impression and the lights keep dimming. You still have power on your side of town?"

"No, we lost it about an hour ago and me with a new shipment of cold cuts in the walk-in in back." Ernie DeVito owned a deli opposite the harbor in Port Jefferson. "There goes this week's profits. But that's not why I'm calling. Have you heard anything else?"

"Not since the last time we spoke," Larry said, watching the light panels above his head finally go black. "Someone get a flashlight," he yelled. He opened the treatment-room door. "Sorry, Jeanie. Seems like the power's out for good. I'll send in one of my girls to take that bib off. We'll have to reschedule for sometime early next week."

He stretched the phone cord into the adjoining treatment room and continued his conversation. "Like I told you yesterday, I called Mercy Hospital and they said that the priest, this Father James, had only suffered a broken leg. He was in traction for a couple of weeks, but since then he's been discharged and is recuperating back at the rectory."

"I don't like this, Larry. What if the cops trace the rented Navigator back to us? We could be charged with hit-and-run."

Like he didn't know. "There's nothing we can do about it, now is there? Look, as I've tried to explain to you a hundred times, if we confess that we were the ones who hit the priest, the cops will run a check and find out who we really are. That means Hornibrook will know we're not mobsters and have absolutely no incentive to pay us back what we loaned his partner."

"You know how nuts this whole thing is? Us, pretending to be mobsters? We should have hired a lawyer and sued." Ernie was living on antacids.

"And then what? Tell our wives that we let a guy we met in a sports bar talk us into loaning him our retirement savings because he said we could double our money in six months. I don't know what your wife will do, but mine will head right to the divorce courts and I'll never see another dime from my practice."

"You're probably right. Your Marlene is a real witch when she gets mad, but then, my Denise is no slouch in that department."

"Yeah, well, I don't know how much longer I can keep my witch off her broom. She has her heart set on one of those retirement homes down in Florida."

"Denise keeps pestering me about the same thing," said Ernie. Their wives were best friends.

"Marlene has asked me at least a half a dozen times this week about the money."

"What did you tell her?"

"Said I invested it in some CDs and if we cash them in before their maturity date we'll lose a bundle."

"She buying that?"

"Until last week. Now she wants me to hand over the certificates so she can go to the bank and wrangle some kind of deal with the manager."

"So, what are we going to do?"

"We're going to have to get that money back, that's what."

"But how? It's been nearly a month since we paid a visit to Hornibrook and still no cash."

"Dr. Pulaski," Larry's assistant interrupted. "I've checked your cal-

endar for next week. You haven't any openings. What do you want me
to do about rescheduling Jeanie?"

"I'll be right there." Larry cupped his hand over the phone and lowered his voice. "Listen, we need to give Hornibrook a call. Remind him
that if he doesn't cough up the money, there's going to be trouble. Why
don't you give him a ring?"

"Me? Why me?"

"Because it's easier for you to call than me."

"Sure . . . I'm just a lowly deli owner and you're the big-time orthodontist. I get the picture."

"Don't start in on that again." He hated when Ernie played that
tune. "Call Hornibrook and tell him that we'll be back for another visit
at the end of the week."

"You're kidding, right?" Ernie asked. "You're not seriously considering going back to Dorsetville."

"You got a better idea?"

Geez, how did he let Larry talk him into all of this? "All right, I'll
call Hornibrook and tell him we'll be up later in the week."

"Tell him we expect the money paid in full or else."

"Or else what?"

"I don't know," Larry thought for a moment then he remembered.
"I saw his boat tied up at the end of the dock. Tell him that if he doesn't
pay us in full, we'll blow it up."

Sheriff Bromley glanced up over his desk. "What is that?" he asked, in-
dicating the large dog leaning against his deputy's pant leg.

"This is Harley," Hill said proudly. "He's attack trained."

"An attack dog?"

Harley looked steadily in his direction.

"Yeah, ain't he something? Got him from Sister Bernadette. He belonged to her uncle, a retired New Jersey policeman. But the guy died
and she didn't know what to do with him, so . . ."

"So of course you took him," the sheriff finished. "Hill, why would
anyone need an attack dog in Dorsetville?"

"To apprehend dangerous criminals," he answered brightly.

"And we have a lot of those in Dorsetville, right?" Bromley ran a hand through his thinning hair. Well, this confirmed it. The man was a lunatic. He changed the subject.

"Listen, I need you to go over to the town green and see if that bag lady Molly is still at the park."

Molly was the only eyewitness the sheriff had to Father James's accident. He planned to keep a close eye on her.

"Sure, Chief. Harley and I will take a walk up there. Check things out. Make certain she's not in violation of . . ." He couldn't think of anything off the top of his head.

"Hill, I've told you a hundred times not to call me 'Chief'!"

"All right, Ch . . . Sheriff. Harley and I will just . . ."

"Hill, shut up and listen *very* carefully to what I'm about to say." Bromley pined for the old days when stupidity was a justifiable cause to fire someone. Now he had to worry about lawsuits and labor unions.

The deputy moved closer.

"I want you to walk up to the town green and find the bag lady. That's the lady with all the bags. Then see if it looks like she might be getting ready to move on. If so, get me on the radio right away. You're to do nothing else. Got that?"

Deputy Hill was mute.

"Hill, is there something wrong with you? I asked you a question."

"Oh . . . it's all right for me to talk now?"

"What???"

"You told me to shut up."

"And now I'm telling you to answer me!" Bromley shouted. Harley barked.

"Be quiet." The dog instantly obeyed.

"Hey, Chief, that was neat how you made him do that. Tell him to be quiet again."

"Hill, you're giving me an ulcer. Did you understand what I've just asked you to do?"

"Yes, sir."

"Good. Then go." He sat back down and riffled through some papers. "And Hill."

"Yes, Chief."

The sheriff looked up over his paperwork and glared.

"I mean Sheriff?"

"Leave the attack dog."

Chapter 7

"Another cup of coffee, Barry?" Wendy asked.

"Sure, why not?" Barry said, hunching over the counter.

Wendy kept one eye on the coffee she was pouring and the other on Barry. "This makes six cups so far. You're normally a one cup kind of guy. You okay?"

"Me? Yeah, I'm all right."

Wendy raised an eyebrow.

"What?"

"Nothing. Whatever it is, it's probably none of my business."

"Are you pickin' on Dorsetville's leading businessman, Wendy?" Harry asked, stepping out from behind the grill.

More like a "misleading businessman," Barry wanted to say. He knew the whole town was counting on his hotel to bring in a surge of new business and help stimulate the downtown. If only they knew the truth!

"Not me," Wendy said, replacing the coffeepot on the hot plate. "But since I'm not needed out in front, I think I'll go in the kitchen and grab another rack of cups."

"While you're back there, would you bring out my mug? I left it by the steaming table."

"The one Nellie gave you?"

"Yes, Wendy, the one Nellie gave me," Harry rested his chin on his chest. He knew where this was going.

"The hand-painted mug that Nellie made *especially* for you last Christmas?"

"Yes, Wendy."

"But, Harry, we have racks full of mugs under the counter. Why would you want that *particular* mug, unless, of course, Nellie might be stopping by?"

"'One of these days, Alice, va-va-voom! Right to the moon,'" Harry said in his imitation Jackie Gleason voice. "Now get out of here."

"Some men are *so* temperamental when they're in love," Wendy teased en route to the kitchen.

"She's a riot," Barry said, laughing. How long had it been since he'd last laughed? It felt good.

Harry looked back over his shoulder. "A real Joan Rivers. I should start charging my customers a cover. So, how's things going down at the complex. Got an opening date yet?"

"Not yet." Barry said, averting Harry's eyes.

Harry wiped his hands on his apron, then leaned over the counter and said quietly, "I heard you're having a rough time. Money a bit tight?"

"Some." There was no use in lying. This was Dorsetville, where secrets came to die.

Wendy placed Harry's mug on the counter.

"Thanks, Wendy." Harry said. "I'm going to get myself a cup of coffee. You want some more, Barry?"

"No, I think I've reached my target heart rate."

Harry filled his mug, set it on the counter, then reached inside his pocket to retrieve a check. He handed it over to Barry. "This should make you feel a little better."

"What's this?" It was made out to Barry Hornibrook in the amount of fifteen thousand dollars.

"Just a little gift from the downtown business community," Harry explained. "We heard you were a little short in cash so we took up a collection."

Barry pushed the check back across the counter. "I can't take this."

"Sure you can," Harry said, stuffing it into Barry's shirt pocket.

"No, I can't . . ."

"Listen, once your place opens all the businesses along Main Street will benefit. So, just think of the money as our way of saying thank you in advance. When things turn around, then you can pay us back."

Just then, Nellie walked through the front door and caught Harry's full attention.

"Hi, Harry," she called, making her way over.

"Hi, Nell."

Harry grabbed a rag and gave a quick polish to the counter, then pulled out a white paper place mat and set it neatly in front of Nellie as she climbed on the stool next to Barry. Barry looked down at the scarred wooden counter around his own cup.

"How about some coffee? I just grabbed some myself. See? Thought I'd use my favorite mug."

Nellie blushed. "Thank's, Harry, but I can't stay. Hi, Barry."

"Hi, Nell."

"You're sure?" Harry said. There was no hiding his disappointment. "I saved a piece of Lori's lemon meringue pie."

"Oh, Harry, you're so sweet. But I really have things to do." Nellie said. "I promise to come back later if I have a chance."

"I don't understand why you're so busy," said Harry, pouting. "It's only August. School doesn't start until after Labor Day."

"There are still things that need to be done," she patiently explained. "Supplies have to be purchased. Books need to be cataloged. I have to submit my teaching schedule, have it approved by the principal." But she didn't add ". . . and get to my second job in Woodstock on time." Instead, she tactfully changed the subject. "Do you have Molly's food? I'll drop it off."

"Yeah, it's right here," Harry reached underneath the counter and pulled out Molly's order. "Pastrami on rye. No cheese. Just like she asked."

"Cheese gives her gas," Nellie explained to Barry.

Barry nodded and went back to his newspaper. By now the couple had forgotten that he even existed, engaging in the mindless chatter of the newly in love.

While the lovers conversed, Barry thought about the folks in Dorsetville. No doubt about it, they were the salt of the earth. Harry worried about what food groups might upset the stomach of a homeless woman. The downtown businessmen had taken up a collection so he could open up his hotel. Even though the check inside his pocket could not make a dent in what he really owed, Barry felt humbled by the offer. He knew that most business people in town barely got by. That fifteen-thousand-dollar check probably represented every last dime they had. No wonder he loved this town so much.

"Barry, would you pass the mustard?" Harry asked. "I just remembered that I forgot to put some on Molly's sandwich."

Barry slid it over.

"That should do it," Harry said, rewrapping the sandwich in white paper. He bent down at the knees and began to rummage underneath the counter. "I put a couple of Grand Union bags down here somewhere. You know the ones, with the handles. Figured they'd be a lot easier for you to cart this stuff across the green." Only the top of Harry's head was now visible.

Nellie turned to Barry and asked, "How is your hotel coming along? I'm afraid that I haven't had the chance to get over there lately."

"Slowly." It was only a half lie.

Harry had found the bags and began to pack Molly's food. "I was just telling Barry how his hotel is going to give our downtown economy a real boost." Harry put a liter of Coke and a couple of plastic-wrapped chocolate brownies in the bag. "In fact, it's one of the reasons I put in a new dishwasher and an extra oven for Lori on the other side. I figured once Barry's place opened, his customers would need a place where they could go to get a *real* cup of coffee and some decent pastries. You know how hotel food can be." Harry laughed heartily at his own joke. "Find a chef yet for that fancy kitchen of yours? Maybe Julia Child's available?"

"Oh, Harry," Nellie said sweetly. "You're such an old tease."

Barry got ready to leave. He dug deep into his jeans pocket for some cash.

"Coffee's on the house," Harry said.

"Thanks. See you two later." They had already forgotten he was there.

He overtipped Wendy and tucked Harry's check under the saucer, where it was certain to be found, then headed outside. As soon as he stepped out onto the sidewalks the heat slammed him in the face. He slowed down his pace and unbuttoned the top of his shirt.

The walk back down to the hotel seemed twice as long. Both the heat and his guilty conscience bore down hard on him. He bent forward, his head no longer facing the open skies, the verdant landscapes. Instead, he marked his travels by the cracks and potholes in the sidewalk.

How many other businessmen in town had made similar investments, like Harry? he wondered. All of which had been based on Barry's ill-fated dreams. What a mess. He should have listened to Cheryl. She was right. He was no Donald Trump.

The Congregational church windows were tightly shut in deference to the antiquated air-conditioning unit stationed outside the basement classroom window. For the last three years, George Benson had told the parish council the unit needed to be replaced. It was noisy and inefficient. The council responded with its customary "We're taking the matter under advisement."

Even Reverend Curtis, a reticent and long-suffering man who made it a point of staying clear of all building-maintenance issues, had sided with George. Just last Sunday, as he was about to deliver his homily, the air conditioner kicked on and the Reverend had been forced to shout out his sermon, aptly entitled, "How to Discern God's Voice Amidst Life's Clamor."

The air conditioner also had a tendency to grow louder the more it was forced to work; and since the temperatures had risen sharply from that morning, it was now working at the same decibel pitch as a heavy metal concert, which was why no one heard Sarah's pleas for help.

Sarah pounded harder on the cubbyhole door, but the hot, humid air had made it swell, trapping her inside.

"Help! Please, someone help me!" Sarah had been shouting for so long that her voice was now reduced to a hoarse whisper. But no one came.

When the other children had piled outside as ordered by Mother Superior, Sarah had stayed hidden in the back of the room. She had reasoned that the cubby was a far better option than the risk of stepping on a snake as she tried to flee.

Inside, the temperature had soared. Sweat coursed down the back of her neck and trickled slowly toward her waist. At times she imagined the droplets were small bugs crawling underneath her blouse. This made her cry even louder.

Finally, she screwed up enough courage to slowly turn the inside handle and push open the door. But it wouldn't budge. She was locked inside. Loss of freedom, of choice, brings with it new terrors, and now Sarah felt its grip take hold, which far exceeded her earlier fear of the snake. She pounded on the door panel and screamed at the top of her lungs until her voice gave out. Still, no one came. Finally, completely exhausted, she slid down to a sitting position and cried in quiet, little tremors that shook her body until her chest hurt.

Where was Mommy? Why hadn't she come? She wanted to go home. It was hot and dark in here and smelled of old sneakers.

Sarah hugged her knees for comfort and the movement caused something to jab her along her outer thigh. She remembered the rosary she had put in her pocket earlier. She pulled out the strand of beads and held it tightly. It made her feel a little less alone. Finally her breathing slowed and her eyes grew heavy from the heat until finally she fell into a deep sleep not even awakening at the sound of Mr. Crawford the janitor's footfalls as he entered the room.

Mr. Crawford chuckled to himself as he went in search of the snake. It reminded him of the things he and his brother used to pull, only it was garden snakes back then, not boa constrictors. The snake, and its suspected owners, had been described to him by Mother Superior. Sounded like the same reptile the Galligan twins had Father Dennis bless on the Feast of Francis of Assisi last fall. He had been there with his grand-daughter Jennifer and her two ferrets. My, those boys could sure get into a peck of trouble.

He didn't have to search long. He found the reptile coiled inside the hamster's glass tank, sleeping peacefully. The hamster was nowhere in sight. He gathered the snake in a pillowcase, turned out the lights and closed the room, stopping briefly at the front desk to gather Mother Superior's canvas bag. He had a feeling that she wouldn't be returning back down here today.

Molly was seated on the park bench just outside the Congregational church, enjoying the remainder of the lunch Nellie Anderson had brought by earlier. The sun had begun to drop down behind St. Ce-cilia's steeples and dusk had darkened the outer fringes of the green. Molly ate the rest of her pastrami sandwich amid a group of seagulls, sharing pieces of crust from the rye bread. For dessert, she had one of the brownies Harry had packed. My, they tasted good. She planned to have the other as her bedtime snack. Shame Harry hadn't packed any milk. Milk always tasted so good with anything chocolate.

She looked up at the clock that stood at the entrance to the park. It was time to get ready. She wiped her mouth with a paper napkin, tied her sneakers with double knots and got up to go. Slowly she walked across the green, climbed the stone steps to the Congregational church and slipped inside.

The Galligan twins weaved across the backyard of the Congregational church, careful to stay well hidden in the thickening shadows. With any luck, they would find their snake, Squiggles, and have her safely back inside the tank before Mother Superior was able to contact their parents. She hadn't believed them when they had said they knew noth-ing about the reptile that had terrorized all their classmates.

"Just call Mom," Dexter had told Mother Superior. "She'll tell you that Squiggles is at home asleep in the tank."

The boys had raced home and disconnected all the phones.

"We just have to keep Mom and Dad away from the phone until they leave for the town meeting," Dexter had explained to Rodney. "As soon as they're gone, we'll reconnect the phones so the baby-sitter can talk to her boyfriend. That way, she won't miss us while we go back to the church to find Squiggles."

Rodney shinnied through a partially opened window at the back of the church and found himself in the sacristy.

"C'mon, Dexter," he whispered. "It's your turn now."

Dexter heaved himself up onto the wooden crate they had found outside the Country Kettle on the way over. Dexter wasn't very coordinated and was having difficulty negotiating his body through the small opening.

"I hope Kevin Brennan was lying about Mr. Higgins taking Squiggles away in his truck," Dexter said, stretching out his hands so Rodney could help pull him through. "There's no telling what he might do with her."

Rodney pulled hard. Dexter slid through, landing in a heap at his brother's feet.

Dexter brushed himself off. "Did you bring Mom's penlight?"

"Yep, it's right here." Rodney ran the beam of light around the room. It fell on a row of cabinets.

"I wonder what's in these?" Dexter asked, not being able to resist opening one of the birch cabinet doors.

"Dex, leave that alone and stop messing around. We're here to find Squiggles, remember?"

"Yeah, I know, but look at all this stuff. Hey, there's a whole shelf of Welch's Grape Juice. They must be having some kind of party."

"Nah, it's for Communion."

"Grape juice?"

"Protestants use that stuff instead of wine," Rodney explained.

"Grape juice instead of wine?" He thought a moment. "I'm glad we're Catholics."

He jumped up onto the counter and opened the top row of cabinets. "Look, they've got all kinds of stuff in here. Social Teas . . . na, I hate those. Graham crackers. Hey, here's a bag of Keebler's chocolate chip cookies. You want some?" He opened the bag and stuffed two inside his mouth. He'd have a case of hives from the chocolate within the hour, but, for now, it seemed worth it.

"Will you get down?" Rodney pulled on his brother's pant leg. Dexter kicked at his brother but missed. "We gotta get back before the baby-sitter finds out we're missing."

"All right, all right." Dexter said, tucking the bag under his arm and jumping down.

"C'mon. Let's get downstairs and look for Squiggles."

Rodney headed toward the back staircase. "You check the classroom and the closets. I'll take the hallway and the janitor's room. You know how Squiggles likes to curl up in dark corners, so check them out first. Dex? Dex?" His brother had disappeared. "Now, where'd he go?" He peered back into the sacristy. "Dexter?" It was empty.

"I'm in here. In the church," Dexter called through a mouth full of cookies. "You gotta see this. It's *really* cool. They got a balcony that goes all the way around. Not just a choir loft like we have at St. Cecilia's."

Rodney found the sanctuary. Dexter was hanging over the railing from the second-floor balcony.

"You know, you could really launch a great spitball from up here." Dexter pretended to take aim at the pulpit.

"Dex! Get down here. We've got to get back."

"I'm coming. I'm coming," Dexter said, racing down the stairs, his heavy sneakers banging hard against the wooden risers. He charged right past his brother and jumped onto the altar area, sending vibrations shooting up the podium; the attached microphone began to reverberate.

"Get off there," Rodney hissed.

Dexter pretended to address the congregation. "My name is Reverend Wisecracker and I'm here to tell you that you're all going straight to hell."

"Dexter, c'mon . . ."

"Wait a minute." Dexter's head disappeared behind the pulpit. He rummaged along the lower shelves. "Hey, look what I've found." He held up a box of matches. "What do you think he uses these for? Do you think Reverend Curtis lights up a pipe when he's preaching?"

"They're probably used to light the candles."

"What? They don't have any altar boys, either? What kind of church is this?" Dexter struck a match. A small triangle of flame flared up.

"Put that out, Dex. People can see through the windows."

"Nah, there's no one outside. Everyone's down at the town hall for the meeting. Even Reverend Curtis and his wife. I saw them leave." Dexter walked over to the altar. "Hey, Rodney. Look at me, I'm the first Protestant altar boy." He pretended solemnity as he lit the candles on both sides of the altar.

"Cut it out, Dexter. We're going to get caught."

Dexter, engrossed in this new game, ignored his brother. Finally, Rodney, the older twin by two minutes, could take it no longer. He ran over and punched his twin in the arm.

"Hey! Cut that out!" Dexter cried, shrugging his brother's arm away and, in the process, knocking over one of the lit candles, which, in turn, knocked over a small vial of oil. Within seconds, the altar was in flames.

"Look what *you* did!" Rodney yelled.

"*I* did? It was *your* fault. You pushed my arm."

The fire quickly spread.

"What should we do?" Dexter screamed.

"I don't know." Rodney stood frozen.

"Big help you are."

Water! We need water, Dexter thought. He raced behind the altar in search of the baptismal font. "Where's the holy water?"

The flames had doubled in size and were now traveling down the sides of the altar and onto the carpet.

"Protestants don't use holy water," Rodney said.

"No holy water either?" Man, what a church! he thought. Okay, there's no water, so what am I suppose to do?

Fire Chief Halstead had visited his fourth-grade class last year during fire-prevention week. If only Dexter had listened instead of drawing funny pictures of the teacher on the back of Holly Chemlin's jacket in front of him. The only thing he could remember was the phrase, "Stop, drop and roll." Dexter dropped to the ground and began to roll back and forth like a fat sausage.

"What are you doing?" Rodney asked incredulously.

"I'm dropping and rolling."

"That's when *you're* on fire, not the building."

The flames had now spread to the back wall. Something exploded. A flash of sparks flew into the sanctuary like a bank of missiles. Several found their mark on the upholstered cushions in the front pews; they, too, quickly burst into flames.

Rodney raced over and pulled his brother back onto his feet. "We've got to get out of here. The whole place is on fire."

"But what about Squiggles?" What if she's still here?" Dexter yelled.

Rodney had a deathlike grip on his brother's arm as he pushed him back toward the sacristy and the open window. "Then she's on her own."

Molly waited until the boys had raced out of the sanctuary before stepping out from behind a dark corner. She watched the flames engulf the altar. The fire was spreading very fast. There wasn't much time. She bowed her head and prayed, asking God to have the town folks hurry along.

Chapter 8

The town hall sat on a small rise that began at the north end of Main Street, which flowed softly like a blanket shaken out in a gentle breeze until it dipped ever so slightly, creating a small gully in front of Stone's Hardware Store before ascending sharply again by John Moran Realty. Finally it leveled out at the top of the hill by Grand Union.

Folks on their way to the town hall this evening had parked their cars in the lot next to Tri Town Auto, a dirt-covered half acre choked with pokeweeds in the summer and encased in ice in the winter. They ignored the diagonal parking slots along Main Street; only newcomers or out-of-towners used these. Unless there was a pounding rain or a blizzard, locals preferred the stroll up the breadth of Dorsetville's main thoroughfare.

This evening was no exception as folks wandered along. To the casual observer it would seem as if they were caught up in some lovely old-fashioned reel, as groups merged, then separated, then merged again, keeping time to the lively rhythm of conversations among neighbors and friends. Occasionally some would step away from the group to peer into the storefront two doors up from the Country Kettle. A new Japanese restaurant was due to open there next week, not that it would in any way impinge upon Harry's clientele, who were stoically opposed to anything other than standard American fare. But that didn't stop some, like Timothy McGree and Ben Metcalf, from pressing their faces hard against the glass, hoping to get a better look inside. The two men jumped back startled, then nearly took off running, when a smiling Asian face appeared on the other side and tried to wave them in.

What had begun as a soft evening's summer breeze had now turned into a blustery wind, wrapping the women's skirts around their legs like plastic wrap and unfurling even the heaviest sprayed hairstyle. Several women had brought their knitting and quilting bags filled with their newest projects. Town meetings were a wonderful place to get the advice of other skilled craftswomen: Should they use this color or that? Insert another stitch along a sleeve or reverse the cable? Which quilting pattern would look best? As the wind intensified, they shifted their treasures to the front of their chests as one would a small child.

The crackle of lightning sounded in the distance, sending husbands scurrying back down the hill to check on car windows while their wives prayed that, should a driving rain arrive, it would blow in the opposite direction of any windows left open at home. The thought of returning home to batten down the hatches never occurred to any of them. Renovations on the town hall had concluded only the week before and everyone wanted a look firsthand.

A grant sought and won by Roger Martin, Dorsetville's mayor, had paid for the entire renovation project, a feat which was certain to assure him reelection this fall. Roger stood just outside the town hall, whose double front doors stood wide open onto the street this evening like a pair of welcoming arms. He cheerfully shook hands, reveling in his constituency's adulation. Many openly admitted they had forgotten the loveliness of the building's architecture, and wasn't he clever in securing the money to bring it back to its former glory?

Everyone conceded that the restoration project was a resounding success, as evidenced now by the brass fixtures on either side of the front door shining like gold nuggets in the evening light, and the crisp, mortared edges of the recently sandblasted brick façade. Once again, the crown moldings on top of the front door, which had been buried under forty years of paint, revealed a beautifully detailed carved cherub, its wings spanning the entire width of the doorway. Only a handful of old-timers remembered its significance—a former citizen's gratitude at having survived the Depression, rising from poverty to economic prominence. It had been his gift that built the town hall.

Ruth Henderson motioned to the angel. Her sister June leaned heavily upon her walker as she, too, paused to look up and gaze. The crowd of people making their way up the front stairs carefully skirted around the two elderly women.

"Good evening, Ruth . . . June," Arlene Campbell said, holding tightly to her husband Fred's arm. "I'd forgotten that angel was there. Beautiful, isn't it?"

"I remember the man who carved it," Fred said. "There was something about him that was . . . I don't know, mysterious, I guess."

"Yes, I remember him, too," Arlene said. "Nice-looking young man. Chestnut hair. Brown eyes. I think his name was Elijah. Whatever happened to him?"

"Just seems to have disappeared," Fred remembered.

"He had other jobs that needed tending," June said, catching her sister's eye, who quietly nodded. They would take his secret to the graves.

"See you ladies inside," Fred said, leading his wife through the opened doors.

Margaret Norris leafed through a stack of magazines as she waited for the town meeting to begin. She was completely at a loss. How did she manage to get on all of these subscription lists?

Ethel Johnson and Harriet Bedford, seated alongside her, were similarly confounded as they rifled through their own filled canvas sacks. Ethel was reading the editorial inside *Soldier of Fortune* while Harriet puzzled over *Popular Mechanics*. Ben Metcalf swapped Harriet's copy of *Ladies' Home Journal* with Sam Rosenberg, after having lost interest in a quiz entitled "What's the Perfect Hobby for You?" Neither decoupage nor candle making held any interest for him.

Sheriff Bromley paused on his way down the aisle to ask Harriet if she was thinking about doing her own car repairs.

Before answering, Harriet closed the magazine and studied its cover. "It's the strangest thing, Al. Margaret, Ethel and I keep getting magazines we never ordered. And every time we call the magazines to complain, they tell us that they have subscription cards filled out in our names." She looked baffled. "It's a real mystery."

"Sounds like someone is having some fun at your expense," he offered, steadfastly ignoring Deputy Hill, seated behind the St. Celicia's crowd, who was trying to wave him over.

"Fun? What's fun about this?" asked Mrs. Norris indignantly. "Do you know how much it has cost in long-distance calls to try to get this all straightened out? It's a good thing I'm dying and won't need the rest of my retirement savings."

"Now, who would do a thing like this?" Ethel asked, pulling out a copy of *Casino Journal*. Like Father James, she had elected to ignore Mrs. Norris's continued reference to her imminent demise, which she didn't believe, not for a minute.

"Hey, Sheriff," Deputy Hill shouted. Apparently the sheriff hadn't seen him wave. "There's plenty of room up here." He moved the Dunkin' Donuts box off the empty chair alongside him and swept away the dusting of confectioners' sugar.

"No thanks. I'm going to keep George Benson company. I'll see you ladies at the social hour after the meeting," he said, then marched down the center aisle, feeling the acid begin to pump into his stomach. Hill had that effect on him lately.

Each day brought new complaints. Just before arriving here, Bromley had gotten a call from Judge Peale. It seemed that Hill had issued the judge a parking ticket for parking in his own space outside the courthouse. Yesterday it had been a call from a blind woman. Hill had ticketed her for jaywalking.

And his wife, Barbara, wondered why his blood pressure was so high.

Hill watched the sheriff take a seat next to George Benson and marveled anew at his boss's keen law-enforcement skills. Instead of having them both sit together, the sheriff had obviously decided to divide the room into sectors. This way, no criminal action would go unchecked.

Hill leaned back in his chair and shook his head in admiration. The sheriff was always thinking. He opened the donut box and polished off the last three while keeping a close eye on the two older women with walkers who had just sat down a few rows ahead of him. Hill waited to see if they planned to keep their walkers in the aisle, a direct violation of the town's safety codes. Lucky for the sheriff, he had brought along his citation book.

Harry Clifford sat toward the front of the hall, next to Lori and Bob Peterson. While the young couple chatted with their neighbors in the front row, Harry adjusted his bow tie, looking awkward in his neatly pressed pale blue-striped dress shirt and navy blue sports jacket. Plaid shirts and jeans were his standard attire.

Nellie should be arriving any minute. He turned around to glance at the back entrance again. It was the third time in less than five minutes. The meeting was about to begin. Where was she?

John Moran asked if the empty seat next to him was taken. "Sorry, I'm saving it for Nellie," Harry said, throwing an arm over the back of the seat.

Was it unseasonably hot in here or was it just him? Harry ran a hand along the inside of his shirt collar. It was already soaked in perspiration. He slid forward, reaching into has back pants pocket for a handkerchief and discovered that he had left it at home. It was probably still lying on his bureau, forgotten in his haste to arrive before Nellie.

"Hi, Harry," Father Dennis said, sliding in beside the nuns from the Sister Regina Francis Retirement Home seated in the next row. He was relieved to discover Mother Superior absent. She was at home, keeping an eye on the residents. "Are you feeling all right?" he asked. "You look a little flushed."

"I'm fine. It's just a little hot in here, is all," Harry said. Someone should tell George Benson that the air-conditioning wasn't working properly.

Harry looked around at the newly renovated room without really seeing it. Later he would comment that it seemed a strange choice of colors for the interior of the old building. Bright aqua and orange, if he remembered correctly. But he really hadn't paid much notice. His thoughts were focused exclusively on Nellie.

How had he lived all these years without her? When he thought of his life before, it seemed as lackluster as plain mayonnaise on white bread. But since Nellie, life was more like New York's Carnegie Deli Reuben.

Recently they had taken a train into Hartford to visit the Horace Bushnell Theater. Bernadette Peters was starring in *Annie Get Your Gun*. They both said it was the best play they had *ever* seen, although secretly Harry had to admit that it was the *only* play he'd ever seen. How had he allowed his life to become so boring . . . so predictable? The couple didn't arrive back at Dorsetville until midnight, causing village tongues to wag for days afterward.

But it was more than just the things they did together that had arrested his heart. It was the way Nellie enriched his life, made it somehow fuller, gave it more meaning. He found the hours without her dragged on interminably and the hours with her sped by at breakneck speed. Nellie had sparked an ember which had illuminated his life with a flame that he never wanted extinguished.

He checked his coat pocket for the umpteenth time, making certain that the jeweler's box was still there. He had picked it up at Sullivan's Jewelers right before coming over. It contained his mother's engagement ring.

Harry swung around again, his heart filled with hope. He held his breath. It was just like he felt every Tuesday night as he watched the ten o'clock news to see if his lottery ticket matched the winning numbers.

Nellie wasn't there. He experienced a sinking feeling, like the way a piece of undigested food lodges in one's stomach. What if she had forgotten their date again? She had forgotten twice last week, and last weekend she had disappeared completely without any explanation. It worried Harry, who tried not to think about the ramifications, like what if she were dating somebody else? Whenever he allowed this possibility to seep into his consciousness, it felt as if someone was tightening a tourniquet around his chest; yet, as much as he had tried to dismiss it, the thought continued to linger in the back of his mind.

Harry had toyed with the idea of parking his car across from her house and watching to see if another man showed up. He had confided both his fears and his proposed plan to Father James, who had strongly urged against it.

"You must trust her," he insisted. "If you want this relationship to grow, you must put aside your suspicions and trust that she will explain her actions when she's ready."

Easy for Father James to say. He wasn't a forty-plus-year-old bachelor in love for the first time with a woman who had suddenly developed a penchant for unexplained disappearances. Oh, she had told him that she had things to do preparing for the new school year. Get her room ready. Plan her courses. And Harry had believed her; that is, until late this afternoon when he had run into her principal, Mrs. Gaines, who said she was looking forward to seeing Nellie again after the long summer.

Harry watched the sheriff settle in beside George Benson. A couple of months ago, he would have sat alongside them, a carefree, albeit boring, bachelor. But now here he was like some lovesick teenager dressed in a sports jacket and tie, sweating like a pig on a barbeque spit, and hoping that the woman he loved hadn't forgotten their date, especially not tonight—not when he had spent all day in front of the mirror practicing his proposal. He took a deep breath and exhaled slowly. He just hoped he didn't lose his nerve by the time she arrived.

When George spied Bromley heading his way, he placed a folding chair in the center of the side aisle for the sheriff in direct violation of the fire code, which, as fire marshal, he was sworn to uphold.

"Hi, George." The sheriff slid into the chair and nearly gagged. "What in heaven's name is that god-awful smell?"

"Aqua-Velva," George said, not at all offended.

"What did you do, take a bath in the stuff?" Bromley moved his chair back a few inches.

George was dressed in his official fire marshal uniform: black tuxedo pants with a gold side stripe, black double-breasted jacket, complete with gold-fringed epaulets, and a white shirt monogrammed FM on both collar wings. George wore it to all town meetings. Said it was part of his contract with the town, although no one could find any mention of this "mandatory dress code" anywhere in the town's charter.

George belched. "Darn cabbage. Had it this afternoon over at Mrs. Hanson's. She had a leaky radiator valve." He belched again, hit his stomach with a closed fist as though to expunge any residue of gas, then looked around the room. "Looks like everybody in town is here. Hope we don't exceed the maximum capacity for the room." George turned back to face the dais at complete peace with his lack of equality in enforcing the state fire codes.

"Heard the board's putting that traffic light issue up again for a vote. How many times have we voted that thing down?" George pondered.

"Four," the sheriff said, adjusting his side holster so he could sit more comfortably.

"Well, I'm still against it," George boomed. Two rows of people turned around, noted it was only George, then resumed their conversations.

"Any leads on who hit Father James?"

"I have a couple," Bromley said.

The most promising one had come from Dorsetville's new bag lady. Molly had witnessed the entire accident and given a detailed description of the two male assailants. The state's crime lab had provided other clues. Amazing what the lab guys could detect from a broken headlight. Make, model and the year of the car were embedded in the glass. The enamel paint flakes left on the motor scooter had provided the vehicle's color. Collectively, the evidence revealed it was a 2001 Lincoln Navigator that hit Father James. Bromley had already begun a

DMV search on all matching vehicles registered within the New England and New York State areas.

"When you find the bums . . . I hope you nail them," George said.

"If it was up to me, I would. But it's not. It's up to the judge. By the way, how's Jim doing?" With the investigation and the ongoing problems with his deputy, the sheriff had yet to find time to visit since the priest had returned home.

"Let's just say Father James won't be doing a lot of genuflecting for a while, if you know what I mean. It will be another six to eight weeks before his busted leg heals and the cast comes off. They had to put a pin in his leg, you know." George spied Chester and waved. "Hey! Chester, over here!"

George watched Chester inch his way down the aisle. Good grief, what's the matter with him? he wondered. The guy looked like death warmed over. His face was drawn, his skin looked gray. He wondered if there was some new kind of virus going around. George moved over. Let Bromley sit next to him. If Chester had something contagious, George wasn't about to catch it.

Mrs. Rochelle Phillips was also the zoning board chairperson. She took her place at the center of the dais and called the meeting to order.

Nigel Hayes, a slight man with auburn hair who still spoke with a heavy British accent even though he had emigrated from Hereford, England, in 1948 stood to read the first docket. "Docket number 105. The zoning board of the village of Dorsetville appeals to institute a traffic light at the intersection of Main Street and Harbor Road."

The entire room immediately exploded into clusters of hot debates. Mrs. Phillips pounded her gravel. "Order! Order! Let's have order!"

By nine-thirty, the traffic light and several other proposals had been voted down. The board now turned its attention to the proposed housing development at the edge of town. Several stood to voice their opinions, including Sam Rosenberg, who agreed that it would help the town's economy but worried that it might be a harbinger of a future trend. No one wanted to see big change come to Dorsetville.

During a small debate among the board over the interpretation of a particular zoning issue, Lori leaned over to speak with Jamie Rupert's mother, Evelyn, who had arrived only a half hour ago.

"Who did you get to baby-sit the girls tonight?" Lori asked.

"Jamie? My mother-in-law." Evelyn had brought her needlepoint pillow and didn't look up to answer. It was the same project she had brought to all the town and school meetings for the last five years. It was still only half finished.

"Mother Rupert had the mumps, so she's immune. We thought it was safe to leave her with Jamie."

Lori was confused. "You let Sarah stay at your house when Jamie has the mumps?"

Now it was Evelyn's turn to appear befuddled. "Sarah? No, Sarah's not at my house."

"She's not at your house . . .?"

"No, the girls' sleepover was canceled. Didn't you get my message?"

"What message?" Lori felt the first rush of fear.

"Oh, Lori . . . I called the restaurant. I left a message with Harry and told him that Jamie had broken out with the mumps early this morning and that I needed to cancel the girls' sleepover. Didn't he tell you?"

Lori was already out of her seat and headed toward the aisle.

Evelyn's face went white. "You mean you never got the message? Oh, dear God. But where's Sarah?"

"Bob, get up! We have to go!" Lori said, climbing over Bob, then Harry.

"I'm sorry, Lori," Evelyn called after her. "Naturally I thought that Harry would give you the message. Oh, dear God. Sarah's been alone all afternoon."

"Lori, where are you going?" Bob bent down to rub his toe. Lori had landed hard on his left foot. "What does Evelyn mean that Sarah's been alone?"

"Jamie has the mumps. Evelyn just told me that she canceled the sleepover this morning. She said she gave the message to you, Harry, but I never got it."

"The message? Oh, no . . ." Harry hit his forehead with the heel of his hand. "I forgot all about it. Oh, Lori, I'm so sorry. Evelyn called right before the lunchtime crowd. I started to write it down when the phone rang again and I had to take an order. Then there was another call, then something happened in the kitchen. I . . . I . . . forgot. Oh, Lori, how could I have not remembered?"

All three crashed into the aisle and raced toward the main exit.

"Sarah's probably asleep somewhere in the park," Bob said, trying to keep his wife calm. "Or she's gone across the street to stay with Mother Superior. Either way, I'm sure she's just fine."

"How could I have been so stupid!" Harry asked.

Bob reached the door first and had just started to pull it open when the shrill, piercing blast of a fire siren rent the air.

For a brief second all conversation stopped, then the room exploded into action. Metal chairs scrapped across the newly tiled floor as volunteer firemen and EMTs rushed toward the emergency doors at the front of the room.

Deep within the crowd someone yelled, "Where's the fire?"

George was directly linked to the town dispatcher through his walkie-talkie. "At the Congregational church," he shouted. "And it's a bad one."

Chapter 9

Father James had been reading in bed when he spied the orange flames illuminating the dining-room wall.

"Dear Lord, what is that?"

He grabbed his crutches and hobbled over to the front window for a better view. "Lord have mercy, the Congregational church is on fire!" He pressed SPEED DIAL for 911.

"Dorsetville Police Station, please state your emergency."

"Betty?" It didn't sound like Betty. "This is Father James over at St. Cecilia's."

"This isn't Betty. Please state your emergency," the voice repeated.

He had a lot of catching up to do when he got back on his feet. "I want to report a fire."

"The fire's location," the operator asked, as though she might be asking the location of a package of Jell-O in Grand Union.

"It looks like the Congregational church on the town green is on fire."

"'Looks like?' Does that mean you're not certain there is a fire or you're not certain of the location?"

"I am *certain* there is a fire and I'm *certain* that it's at the Congregational church. Please send someone right away."

"Is there anyone there that could verify the fire's location?"

"I don't need it verified," he said hotly.

"We wouldn't want to dispatch the fire trucks to the wrong address, now, would we?" she asked, as if speaking to a child.

Betty would have never spoken to him like this.

"Neither would I!" he shouted. "But if you don't send someone shortly, there won't be anything left to save." Thank goodness the winds had died down or the entire area would be in peril.

"You don't have to be so testy. I'm only doing my job," she countered. "This is the last time I cover for my cousin Betty so she can go to a town meeting."

She hung up before he could apologize.

The town hall had emptied in minutes as both volunteer fire and ambulance workers crashed through the emergency doors. Some scrambled into their cars and switched on the brightly colored strobe lights mounted on their dashboards—green for ambulance, blue for fire—and raced up the hill to secure the scene. Others rocketed to the firehouse next door, hustled into their yellow fire gear and got ready to roll. Within six minutes of the first alarm, a hook and ladder and two tankers sped out the massive garage doors and charged up to the top of the hill. By the time they arrived, Sheriff Bromley's men had cordoned off the scene.

"Back up. Let the trucks get through," Deputy Hill told the crowd gathered outside.

All twenty-four residents of the Sister Regina Francis Retirement Home were among them. They shifted back onto the sidewalk.

Mother Superior, who had been in the midst of balancing the books when the first alarm sounded, rushed outside.

"I want everyone back in the house," she ordered, spreading her arms and shooing them forward like a mother duck gathering her young. "It's much too dangerous out here."

Sister Joanna, self-proclaimed group leader, adamantly refused. "We're not going. This is the most excitement any of us have had in nearly fifty years."

The fire trucks screeched to a halt in front of the scene. Firefighters tumbled out of the cabs and jumped off running boards, quickly melding into the tangle of men and equipment already scattered around the church. A quarter-mile length of hose was quickly connected to one of the two tanker trucks. Dorsetville had no water mains. Everything came from wells, which meant there were no fire hydrants. When one tanker had been drained, it would make its way down to the river to refill.

Someone yelled, "Ready to roll."

Water coursed through the hose, seeming to give life to this inert length of black rubber. The men on the other end held steady, their thick leather gloves clamped tightly as the water rushed along its length, finally emerging in a powerful gush.

George Benson's role of fire marshal would begin in earnest after the blaze, but for now he lent his support to the fire chief, Billy Halstead. The two men had fashioned a command post on the hood of Billy's fire-engine red Ford Bronco that had FIRE CHIEF written in two-foot-high white lettering along the side-door panels. Even in this thick smoke, the lettering could still be read.

Billy had a walkie-talkie directly linked to the four sector captains in one hand, and a cell phone in the other connected to the neighboring Woodstock firehouse. The dispatcher over in Woodstock had just notified the chief that their trucks' ETA was thirty minutes.

"Tell them that's not good enough," he yelled over the roaring blaze and the shouts of his men. "We need them here in twenty, tops, if we're going to contain this thing." Where was the rain that had been promised?

George stood steadfast, eyes riveted on the church's interior, watching the fire begin to roll in a slow boil, like a pot of stew. A side window exploded, propelling shards of glass and wood into the side yard. Shouts of "Get out of the way!" rang through air.

George stood a safe distance from the flames watching the fire, trying to guess its next move. No matter what modern technological advances were made in the field of fire fighting, a trained firefighter's eyes were still the best weapon. A fire could shift in a heartbeat, turning from a simple open flame to a raging inferno, consuming everything in its path, including firefighters. The men fighting this blaze depended on the chief and the fire marshal to keep them out of harm's way.

George watched as two firemen burst out the front doors of the church and hustled down the steps. Each had an arm around a woman whom he immediately recognized as the bag lady Molly.

"What in the blue blazes was she doing in there?" he yelled as the men approached.

"She wouldn't come out until we promised we'd start a search," John Moran explained, taking off his mask. John was a senior member of the fire department and sector captain, a volunteer since high school.

"A search for what?" George asked.

"There's a child in the basement of the church," Molly told him. "You need to hurry. There isn't much time left."

"A child?" George felt his heart drop down to his feet. "What child?"

"George?" Sheriff Bromley shouted, the Petersons racing close behind. "We've got trouble. Lori and Bob think Sarah might still be inside the building."

"God help us," George whispered, noticing that Lori's body was shaking so hard she looked as though she was having a seizure.

Molly reached out a comforting hand. "Don't be afraid, my dear. Everything is going to be all right."

There was something in the woman's eyes that made Lori want to believe her. "My baby's in there and it's all my fault," she told the woman, then fell into her husband's arms and sobbed.

"It's not your fault," Bob said, working feverishly to hold rein on his own emotions. He grabbed Lori and clung tight. "It's not anyone's fault."

"If she's inside, we'll get her out," George said, praying somehow that statement might be true. He watched heavy black smoke rising in plumes, riding on thermals of liquid heat. Not a good sign. It meant that the building was already past saving.

George tapped Billy on the shoulder. "Chief, we have a new problem. The Petersons think their daughter Sarah might be trapped inside."

Billy Halstead was a young father with two little girls of his own. His immediate reaction was to begin an expansive search, using every available fireman. But that would have been pure lunacy. He had a re-sponsibility first for the safety of his men. There was another explosion. Billy shouted into the walkie-talkie. "Sector captain 102, this is the chief. We have a new development. We need volunteers. A two-man team. We're going in to search for a missing child."

If no one responded, he'd go in himself.

Chester Platt didn't hesitate when Frank Moran asked for volunteers.

"It's burning fast. I won't kid you. This one could be a killer," Frank Moran told the three men and Nancy Ferguson who had answered the call for volunteers. "I think those who have young families might be better off stepping back on this one."

Two of the volunteers nodded sadly and walked back to their pre-vious posts. Chester Platt and Nancy remained.

"You two sure about this?"

They nodded.

"All right, then, let's get ready."

By the time Chester and Nancy had reached the basement of the church, the temperature had risen to one hundred and ten degrees.

Nancy knew the layout. Her sons had gone here to Sunday school. "There are two large classrooms on the right. The rest is storage space," she said.

They were on their knees, crawling along the hallway. The floor tiles were buckling, hot, melted glue oozing out. Visibility was zero. Smoke filled every nook and cranny.

Chester's hand came to rest on a large metal can. He edged closer with his flashlight and had to put his nose up against the container to read the label. It was cleaning fluid. Chester relayed the information to Nancy. She nodded, the unspoken threat duly noted. She called it in to the chief. If ignited, it could seal off their only escape route.

Chester fought to stay focused. The heat was suffocating, making the force of each breath compound the stress on his already weakened lungs. He could feel the now familiar trickle lurking just in back of his throat. *Dear God*, he prayed, *let me get through this without a coughing fit.* These episodes left him gasping for breath. If one started here, he'd suf-focate for sure. Thankfully, the codeine Doc Hammon had given him was still holding.

They began a methodical search of the first classroom. Visibility was less than two inches. Both firefighters knew that Sarah could be within a breath of discovery; yet with the thick, impregnable wall of smoke, unless they literally stepped on her, she would not be found.

Nancy tapped Chester on the shoulder and pointed toward the ceiling. The floorboards overhead had begun to glow.

"We'd better give it up," she said. "The floor joists are about to give way."

Chester nodded.

"Chief, we're coming back up," he relayed.

"Roger," the chief replied, doing a poor job of hiding the disap-pointment in his voice. But as an experienced firefighter, he knew that there came a time when further search was futile. The only thing to be gleaned was the loss of two firemen in addition to the child.

"Come back in," he told them. "You've done all you can do. And hustle."

Chester tapped Nancy on the shoulder and pointed up. She nod-ded and started back. Chester followed as far as the stairs.

"I'll meet you up top," he told her.

Chester watched her disappear into the black smoke and then turned to head back down the hall.

Sarah had fallen asleep tucked in the cubbyhole but had awakened when smoke began to seep through the vents in the door. She coughed and rubbed at her eyes. They had begun to burn.

"Mommy," she whimpered. "Where are you?"

Upstairs she could hear a loud roar, like a freight train. The building seemed as though it were shifting right above her head. She clutched the strand of beads closer to her chest. It had begun to hum.

Chester heard the overhead floorboards shift. He figured he had only minutes tops before the whole building came crashing down. His chest felt as though it were on fire; his pants legs were scorched through from the heat of crawling along the floors and his knees had begun to blister.

Lord, I need Your help, he prayed. *If Sarah is trapped down here, please help me find her before its too late. I'll gladly sacrifice my life for hers, just keep Sarah from harm.*

Chester would never be able to explain what happened next in words, for neither language, nor logic, could contain what he was about to experience.

Suddenly, he was filled with an overwhelming feeling of peace and well-being, although such a state was completely in conflict with the scene that surrounded him—the roar of the flames overhead, the thick black smoke, the heat bearing down on him like a blast from a furnace. Yet all fears had vanished and the rush of adrenaline he usually felt at a fire had been replaced with complete calm.

A "presence" entered the room and stood beside him, filling Chester with confidence, a surety of faith unlike anything he had ever known. He heard a voice inside his head. It said, "Fear not, for I always walk beside you."

A small light appeared in the far corner of the room. Chester watched with a strange sense of detachment as it began to glow. At first it was hazy, like light refracted through a thick glass bottle. But then it moved forward, cutting through the dark smoked-filled room like a laser. Chester got off his knees. He could see clearly now to the other side. The light was originating from one of the children's cubbies.

Chester rushed forward, shoving desks and chairs out of his way. The wall of smoke remained divided, as though it were encased behind glass. He reached the cubby door within seconds, grabbed hold of the handle and yanked it open. Sarah tumbled out into his arms.

"Mr. Platt," Sarah cried, and threw her tiny arms around his neck so tightly that he nearly choked.

"It's all right, Sarah. I've come to get you out of here."

The upstairs floorboards across the hall crashed down, shaking the building with a terrifying tremor. Sarah screamed and covered her ears. The rosary she was holding flew out of her hand and disappeared into the darkness.

They had barely seconds left.

Lord, I need Your help, he prayed. *Show me the way out.*

The light moved upward, revealing a bank of windows just above the row of cubbyholes.

"Hold on," he told Sarah. Wasting no time, he scrambled up on a nearby table and onto one of the storage units.

"Cover your eyes."

He ripped the small ax from his utility belt and slammed it against the nearest window. The pane shattered outward and a blast of cooler air rushed in.

"You made it!" Nancy screamed, tears welling up. She had been standing just feet away when the window shattered and Chester's arm had poked through.

Chester tore off his mask. "Here, take her." He pushed Sarah through the small opening. Within seconds, dozens of hands were reaching out to pull the child to safety.

"Take off your gear. You're never going to fit through," Nancy shouted. "Hurry!"

Chester tore at his protective jacket, shedding it within seconds. The fire was right behind him, approaching like a speeding train.

"Give me your hands," Frank Moran yelled. "She's about to go!"

Chester reached up. Frank pulled on one arm, Nancy the other and both yanked for all they were worth. The building was crashing around his feet as they pulled him through the opening and along the slick, wet grass. They didn't let go until Chester was a safe distance away.

"Don't you *ever* do that again!" Nancy screamed, then scooped him up in her arms and gave him a hug.

Chester smiled weakly and was about to reply when an explosion shook the ground they were standing on. The church had imploded. A powerful rush of flames shot up twenty feet in the air. Seconds later the structure collapsed, falling down into the basement where Chester and Sarah had been only moments before.

Chapter 10

The morning after the fire, Father James gazed out the dining-room window with a sense of remorse so deep that he had to choke back a tear. There was nothing but blackened timbers where once the Congregational church had stood.

The skies were gray. It had started to rain a little after midnight, coming down in torrents that drove water underneath the window sash in Father James's makeshift bedroom. It was as though heaven itself heavily mourned the loss of this historic old church. If only the rain had arrived earlier.

His heart went out to Reverend Curtis and his congregation. He could think of no greater heartache for his people than to lose their place of worship. He remembered the recent near loss of St. Cecilia's and how it had nearly devastated his parishioners.

Dear Father, please extend Your grace to those who are so filled with sorrow this morning and keep us here at St. Cecilia's always mindful of their needs and how we might help lighten their loss.

He would call Reverend Curtis, offer St. Cecilia's basement for his services until the church could be rebuilt. Unfortunately, that meant Father James would have to stop procrastinating about a color for the basement walls. Chester had been hounding him for weeks, but, as with everything, Father James could not decide.

"Painters need to finish the walls downstairs before we can varnish the floors," Chester had said just last week. "It's nearing the end of August and Mother Superior has scheduled religious education classes to start down there the third week in September. How about a nice off-white?"

But off-white might show more dirt than, say, robin's-egg blue or lemon yellow, he reasoned, which meant that the area would have to be repainted in just a couple of years. Of course, he could choose the blue or the yellow, but then those colors would clash with the curtains Mildred Dunlap had made. At least, that was his understanding, as told to him by Mrs. Norris. Father James had no sense of color, which was why he said a silent prayer of thanks each morning while dressing that, as a priest, his color choices were extremely limited.

Of course, Father James could have the curtains changed, but that might offend Mildred, not to mention the added expense. It was quite a quandary, but one he had to resolve before he could offer the downstairs room to Reverend Curtis. Maybe Father Dennis might have an idea. He reached for the yellow legal pad he kept by the side of his bed to jot down a reminder but couldn't find it. No doubt Mrs. Norris had moved it.

"Blast that woman!" he swore under his breath.

Since the dining room had been made into his bedroom, Mrs. Norris felt free to arrange things to her liking not his; consequently, he could never find anything he needed. She kept packing his shaving gear in the bottom drawer of the sideboard, moving his favorite books off the chair next to the bed to the large serving table underneath the front window—twice he had been all settled in for the night only to discover his copy of Catherine Marshall's *A Man Called Peter* was across the room—and she insisted upon packing his undershorts in a cardboard box under the bed.

"Can't leave personal things like that out for just anybody to see," she reasoned while helping Father James to his feet, who was now reduced to crawling around like a toddler whenever he wished a change of clothes.

Outside his window, Father James spied George Benson's van and

Sheriff Bromley's Chevy Cruiser pull up in front of the fire scene; seconds later, Chester Platt's pickup truck pulled in alongside. The three men got out of their vehicles, doors slamming in rapid succession like gunshots. George led the retinue carrying an arson investigation kit. The others followed behind.

Timothy had popped in before morning Mass to bring Father James up to speed on the fire.

"George says it looks like it was set. I guess he and the Reverend went over the place a few weeks ago for their annual fire inspection, so chances are it wasn't started by something like faulty wiring," Timothy said.

"Sheriff Bromley thinks Molly might have started it. She was still in the building when the firemen got there. Bromley's locked her up until he can finish the investigation. But, I'll tell you this, no one in town is happy about it. Heck, if it weren't for her, Sarah Peterson might have died in that blaze."

Father James couldn't bear to even think about such a possibility. The Petersons had been through enough these last few years.

Timothy leaned back and rubbed his chin. "None of the gang think Molly did it." (The gang consisted of him, Ben, Sam, Father Keene, Fred and Arlene Campbell, Ethel Johnson and Harriet Bedford.)

"Now, I ask you, would she set the place on fire then hang around to tell the firemen that a child was trapped downstairs? We don't think so. No, it had to be somebody else. But who?"

Father James discussed it further with Bob Peterson when he and Sarah arrived later that afternoon for a visit. Sarah was dressed in a pink polo shirt and bib overalls, her hair done up in braids, looking as though she were ready to milk cows.

"How are you this afternoon?" Father James asked. The child had been through quite an ordeal.

"I'm fine, Father James," she said, her tongue playing with a front tooth that had begun to come loose.

"That was quite a scary fire last night," Father James offered, watching her expression closely.

"Yes, but Mr. Platt came and got me."

"Mr. Platt is a wonderful fireman," Father James agreed. "It was lucky that he was able to find you in all that smoke."

"It was easy," Sarah said, taking another cookie from the plate. "He just followed the light the rosary made."

Father James looked quizzically at Bob.

"She insists that the rosary Sister Claire gave me glowed with a bright light that helped Chester find her."

"I see," the priest said quietly.

"I haven't spoken to Chester about it yet," Bob said.

"Well, whether it did or not, it's still a miracle that Sarah's alive," Father James said, reaching out and drawing the child close. Sarah hopped up and settled comfortably next to him on the bed.

"Some of the credit goes to Molly."

"The bag lady?" Father James asked. "Yes, Timothy was here earlier. He said she was the one who told the firemen Sarah was trapped inside."

"If it weren't for Molly . . ." Bob paused, too overcome to go on.

"Can I have another cookie?" Sarah asked.

"No, sweetheart, I think you've had enough," Bob said, searching his pants pocket for a handkerchief.

While Bob searched, Father James snuck Sarah a cookie. The child's face lit up with a smile. How innocent and forgiving children are, he thought. No wonder the Lord said their angels always have access to the Father.

"I think the town should do more to help this poor woman than to condemn her," Bob said, wiping his nose with two rough swipes. "Even if—and let me tell you that in my mind it's a big 'if'—she did set that fire, shouldn't we try to find ways to help her? Find her a place that can help meet her special needs? I don't think throwing her in jail is the answer."

Father sipped his cup of Earl Grey tea, something he had just discovered in a box that had come with a fruit basket. It was almost as good as drinking coffee. Well, almost.

"I agree," he said, replacing the porcelain cup on its saucer. "I also think that our town should be the one to help her. We shouldn't try to pack her off to the state mental facility up in Hartford. Her presence in Dorsetville is a blessing."

"How's that, Father?" Bob asked.

"Molly's presence is a reminder that we are each responsible to answer Christ's call to feed the hungry and shelter the needy. It's easy to become indifferent to the plight of the poor when they don't live among us.

"But we are *our* brother's keepers. Not the state nor the government, which is why the welfare system can be so insidiously evil. It removes our personal burden to care for those less fortunate."

He often had watched Molly from his new "bedroom" window, and on several occasions Father Dennis had extended an invitation to her to come visit. Father James hadn't yet thanked her for her help during his accident.

Father Dennis relayed this information, but Molly said she was only doing her job. There was no reason to thank her. A strange kind of response, Father James felt. But perhaps like many street people she was mildly delusional or mentally challenged. As soon as he could handle his crutches without fear of falling flat on his face, he would walk over to offer a personal thank-you just the same.

Father James, therefore, was even more saddened when several days later Molly was officially charged with arson.

Something strange was happening to Chester Platt's lungs and he thought he had better pay Doc Hammon a call.

"I don't understand it," the doctor said. He sat puzzling in front of a new set of X rays his technician had just developed. He compared them with the set he had taken only the previous week. "It's as though I'm looking at two entirely different pairs of lungs."

Chester walked over. The X rays on the right showed several dark masses. The ones on the left were clear.

"What does it mean?"

"It means that your cancer has disappeared," the doctor said, flicking off the light.

"Disappeared? But . . . how?"

"Darned if I know."

"You're sure about this?"

The Doc hunched up his shoulders. "As sure as I can be without opening you up and looking inside." He studied Chester quietly for a long time. "It's the darnedest thing I've ever seen. Last visit your lungs were filled with fluid, which was why you were constantly coughing. Now they're clear. It's as though you've been given a completely new set of lungs."

He sank down on the stool in the corner of the room and looked up at Chester, completely perplexed. "I'm darned if I know what's going on. But this much I do know: there's absolutely no medical explanation for what has just taken place."

Chester walked out of the medical building feeling like a man on death row who had just been granted amnesty. He was so entrenched in his thoughts, the miraculous healing he had just received, that he didn't notice Nellie Anderson waiting to take his parking space. The lot was full and she was already late for her second job over in Woodstock.

"Chester, are you pulling out?"

Chester was thinking about that trip down the Mississippi his wife Patricia had always talked about. Maybe he'd drive to the travel agency over in Woodstock and book it. He dug down deep inside his jeans pocket for his car keys. Wouldn't Patricia be surprised? But not half as surprised as when she learned that Doc Hammon had just given him a complete bill of health.

He pulled out his keys and hopped into the cab of his truck. The rosary he had found while he and George had searched through the church ruins slipped to the ground unnoticed.

Nellie waited for Chester to pull out, then parked in his space, trying to hold rein on the anger she felt toward Doc Hammon's new medical technician. The woman had flatly refused to get Doc to call in her prescription, even though it was the same one she'd had for nearly twenty years. For goodness' sake!

It was just one more thing that made her insides churn like a KitchenAid mixer. She had been at the school since eight o'clock this morning setting up. She had told Harry she had been arranging her room for weeks. Truth was, she hadn't even started. She had been using that time to write a children's book, another secret she was keeping from him.

Now she was on her way over to Woodstock to clean offices until nine that night. Afterward, she would speed home and try to get some more work done on her book.

She looked at her watch. It was nearly four-thirty. Good grief! She was already late for her second job. She had hoped to stop over at Harry's en route to Woodstock. She needed to apologize for standing him up last night. But one of the offices had thrown a birthday party for an employee and the place was a shambles. It was after eleven before she pulled into her driveway, too tired to even pick up the phone.

But apologies would have to wait. She was already late for her job, and now this stop at Doc Hammon's was only going to make matters worse. Nellie carefully put her keys in her purse. She definitely did not want to risk locking them inside her car, something that she did so often that friends joked she was on a first-name basis with the tow-truck driver from Triple A.

She closed the car door, took two steps and spied something lying on the pavement. It was a rosary. Nellie picked it up. The blue beads were the color of a soft spring sky and the crucifix, so intricately cast of silver filigree, felt surprisingly heavy in her hand. Someone was certain to be saddened by its loss.

Nellie stuffed it inside her purse and rushed to make her appointment. She'd try to find the owner later.

Father James cradled the phone with his neck while trying to force a hand down into his cast to relieve a maddening itch. "So, how's the children's book coming?" he asked Nellie the next day.

"Just wonderful, Father James," she sang. "Perhaps a little *too* wonderful. I just wish I had more time to write."

He couldn't reach the itch. He grabbed for a pencil and shoved it inside the cast, but it was also several inches too short. Spying a yardstick lying on the nearby sideboard, he began to inch his way over to it.

"'*Too* wonderful'?" he said.

He stretched. The yardstick was only a fraction of an inch out of his reach but a new roll of fat prevented him from bending any farther. He really had to go on a diet when the cast came off. Elastic-waist sweatpants gave one a false sense of confidence. But who could resist the parade of casseroles, cakes and pies that marched through his makeshift bedroom?

Harriet Bedford's New England clam chowder laced with sherry. Lori Peterson's famous Haddam Hall gingerbread with lemon sauce and apricot scones made with real whipping cream. Ethel Johnson sent over Yankee pot roast at least every two weeks, and Nellie was just as faithful with her beef brisket. Father James felt to refuse these thoughtful gifts would give offense and he didn't want to do that, now, did he? He even felt it his priestly duty to sample the Henderson sisters' lavishly decorated wildflower cakes, making certain always to check for bugs before shoveling a forkful into his mouth. He'd once eaten a spider in undue haste.

"I'm afraid that I've missed another date with Harry," Nellie confided. "I got so caught up in the story line—the place where the little Christmas tree is about to give away his second chance to be taken home—that when I looked up it was after eleven o'clock. I was supposed to have met Harry at seven."

"I know we've talked about this before," he said, "but have you reconsidered telling Harry the truth? Let him know the reason you've missed a few dates is because you're caught up in writing a book, not to mention the fact that you've taken a second job."

He threw his upper torso over the side of the bed and snagged the yardstick. He got it! He shoved it down inside the cast with triumphal satisfaction. *Ah . . .* that felt so much better.

"I don't want Harry to know about the cleaning job."

"But he might want to help."

"That's exactly why I can't tell him."

"Then at least let him in on the children's book. It would help explain some of your absences."

"I can't, Father. How would I tell him that I'm writing a children's book because God gave me the idea in response to my prayer to find the money to save my family home? Now, I can say that to you, but just think how it would sound to Harry. Like I've bought the farm, right?"

When she put it like that, he admitted that it did sound a little crazy.

A school bell rang in the background. "I want to keep this whole thing to myself until the book is finished and I've found a publisher. Then it will be my great pleasure to tell the world the wonderful story of God's faithfulness and His miraculous saving power."

"I like your confidence," Father James admitted openly.

"It's not confidence in me, Father. It's confidence in God's saving grace."

"That's the only type worth having," he conceded.

"Mrs. Norris, may I please see a copy of the church bulletin before it goes to the printer?" Father James yelled from his bed.

Mrs. Norris appeared in the doorway, wiping her hands on a terry-cloth towel. "Was that you howling for me?"

"I wasn't 'howling,'" he said indignantly. "I just wanted to see the church bulletin before it goes to the printer."

"Why didn't you use the bell I put on your nightstand?" she asked, completely ignoring his query about the bulletin.

"The what? Oh, the bell? It's here someplace. Do you have it?"

"Have what? Look what you've done to this beautiful quilt."

Beautiful quilt? This was the same one that she insisted was completely inappropriate for a priest to own. The pattern was called the Drunkard's Path and it had been a gift from the Clothesline Quilters. ("They gave Reverend Curtis a nice Irish Chain when he had lumbago," Mrs. Norris had complained when it was delivered.)

"You've got all the bedcoverings bunched up underneath your cast," she said, yanking the offensive quilt right out from under his leg and giving the quilt a sound shake. His cast sank down into the featherbed mattress like a stone in a pond.

"The church bulletin," he said, trying to get settled again.

"Bulletin?"

"Yes, Mrs. Norris, the *bulletin*. I heard Fred Campbell drop it off this morning."

If only Doc Hammon would allow him to increase the time he could spend on his crutches instead of being dependent on everyone for the simplest things, then he would get the blasted thing himself!

"Oh, that. It's already gone to the printer."

"Gone to the printer?"

"That's what I said." She placed the properly folded quilt at the foot of the bed. "Father Dennis took it over early this morning. Might as well straighten up since I'm here," she said, turning her attention to his nightstand.

Before Father James could protest, she had closed his copy of *The Editor's Boy*, by his favorite naturalist, Hal Bortland, without benefit of marking his place, and stacked it among a pile of other books. Now it would take him most of the morning to find where he had left off.

"Here's the bell," she said triumphantly. She gave it a shake, as though to test if it still worked.

He would not be sidetracked. "What if I want to make some changes?"

"Changes?"

"To the bulletin." Two more weeks of this and he'd be a madman.

"You don't need to make any changes. Father Dennis has already gone through it and says it's fine."

Fine? He doubted that. Although Father Dennis had many wonderful attributes, and had been a godsend during these last few weeks, copyediting was definitely not one of his strong suits.

An insert in the previous week's bulletin read, "Mrs. Johnson will be entering the hospital this week for testes," and the week before that, in bold black type, an announcement stated: "Weight Watchers will meet at 7 P.M. in the church's basement. Please use the wide double doors at the side entrance."

That one, in particular, brought several angry phone calls from the women who ran the program. "Was that supposed to be funny?" they asked. Even the Henderson sisters, who had just joined Weight Watchers under Doc Hammon's orders to lose forty pounds apiece, still weren't speaking to him.

"I wish *some* people would get my approval before they go off and do things on their own," he said petulantly. "After all, I am still the pastor here."

Mrs. Norris yanked the pillow out from behind his head and fluffed it up. "In that case, do I have your *approval* to serve chicken pot pie for lunch?"

He ignored the barb, grabbed his book off the nightstand table and began to read. It wasn't until she left the room that he noticed he was holding it upside down.

Although Mrs. Norris continued to set his teeth on edge, Father James was grateful for her suggestion that his bed be moved downstairs.

In the hospital, the days had gone as slowly as a walk through molasses. He had marked the passing of time by the three meals and two snacks served each day. And although people came to visit, no one seemed terribly comfortable there. In fact, most looked relieved when it was time to go. The hospital atmosphere did not lend itself to good conversations. But now that he was stationed in the rectory's dining room, people came through in droves and, more important, stayed to chat.

Timothy McGree, St. Cecilia's head usher, dropped by each morning after Mass to update Father on the town's latest gossip.

"That Japanese restaurant is opening up this Friday," Timothy informed Father James on Monday.

"Really?" Knowing that most people in Dorsetville might feel they were not being faithful to Harry Clifford by trying a new restaurant, he asked, "How do you think it'll go over with the village folk?"

"Opinions are divided," Timothy said, looking like a test pattern in this morning's outfit: an orange-and-lime-checked shirt he'd found at Secondhand Rose and a black-and-white herringbone sports jacket with lapels as wide as a barn door.

On Tuesday, Timothy had discovered the people's last name, Yokohama, and that twelve of them had rented the old Hawkins farmhouse. Apparently they had been living there for several weeks.

"Ethel and Arlene dropped over with a cake." (These two women were Dorsetville's self-appointed welcoming committee.) "Said they spoke to the mother. She stays home while the others work over at the restaurant. Ethel convinced the woman to let her take her to the senior center for bingo." Timothy scratched his head. "Which reminds me. When are you planning on finishing up the basement of the church? Our P.A. system is a lot better than the one over at the senior center. Ben swore he lost last week's ten-dollar pot because he'd heard 7 being called when it was 11."

Father James told him that the basement should be finished in about two weeks. He had finally decided to delegate the whole decorating issue to Mrs. Norris and Arlene Campbell.

"You expect two women to come to an agreement on decorating?" Timothy asked incredulously.

"Yes, and now I don't have to think about it again," Father James said rather smugly.

Timothy just shook his head. "Father, what you don't know about women would fill a book."

On Wednesday, Timothy was back with a copy of the Japanese restaurant's menu. He had snagged one from the printer when he had gone over to pick up the church bulletins. The two men reviewed it over a piece of Mrs. Norris's prized malted chocolate cake.

"What's sushi?" Timothy asked, helping himself to a second piece of cake.

"Raw fish," Father James offered, holding out his plate. "I'll take another slice."

Timothy paused with the cake knife in hand. "Raw fish? Who in heaven's name would want to eat raw fish?"

"It's quite popular in New York," Father offered.

"Well, this ain't New York, Father," Timothy reminded him.

On Friday, Timothy came with news that George Benson, in his capacity as fire marshal, had refused to allow the restaurant to open until the owners installed a new sprinkler system. George confirmed this the next morning after Mass. Father James was still having trouble adjusting to the thought of George as a Catholic.

"Can't be too cautious. Everyone knows these people cook with enough oil to lube a fleet of buses. Last thing Dorsetville needs is another three-alarm fire," George said.

Men from Chester Platt's construction crews also visited daily, passing through with heavy rolls of electrical wire, five-gallon buckets of Spackle, boxes of power tools. Much to Father James's delight, they also came to share their midmorning breakfast sandwiches of bacon, double egg and cheese on hard rolls smothered with butter and Thermoses filled with the Country Kettle's fragrant black coffee, which he sampled freely when Mrs. Norris wasn't looking.

And, while Timothy kept the priest apprised of the goings-on around the town, the workmen kept him current on the renovation. It was a lucky thing, too, because there seemed to be a conspiracy of silence among Father Dennis, Mother Mary Veronica and Mrs. Norris.

"No need to bother you with trifles," they assured him.

Trifles? he thought peevishly. These trifles were adding up to hundreds of thousands of dollars—money that, as St. Cecilia's pastor, he was personally responsible to see got spent properly. Even more disturbing was the open admiration the laborers had developed for Father Dennis and Mother Superior, who were now working as a team.

"The crews love working with those two," said Sirius Gaithwait, head stonemason, a short, stocky fellow with coal black hair and arms the size of ham shanks. "But Father Dennis should really see a gastroenterologist for those hiccups. Never saw anyone so plagued by them in all my life."

In between bites of his Italian sausage and peppers on a hard roll, which Father James happily shared, Sirius added, "They're quite a team. On Monday morning, they give us a list of exactly what they want done during that week. Never any changes, which means no more delays. They keep right on top of us, too. No unscheduled coffee breaks when they're around. In fact, if Mother Superior saw me here with you right now, she'd give me one of what we guys call her 'Darth Vader' looks." He laughed. "Yep, there's no messing around while those two are in charge."

Unlike me, Father James silently admitted, openly piqued.

"The way things are now moving along," Sirius concluded, "we'll have the renovations finished by Thanksgiving. That is if the women can come to some kind of an agreement on the paint color for the basement."

Father cringed. Having Arlene Campbell and Mrs. Norris choose the colors for the church basement seemed like such a good idea at the time. After all, who knew more about color than women? And these two had always worked together well on other church projects. Apparently, however, Mrs. Norris liked pastels while Arlene favored fall colors, which resulted in a stalemate. Both continually asked Father James to take sides in this debate. He refused. Work it out among yourselves, he insisted. But it seemed they couldn't. In fact, last he heard, neither was speaking to the other, and now the painters were farther behind schedule than ever.

But at least everything else seemed to be coming along. The Dorsetville garden club had replanted all the beds along the exterior of the church as quickly as the scaffolding was taken down. All that was left to plant was the bed of hostas along the shady north side of the church.

And the Clothesline Quilters' sewing machines hadn't stopped humming all summer. They had taken it upon themselves to make quilted seat cushions for all of the pews. Even the Knights of Columbus kept busy, throwing a monthly pancake-and-sausage breakfast for all the volunteers and crews. Father Dennis always volunteered to help.

Father James should have been thrilled with the way things were speeding along, the way his church had come together as a community to help with the renovation during his convalescence. But instead, he fell into a blue funk. Somehow, he felt usurped, stripped of his power, his position; he felt unneeded, as if he had been overlooked. And try as he might to shove these petty feelings aside, he could not. In fact, they seemed to grow in intensity each time Mrs. Norris came to his room to give an update of the tasks completed.

Then one night as he lay in bed, his *Thompson Chain Reference Bible* propped up on his chest, his eye happened to fall upon a passage in the book of I Corinthians that filled him with remorse. The passage dealt with the diversity of gifts given to man through the love of the Father: "Are we all prophets? Are all teachers? Do all work miracles?" To which Father added, "Do all have the gifts needed to renovate a church?"

Saint Paul urged the early Christians to celebrate their diversity of gifts. Everyone has been given a special talent by God, the apostle said. But not all possess the same talents; and this is exactly how it should be, he insisted, in order to build up the body of Christ, to be effective in the world.

One thing was for certain, Father James had no talent for renovating a church. Which was the right floor tile? Lighting system? He hadn't even been able to make a decision on a simple thing like paint color. If he had, Mrs. Norris and Arlene Campbell would still be talking. But never having been involved in a similar project, how was he supposed to know these things? And so he had delayed making any decisions, which had increased the costs and caused a rift between two of his flock.

Hadn't he prayed for God's help, and hadn't God sent Mother Superior and Father Dennis to direct the project and his parishioners to offer their talents to do things he couldn't? But instead of Father James's being thankful for the gifts they so kindly shared, he allowed resentment to fester.

Dear Lord, forgive me, he prayed, his face reddening with shame. He was almost embarrassed to ask for forgiveness. He, of all people, should have known better than to let anger and jealousy enter into his heart, to give Satan a foothold. But he also knew that as long as he was mortal, he would be subject to sin and failure. Fortunately, his Heavenly Father always stood with open arms. He continued with his prayer:

I come humbly into Your presence with a penitent heart. Lately, I've allowed bitterness to seep into my soul. You sent Your servants to help me accomplish that which I was incapable of doing; and I shamefully admit that their efficiency has made me feel threatened. I no longer felt I was in charge.

That's dangerous thinking, Lord. Straight from Satan's lair. Since the Garden of Eden, Satan has tried to convince man that personal power was something to be sought after, fought over to retain at all costs. And those costs have been high. Broken relationships. Unethical business dealings. Wars.

But I know that true power comes through relinquishment. The Cross taught us that. You, who were God, relinquished Your power to man, in order that we all might be saved.

So let me not fear that Father Dennis and Mother Mary Veronica or any of the others who have so generously offered their time and talents will infringe upon my position. Instead, let me openly and joyously pray for their success. Give me the spirit of thanksgiving for the gifts You have instilled in others and which I lack.

And, Lord, most important, let me always remember that we are all members of the same body, working to share Your great gift of salvation with others who, I must add, would be more greatly received in a church that was not going to fall on everyone's heads.

Chapter 11

Mrs. Norris arrived early the next morning in an effort to get Father Dennis out of bed, fed and ready for seven o'clock Mass.

"Father Dennis," she called from the bottom of the back staircase. She didn't try to hide her exasperation. "It's almost six-thirty. Mass starts in half an hour."

"I'm getting up," he fibbed.

If she had an extra ounce of energy, she'd march up those stairs and pull him out from under the sheets. But she hadn't. In fact, she felt as though the very life force had been drained from her body. Even breathing had become an effort. She wondered how much time she had before the Lord came to call her home.

Charlie Littman dropped the mail through the back-door mail slot, calling, "Morning, Margaret."

"Morning, Charlie," she called back, not bothering to open the door.

She felt a new pain shoot up along her upper back as she bent down to pick up the mail. Were her kidneys beginning to shut down? She had read that they were the first of the major organs to go.

Mrs. Norris leafed through the mail on her way to the stove. Bills. Advertisements. A Patrick Baker catalog, which reminded her that Father James needed to order a new set of collars. The way he was gaining weight, he'd also need a few new pairs of pants. She had tried to tell him to stay away from the sweets, but he persisted. The man could live solely on a diet of coffee and cake. Father Dennis wasn't much better.

There was a time she would have worried herself sick over these priests, but now . . . What did it matter? She would soon be joining the Lord and these priests would be some other housekeeper's cross to bear.

Sorting through the mail, she was reminded of the letter from her cousin Portance, still tucked inside her sweater pocket. It had arrived yesterday, but she had been too exhausted to read it. She stood quietly, listening for any indication that Father Dennis was moving about upstairs. Silence. She exhaled in utter defeat. She was too tired to climb those stairs and shake him awake. Let him celebrate the morning's Mass in his pajamas, for all she cared. It would serve him right.

Mrs. Norris filled the coffeepot with Maxwell's French Roast. Father James would be finished with his prayers soon and begin to bellow for his morning brew. He had taken to completely ignoring Doc Hammon's orders. Just another thing she had decided to let ride.

She switched on the coffeepot, then walked over to the kitchen table, pulled the letter out of her sweater pocket and collapsed in a chair. Apparently, she had plenty of time to read it. There still was no movement overhead.

> Dear Margaret,
>
> Your Aunt Sally and I just got back from Branson. We had a wonderful time. (That Bobby Vinton plays a mean accordion.) We took the bus with a group from our senior center. Boy, can those people party!
>
> On the way home, Sally and I got to talking about your recent interest in family genealogy and she helped me see that I had gotten things a little mixed-up.
>
> I'm afraid that I sent you your Cousin Rachel's family history. She's the one related to your Great-uncle Willaby on your grandfather's side. That's the uncle who married into the family of circus performers—lion tamers and high-wire performers—which is probably why so few of them lived past sixty.

Anyway, your Aunt Sally gave me the correct documents which I have enclosed along with this letter.

As you can see, you come from the Jacob's side of the family, all of whom were as strong as horses. (In the late 1800s, several of the women gave birth out in the fields while gathering the corn.) Phoebe Jacob lived to be one hundred and three. I hope this clears things up a little.

Write again soon, dear, but don't expect a quick reply. Sally and I are awfully busy. We've booked a singles' cruise for next month and have joined a daily aerobics class to get back into shape.

Love,
Cousin Portance

Mrs. Norris stared at the letter, then read it again. And yet again. Could it be true? She was *not* going to die? Imagine that! Her silly Cousin Portance had sent her the wrong side of the family tree. In fact, she'd probably live to be one hundred. Didn't her father always say that she took after Phoebe?

Mrs. Norris briskly pushed the chair away from the table, rising like a phoenix. She could feel the blood coursing through her veins, her heart beating strong and steady in her chest. She walked over to the back door, flung it open, stepped out onto the porch. She did a few deep knee bends. Her arthritis was gone. Must be coming into a dry spell, she thought.

What a glorious day it was going to be. The sun was shining; the air was clean with just a hint of wild phlox. Why, she felt like a teenager again. She took several deep breaths. Too bad there wasn't time for her to take a brisk walk around the town green. Oh, well, that would have to wait. There was work to be done. She had been idle for too long.

She marched back into the house, slammed the door behind her and headed toward the back stairs. It was nearly quarter of seven and Father Dennis still hadn't come down.

"Father Dennis! Get up this minute!" she clamored. The stair treads creaked loudly as she pounded up to the landing. "This is your final warning. You've got one minute to get your lazy self out of that bed or I'm coming in and dressing you myself."

Halfway up the staircase, Mrs. Norris decided that right after she had roused Father Dennis out of bed, she'd give Arlene a call. It was time to stop all this bickering over the church basement's colors. She had no intention of living out the next thirty or forty years not speaking to one of her best friends.

Postman Charlie Littman shifted the forty-pound sack of mail to his other shoulder as he trudged up the pathway to Reverend Curtis's home. He tried to divert his eyes from the charred ruins that had once been a church. Generations of Littmans had worshipped there for over one hundred fifty years. Now it was just a pile of rubble.

Charlie swung his bag toward his chest, reached in and grabbed the reverend's mail. He quickly thumbed through the letters, making certain that each was addressed to the Curtis home, 137 Church Street. Also included among the mail was a copy of the *Dorsetville Gazette* with a front-page story about the fire. He batched everything together with a rubber band. All except the two magazines, each wrapped in a plain brown paper. Charlie was no fool. He knew what they contained: adult magazines. Reproachful! He handled these with the utmost distaste. If only Charlie wasn't sworn as a government official to keep all official postal matters private, he'd march right to the church council and have the Reverend Curtis kicked out. Imagine, a pastor—a man of God—reading such filth! Why, it made him weak at the knees just to think about it.

Charlie stuffed the mail into the white metal box next to the front door, then quickly stomped back down the stairs as though depravity was contagious. He didn't even dare breathe until he had hit the sidewalk. Only then would he turn and pause. His eyes took in the church ruins. It was a shame, a pitiful shame, that parishioners had to suffer such a tragic loss due to the sins of their pastor. There was no other plausible explanation. Hadn't the church stood unscathed for over two hundred years until *he* came along?

Charlie hitched up the mail sack and started across the street. He couldn't stand here all day filled with regrets. He had work to do. He reached inside his sack and pulled out the next delivery as he headed toward the Sister Regina Francis Retirement Home. In his hand he held two magazines addressed to Mother Superior: *Hot Rod Digest* and *Celebrity Hairstyles*.

"It's arson. No doubt about it," George Benson said, passing Sheriff Bromley the state's official lab report.

Just as the sheriff began to read the first sentence, Betty's voice sounded on the intercom. "Al, the Henderson sisters are on the phone again."

"Sic 'em on the highway department."

Harley, asleep in the corner, heard the words "sic 'em" and began to growl. The German shepherd had become a police station dog—or, more accurately, the sheriff's dog, after Deputy Hill's landlord threatened to have him evicted. Apparently his lease had a no pets clause.

"Quiet down," said the sheriff. Harley lay his head between his paws and went back to sleep.

"They're not calling about the missing black-eyed Susans along Route 7 this time," Betty informed him.

"Then *what?*"

"They want to file a formal complaint about Molly's arrest." Getting no response, Betty continued: "It's the fortieth call I've gotten today. A lot of people are upset that you locked her up."

"Yeah, well, you tell them I'm upset, too. We've got an arson report here saying that the church was deliberately set on fire. You know of anyone else in town that would torch a church?"

"I'm just telling you what people are saying."

"Betty?"

"Yes, Sheriff?"

"Don't bother me again."

"Right."

Bromley went back to the report. "You're positive that the fire didn't start on its own?" he asked George.

"Electrical was sound. Ted Jefferson checked all that stuff before issuing a permit for the Bible camp."

"Then it started . . . how?"

George tipped his chair back. "It's hard to be sure, Al, but if I had to guess, I'd say someone was playing with matches and the place just caught fire." George was dressed in coveralls stained with grease and smelling like fuel oil. The sheriff got up and opened a window.

"We both know that building was tinder dry," George continued. "A spark from any source could have set it off. In fact, I told Reverend Curtis last year that they should put in a sprinkler system, but no, he said they didn't want to ruin the church's historic charm, and since the building was 'grandfathered' I couldn't insist. All I can say is that we were lucky to get a little rain earlier in the evening, enough to keep the woods from going up. If that had happened, we might have lost the entire town."

"There's no sign of any type of incendiary?" Bromley asked, distancing himself farther from George and the fumes. Apparently George's "eau de cologne" bothered Harley, too. He sniffed the air, got up and moved to the other side of the room.

"Nope," answered George. He was silent for a few seconds before asking, "How long can you keep the bag lady without any hard evidence that she started it?"

"A few days."

There was a knock at the door. Harley's ears went up. He watched the door intently as it opened.

"Sorry, Al," Betty said, "but Kim Leyden from the *Dorsetville Gazette* is outside. She wants to talk to you about the fire investigation."

"Have her talk to George," Bromley said.

George puffed up with self-importance. "Tell her she'll have to make an appointment."

Betty continued to stand in the doorway.

"Good God, Betty! You're starting to act like Hill," Bromley bellowed. "What else?"

Betty Olsen had worked for the department for thirty years and was completely unfazed by the sheriff's tirades.

"There's several women's groups outside. They want to see Molly."

"What kind of 'groups'?"

"The Clothesline Quilters want to deliver some quilts. The two women who run Secondhand Rose are here with several bags of clothes and the Dorsetville Beautification Committee has decorated a Grand Union shopping wagon with ribbons and flowers. Said the Grand Union store manager donated it."

The sheriff stared at her blankly.

"You know. So she can carry around her shopping bags."

The sheriff hung his head in his hands. "It's going to be a long day."

Father James sat uncomfortably in the confessional, his leg cast jutting out from underneath the red velvet curtains at an odd angle and into the aisle, his new crutches leaned up against the outside. Mrs. Norris had decided to do the fall cleaning. His room had been completely torn apart. He had been given instructions not to return for at least an hour.

As the priest waited for the next penitent, he looked up into the grate embedded in the ceiling. It was a habit he had gotten into ever since a secret room had been discovered directly above the confessional. The room could be accessed by a hidden panel at the top of the choir staircase, and had been used by young Matthew Metcalf two years ago when he and his grandfather's friends had decided to use a holographic image of the Blessed Virgin Mary to replace a broken statue.

Someone entered the chamber to his left. He gave them a few moments to get comfortable, then slid back the small wooden door, revealing a wire screen. It was one of the Galligan twins. He was not certain which one.

"Bless me, Father, for I have sinned. It's been a month since my last confession," the boy intoned.

"I'm listening," Father James said softly, always thrilled to have the young members of his parish use this much-neglected sacrament. Since the Galligan twins were altar boys, it thrilled him even more.

The boy rambled off his sins as though he were reciting items off of a shopping list. "I lied about a dozen times. I was disrespectful to my parents about four times. I stole a candy bar from Grand Union, and I also broke the seventh commandment."

Seventh commandment?? Father James silently counted off. One . . . You shall have no other gods before Me. Four . . . Remember to keep the Sabbath. Six . . . Do not murder. Seven . . . Do not commit adultery. Adultery???!!!

He cleared his throat. "What commandment is that, Rodney . . . or is it Dexter?"

"I'm Rodney. Gee, Father, you're a priest. Don't you know the Ten Commandments?"

"Yes, Rodney, I know, but I just wanted to know if *you* know." Great save.

"Thou shalt not steal."

"Oh . . ." Father James sighed with relief. "Rodney, for the future that's the eighth commandment. Now, go on."

"Could you tell me how much I owe for each of those sins, Father?"

"Owe?"

"Yeah, like how many Hail Marys or Our Fathers for each of them. I like to know which prayers I'm praying for each sin."

"Oh, I see. Well, why don't you say five Hail Marys for stealing the candy. I do hope you know how wrong it is to steal. And two Our Fathers for the others."

"Okay."

Rodney paused.

"Is there anything else you wish to confess?" Father asked, his hand poised midair ready to give absolution.

"Yeah. But before I confess, I just want to go over the rules again."

"Rules?"

"You know, like I can tell you anything in confession but you can't tell anyone what I've told you. Is that right, Father?"

"That's right. Anything you say here stays between us and God. Is there something else that's weighing on your mind? If so, this is the place to get rid of it."

"Well . . . yeah . . . there is something."

"All right, then. Let's have it. I bet it's not half as bad as you might think."

There was a moment of silence before the boy spit out the sin in one quick breath. "I confess that I started the fire that burned down the Congregational church."

Father James slid off his seat and crashed out into the church aisle.

The boys both watched Chester Platt go inside the church. As he passed, he waved and shouted out a hello. He wore the biggest grin the twins had ever seen on any adult's face.

"Maybe he won the lotto," Rodney postulated. Then he turned to his brother. "So, did you tell him?"

Rodney had waited outside of the church, having won the coin toss. The twins figured since they looked alike, there was really no need for them both to go to confession.

Dexter smiled an evil grin. "Yep. Told him I was you."

Rodney punched his brother in the arm. "So what did he say?"

"Said that you've got to say five Hail Marys for stealing candy again and I've got two Our Fathers."

"No, I mean about the fire? He's not going to tell, is he?"

"Nope. He can't," Dexter said, bending down to pick up a stone. He hurled it across the street. "It's against the laws of the Church, he said."

"Good." Rodney was relieved. "So? What's our penance?"

"We have to say the Rosary three times a day until we confess to Sheriff Bromley that we were the ones who started the fire."

Rodney laughed. "Yeah, like *that's* going to happen."

Chapter 12

"What do you think it is?" Father James whispered to Father Dennis across the breakfast table as he stared down into his plate. Mrs. Norris was washing dishes in the kitchen sink, safely out of earshot.

"A pancake?" Father Dennis poked it with his fork. "But what are these other things?" His stomach began to growl. "Excuse me."

On having discovered that she was no longer in peril of dying, Mrs. Norris had embarked upon a health kick with the zeal of a new convert, deciding to make the most of the many years she had left.

Unfortunately, she had included the priests in this new regimen comprised of no sugar, no white flour or fatty foods—everything the two men liked. Things had grown so bleak that Father Dennis hadn't taken anything out of the refrigerator since she had begun ("I'm afraid people would ask me to return it," he lamented); and Father James, who had been eagerly awaiting permission to use his crutches, had found midnight forays into the kitchen hardly worth the effort.

Father James took a sip from his coffee cup and gagged.

"What in blazes is *this?*" he wailed. It tasted like roasted tree bark.

Mrs. Norris raced over. "It's Postum. Do you like it?" She hovered, carafe poised, ready to pour him another cup.

"No," he said decisively. Why was the Lord testing him? Hadn't he suffered enough?

"The woman at Morning Sun Health Foods store showed me an article about the effects of caffeine. Why, it's a wonder your intestines aren't in a permanent state of decline, with all the coffee you drink."

"I don't drink *that* much . . ." Father James started to protest but she silenced him with an upraised hand.

"I've seen parishioners sneak cups of coffee from the Country Kettle into your room when they think I'm not looking."

How did she always seem to reduce him to a mere child? He resented this and spoke out. "I *like* caffeine, Mrs. Norris, and, although you are welcome to embark upon any health plan you choose, I would appreciate it if you would leave me out of your new regimen." There! He had told her. He took a deep breath and began again in a more civil tone. "Now that we've got that all settled, I'd like my cup of coffee, please."

"No," she said plainly.

"No?"

"I threw out all the coffee and tea."

"You threw it out??!! But why?"

"Do you have any idea what it does to your nervous system, not to mention your intestines?"

He wished she'd leave his intestines out of this.

"No, and I don't care. I just want my coffee or tea or . . . something familiar." He felt the joy go right out of his morning.

"Well, there isn't any." She placed the carafe in the center of the table. "You'll thank me for it later."

He doubted that.

She grabbed the wash basket off the top of the washing machine and headed outside to hang a load of curtains. She had stripped the rectory bare and was giving everything a thorough cleaning.

"Eat up before your tofu breakfast links and wheat germ cakes get cold."

The two men sat alone in silence, each staring even more forlornly into their plates. So that's what it was.

"Father Dennis, will you please give the blessing?" Father James said in utter defeat. He bowed his head and waited. And waited. No prayer issued forth.

"Father Dennis?"

Father Dennis looked up with mournful eyes. "Would you mind saying the blessing over the food this morning, Father James? If I tried to tell God I was thankful for this, He'd know I was lying."

Father James sat in the front pew with his parishioners, waiting for the Mass to begin. Father Dennis was presiding until he was mobile again.

How restful and lovely the sanctuary felt this time of morning. The newly completed interior renovations added to these feelings of peace and tranquillity. The ceiling had been covered with a new coat of plaster and painted a pristine white. Gone were the cracks and crevices that had scarred it for so long, which made the refurbished gilding along the crown moldings shine even more brilliantly. Below, the marble floor had been resurfaced and polished until it sparkled like glass; and the pews, with their new coats of shellac, appeared golden in the light, as if they, too, were gilded by an artist's brush. Just the walls remained to be finished. Painting was to commence today, a soft, saffron yellow.

Father James was pleased that Mrs. Norris and Arlene Campbell had finally come to terms on the color for the basement, although neither would tell him what they had chosen.

"We want it to be a surprise," they said.

Father James was always a little leery of surprises, but tried to think positively. He just hoped that Chester Platt's men still had ample time to finish the job. Reverend Curtis and his congregation were using the Salvation Army's storefront mission this Sunday but expected to switch over to St. Cecilia's basement early the following week.

Early morning had always been Father James's favorite time of day. Even as a youngster. There was something magical about a new dawn, a sense of discovery, miracles waiting to be born. Apparently the psalmist David felt the same. "Early will I rise to greet you," he had written.

Although it was only seven-thirty, several candles already flickered in front of the statues of the Blessed Virgin Mary and Saint Anthony, many, he suspected, lit by the sea of nuns in their blue habits seated to the right of the altar. They were softly reciting the Joyful Mysteries of the rosary, their fingers counting off the beads, which tapped softly against the wooden pews.

Father James offered up his own silent prayer.

Dear Father, please help these dedicated women find the money they seek to open another retirement home so other religious, like our dear Father Keene, may live out the rest of their days in peace and safety. I beseech You on their behalf to send the circumstances, events and people needed to bring the miracle they seek to fruition.

"Good morning, Father James," Ben Metcalf whispered, sliding into the pew behind him.

Father James turned with a wide smile. "Good morning, Ben. How are you this wonderful morning?"

"Not too bad," Ben said, pulling the kneeler forward and painfully sliding onto his knees. His arthritis was acting up again. He whispered into Father's ear, "Please pray for me, Father. I have a job interview right after Mass."

"A job interview?"

"Well, it's not *exactly* a job."

"Oh?"

"It's more like an apprenticeship. I'm applying at WKUZ as a cameraman-in-training for their public access station. They produce Jim Moran's *Dorsetville News* and Mildred Dunlop's show, *Crazy About Crosswords*."

"Can't say I've seen any of them."

"Well, none of the shows are really very good, but it's something to do."

"Do you think you'd like running a camera?"

Ben shrugged. "Don't know. I just thought I'd give it a try. One of the guys down at the senior center ran the camera until he got cataracts. He said it was kind of interesting. He's the one who told me about the opening. So, will you pray for me?"

"Fervently!"

After Mass, Father James braved a walk to the Country Kettle. He was a desperate man. He needed coffee and recognizable food.

Hobbling on crutches, it took him twenty minutes to finally reach Main Street. He paused where the road leveled out in front of Second-hand Rose to massage his lower back.

"Just ten more feet," he said, cheering himself on. Ten more feet and he'd be greeted with the aroma of freshly brewed coffee, Lori's just-baked cinnamon buns, Harry's golden home fries. Ah, he could almost taste it.

Minutes later, he came to the front door of the restaurant, hopped up onto the granite step and flung the door open wide with the tip of his right crutch. Having made it this far, Father James couldn't have felt more satisfaction than if he had climbed to the top of the Matterhorn. He stepped inside, closed his eyes and breathed in deeply, anticipating the heavenly aromas that urged him on. Instead, he nearly choked. The air was filled with the noxious odor of charred home fries and burned bacon grease.

What had happened? He edged a little farther into the restaurant; his eyes began to sting from the smoke that filled the place. Through a heavy haze, he could make out Harry's figure standing in front of the grill. Nancy Hawkins was beside him with a fire extinguisher in hand. Several other members of the Dorsetville Fire Department looked on from across the counter. Chester Platt was one of them.

"Thanks, Nancy," said Harry, as he began to scrape the blackened mound of fries into a metal pan.

His face was covered in red blotches from both the intense heat and embarrassment. It was the first time in all the years he had run the place that he had ever set the grill on fire.

"No big deal," Nancy said, standing the fire extinguisher on the floor. "We got it before it could do any real damage. Chester? Will you run over to the firehouse and get a couple of big exhaust fans? We gotta suck some of this smoke out before Harry, here, dies of smoke inhalation. I'd go, but I have John Moran's Lumina up on the lift and he needs it back by twelve."

"Sure thing." Chester finished his coffee in one giant gulp, then headed toward the front door, nearly colliding with Father James.

"Sorry, Father. I'd better be more careful. I wouldn't want to break your other leg," Chester said, laughing, then motioned toward the grill. "Isn't this a pip?"

"What happened?"

"A grease fire. But we got to it before it did any real damage."

"Thank the Lord you were here," he said in earnest. "Seems the Lord is using you a lot lately."

Chester smiled. "I'm grateful to be of service." Then, changing the subject, he added, "Looks like you've finally got the hang of those crutches."

"Trying," he said, eyeing an empty stool. Smoke or no smoke, it was going to feel great to sit down.

"You need any help before I take off?"

"No, I think I can manage," he said bravely.

"All right, then. I'll see you later." Chester bounded out the front door, teeming with youthfulness and vigor.

Father James turned to watch him leave and issued another prayer of thanksgiving. It had been several weeks since Chester had slipped into his confessional to share the good news that his cancer had miraculously disappeared. The priest still got goosebumps when he thought about it, especially the conversation that had come afterwards with Doc Hammon.

"I'd like to take the credit, Jim," Doc had said. "Tell you that some wonder drug I administered was responsible for the disappearance of Chester's cancer. But, truth is, I can't. No, I think the reason behind Chester's recovery can be found more easily in your realm of expertise than mine."

Father James watched through the front window as Chester hopped into his pickup truck. Praise bubbled up inside of him.

How great is God's love? His mercy endureth forever, he recited silently.

While Wendy busied herself clearing some tables of spilled coffee cups, Lori and two other waitresses opened all the windows and began using menus to fan the smoke out. By the time Father had maneuvered his way around a nest of wooden tables and collapsed onto a stool, the air was almost breathable.

Harry had his back to the priest and was working hard at cleaning the blackened mess off the grill.

"What happened, Harry?" Father James asked, leaning his crutches against the counter.

"A can of Crisco got too close to the flame," Harry said, not bothering to turn around.

He scraped a pile of charred bacon into a plastic twenty-gallon garbage can, most of which spilled on the floor. Wendy tried to get by with a pan of dirty cups and saucers and slid her heel on some bacon grease. She sailed across the floor behind the counter, arms flailing.

"Harry! Are you trying to kill me?" she screamed.

"What are you doing back here, anyway?" he snapped. "Can't you see it's still a mess? Stay out of here until I get this stuff cleaned up unless you want to get hurt."

Wendy slammed the pan of dirty dishes down on the counter. Father James nearly jumped out of his stool. There was fire in her eyes. She marched back to Harry and stuck out her chin in his face.

"You think I'm back here because I miss you? A customer just walked in and wants some oatmeal, *which* is in the steam table in the back, *which* means that I have to walk past here to get it. Or would you prefer I just tell him to just go on home until you're finished cleaning the grill?"

Father James watched the exchange, feeling slightly anxious. Wendy came from New York City. Nobody in Dorsetville messed with Wendy.

"I don't care what you tell him," Harry shouted. "Just get out of my way."

Lori magically appeared and placed her body in between them. "Let me finish this up, Harry." She took the spatula out of his hands. He gave no resistance.

"Wendy, get your oatmeal. Just be careful. Harry, sit down and have a chat with Father James. I'll get Pedro to help me clean up this mess."

"Fine!" He stomped around the counter like a schoolchild who had been sent to the back of the class. He crashed onto the stool next to Father James.

"Looks like you've had a hard morning, friend," Father James said, patting his friend's shoulders.

"I've had better," said Harry. "Wendy?"

Wendy swung the bowl of oatmeal over Harry's head. Father James held his breath.

"Sorry I shouted."

"That was shouting?" she quipped. "Not where I come from."

Harry gave a weak smile. "On your way back through, would you get me some coffee? Father James could use a cup, too."

"Sure thing. You want your *special* mug?" She teased.

"Any mug will do," Harry smiled.

Father James watched Lori and Pedro, the dishwasher, vigorously scrub the grill with wire brushes, hoping she hadn't overhead. This morning he needed something stronger than herbal tea.

"The fire could have been worse," he offered, hoping to lighten Harry's mood.

"Yeah. I suppose."

"Looks like there wasn't much damage."

"Just to my pride."

"I'm certain that will mend," Father James offered. "Ah, coffee. Thanks, Wendy."

He took a quick sip from the white porcelain cup, secretly wishing that Wendy had chosen a mug instead. That way, he might have gotten several good slugs before Lori turned around and discovered that he wasn't drinking tea.

Harry kept his voice low and confided miserably, "I think Nellie has found someone else."

Reluctantly, Father James placed his cup down on the counter. "Now, Harry, we've talked about this before."

"Yeah, I know, and you told me there was no basis for my fears. But now it's different."

"How's that?"

"She's canceled two of our dates in a row, and last night she called fifteen minutes before we were supposed to go out to dinner to say she had a headache and was going straight to bed. I couldn't sleep, so I took a walk around eleven o'clock. I caught her just pulling into her driveway. Some headache!"

"Maybe she couldn't sleep and decided to go for a drive?" Father James offered. If only he could tell Harry the truth.

The phone rang as Harry sipped from his Warren Kimble mug.

"Country Kettle Restaurant and Bakery," Wendy answered. She scribbled down an order.

Harry walked around the counter and poured himself another cup of coffee. "You want some more?"

"Yes. Er, and do you think I might have a mug?" Father James asked hopefully.

"Sure." Harry reached beneath the counter and pulled out a large brown mug in the shape of a barrel. Father James looked on happily as Harry filled it to the brim.

"Nellie says that nothing has changed," Harry said, replacing the glass coffeepot on the hot plate. "Says she still cares for me. But it's getting harder and harder to believe. I tried calling when I got home and her line was busy. I called until midnight. Still busy."

"Maybe she took it off the hook."

"Maybe she was talking to the guy she went to meet."

"Now, Harry, you have no evidence that Nellie is seeing another man."

Harry wasn't interested in reasoning. "I'll tell you this," he said with male pride. "One more excuse . . . one more broken date and it's over between us. We're history. I'll go back to being a bachelor, which was a lot less stressful than all this . . . this . . . romance stuff."

Wendy slapped a two-page order in front of Harry's mug. "That was Chester Platt. Says he'll be here with the exhaust fans in about ten minutes. He also wants an order of thirty-eight double egg and bacons on a roll for his crew."

"Great! Just what I need," Harry slugged down his coffee. "Lori, that grill ready to go yet?"

"In about five minutes," she said, rinsing a dirty cloth into a pail of soapy water.

Wendy looked at Harry. "How about letting me help Lori with the grill for a while? The other waitresses can take care of the customers."

"I suppose," Harry said.

Wendy turned to Lori and said loud enough for everyone to hear, "Harry's mind just hasn't been on business since he fell in love."

Harry turned as red as a beet before storming into the back kitchen.

When Father James left the Country Kettle, he should have headed straight back to the rectory; he was already nearing exhaustion, but he chose to go on to the town hall instead. Somehow, he had to try and talk Sheriff Bromley into continuing the investigation of the church fire. He also had to find a way to convince the Galligan twins to confess.

Thankfully, the town hall was only a few doors away. He continued his slow gait, pausing every few steps to catch his breath. He really should consider going on a diet. Lately, it felt as though he had a twenty-pound sack of potatoes strapped around his waist. He couldn't remember the last time he had seen his feet from a standing position. Maybe instead of lambasting Mrs. Norris for her new health regimen, he should join her. He thought about that for a moment. Nah . . .

Arriving at the town hall, he prudently decided to take the handicapped ramp, which brought him to a side door and the community bulletin board. A poster of Dorsetville High School's upcoming George Gershwin musical revue was on display. Father James noticed that Matthew Metcalf and Stephanie Costello had the leads. He would have to make a note of it. He thoroughly enjoyed high school plays. Had been quite a thespian back in his own high school years. Officer Krupke in *West Side Story* was the role that got him the most acclaim.

Father James hit the "handicapped" button, which automatically swung open the large double doors, and he stepped through. For a brief moment, he felt like Alice in Wonderland just stepping through the looking glass. Nothing appeared as it should. Although the outside of the building had been faithfully renovated to reflect its original 1930s design, the inside resembled a futuristic, fast-food restaurant where bright primary colors and plastic furniture prevailed.

Gone were the flaking sea green walls, the gray-tiled floors of indeterminate pattern and the water-stained ceilings. The walls and floor were now an antiseptic white, with lively, color-coded stripes directing visitors to various departments. Even the sagging chairs—one of which had held Fred Campbell prisoner for the better part of an afternoon—had been replaced with molded-plastic forms in an array of sandbox colors.

The town hall's interior was another one of Roger Martin's improvements, and he felt certain it would increase his chances of reelection this fall. There was only one slight hitch: the building's interior hadn't quite turned out the way Roger envisioned it when he let his wife talk him into hiring her cousin.

"The guy's in the business. He'll save us a bundle," Roger had proclaimed to all his constituents. He was *already* campaigning for reelection.

"My wife's cousin promised to get us everything at cost. And remember, just because we have it doesn't mean we should spend it." With those words he experienced an epiphany, and a campaign slogan was born. Fiscal restraint was always popular with the voters.

But the cousin, it turned out, was a display assistant for Toys "R" Us. His design scheme centered heavily on primary colors and plastic, leaving many feeling that walking into the town hall was like walking into a box of crayons.

Creamsicle Orange denoted the town clerk's office. School Bus Yellow, the town treasurer's and tax office. Easter Egg Purple, the building department. Grass Green, the health department. Fire-Engine Red was the fire marshal, Heron Blue the police department.

Building inspector Tom Pastronostra had taken to riding his grandson's tricycle throughout the building whenever Roger was around. He was still miffed over Roger's budget cuts to his department.

"Hi, Betty," Father James said.

By the time he had found his way to the back of the building, he was certain that he would go color-blind. More unnerving, however, were the blisters that had begun to form in his armpits from the crutches. Doc Hammon had warned him to use them properly.

"Use your arms to lift your body, not your armpits to support your weight."

But then, Father James wasn't very good at taking his doctor's advice, on several counts.

He headed toward the nearest chair. "Is the sheriff around?"

"He's on a long-distance call, Father." The console lit up with another call. "Dorsetville Police dispatch," Betty answered. "Please state your emergency. Oh, hi, Arlene. Wait, let me switch you over to a free line. Excuse me, Father. This will only take a minute."

"Go right ahead, Betty. I'll just sit down over here and rest."

He collapsed into an electric blue chair. He sure hoped the sheriff could give him a ride home.

"Arlene, you still there?" Betty picked up the other receiver. "Yes, I gave Molly your muffins. She loved them and insisted that I take one for my coffee break. Did I like them? I'll say. You put something different on the top this time. Candied ginger? Well, it made all the difference in the world. I definitely think they will give Gloria Puma's lemon spice muffins a run for the money at this year's county fair. Yeah . . . it's a shame about Molly being locked up. She seems like such a nice old lady.

"Sure I can drop your plate off on the way home. I get off at three. See you around then. Well, gotta go, Arlene. I have to let the sheriff know Father James is here." Betty placed her hand over the receiver. "Arlene says hi."

"Tell her hi back," he said, leafing through a six-year-old copy of *National Geographic*.

"I'll tell Molly you called, Arlene, and that you were thrilled she liked your muffins." Betty hung up.

"How is Molly doing?" Father James asked.

"Okay, I guess," Betty said, leaning over the counter. "I mean, she never complains or anything. But I imagine that being locked up in jail is no picnic, especially for a woman her age."

"Does she get many visitors?" Now that he was mobile again, he planned to visit every day.

"Does she have visitors?" Betty laughed. "Does the Pope say Mass? Why, it's been a zoo around here ever since she arrived. The Clothesline Quilters come three times a week. The sheriff lets them set up their quilting frame inside Molly's cell. You should see those needles fly. They're just about finished with their first quilt."

That made him feel better. The quilters were a lively, upbeat group of ladies. He couldn't think of a more uplifting bunch of visitors.

"And the Dorsetville Historical Society comes on Mondays and Fridays. They arrive around two o'clock and stay for about an hour."

"The Historical Society?"

"Yes. They're doing research on vagrants that have passed through Dorsetville. They want to include Molly in their paper."

That should be a short text, he thought.

"Sergeant Bradford from the Salvation Army comes regularly," she counted off another finger. "So does Reverend Curtis, even though it was his church that got burned down."

That didn't surprise him. Even if Molly *had* started the fire, the Reverend would be the first person to offer his forgiveness.

Sheriff Bromley was on the phone with Captain Paul Lance from the Suffolk County Police Department on Long Island.

"I think we've found the car that was involved in that hit-and-run accident up your way," Captain Lance said.

"Let's have it," Bromley said, reaching for a yellow pad. Adrenaline began to pump. He knew it would only be a matter of time before he caught the scum that had run down Father James.

"We traced it to an Avis Rental Company in Patchogue. The rental agent said it went out on the morning of the twenty-ninth. Two guys. They match your witness's description. But here's the clincher. The guy says it was returned with a smashed right headlight and some damage along the front bumper. The men told him some story about hitting a deer. They paid cash for the damages. Didn't want the rental guy to file a claim."

Sheriff Bromley began to feel an immense sense of satisfaction. They had got them!

The captain spoke to someone in the room, then returned to their conversation. "Bromley, you still there? Listen, I just sent a truck over to pick up the vehicle and bring it back here to the lab. If the paint on the bumper matches that on the motor scooter your priest friend was driving, I think we've found your men."

"Hot dog!" the sheriff shouted. Harley bolted upright, ready to do battle. "Sit, boy. It's all right," he told the dog. "Great work, Paul. I owe you one."

"Can you get me an interstate warrant?"

"I'll have it in my hands when I arrive. I can get there first thing tomorrow morning. So, who are these creeps?"

Papers rustled on the other end of the phone. "One is an orthodontist. Dr. Larry Pulaski. He's part owner of an orthodontic clinic. I can tell you, the guy makes a nice income. My two kids got braces from that place. Cost me half a year's salary. The other guy owns a deli on Main Street, also in Port Jeff. Name's Ernie DeVito."

Good, the men were businesspeople, which meant it was highly unlikely they'd try to skip town. And now that he had Molly, his star witness, safely under wraps downstairs, he'd nail these bums. At times like this he loved this job.

"Nine o'clock tomorrow morning good for you?" he said.

"Fine with me. We'll be expecting you."

The sheriff hung up and leaned back heavily in his chair, his arms tucked behind his head, a wide grin spread across his face. It had taken him six weeks—six . . . *long* . . . weeks—of intensive police work, but it had finally paid off. He felt an inner sense of pride. He hadn't lost his edge.

"Want to go for a ride tomorrow?" he asked Harley.

The dog got up and began to wag his tail.

Who knows? He might need an attack dog after all.

Clyde Hessler sat in the rental car, a white Chevy Cavalier, with his blue baseball cap turned backward and his sunglasses hiding his red-rimmed eyes. He hadn't slept much these last few days, having spent most of his time hiding out here—a small back road overlooking the Hawkins farmhouse—trying to catch a break. He needed to get into the barn, where a million dollars was buried in a cash box. Part of it was money taken from the construction loan at the hotel complex. The other two hundred fifty grand came from the two losers out on Long Island. What a pair of buffoons, Clyde thought. It was the easiest mark he'd ever made.

He flicked his cigarette out the car window. He had been here since early that morning and was already on his second pack. He tried to stretch out his legs, cramped from being in the same position all morning. Darn that old Japanese lady inside the house. Didn't she ever take a walk or something? Whenever he looked through his binoculars, there she was, seated by the kitchen window. He wondered what she could find so interesting to look out at all day long.

He reached down and massaged his legs. God, he was bored. How did cops spend entire days crammed inside a car doing surveillance?

Well, there was no use complaining. If he wanted his money, he had to wait it out. Besides, the old broad had to leave sometime and, when she did, he'd sneak back inside the barn, dig up the loot and hightail it out of this one-horse town.

Chapter 13

"I'm sorry, Mr. Hornibrook, but after reviewing your file I'm afraid the bank can't offer you a loan," said Mr. Hennings, Woodstock Savings and Loan's senior loan officer. "Our research shows that there's a first mortgage on your home for"—he shuffled through the open file—"forty-five thousand dollars. Borrowed from Webster Bank in Dorsetville."

Mr. Hennings, a sober-faced, drab little man who always dressed in gray, looked over his black-rimmed glasses. "Webster Bank is an excellent organization. I know Frank Webster personally. His father started that bank in the twenties and through pure grit kept it going during the Depression when more established institutions failed. Fine family, the Websters." He cleared his throat. "Well, yes . . . that's getting away from the matter at hand, now, isn't it?"

Mr. Hennings sat back in his chair and studied Barry Hornibrook, who sat quietly staring down at his shoes. "Your credit report lists several other outstanding loans," Mr. Hennings continued, running his finger down the columns on Barry's application form. "Let's see . . . you owe several million in construction loans. That's quite a lot of money, now, isn't it, Mr. Hornibrook? And yet, you still need to borrow more?"

"Cost overruns," Barry lied. "You know how that happens on a project as large as this." He tried to keep the sound of desperation out of his voice as he concluded, "I'm good for the money, Mr. Hennings. Ask anyone. I've never defaulted on a loan in my life."

Mr. Hennings removed his glasses and placed them carefully on the desk. "Your credit history isn't being disputed, Mr. Hornibrook. It's the vast amount of money you owe versus the income projections for the hotel that concerns us," he explained. "Your hotel complex is a new business, and few businesses see a profit for at least the first three years. We've reviewed your records and, honestly, Mr. Hornibrook," he referred to the paperwork on his desk, "we don't see how you can afford to run the facility—salaries, insurance, taxes, things like that—and still have enough to pay off your original loans, plus the one you are requesting from us."

Applying for a new loan had been a long shot; still, Barry had hoped for a miracle. Now, however, even that hope had just vaporized. It was evident that Mr. Hennings was not going to approve his loan, which meant that Barry had run out of options.

The mobsters were expecting him to wire the money by noon, all two hundred fifty thousand of it. Without the cash, he was officially a dead man. He wondered how it would end. A bullet? Car bomb? Buried alive in a vat of cement? He suddenly felt dizzy, inched forward in his chair and hung his head between his knees. His heavily sprayed coil of hair fell forward, revealing a bald crown. He was too desolate to care.

"Are you all right, Mr. Hornibrook? Can I get you a glass of water?" Hennings rose swiftly from his chair.

"Yeah, that would be good. It's just a little hot in here, is all."

"Yes, sometimes it does get a little stuffy in this office." The bank officer raced around his desk and headed straight for the door. The last thing he needed was for the man to faint dead away in his office after being denied a loan, especially when the Woodstock Savings and Loan billed itself as the "People-Friendly Bank." "You stay there. I'll be right back."

Barry sighed. Maybe Chester was right. Maybe he should let Sheriff Bromley know what was going on. Maybe he could put him under police protection. Maybe. Maybe. Maybe. Maybe the mobsters would still kill him. Didn't they have ways of killing informants with or without police protection?

Barry felt the bile in his stomach begin to move up his throat. He should just let the mobsters kill him, get it over with. At least that way, his wife could collect the insurance money, which was enough to save their home and maybe pay back some of the money he owed friends. He wished Mr. Hennings would get there with that glass of water. He really did feel faint.

Mr. Hennings was racing back to his office when he spied Nellie Anderson seated in the waiting area. Good grief, another difficult interview. He had almost forgotten. Ms. Anderson had come to discuss the foreclosure on her home. The papers were due to be processed that afternoon.

She spied him and nodded. "I'll be right with you," he said hurrying by. Good Lord, he thought, the woman looks as pale as Mr. Hornibrook. He hoped she wouldn't fall apart, too. Why couldn't these Dorsetville folks keep their business in their own town?

The interview with Mr. Hennings did not go well, but then Nellie hadn't really expected it to. The fifteen-thousand-dollar balloon payment due on the mortgage was past due and she had no cash reserves left after her mother's funeral to pay it. The bank had been generous in allowing her an extra ninety days, but now time was up and they were demanding payment in full. She didn't have it, not that she hadn't tried to get it: she had been living on nothing for nearly two years.

She refused to buy any new clothing, not even from the discount stores. She brought all her meals to school, clipped coupons, even had her hair styled by the students at the beauty school over in Waterbury, which was why it seldom was colored uniformly or layered evenly. But even with these economies, she had squirreled only a few thousand dollars away, a far cry from what was due.

Even her second job cleaning offices over in Woodstock several nights a week couldn't help bridge the financial gap. Still, she persevered, refusing to give up. Lately, she had tried to increase her office-cleaning hours, filling in for people when they didn't show up. Unfortunately, it had meant canceling several more dates with Harry. She had hated to do it, hated the sound of his disappointment, then disbelief, over her rather lame excuses.

"I have several papers to grade," she would lie. "I have a terrible headache." Or, "I think I'll go to bed early tonight."

She knew she should come clean. Tell him the truth. But something held her back. Perhaps it was pride.

Up ahead, a squirrel began to cross the road. She lifted her foot off the accelerator; the car began to coast as the small rodent dashed one way, then another. Finally, he spun around and ran back the way he had come.

If only she could drive over to Harry's and fall into his arms. Just the thought of being locked in one of his tender embraces made her feel better. She had missed those comforting arms these last few weeks. But she just couldn't tell Harry what she was doing at night. First, she was too embarrassed; and second, she was convinced that if Harry knew her predicament he would insist on helping even though he was probably as strapped financially as she was. Hadn't he just enlarged the restaurant, opened a bakery, hired a bunch of new waitresses? Of course, once Barry's hotel opened all downtown business was bound to increase. Harry would recoup his money in no time. But still, this was her problem. She just couldn't burden Harry with it.

A sign up ahead cautioned that roadwork was in progress. Once again she slowed down.

But not telling Harry the truth, had she risked losing him? A part of her wondered if it wasn't already too late. It had been nearly a week since Harry's last call. He had probably grown tired of her excuses. But what could she have said? She was working two jobs and, in between, using every spare moment to write her book. And, as unlikely as it may have appeared, she was convinced that God would use this little book in a powerful way.

She flicked on her turn signal at the Route 7 turnoff, even though no one was behind her. She drove the familiar back roads by rote, roads that wound their way down the mountain from Woodstock like an unfurled ribbon into the little valley town. Sam Rosenberg's old Plymouth Duster passed by on his way to deliver noontime meals. Sam waved. She honked back.

Her mind was awhirl with fearful questions: What would she do if Harry had tired of her excuses? Said he didn't want to see her again? The thought made her feel weak at the knees. She loved him so completely, this man who had somehow managed to take her dull, uninteresting little life and suffuse it with new meaning and joy—a joy that was apparently written all over her face. How many people had told her that she looked "different," younger? A dozen? Two dozen? One of her colleagues had even mentioned that she seemed to literally bound into a room these days. Harry had done all this for her.

Their relationship had started a few months ago when Harry stopped her after Mass to ask how she was faring. "How are you doing, all alone up at that big place?"

When her mother had died, Nellie had been left with the family homestead: an eighteenth-century saltbox, in constant need of repair, and fifty acres of land. Just keeping up with it, and her job, seemed to tax all of her strength.

"I'm managing," she replied. Harry stood well over six feet tall. She was only five foot two. She had to bend her neck all the way back to look up into his face.

He cocked his head to one side as if to say, Are you really?

"Well . . . kind of," she amended.

"It's not easy being alone."

At that moment, she realized she had never really studied Harry's face before, even though they had known each other since childhood. She was surprised at the depth of compassion and gentleness in his blue eyes.

Harry walked her home that day after church. They talked about his restaurant and her students. They spoke of the difficulties in being an only child and the loss of one's parents. They laughed over the happy reminiscences of their youth in Dorsetville, both agreeing that it had been the best of childhoods.

"May I check out the house before you go in?" he asked, even though they both had lived in Dorsetville all of their lives and knew such precautions were entirely unnecessary.

She placed her house key into his thick hands, inwardly delighted at this old-fashioned show of gallantry. Before he left, he shyly asked her to a movie. She said yes, which led to an outrageously expensive dinner afterward at Carmen Anthony's Fish House in Woodbury; and, before long, they were seeing each other on a regular basis. Their love steadily grew, although neither seemed to be able to say the word. It seemed a commitment both were hesitant to make. That was okay with her. She was in no hurry, or so she had told herself.

She neared the bend in the road where St. Cecilia's spires peaked through the treetops. If only there had been some kind of formal understanding between them, how much harder it would have been for either to have walked away without a word.

Nellie turned onto School Street, drove a hundred yards, then pulled into the parking lot behind the school. It was almost ten o'clock. She collected her things and made her way through the back entranceway, trying to force her mind back on her work. Thankfully, her teaching assistant, Kitty Hawkins, an eager twenty-year-old senior from the university, was helping out today. The kids loved her and were quiet as mice as Nellie entered the room.

"Look, Miss Anderson," ten-year-old Jennifer Crawford said, placing a hard-boiled egg on top of a heated glass vial. "Look what Miss Hawkins taught us."

Within seconds, the egg was sucked through the opening. The children clapped with delight and Miss Hawkins beamed with satisfaction.

Fortunately, the rest of the day sped by. Nellie stayed late to grade some papers. She had the night off from her cleaning job. She drove home, parked the car and pulled the trash cans in from the curb. The garbage man had refused to take several cardboard boxes again, even though Nellie had broken them down. She would have to make a special trip to the dump this weekend. Just what she needed: one more errand.

Dinner was a can of Progresso Split Pea Soup and toast. She threw in a load of laundry, mopped the kitchen floor and laid out her clothes for the next day. By then it was eleven o'clock and time for bed.

But sleep was elusive. Thoughts of Harry, then of the imminent foreclosure, kept revolving around her head like an endless videotape loop. Finally, she got up and made herself a cup of chamomile tea. While she waited for the teapot to boil, she looked around the familiar kitchen, the worn oak table her grandfather had made, the red checked curtains she and her mom had hung, the beehive oven that still worked and was used every Christmas to make St. Lucien's bread. Suddenly the emotions she held in check broke loose in a rush of tears. What was she going to do? This was the only home she had ever known. She grabbed a handful of napkins from the top of the refrigerator, stuffed several in the pockets to her robe and used one to blow her nose.

What did Father James always say? "God is never nearer than when we walk through a valley. To feel His presence we only need to allow Him to lead."

Perhaps that was her problem. She hadn't allowed God to lead. She was so busy fixing things—taking a second job, dealing with the bank—that she hadn't given God a chance. Worse still, she had dismissed the answer He did send: the children's book. It was the most wonderful book she had ever read, and it gave her a chill just to think she had written it. She never had any inclination to write before. But the idea had just fallen from the skies hours after she met with Father James to tell him of her dilemma.

She brought Father James beef brisket and stayed to visit the day he got home from the hospital.

The priest reluctantly turned the casserole over to Mrs. Norris, hoping that Father Dennis wouldn't give it away before he got a chance to sample it.

"You make the best brisket in the county," he said. "I can almost taste it with a side of cabbage and a nice plump boiled potato. Ah, it's one of my favorites. Bless you, my child." Then, noticing her quiet mood, he asked, "Is there anything wrong, Nellie?"

Suddenly her face filled with sadness. "Father, I just received a letter from the bank. They want to foreclose on my home."

"Foreclose? Oh, Nellie, why didn't you come to see me sooner? Perhaps the church could have helped."

"I suppose I kept hoping for a miracle. I'd get a raise. Win the Lotto," she tried to laugh.

"Instead of playing the Lotto, I think people would be better served if they placed their bets solely on Jesus," he said decisively. "In my opinion, they'd get much better odds."

"That's exactly why I'm here, Father," Nellie admitted. "I want to confess that I haven't done that. Not even when my mother was so ill. Oh, I asked for His help with Mom's care, but I really didn't *expect* it, so I went about taking care of things myself. Cashed in my pension fund. Used up my savings."

She had promised herself she wouldn't break down and cry, yet here she was on the verge of tears. She fumbled in her purse for a handkerchief.

"And now it looks as though I might lose everything. A lot is due on the mortgage my mother took out when my father was so ill. I just don't have the money." She scrounged around deeper in her purse. "Oh, why can't someone design a purse where you can find things?"

Father James handed her his handkerchief.

"Thank you, Father." She dabbed her eyes. "Did you know that I'm the sixth generation Anderson to have lived in that house? I can't imagine losing it."

"What makes you think that God wants you to lose it?"

"I don't know. It's just that . . . I just assumed that God had more important things to look after than my money problems."

"Then you assumed wrong," said Father James sadly. Doesn't *anyone* listen to His homilies?

"In the Gospels, a blind man yells out from the crowd, 'Have mercy on me, Son of David,' and the apostles tell him to hush up. But Jesus turns and asks how He can help. In another instance, a child rushes up to Jesus, probably with a childlike request, but once again the apostles push the child aside. Jesus rebukes them. 'Do not prohibit the children from coming to me,' he admonishes, 'for their angels always have access to my Father in heaven.' Our Lord was saying that no matter how small or childlike our requests are, He wants to help."

"Even with money?" she asked.

"Even with money," Father James insisted. "You need it to live, now, don't you? Without money, how are you to pay your taxes or buy groceries. Or . . . support the Church, so we priests can live in style?" he joked. This made Nellie laugh.

"I suppose you're right," she agreed.

He continued, "Throughout the ages, men have continued to try to limit Jesus' generosity. And time and time again, Jesus shatters their preconceived notions of what is important to God. 'Aren't two sparrows sold for a penny?' He asks in Matthew. 'And yet not one falls to the ground without my Father's notice.' Jesus is trying to tell us that *everything* about our lives is important to our Heavenly Father. You might say that God likes being actively involved just as any good parent would."

"If I only could believe that," Nellie said wistfully.

"You can," Father James assured her. "Nellie, I've known you for a long time, and I've seen what a good steward you have been of all that God has given you. You spent all you had in making your mother's last days as comfortable as possible. Would you have abandoned your mother in her need?"

"Absolutely not!"

"Then what makes you think that your Heavenly Father will abandon you in yours?"

"I . . . I don't know," she said, wiping away her tears.

Father James reached across and took her hands into his. "Jesus said we are not to worry about what we eat or what we wear or where we will sleep, for the Father knows we have need of these things. Earthly needs, Nellie. Not just spiritual needs. God only asks that we be good stewards of all that He entrusts into our care, and you have done that."

"Oh, Father James, you make it sound so simple," she said.

"But God's love *is* simple, Nellie. It's man who makes it complex by trying to delineate what God deems important. In God's eyes, *all* of our needs warrant His attention, not just *some* of them. *All* of them—and that includes finding a way for you to pay off your mortgage *and* keep the homestead you love so dearly."

"Oh, Father, I want so desperately to believe that!"

"Then *choose* to believe it," he challenged.

"Just choose?"

"Yes, Nellie, all faith begins as a choice. You can either choose to have faith, or you can choose to doubt. It's up to you."

She thought a moment. "Father James, I choose to have faith." She blew her nose and stuffed the priest's handkerchief inside her purse. She would launder and return it later.

"Now what should I do?" she asked, looking expectantly at Father James.

"Well, for starters, we're going to pray and ask God to forgive you for your lack of trust and for not coming to Him in the first place. Then we're going to place the whole thing in His hands and wait for Him to come up with a plan."

"Do you *really* think He'd do that?"

"Think so? I absolutely *know* so!" Father James rose several feet off his bed with the conviction. "Look at what He's done for St. Cecilia's. The archbishop ordered the church closed. The town was ready to condemn the property and demolish the church and rectory. If ever there seemed a hopeless case, that was it. Then what happened?"

"God sent a miracle." Nellie smiled, remembering all the miraculous events that helped to save the church.

"Exactly!" Father James said brightly. "And if He could do it for us, He can do it for you. Now bow your head and pray with me. We're going to ask God for another miracle, and for the faith needed to see it happen."

Nellie double-checked the stove, then turned off the light and carried her cup of tea up the back stairs. Her tabby cat, Theodore, followed fast on her heels, protesting loudly as they went. He had come downstairs in hope of a saucer of milk that hadn't materialized.

"How is the children's book going to provide the large amount of money that I need?" she asked Theodore, slipping out of her robe and climbing into bed. The cat ignored the query, instead establishing himself on one of the pillows.

It certainly didn't make any sense, she conceded. Even if she did have a way of getting it published, which she hadn't, she knew that the wheels of the publishing world ground slowly. It would take several years before it was actually printed and she realized any money from the sales. She switched off the bedside light. But hadn't Saint Paul said that spiritual things are spiritually discerned. That meant that she must not try to rationalize how God might meet her need.

All right, Lord, she prayed aloud, sliding under the covers. *I don't understand it. It makes absolutely no sense, but I will finish the book tomorrow. Then it's up to You to decide what You want done with it.*

Good as her word, Nellie was dressed and seated in front of her computer by 6 A.M., although she was getting precious little done. The view outside her window proved too much of a distraction.

A silvery mist still covered most of the ground like a soft blanket, and the slanting rays of the sun brushed against the tips of the leaves, which were ringed with rich cranberry reds, butter yellows and golden browns. Fall was Nellie's favorite time of year, and she had to muster every bit of her resolve not to run upstairs, riffle through her mother's quilts and air them out on the clothesline. There was nothing like the smell of bedcoverings tossed in the autumn breeze to ensure a night of sweet dreams. If it could be bottled, no one would need sleeping pills.

"No more dawdling," she said out loud, causing Theodore, nestled in her lap, to wake with a start. "It's all right, dear," she told him, stroking his ruffled fur. "I was only saying that I have just one hour left of this glorious morning before I have to get ready for school and I mustn't waste it."

Theodore arched his back slightly and stretched out a back paw in some mystical feline dance, as though to say, Either way, it makes no difference to me. He stood up, shifted position, then hunched over and began to clean himself, all the while his mistress staring at the computer screen.

One more paragraph to edit and *The Christmas Tree Who Wished for a Star* would be finished. In a way it saddened her to see it completed. Never before had she felt such closeness to God as she had while writing this story.

It was the tale of a tiny Christmas tree along with three other outcasts. As Christmas Eve quickly approaches, the tiny tree is given three opportunities to be taken home and allowed to wear a coveted Christmas star; yet each time, he elects to give away his chance to his friends. In the end, God rewards him for demonstrating the true meaning of Christmas by crowning him with the Bethlehem star.

Nellie knew that this story was special from the moment the very first line had marched across her computer screen seemingly all on its own. She also felt humbled that God had entrusted it to her care.

But she was enough of a realist to know that not everyone would understand the hope she had pinned on this little tale. Her coworker Martha LaClaire's reaction one lunch break was probably typical when Nellie had told her she was writing a book for children.

"You're wasting your time. It's impossible to get published these days," Martha said, spearing bits of macaroni and cheese off a plate on her blue plastic tray.

"First, you'd need to find a literary agent. Publishers no longer read unsolicited manuscripts," she continued, slashing a hole in the tin covering on her chocolate pudding with a metal fork. "And since you're a new writer, what literary agent is going to want to represent you?"

As much as the comments had unhinged her, Nellie knew Martha was right. She knew the statistics. Over one hundred thousand manuscripts were received by literary agents and publishers every year, of which only a few hundred ever made it into print.

Dear God, she prayed, *if this is going to work, You have to find me a lit-*

erary agent and a publisher who are willing to take a risk on a new author. And God? She hit the print button on her keyboard. *Please hurry. There isn't much time before the bank forecloses.*

Then, for some reason she could not fathom, she pulled the rosary she had found out of her purse, knelt down beside her chair and began to recite the Glorious Mysteries.

Chapter 14

I t wasn't much of a boat, a twenty-six-foot Skiffcraft, dented and rusted in a couple of spots, that he had bought used in the early eighties with some casino winnings he never told Cheryl about. He and Chester had gone down to the Mohegan Sun for the day and played the slots.

Barry bought it the next week from a guy in Old Lyme and christened it *The Great Escape*. It was the best money he had ever spent.

Every spare dime he made went into the boat. Paint. New decking. A new 260-horsepower engine. The thing purred like a kitten. Last year he had even replaced the Bimini top, which made the boat look a little less shabby. Still, it could never compete with the "Yuppie Crafts" New Yorkers used to ply the river with on summer weekends. But he didn't care. What mattered most was that it was a dependable craft, felt solid and got him where he wanted to go. And right now, that was anywhere other than here.

Barry headed straight for the boat the moment he arrived back at the hotel after returning from the bank. He pitched his sports jacket into the cab of his truck and started across the hotel's front lawn, which swept down toward the river. What a great day for fishing, he thought. No wind, temperature hovering around the seventies, autumn foliage reflecting off of the water. God, it was beautiful . . . the grounds . . . the hotel complex . . . the marina. For just an instant he paused with a surge of pride. His vision had created this. He had taken a couple of broken-down buildings and a scruffy piece of property and fashioned it into a first-rate hotel complex. He wished his father was still alive. He would have been proud.

He resumed his pace, enjoying the way his boat rocked gently against the pilings. Barry hopped on board. It was almost eleven forty-five. He had promised to wire the mobsters their money, in full, by noon. In sixteen minutes they would know he had lied. Then what? Memories were stored on this boat and he grabbed for one, like a life preserver, before fear could drag him under.

He remembered the morning George Benson had nearly toppled overboard as his rod bent under the weight of his catch, screaming, "This will win me this year's trophy for the biggest bass for sure!"

Chester, John Moran and Billy Halstead had been on board and nearly choked with laughter as George's "bass" turned out to be an old cooler filled with empty beer cans.

Barry lifted up the hatch and checked on the engine. There was nothing that really needed to be done; still, he moved some wires around, fiddled with some gauges. Busy work.

A seagull screeched overhead. The sound made him nearly jump out of his skin. I gotta calm down, he told himself, before I have a heart attack. Barry leaned against the hull and reached inside his shirt pocket with shaky hands for his pack of Marlboros. He'd gone back to smoking. He struck a match across the wooden railing, cupped his hands to block the breeze and sucked, watching for the tobacco to catch. Finally, the tip of the cigarette glowed red. He inhaled deeply, closed his eyes and waited for the nicotine to kick in. Hopefully, it would help to take the edge off his frayed nerves. His eyes came to rest on the gas tank. Might as well check that out, too, he thought.

He unscrewed the cap, indifferent to the lit cigarette dangling from his lips. The tank was half full, but, needing something to do, Barry decided to top it off. He kept a couple of five-gallon tanks inside a metal storage shed at the edge of the property. He flipped the cigarette into the water and hopped over the side of the boat onto the dock. The shed was hidden behind a row of hedges just about twenty feet from where he was moored. En route, he noted that the patch of poison sumac at the edge of the woods that he had sprayed last week was still thriving. If only his front lawn at home was as hardy as this stuff. He'd grab the weed killer and give it a blast on his way back from the shed.

Barry unlocked the padlock and pulled on the door. Metal sounded against metal as it swung open on its rusty hinges. He walked in. One whiff of the musty canvas beach chairs stored inside and he was in trouble. His allergies had kicked in, making his nose feel as if it had been clamped shut by a vise. God, how he hated being over fifty.

But he was determined to get what he had come for. A shaft of light cut through the interior darkness. Barry waited, letting his eyes adjust after the bright sunlight. He easily spied the orange gas tank; it stood just inside the door. He grabbed hold of it and swung it outside. The weed killer, however, was stored somewhere along the back wall, next to the boxes of fireworks. What was he going to do with all of those, anyway? He had bought nearly thirty boxes last year while passing through North Carolina. That's when he had no doubt that he would be alive for the hotel's grand opening.

He moved a small bale of chicken wire and carefully began to wade his way through the tangle of discarded tires, old batteries and gardening tools. He really had to get someone to clean this place out. He stepped high over a tangle of garden hose, but he didn't step high enough. His foot caught, pitching him forward. He reached out to break his fall and caught the handles of an old jet ski, bringing it down on his right knee. Swearing, he rubbed his leg, more determined than ever to find the weed killer. He moved a few things around on the shelves and managed to stir up quite a bit of dust. His eyes began to itch. He sneezed three times in rapid succession. From past experience, Barry knew he had just launched a full-fledged allergy attack. Great! Just great!

He grabbed for his handkerchief and headed back outside. Where had he put that bottle of Allegra? Maybe in his desk drawer back in the office? Barry headed for the hotel, feeling more miserable with each step. He'd have to come back later and lock up. Right now he had only one thought. Relief, before the mobsters arrived to kill him.

The Galligan twins watched Barry track back up to the hotel, sneezing and wheezing as he leaned into the steep incline. The boys were hidden from view just a few yards from the shed near the sumac patch.

Rodney and Dexter had skipped school, and, although it wasn't yet noon, they were already bored. So far, they had gone fishing with spears made out of crudely hewn twigs, attempting to imitate some primitive culture they had seen on the Discovery Channel. They were unsuccessful. Next, they snatched some bras from the nuns' clothesline and dumped them in the backseat of Father Dennis's car. Dexter wanted to hang around and watch the priest's face when he found them, but Rodney was itching to move on. Finally, they wound their way through backyards and side streets until they came to the edge of the woods by the hotel, arriving just in time to see Mr. Hornibrook race back up to the main building, leaving the shed door open. The twins wasted no time rocketing out of hiding and into the shed.

Dexter moved a few things around, looking for something of interest. Finding nothing, he began to wend his way toward the back of the metal building. Then he saw it: the silhouette of a jet ski. He made a mad dash, hoping to get there before Rodney spied it. But Rodney had already seen it. Both boys raced forward. Dexter caught his foot in the same unwound coil of hose that had snared Barry and landed face first on the dirt floor. He started to whimper. But Rodney ignored him, seeing this as his opportunity, and hopped on the jet ski first.

"*Rummmm, rummmm.*" Rodney pretended to lean into an imaginary curve.

"Be quiet, you nerd, before someone hears us," Dexter said, untangling his foot from the hose. How could he divert his brother's attention so he could take his place? "What's that over there?"

"I didn't see anything." Rodney was smart to his brother's tricks.

Just then a water rat scurried out from underneath a piece of canvas. Rodney jumped down off the ski.

"Quick, get something to put it in," he said, moving a stack of boxes from off the shelving where the rat had disappeared.

Dexter thought about jumping on the jet ski, but the chance to catch a water rat was just too enticing.

"Here, hold these." Rodney handed Dexter the boxes.

While his brother searched for the rat, Dexter read the large red, white and blue lettering written across the front. "Hey, Rodney, look at this."

"Look at what?" Rodney's head had disappeared between two shelves.

"Rodney, never mind the rat, look at this."

"This had better be good. I almost had him." Rodney slid out.

Dexter pointed to the lettering, GALAXY FIREWORKS. 20 BLUE THUNDER ROMAN CANDLES.

"Jeeping willies!" Rodney snatched it out of his brother's hands. "Real fireworks. How cool is that?"

Dexter snatched it back. "Let's take a couple outside and shoot them into the river."

"You can't see fireworks in the daytime, you moron."

"I *know* that. I just wanted to test a couple. See if they work."

"I don't know, Dex."

"Listen, no one is going to see us. There's no one around here except Mr. Hornibrook, and he went inside the hotel." Dexter dropped the box on the floor and removed the lid. "So, how many should we take?"

"I don't know. They seem kind of big. Maybe two or three."

"Right." Dexter said, stuffing two Roman candles down his pants leg and tucking four more under his arm.

Nellie arrived at eight-fifteen, forty-five minutes before classes started, in order to use the copier in the school's main office. She had downloaded a dozen names and addresses of New York City literary agents from the Internet. She planned to send each one a copy of her manuscript.

When she arrived, Alice, the principal's secretary, was already busy at work. It looked to Nellie like a new student was transferring in. A nice clean-cut boy. He stood alongside his father, who was busy filling in forms.

"Alice, I need to use the copier, do you mind?" Nellie asked.

"Go right ahead. Mrs. LaClaire was about to run something off but forgot some papers back in her classroom. Might as well use it until she gets back."

Nellie placed the fourteen-page manuscript into the feeder. She hit PRINT. Instantly, a wide beam of light began to move from left to right underneath the cover. While the copier continued to hum along, Nellie took out her change purse and dropped several quarters into the jar Alice kept to the right of the copier for non-school-related copies.

"Miss Anderson," Alice called. "While you're waiting, may I introduce you to your new student, Brian, and his father, Mr. Seymour. Brian is transferring from a school in Port Washington, Long Island."

Nellie walked over to them.

"This is Miss Anderson, our fifth-grade teacher."

"Nice to meet you both," Nellie said.

Brian was a small, neat little boy with black-rimmed glasses that rode the tip of his nose. His father was a tall, thin, collegiate-dressed man, the type that rode expensive European bicycles on weekends. He reached out to shake her hand.

"I hope your family doesn't find country life too quiet after living on Long Island," Nellie said. "I have some friends who live in Oyster Bay. I'm afraid it's a much faster pace of living there than it is here in Dorsetville."

"We chose Dorsetville because it is quiet. Didn't we, Brian?" Mr. Seymour said. His face appeared drawn with sadness.

Brian nodded.

"We're looking for a change," he explained. Gathering his son closer, he went on. "We lost Brian's mother two years ago and thought a new start might help us finally get on with things."

"I see," Nellie said, her heart going out to the boy. "I lost my mother, too, Brian. She died last year. I know how sad you must feel."

"Do you still miss her?" Brian asked shyly.

"Every day," Nellie replied. Several seconds of awkward silence followed. Finally, Nellie asked, "Do you like to read, Brian?"

"Yes, ma'am."

"Then I think you're in for a treat. Our class is about to start a new book today. *Harry Potter and the Sorcerer's Stone.* Have you heard of it?"

Brian's face charged with emotion. "Heard of it! Who hasn't? Harry Potter books are my favorite."

"He's read every one of them at least three times," Mr. Seymour said, ruffling his son's hair.

Now that the lines around his eyes had softened with a smile, Nellie realized he was quite a striking man.

"Isn't it great to find an author who inspires children to want to read? I only wish that J. K. Rowling was one of my clients," he said.

"Clients?"

"I'm a literary agent. Children's books, mostly. That's why I feel so strongly about the Harry Potter series. Anything that can fire up a child's imagination and make them love reading, I'm all for it."

"Excuse me, Nellie. I hate to interrupt," said Martha LaClaire, who stood to the side, her arms full of papers. "Are you through with the copier?"

"Oh, yes, I'm sorry. I'll get my things."

"No need. I've already done it. Here. I didn't want to get them mixed up with mine." Martha glanced at one of Nellie's title pages. "Is this the children's book you were telling me about? *The Christmas Tree Who Wished for a Star*? I like the title."

"Are you a children's writer?" Mr. Seymour asked.

"This is my first book," Nellie said, her cheeks blushing slightly. She didn't want him to think this was a setup; but, then, how would she have known that he was a literary agent?

"Mind if I take a look?"

"No, please, go ahead." She handed him a copy.

He studied it quietly, then asked, "May I take this with me? In my rush to get out early this morning and sign Brian up for school, I left my briefcase at home with all the manuscripts I had planned to read. This will give me something to study on the train ride into the city."

"Mind? No . . . Not at all." Nellie's mind was reeling. What were the chances of her meeting a literary agent in the school office where she taught? She felt a chill. Father James always called these moments "God-oincidences."

"Mr. Seymour, may I ask what literary agency you represent?" Maybe she could look it up later on the sheet she had pulled down from the Internet.

"The Kellerson's Literary Agency. Do you know it?"

Know it? It was the biggest literary agency in New York City, with a stable full of best-selling children's authors. But before she could reply, a cosmic explosion from the riverfront shook the school so hard that the windowpanes rattled.

Chester Platt had climbed onto the top of the twenty-foot scaffold and was preparing to inspect the stone masonry Sirius Gaithwait had just finished on the back side of St. Cecilia's when the blast shook the scaffolding so hard it nearly pitched him over the metal railing. Miraculously, he had managed to hold on to his cell phone. Barry was on the other end.

"What in blazes was that?" Chester asked. "Barry? You all right, man? It sounded like it came from over your way."

"Holy smoke!"

"What is it?"

"All the windows have been blown out of my office. There's glass everywhere."

"What the heck happened?" Chester asked. Sirens blared in the distance.

"Oh, no . . ."

"What is it?"

"They blew up my boat. Those mobsters blew up my boat! I loved that boat."

"Mobsters? What mobsters? Someone blew up your boat?"

"They said I'd better pay up or else."

"You're losing me here, buddy. You sure you didn't get hit on the head with something? Listen, I'm coming right over," Chester began to climb back down the scaffolding as the sharp blare of Dorsetville's hook and ladder sounded from Main Street. "You stay put. I'll be right there."

"Chester?"

"Yeah, buddy?"

"When you get here, I think you had better drive me over to the sheriff's office."

Sheriff Bromley nearly dropped his coffee mug when he heard the blast.

"What the . . . ??!!" He tore open the interrogation/conference/lunchroom door and bellowed down the hall. "Betty, what was that? It sounded like an explosion."

"Don't know, Al," she yelled from out front. "But everyone else wants to know the same thing. The switchboard is flooded with calls. Hello, Dorsetville Police Dispatch. Oh, hello, Ethel. No, we don't know what that was. I'm sorry it scared Honey so badly that she won't come out from under the bed. I'll call you back as soon as I find out anything."

Bromley looked back inside the room where Ernie DeVito and Larry Pulaski were seated, staring down at their hands. Neither one had moved or said a word since he had brought them up from lockup.

The sheriff had a sobering thought. "Where's Hill, Betty?"

"He went to the Country Kettle. Today's Wednesday," she yelled.

"Wednesday?"

"Apple strudel. Lori Peterson bakes apple strudel every Wednesday morning. It's Hill's favorite."

The switchboard lit up again.

"Send him out to investigate when he gets back."

"Did I hear you right, Sheriff? You want me to send Hill?"

"He's the only one I've got to send. Pathetic, isn't it? Listen, when you get a chance, bring Molly up. I want her to see if she can I.D. these guys."

"Sure thing, Sheriff. As soon as this switchboard calms down, I'll get right on it."

Bromley walked back into the room, which looked more like a setting for a country inn than a police station. Sheer crisscross curtains hung behind panels of calico. The windowsills were filled with potted plants, which changed with the season; mums were now in residence. A needlepoint sampler, which read GOD IS ALWAYS LISTENING, SO BE CAREFUL WHAT YOU SAY, hung over a skirted table that held the coffeepot and several mugs employees had brought from home. Above the table was a corkboard filled with photographs of children and grandchildren, last year's picnic at Judge Peale's, a recent birthday party for Deputy Hill. Yesterday, the sheriff had added a photograph of Harley snoozing with one of Barbara's cats.

Bromley walked over to the coffeepot, filled his mug to the brim, shoveled in four heaping teaspoons of sugar, then sat opposite the two men.

"Now that you've had a night in the brig to think things over, are you two ready to tell me what happened the morning of August twenty-first?"

Armed with arrest warrants, the sheriff and Captain Lance, of the Suffolk County Police Force, had waited outside the men's homes until nightfall. Around 1 A.M., they had paid a surprise visit. The men were still wearing the pajamas they had on when the officers had arrested them.

Bromley sipped his coffee while studying their faces. Dr. Larry Pulaski and Ernie DeVito didn't look as though they were especially pleased to be here.

"We're not saying anything until our lawyers arrive," Larry said, never looking up from his folded hands.

"Fine by me." Bromley hiked up one cowboy-booted leg and hitched it over the other. "Lawyer or no lawyer, I mean to get the truth out of the two of you."

"We don't know what you're talking about," Larry insisted with as much passion as he could muster, considering everything he had said since being picked up last night was a gross lie.

Bromley, however, had not been fooled.

"So you told me." Bromley sipped his coffee slowly. "But, you know . . . I'm having a real hard time believing you guys. In fact, I'd be willing to bet my life's savings that you were the ones who ran down our local Catholic priest and left him lying by the side of the road."

"I'm telling you, you've got the wrong guys," Ernie said, feigning sincerity but not faring much better than Larry.

"Ernie, we don't have to say anything until our lawyers arrive," Larry cautioned.

"You mean *if* they arrive."

Larry leaned over and asked quietly, "What do you mean 'if'?"

"Our wives are fuming over this mess. Neither will be in a rush to bail us out."

"Stop worrying. They'll show up."

Bromley shifted tactics. "How about a cup of coffee, Ernie? It's fresh. Made it myself just before you guys came in."

"That sounds good." Ernie felt like crap. He hadn't slept, nor shaved and his breath tasted like the pepperoni-and-onion sandwich he had eaten for a snack the night before. He could use a cup of coffee.

Larry glared at him. "Be careful," he hissed.

"How do you take it?" Bromley asked, reaching for Deputy Hill's mug.

"Two sugars. A little milk," Ernie replied. Suddenly feeling a little less hostile toward the sheriff, he added, "Listen, we've been telling you the truth. It's just like we told you last night. We rented the Navigator on the day your priest was run down, but we never drove it off Long Island. If it was involved with his accident, we don't know anything about it. Maybe the rental guy loaned it out to one of his friends after we brought it back. Maybe he figures he'll put the blame on us." This seemed feasible, didn't it? He wasn't much of a liar.

"I see," Bromley said, pouring Ernie's coffee. "There's only one thing wrong with that story."

"Oh?"

The sheriff placed the mug on the table. "We have an eyewitness who saw you two at the scene."

Ernie looked at Larry.

"It's just a trick," Larry warned. "There is *no* eyewitness because we weren't involved, *remember?*"

"A trick, uh?" Bromley called out down the hall, "Betty? Bring Molly up here."

"Don't buy it," Larry warned Ernie, who looked as though he were about to crack. "It's a sham. A con game. The sheriff's got someone who's going to pretend that they saw the accident."

"That's what you think, huh, Einstein? Well, you're wrong. This woman saw everything. How you two ran right into Father James. How you got out of the car and one of you checked his pulse. I'm assuming that was you, Doctor Pulaski."

Less sure of himself, Larry looked away.

"Then she saw you two get back into your vehicle and drive off."

Larry had done some research just before they had been arrested. "Even if it were true, which it is not, leaving the scene of an accident is only a misdemeanor. Not a *felony*."

"In my book, it should be," Bromley assured him in his legendary Rottweiler voice. The men sat farther back in their chairs. "But, you see, here's the thing. You guys picked the wrong town to mess with. We don't like outsiders coming in here running down our Catholic priests, then acting as though it were nothing more than a parking ticket."

"No . . . he didn't mean to imply . . ." Ernie jumped in.

"I know *exactly* what this scumbag was implying," Bromley growled. "But you're not in Kansas anymore, Dorothy. You're in Dorsetville, a town that takes care of its own. In a few hours, you're going to be brought before Judge Peale. He's sat on the bench here for more years than most of us can count. He loves this town, and he's also very fond of Father James. So, here's the thing. The judge can charge you with anything he wants. He can also set a bail so high that even the Queen of England couldn't meet it. And since this is such a small facility, we'll have to send you guys up to the state penitentiary in Cheshire while we run an investigation. You've heard about those kind of places haven't you?" He watched with enormous satisfaction as the men's faces turned a ghastly white. "Of course, you might be up there for a while. Investigations like this can take a year. Maybe longer."

"I told you we should have stopped," Ernie shrieked. He had seen stories about prison life. He was not about to be some inmate's boy toy.

"Shut up!" Larry shouted.

"You know, I'm just about fed up to here with listening to you. It's because of you we're in this mess."

"I said shut up!"

"Or what? You'll run me over, too?"

"You dumb idiot!" Larry shot out of his lightweight molded-plastic seat, sending it scurrying across the room and rushed for Ernie's throat.

"Sit back down!" Bromley shot up out of his chair, placing his six-foot four-inch, three-hundred-pound frame in between them. He grabbed each man underneath an arm and forced them back down into their chairs.

Betty peeked her head in. "You ready for Molly?"

"You two idiots finished?" he asked, waiting to make certain that no one was going to move, but it seemed as though the two men had exhausted their anger. "All right, then. Betty, bring her in."

Molly walked into the room, looking more like a grand dame than a bag lady. She was dressed in a moss green flowered dress with a matching linen jacket, courtesy of Secondhand Rose. Setting off the outfit was a triple strand of Kmart pearls with matching clip-on earrings (Mildred Dunlop's cast-offs). Molly walked past the sheriff and faced the two men seated at the table. As she moved, she left a trace of Chanel No. 5 in the air.

The men avoided her eyes, looking as though they wished the floor would open up and swallow them whole.

Bromley carefully lowered his voice. He didn't want to scare her. "Molly, would you like a cup of tea? Hot chocolate? Are you hungry?"

"No, I'm fine," she assured him.

"Molly, can you tell me if these are the two guys you saw get out of the car that hit Father James?" the sheriff asked. "Now, take your time. There's no reason to hurry. I want you to be certain."

Molly carefully studied their faces. "Yes. They're the ones. Except they weren't dressed in pajamas that day. They were dressed all in black."

"Oh, God! We're dead meat," moaned Ernie.

Betty knocked on the doorframe, then leaned her head inside the room.

"What is it, Betty?"

"Two things. First, their wives are here," she consulted a piece of paper in her hand. "Denise DeVito and Marlene Pulaski." She handed the paper to the sheriff. "But if I were you, Al, I'd strongly suggest you frisk them for weapons before they're allowed to see the prisoners. And the second thing is, Barry Hornibrook is here and wants to talk to you right away. Seems that explosion earlier was his boat blowing up. He says he knows who did it."

Bromley placed the piece of paper on the table. "All right, put the wives in my office and tell Barry I'll be with him as soon as I finish with these two." He turned to Molly. "Thank you for your help, Molly. Your testimony means a lot to this case."

She studied the sheriff quietly for several seconds before inquiring, "Have you asked Father James what he wants you to do?"

"What do you mean?"

"Are you sure Father James will want to press charges?"

The sheriff looked at her blankly. Where was she going with this?

Molly turned to the prisoners. "Why *did* you run away?"

"We were just scared," Ernie said. It was the first truth he had uttered since the previous night and it felt enormously good. "You have no idea how awful it's been, having this thing on our consciences. We'd do anything to have a second chance, to make this right. I swear."

"I've gotten to know Father James over the last few weeks," Molly told the sheriff. "He strikes me as a man filled with compassion and forgiveness. Maybe you'd better talk with him first before charging them two."

Larry grabbed hold of the suggestion like a life preserver. "What if we talked to Father James? Tell him how sorry we were for causing all this trouble? Offer to pay for his medical bills?"

"Maybe we could do some community service," Ernie added hopefully.

Bromley folded his massive arms across his chest and grew silent while the two men held their breath. The sheriff had known Father James for several years, and, as much as he would have liked to see these idiots pay for what they had done, he knew Father James was quick to forgive. He'd probably never go along with pressing formal charges.

"All right, you've got the right to make one phone call each. You can either call your attorneys, or you can call Father James."

"If I was you, I'd call the priest," Molly said sagely.

Moments later, Bromley was leading the two men in handcuffs toward Hill's desk so they could make a phone call, when Barry Hornibrook intercepted them as they rounded the station desk.

"You've caught them!" Barry shouted. "Holy smokes! You've got them!"

The two men froze in place.

"I know," the sheriff said. "They just confessed to hitting Father James."

"They're responsible for doing that, too??!!"

"Come on. Get going," Bromley said, trying to prod the prisoners along. "Barry, what do you mean 'too'? What else have they done?"

"I thought you knew. They're the ones who just blew up my boat."

Chapter 15

While Larry Pulaski and Ernie DeVito sat in the Dorsetville jail, nervously awaiting Father James's arrival and word of their fate, their wives tried to pray from the front pew of St. Cecilia's surrounded by painters, high on ladders, who were putting the finishing touches on the walls. Neither woman, however, was having much success.

Marlene Pulaski couldn't stop wondering how Larry had managed to get into this mess. What had he been doing up here in Dorsetville, anyway? And why hadn't he stopped when he had hit the priest? She and Denise had both asked their husbands these questions earlier through jail bars, but neither had been able to provide satisfactory answers.

Marlene shifted her weight onto her other knee. She had heard that men Larry's age sometimes did stupid things in order to regain their lost youth. Some took mistresses; others bought sports cars. Larry *had* been acting weird ever since he had turned forty. But still, why would he rent one of those huge SUVs—the kind that Tony drove on *The Sopranos* (his favorite show)—and drive it all the way up here to New England? If he was going to have an affair, wouldn't it have been a lot easier to choose a mistress who lived closer? And why had he brought Ernie along? Everyone knew Ernie lived in mortal fear of his wife, Denise. This was the woman who once brought down a brawny sanitation worker because he dumped garbage on the hood of her Cadillac. No, if Ernie had been along, it couldn't have been women.

But then, what? Sure, Dorsetville was a cute little town, but it was hardly worth a two-and-a-half-hour drive to visit.

Then there was the matter of the accident. Larry was a doctor. Well, all right, an orthodontist, but even *he* knew that when you ran someone over they got hurt. They might even die. So, why did he leave the priest on the side of the road and leave the scene without calling for an ambulance? Nothing made any sense.

She looked over at her best friend, Denise, whose mouth was set in a hard line. Apparently, she wasn't having any more success at praying for Ernie than Marlene had had for Larry. Marlene studied her closely. She knew that look. Lucky for Ernie he was safely locked in jail.

Denise made the sign of the cross and sat back in the pew. "It's no use," she whispered. "I can't pray for the bum. I keep getting images of Ernie being dragged behind my car on the Long Island Expressway and I'm the driver."

"Yeah, I know what you mean," Marlene said. She reached inside her leather bomber jacket for a pack of gum. "You want a piece?"

"Sure." Denise quickly turned the gum into a soft mass and began to make little snapping sounds. "Can a priest sue?" . . . *Snap* . . . "I mean, is it against their vows or something, right?" . . . *Snap* . . . *Snap* . . . Denise deferred to Marlene in all things Catholic. Marlene had gone to Catholic school.

"Who knows? These days everybody sues everybody. Larry thinks it's because of those darn lawyer infomercials. You know the ones. 'If anyone has ever stepped on your toe . . . see us. We'll get you the money you're due.' Gives people ideas." Marlene folded her arms across her ample bosom and thought for a long moment. Finally, she said, "If Father James does decide to sue, we will probably lose our home. I should give my brother a call."

"The accountant?" . . . *Snap* . . . Denise asked, pulling an emery board out from her purse.

"Yeah. Maybe there's a way of protecting our assets."

"From the Church?"

"Well, no one can protect them from God." Sometimes Denise can be so dense, she thought.

Two nuns in blue habits entered the sanctuary. Denise watched them genuflect before the host, then begin placing fresh flowers in the vases around the altar. She ran the emery board across a heavily lacquered thumbnail, ignoring the occasional disapproving looks from the nuns.

"Did you notice my new nail color?" . . . *Snap* . . . "Purple Passion," Denise asked, holding out her hand.

"Looks a little on the red side to me," Marlene said. She studied her own nails. They did look a little rough around the edges. She opened her gallon-size purse in search of her emery board. Where was it? She pulled out a bag of miniature Snickers, an empty can of Pringles and a twenty-three-ounce-size bag of Cheez Doodles and set them on the pew.

"It's this candlelight. Throws off the color," Denise explained. "Good thing I got my nails done before all this happened. It could be days before we get back to the Island."

"Yeah, and I don't think a town like Dorsetville has a lot of nail salons," Marlene offered. There it was! She detached an old Life Saver that had stuck to the emery board and began to file away. "I don't know how the women around here can live in such primitive conditions."

"Me neither. Heck, the nearest mall is practically twenty miles away."

The women studied the nuns in silence for several minutes. Finally, Denise leaned over and asked, "You think we should light some more candles?"

"We've lit all the ones under the Blessed Virgin and Saint Anthony. Saint Joseph doesn't get involved in these kinds of things. He's in charge of selling people's houses."

Since Marlene knew these things, Denise didn't question. Instead, she said, "What are we going to do if there's a trial?"

"We'll have to hire some lawyers, I suppose."

"Lawyers? Do you know how much that's going to cost?" Denise hadn't considered this possibility. It was not a welcome thought. "The other night, I was watching *Family Law* and saw a client asked to pay a fifty-thousand-dollar retainer."

"Denise, that's just a television show. It's not real."

"I *know* it's not real, but they hire real lawyers to advise them on things like that so the show is authentic and everything. If they quoted fifty thou, then that's what it must cost to retain a lawyer." Denise's weekly schedule revolved around her many favorite television shows and news gleaned from reading the *National Enquirer*.

"How are we supposed to get our hands on that kind of money?" Denise asked.

"Mortgage our homes, I guess."

"Well . . . that's not an option for us. Our home is already heavily mortgaged," Denise said. "We took out a second one to help pay for Ernie Junior's college tuition. All we've got left is the savings we were going to use for our retirement home and I'm not giving that up."

Denise had just picked out the perfect retirement home from a brochure the realtor has sent up from Marco Island, Florida. It was a brand-new subdivision that bordered a small lake, and, according to the realtor, the homes were selling fast. Denise would strangle Ernie if he caused her to lose this once-in-a-lifetime opportunity.

"This whole thing makes me so mad I could spit!" Denise railed. "In fact, I have a good mind to let him rot in jail." . . . *Snap* . . . *Snap* . . . *Snap*.

The two nuns looked over at them and frowned.

"Sorry, Sisters," the women chimed in unison.

"That's not such a great idea," Marlene whispered.

"Why not?"

"Because if they get locked away for good, you and I are going to have to find jobs."

"Jobs?" Denise screeched. The nuns lifted their fingers to their lips.

"Sorry, Sisters."

"We need *some* way of supporting ourselves," Marlene insisted.

Denise looked stricken. *Snap* . . . *Snap* . . . "But I've never worked before. Who would hire me? McDonald's?"

"I've never worked before either. Maybe we could create some kind of business of our own. Like . . ." Marlene tried to think of something.

"Like shopping?" Denise quipped. "It's really the only thing we're good at."

The women sat silently, watching the nuns replace a basket of flowers underneath the Blessed Virgin's statue.

"Let's face it," Marlene said, "we need help."

"That's an understatement." . . . *Snap*.

"You know, the nuns back in school used to tell us stories about real people . . . you know, like us . . . who needed a miracle, and how they prayed to a special saint, or something, and everything worked out."

"We've already lit every candle in the place, except Saint Joseph's, and you said his doesn't count. Shouldn't that be enough?"

"Nah . . . you've got to pray, too. Maybe say a novena."

"We tried praying, remember? And besides," . . . *Snap* . . . "don't the saints kind of favor the people who go to Mass all of the time? We like to sleep in on Sundays, then go to brunch, remember?"

"You're probably right." Marlene looked over at the nuns. "But my Nana always said that nuns and priests had direct access to God. Maybe we can get them to pray for us. You know, offer to make a donation or something in exchange for their prayers."

"Like 'Rent-a-Nun'? That's a great idea, but do they do things like that?"

Marlene shrugged. "I don't know, but it's worth asking. Move your feet."

"Where are you going?"

"I'm going to go rent us some nuns."

"You're kidding, right?"

"No, I'm not. We need help and I'm not living out my retirement years sucking fumes from the Long Island Expressway." Marlene's home was only a quarter of mile away from the LIE. She slid out into the aisle. "Yoo-hoo, Sisters. May we have a word with you?"

"Sister Joanna, what is this?" Mother Superior asked, watching an animated nun dance across their order's Web page.

"Isn't that a hoot?" smiled Sister Joanna, her dentures slipping. She was their resident Web page designer, having taken to computers like a duck to water ever since her first computer class at the senior center.

Matthew Metcalf was the instructor. It was part of the teenager's community service that had been leveled by Judge Peale.

But the Web page that Mother Superior was now viewing was vastly different from the one Sister Joanna had originally designed under Matthew's tutelage. That one had borne an oval image of the Blessed Mother surrounded by their order's name and a short history of the Daughters of the Immaculate Conception of the Blessed Virgin Mary, as well as information about the Sister Regina Francis Retirement Home. Now the site opened with an animated blue-clad nun dancing to "Your love Is Lifting Me Higher." Sister Joanna thought it was a riot. Mother Superior did not.

"Sister Joanna, may I remind you that our order is one of piety, charity and good works—all rather serious, deeply spiritual issues. What will the public think when they come upon this?"

Sister Joanna steadied her walker and looked disapprovingly at the prioress. "They'll think that this is a 'happening place.'"

Mother Superior exhaled audibly. She really did have to talk to Sister Claire about limiting the amount of time their residents spent in front of the television. Sister Joanna was beginning to sound more and more like one of the characters on *The Hood*. "May I have this morning's e-mails?"

Sister Joanna passed them over. "Four more nuns and another priest looking for a retirement home."

"Write back and say that we'll put them on a waiting list."

"How many does that make?"

"One hundred and four," answered Mother Superior, already busy with another task.

"One hundred and four? Well, the good Lord had better do something soon. At our age, there ain't a whole lot of time left to wait."

"I agree." Mother Superior said.

The elderly nun turned to leave.

"And Sister Joanna?"

"Yes?"

"Don't forget what we talked about. You are to change the Web page back to its original design."

"I never agreed to any such thing."

"Sister Joanna . . ."

"All right, I hear ya." She ambled toward the door, calling back over her shoulder as her walker thumped along. "I'll change it, except for the dancing nun. She stays."

The increasing need among elderly clerics for retirement homes was much on Sister Bernadette's mind this morning as she pulled out the last of the impatiens that bordered the front walk. She planned to replace them with a flat of chrysanthemums that Harriet Bedford had just delivered. Harriet's nursery grew the loveliest chrysanthemums in the entire county. Sister Bernadette was especially fond of the deep crimson ones.

Sister Bernadette snapped off a small cylinder, cut away the black plastic and freed one of the plants. Next, she sprinkled some dry cow manure into the hole, worked it around with her garden prongs, then moistened the soil with her sprinkling can before tenderly placing the plant in its new home. This was the nun's favorite part of gardening and she took her time, feeling a sense of connection to the rich earth. She never wore gardening gloves.

As her busy hands planted, her mind was free to wander back to the conversation earlier that week at breakfast. When she and the other sisters had returned from chapel, Sister Claire was already seated at the kitchen table, the notebook in which were listed the names of those waiting for admission into the home open beside her.

"We've received over a dozen queries for rooms just this week alone," she reported after grace.

"It deeply saddens me to see so many turned away," said Sister Theresa, reaching for the pitcher of milk.

"I know. I feel the same way," Sister Claire said sadly, "Which is why we must keep up with our prayers, Sisters. Many of those listed here will be retiring this year. Some have no place to go."

Sister Bernadette had mentioned all of this to Molly during her visit yesterday. Their order had been delegated by the Dorsetville Women's Club the task of supplying Molly with fresh toiletries.

Molly had sat quietly, spreading lavender-scented hand lotion on her hands while she listened to Sister Bernadette explain that the nuns had begun a novena to the Blessed Mother.

"Tell the Sisters to keep on praying, and don't give up," Molly encouraged. "God cannot refuse a persistent prayer."

"We don't plan to give up. If nothing else, our order is tenacious," Sister Bernadette assured her.

"That's the spirit!" Molly said. "People often lose hope if their prayers aren't answered in a few days or weeks or months. But remember the Lord's parable about the persistent widow?"

Bernadette quoted, ". . . because this widow keeps bothering me, I will see that she gets justice, so that she won't eventually wear me out with her coming!"

Molly smiled. "I never read that story without laughing. I can just picture that widow, stalking out that judge's home. Coming again and again. Disturbing his neighbors with her persistent knocking and shrieking, 'I know you're in there. You can't hide from me!' Finally, the judge couldn't take it anymore and he shouts, 'Woman, I'll give you whatever you want, only leave me alone!' "

"More people should be like that widow. Hold on until God has time to act in their behalf." Molly's face turned sad. "But I'm afraid that most people are quick to label God indifferent because what they have prayed for hasn't yet arrived. They don't really believe in His unlimited mercy, compassion and love, or that He takes a personal interest in every one of their requests. If they did, they'd hold out until their prayers were answered.

"That's what Jesus tried to teach people throughout His ministry. He was God among us and never once did He refuse anyone's request or withhold a blessing. In fact, Jesus said that God already knew our needs before we prayed, so why were we worried? Would God give His children a stone when they asked for a fish?"

Sister Bernadette settled deeper into the slipper chair inside Molly's cell. She loved to hear this strange woman speak of the things of God. There was a personal intimacy with the Lord expressed by her words that the nuns envied.

"Jesus continually held out a compassionate hand and spoke miracles into being on people's behalf. So, what makes people think that the Father Jesus served is any different from the Father we serve today?"

Molly riffled through the basket of toiletries, lifting out a can of gardenia-scented talcum. She studied it for several seconds before continuing. "Delays are not denials. It doesn't mean that since He hasn't sent a speedy reply that a request has been refused. Sometimes delays are necessary so God can put certain things into motion."

"Like lining up the right set of circumstances? Or putting the right people in the right place at the right time?" the nun asked.

"Yes. And don't forget about the angels," Molly said, sprinkling on some talcum. It smelled heavenly. She wondered if Sister Claire could bring some bubble bath next time.

"Are you sure you have gotten the proper permission to take this camera?" asked Sam Rosenberg as he helped Ben Metcalf pack the Sony DVCAM into the Plymouth's backseat. Timothy McGree held open the door. They were parked outside the WKUZ public television station.

Sam had not completely recovered from their last escapade when they borrowed the university's laser without permission, which nearly resulted in the three men being charge with grand larceny. This time, Sam was going to make certain Ben had gotten the proper authority.

"There's no need to worry, honest, Sam," Ben assured him as he carefully positioned the camera securely on the backseat. Sam had never gotten the hang of using the power brakes. Sudden, jerky stops were frequent.

"I got the okay from the station manager, Carl Pipson, himself. He's scheduled me to work on John Moran's show tomorrow. We're taping right here in town, and, since I've never worked the camera outside the studio before, Carl thought I could use the practice."

"So you'll practice, right, Sam?" Timothy said.

"Right. So how can we help?" Sam asked.

"Carl suggested I film that new Japanese restaurant," Ben said.

"The one near Harry's place. The station is trying to get him to advertise. Carl said if I do a good job, they'll air it as part of a downtown promotional piece they're putting together."

"Sounds like an important assignment," Sam said.

Ben blushed. "It's no big thing."

"'No big thing,' he says," Sam echoed. "Our friend is suddenly a television cameraman and he says it's 'no big thing.'"

"Let's see if I can pull it off before you start filling my head with praise," Ben laughed.

"We have every confidence in you," Timothy said, thrilled that his best friend had finally found a new hobby he obviously enjoyed, and one he hoped would make him miss his grandson a little less. It sure made him feel good to see the sparkle back in Ben's eyes.

"So, shall we get started?" Sam asked. "I'm ready." Sam fished inside his coat pocket for his car keys. "Let's go pick up Father Keene at the home. He might like to take a ride."

It took the sheriff the better part of the morning to straighten out the whole mess between Barry Hornibrook and the two men from Long Island. Apparently Ernie DeVito and Larry Pulaski had been conned by Clyde Hessler just like Barry. If only Hornibrook had come to see him earlier he could have alerted the surrounding sheriffs, maybe gotten a lead on Hessler before he fled the state. The guy was probably a million miles from here by now, living high on everyone's money.

The sheriff still couldn't believe that the two schnooks downstairs had just handed Hessler two hundred and fifty thousand dollars. A guy they had met in a sports bar. How stupid was that? The dumb things people did never ceased to amaze him.

Together, Hessler had gotten away with a cool million. What made people trust guys like Hessler? he wondered. He had known Barry all of his life. The guy wasn't stupid. Why did he take Hessler, basically a stranger, in as a partner then entrust him with the bank account? And although Bromley didn't particularly like the two Long Islanders, they seemed like reasonably educated men. You'd think they would have run some kind of background check on the guy before forking over that kind of dough. But then, if he could figure out why people did what they did, he would be out of a job.

The sheriff opened the polystyrene container that held the corned-beef-and-sauerkraut sandwich Harry had just delivered. On top were two envelopes of mustard. On the side sat a container of Harry's home-grown horseradish, so fresh that just smelling it made your eyes tear. The sheriff loved it.

While fixing his sandwich, he wondered who had blown up Barry's boat. And why? George Benson, who had left a few minutes before, didn't have a clue.

"It looks like someone threw a lighted article into the gas tank," George said, falling into the chair next to the sheriff's desk. Bromley noticed the trail of mud George had tracked in. At least he thought it was mud. With George you never knew.

"I spoke with Barry, since you asked," George said. "He doesn't know anything. At first, he thought it was those two guys you arrested for running down Father James. Now that you've ruled that out, Barry doesn't know of anyone else who might have wanted to blow up his boat."

"Did he give you anything we could use?" Bromley asked.

He hadn't yet questioned Barry. He planned to take his statement later when things around the station calmed down. It had been a hectic morning, and it didn't seem as though it was about to get any better. Father James was due in soon and the prisoners' wives were demanding visitation rights. Which reminded him, he'd better have Betty make certain a deputy was stationed inside the room, and doubly certain that that deputy wasn't Hill.

"No. Barry said the boat was in one piece when he had headed back to his office. Something about an allergy attack. Anyway, just before that, he had decided to top off the boat's gas tank and went to get some gas he stores in the shed. That's when his allergies flared up, so he headed back to the hotel. Several minutes later, his boat blew up.

"My guess is that someone came along and dropped a match in the tank." George scratched his head, "Of course, that wouldn't explain how they got safely away without blowing themselves up along with the boat. Oh, well . . . we're just going to have wait until we can dredge the river and haul the thing out. Maybe we'll find some clues then."

Bromley finished preparing his sandwich just the way he liked it. Double mustard on one half. Horseradish on the other. Well, he knew that Pulaski and DeVito hadn't blown up Barry's boat. They had been with him when the blast had happened. Of course, they could have hired someone. Barry said they had threatened it but the sheriff thought this highly unlikely.

He began to move the sandwich toward his mouth, then paused. Imagine Pulaski and DeVito pretending to be mobsters in an effort to get Barry to pay off Hessler's loan. How did people come up with this sort of stuff?

He bit into his sandwich and started to chew. The sharp bite of the horseradish began to work its way up his nasal cavity. His eyes had already begun to water. God, this stuff was potent. He loved it! He grabbed for a napkin and blew his nose.

"So what do you think, boy?" Bromley asked the German shepherd, lying near his office door. "Got any clues?"

He lopped off a piece of corned beef smothered in horseradish and hurled it in the shepherd's general direction. Harley stretched his neck without getting up and caught it in midair. Bromley waited to see if the dog rushed for his water bowl. Harley didn't flinch.

"Dorsetville used to be a nice and peaceful place," he said, patting his knee. Harley scrambled to his feet and came over to sit by his side. He looked up hopefully toward the sandwich. The sheriff tore off another piece.

"I guess even our town isn't immune to crime anymore," he told his canine friend. "Before you know it, people will have to start locking their doors." Bromley didn't even own a house key. He doubted anyone else in Dorsetville did either.

Father James started Thursday in a chipper state of mind, seated in Doc Hammon's office waiting for the cast to be removed. He felt like a man who had done his time and was about to receive his pardon.

"Father James?" the receptionist, Shirley Olsen, called. Shirley was married to Betty Olsen's brother and had worked for Doc Hammon since graduating high school thirty-eight years ago. Although both she and the Doc were married to other people, it was hard not to think of them as a couple.

"You can go in now. Examining room number three. Our new technician, Darlene, will lead the way."

"This way, Father James," said Darlene, a tall, thin woman who appeared the model of efficiency. Darlene took Father James's blood pressure and weight. He deliberately looked the other way as the technician continued to move the metal weights to the right. Ignorance is bliss.

"Good morning, Jim," the doctor said. "I'll take over from here," he told Darlene.

"Very well, Doctor. Just remember that you have a patient in exam room number two. You're twelve minutes behind schedule."

"Is that all?" the doctor laughed. "It's only Charlie Littman, complaining about his back again. What does he expect after decades of lugging a forty-pound mailbag around town? Just tell him to lie down and give him a newspaper to read. He'll be asleep before you close the door."

"If you say so, Doctor," she said. Her expression showed she thought this a poor way to run an office.

Doc Hammon bent over a small metal sink and began to wash his hands. "I bet you've been looking forward to this day."

Father James balanced against the exam table while he placed his crutches up against the wall. "I can't remember an event that I've anticipated more."

Doc smiled, dried his hands, then began to slip on a pair of latex gloves. "Amazing how we take our mobility for granted until it's taken away."

"I can assure you that I will never take it for granted again," Father James said in earnest. "I hate to admit this, but before my accident, I never spent a lot time thinking about the challenges of the handi-capped."

"Few do," Doc said, perching on a low stool with wheels.

"But I learned that even the simplest things like taking a bath or getting dressed require Herculean effort. Of course, I was lucky. I had Mrs. Norris and Father Dennis to help me out. I can't imagine having to manage on my own." He slid up onto the exam table.

Doc checked the vacuum hose on the blade used to remove casts. "I always tell my patients to take good care of their neighbors, relatives and friends because you never know when you might need them." He donned a pair of safety glasses.

"Excellent advice. Mind if I use it in one of my sermons?"

"With my compliments. Ready?"

The priest nodded, then watched as the doctor threw the switch that started the blade rotating. Doc Hammon moved it closer to his cast. Father James tensed up.

"You want to relax a little, Father?"

"That blade looks rather dangerous." He had to shout to be heard above the sound of the motor.

"This? No. It only cuts the upper layer of the cast. It doesn't get anywhere near your skin."

How much in life we take on faith, Father James thought. He closed his eyes as the blade began to vibrate against his cast.

It took less than five minutes for the doctor to finish. He switched off the machine. Father James finally opened his eyes. Doc Hammon rolled his chair back to the counter, grabbed hold of what looked like a small tire iron, then rolled back and inserted it into the cast along the cut. Several quick movements and the cast cracked open like an egg. A few snips more and the cloth beneath also fell away.

Shirley stepped inside the room. "I'm sorry to bother you, Doctor, but Mrs. Galligan is on the phone."

"What have the twins done now?" the doctor asked, laughing.

"Apparently they've developed a terrible rash. She says they're itching themselves raw and is afraid to bring them to the office in case whatever they have is contagious. She wants to know if you'll drop over as soon as you're finished up here?"

The doctor peeled the cloth away and, to Father James's amazement, his leg had shrunk two sizes.

"Tell her I'll be done here around eleven. I'll stop over after that." The doctor slowly rotated the priest's leg to the left, then to the right. "How does that feel?"

"Feels great," Father James said, starting to slide off the table.

"Whoa!" Doc Hammon cautioned. "It'll be a few more weeks before that leg can bear up under your full weight. The muscles have atrophied while you were in that cast." He handed him the crutches. "I'm afraid you're going to need these for a little while longer."

"How long?" Father James couldn't hide his disappointment. He had expected to walk out under his own steam.

"With therapy, six weeks, tops. I'll call upstairs. Make an appointment for you with the physical therapist. Hang in there, Jim. You're down to the wire. Everything will be back to normal in no time."

Doc Hammon opened the exam door and stood aside to let Father James through. "Make an appointment with Shirley. I want to see you back here in a week."

Father James had limped forward a few feet when he stopped. He suddenly had an idea. "Doc? You're going out to see the Galligan twins, right?"

"Yes, after I finish up here. Why?"

"Mind if I ask you a favor?"

The doctor turned around. "What do you need, my friend?"

"Let's just say I need some help in motivating the twins."

Chapter 16

By nine-thirty that morning, Ben Metcalf had filmed the mayor in his new office, Molly in the town jail, and the new Japanese restaurant. Since the station manager had given him permission to keep the camera until noon, he was eager to keep on filming.

"The more practice the better," he told Mr. Yokohama, the Japanese restaurant owner, as he packed up to leave.

"You go practice at my house," Mr. Yokohama suggested, then explained that there was a stray cat that had just had kittens inside the barn. "When I call landlord, Mr. Hawkins, he says no want cats. You go to barn. Take picture. Put on television. They find home," he said, smiling broadly at this clever idea.

"Why not?" Sam Rosenberg said. It wasn't as though anyone was in a hurry this morning. Timothy had nothing to do. Father Keene had a doctor's appointment at twelve, but Sam could easily drop him off on his way to the senior center to pick up his Meals-on-Wheels delivery. "What do you think?"

"I'm all for it," Ben said.

"Me, too. I think it's a fine idea," said Father Keene, who had been studying a small wisp of a woman rolling sushi behind the counter.

The men thanked Mr. Yokohama for the suggestion as they left. Sam's car was parked right out front, so it took only a few minutes to carefully repack Ben's equipment and hop inside. Across the street, Deputy Hill was trying to justify to Mrs. Phillips why he had given her a ticket for parking eleven and a half minutes in a ten-minute parking zone. On any other day, the men would have intervened, asking the deputy to reconsider. Twice they had saved Mildred Dunlop a parking fine when she had double-parked outside the Smoke Shop to run in and pick up a new supply of the crossword puzzles. The shop owner, Dick Dwyer, saved unsold newspapers and magazines for Mildred.

But today, none of the men felt like confronting Deputy Hill, who had a tendency to talk on and on and on. Sam was the only one not bothered by it. He just turned off his hearing aid. Besides, they had things to do. Ben had promised to get the camera back before noon and there still was the Hawkins place to film.

Sam maneuvered the Plymouth down Main Street and made a right onto Library Road, which led along the base of the mountain range that surrounded the town. He was a competent driver who, like his passengers, was more interested in the journey through the ever-changing landscape than actually arriving at the destination within a certain amount of time. Today was an especially good day for meander-ing along back country roads, many of which were dirt lanes no wider than a cow path.

The men grew quiet, comfortable in their long friendship, as they drove along. A slight, cool breeze blew in through the open car win-dow, ruffling their hair.

An early cold front last week had hastened the advent of fall, tip-ping the countryside in color. It would intensify over the next two weeks until the valley was surrounded, ablaze. Each man savored the landscape and committed it to memory, knowing that by March this spectacular moment of beauty would help to offset winter's hard edge and the icy pathways that forced them indoors.

"Here we are," Sam announced, pulling into the Hawkins's drive-way, a deep-rutted dirt road hemmed in by abandoned farm equipment scattered along its length. The barn lay up ahead, toward the rear of the property. Sam took it slow, doing his best to avoid the deep potholes.

Neither the barn nor the farmhouse fronting the main road had seen a coat of paint in nearly two decades. Once white, both buildings had weathered to a blotchy gray. The wood-shingled roofs had been patched so many times with a variety of materials—tin, asphalt shingles, clapboard planks—that they looked as though they were molting.

Finally, Sam pulled the Plymouth in front of the barn door and turned off the engine. The four men slowly got out, bones cracking and creaking, to survey the place.

"Maybe I should take a couple of shots of the outside," Ben said, walking back and forth, trying to settle on the best angle. "It would make a nice opening shot. I could set up the tripod here. It wouldn't take more than a few minutes to get this on tape, then we could move inside and film the cat and her litter. What do you think?"

"Sounds like a plan to me," Timothy said. "Sam, you want to open the trunk. Ben, you get the camera. I'll grab the tripod."

"Should I go inside and scout out the place? See if I can find the litter?" Father Keene offered.

"Good idea," Timothy said, as he set the tripod on the ground. "Just be careful. If you fall and break anything, Mother Superior will have our heads."

"I'll invoke the protection of Saint Michael," he assured them, making the sign of the cross.

As Father Keene entered the barn through the large front door, it was as if he had stepped back in time. A gentle flutter of memories began to stir. He stepped in farther.

The interior was near ruin from years of neglect—stalls whose gates sat at odd angles, rusted hinges having long since given way under their weight; a bank of old-fashioned milking equipment with hoses decomposing on the ground. But Father Keene saw none of this; instead, his mind superimposed the image of Mr. McNally's barn, where he had spent so much of his youth milking a seemingly endless succession of cows.

These were fond memories, ones that he had replayed often throughout his adult life, like a favorite orchestra score—the soft, rolling hills and hedgerows, the tinkle of the cow bells, the earthy scent of straw and wet fur, the mist rising off fresh manure.

On Patrick Keene's thirteenth birthday, his mother had hired him out to a dairy farmer, Mr. McNally, who lived twenty miles away. It was the first time he had ever been away from home. His young heart had beaten wildly as his plied the back roads not at all certain what he might encounter at the end of his journey. He only knew that whatever it was, there was no turning back.

In all the seventy years since then, Father Keene had never forgotten that day or the long walk. It had been seared on his consciousness like the imprint of a branding iron.

The young lad had stubbornly placed one foot in front of the other, reaching deep down for the courage to go on even though only uncertainty lay before him. Would the McNallys be kind or hard taskmasters? He had heard stories from others, lads who had run away, banished from their families for not sticking it out regardless of the beatings. Often a son's wages were the only thing that had kept a family from starvation.

He had just passed a young boy in the village, younger than himself, who had run away from his master. The boy showed him scars on his calves where a pan of scalding water had been thrown at him for not jumping up fast enough when he was called. The scene was recounted most vividly and it had shaken young Patrick to the core. Worse was the knowledge that if a similar fate befell him, he must endure it. He had promised his mother to take care of her and his siblings. He would rather suffer any amount of torment than forsake his family.

His father had died the previous year, leaving him, the oldest, as head of the family. His mother took in washing and he and his younger brothers sold peat door to door. It was a meager existence at best. They were not alone in their misery. Dozens of other widows with children to raise bore the same heartache. But the Keenes were luckier than most because Patrick, at thirteen, was old enough to work.

"'Tis the only way to keep your brothers and sisters from starving," his mother had said with tears streaming down her face. "If there was only some other way, my lad . . ." The words drifted off and disappeared like steam from a kettle.

Patrick didn't complain. Like most children during that bleak period of Ireland's past, he was resigned to whatever fate brought his way and kept his disappointments to himself, like his secret wish to become a priest. But what good was it to dream of things that can never be? he asked himself, jumping over a small stream. It was better just to pluck the thought from his consciousness like one would a thorn or briar.

But no matter how hard he tried to jettison the thought from his mind, it refused to be expelled. It had been a dream of his for so many years that it had become an integral part of him, like the freckles that abundantly covered his face.

But young Patrick had not yet discovered the ways of the Lord. He did not know that God had not asked him to abandon his dream. In fact, God had already begun to prepare him for the priesthood by beginning the work of patience, a grace that is needed to support all great visions.

But thoughts of the priesthood were put aside as Patrick settled in on the farm. Mr. and Mrs. McNally proved to be a gentle, devotedly Catholic couple, and soon his days moved to the beat of a gentle rhythm dictated mostly by the needs of Mr. McNally's large herd of cows.

Chores began at four-thirty in the morning with the milking. By six, Patrick was shoveling and washing out the stalls. The rest of the day was spent doing whatever chores needed to be done—heaving bales of hay into the feeding troughs in preparation for the next milking, hoeing weeds from the fields, planting and harvesting corn.

All in all, it was a good life, and Patrick was especially proud to know his hard work helped feed his family.

Mr. McNally, a patient and kind man, and his wife, the epitome of compassion and charity, were a childless couple and Patrick became the son they never had. Within two months of his arrival, the boy was moved out of the barn and into a small bedroom off the pantry in the main house. Privacy was a luxury the poor rarely enjoyed and the gift of a private room filled Patrick with unbridled joy.

On his seventeenth birthday, Patrick was asked to blow out the candles on his birthday cake and make a wish.

"I bet I know what you wished for," Mr. McNally teased. "A day you can sleep in till six."

"Now, don't tease the lad," Mrs. McNally said, watching Patrick loop the scarf she had knitted around his neck.

Patrick smiled, then said shyly, "I wished to become a priest."

The couple remained quiet, their eyes slowly filling with tears.

Mr. McNally cleared his throat and addressed his wife in a quiet voice. "Imagine that, Ma. Our boyo here want'en to be a priest."

"'Tis a grand and noble plan," his wife conceded.

"A grand plan that has no way of ever happening," Patrick admitted. "Even if I was accepted for the priesthood, who would support my family? No, I'm afraid that was just a wasted wish."

"I wouldn't give up as easy as that," Mrs. McNally said. "God has placed this dream in your heart, and when God calls He always makes a way."

Several days later, Patrick came in from his early morning chores to find the couple all smiles.

"Come over here, boyo, and sit down," Mr. McNally said, pulling up a chair. "We've got something to share with you."

Patrick took a seat by the kitchen table.

"I think God has given us a plan so you can become a priest," Mr. McNally said plainly.

"He has?"

"You tell him, Da," Mrs. McNally laughed, seeing the surprise on Patrick's face.

Mr. McNally joined the boy at the table. "We want you to write your family and ask them to come here and live."

"Here?"

Mrs. McNally smiled. "Yes, here. They can live in that little cottage at the back of the glen. It's been sitting empty for years and years. It needs a family to fill it up again."

"I thought I was telling the lad?" Mr. McNally said, piqued.

"Well then, get on about the telling," she said, jabbing him in the arm with a wooden spoon.

"As I was saying . . . there's a cottage your family can have in ex-change for some chores around the farm. Your brothers can take over the milking. And one could bail the hay, the other help with the plant-ing."

"And your ma could help me here in the house," Mrs. McNally added. "She can also lend me a hand with the washing and ironing, and the canning in the fall. In exchange for all that your family could live in the cottage rent free."

Patrick felt stunned. Was this the answer he had sought from God?

"They won't starve around here, that's for sure," Mr. McNally added. "There's always extra milk and eggs lying about. And your family can put in a vegetable garden. That glen has good, fertile soil. If planted properly, it will supply them with food right through the winter."

"And this way, you'll be free to go to the seminary," Mrs. McNally said. "We've already talked to the village priest. He's willing to write you a letter of recommendation."

Patrick tried to find words to express his deep feelings of gratitude, but few would come. Finally he settled on "How can I ever thank you for such a kindness?"

"No need to," Mr. McNally said. "The missus and I have been greatly blessed over the years, and we've always wanted to share those blessings. What better way than to help out a family so their eldest can become a priest?"

And so Patrick's family came to live on the McNally farm. His brothers eventually married local girls and filled the house with chil-dren and laughter, giving the McNallys the grandchildren they never had. Mr. McNally lived into his eighties, dying at home, just slipping away one day as he was hefting a spool of barbed wire. Mrs. McNally lived four years after that.

When she died, Father Keene received a letter from her solicitor informing him that he had inherited the farm. He sold it and sent the proceeds to the local parish to help those wishing to become priests.

"Sheriff, you've got three phone calls," Betty announced over the intercom.

"Tell them to call back," he said.

"They sound kind of important," she insisted.

"Go on."

"Mother Superior is on line one. She says Father Keene left this morning with Sam, Timothy and Ben and they haven't returned yet. He has an appointment with Doc Hammon in about thirty minutes. She doesn't want him to miss it.

"And Mrs. Hopkins, over at the senior center, is on line two. She says Sam Rosenberg hasn't showed up to pick up his meals and she's worried. Says it's the first time in sixteen years he's been late.

"The station manager over at WKUZ is on line three. He says Ben borrowed their . . . what did he call it? . . . I wrote it down someplace . . . Oh, yes, here it is. He borrowed the Sony DVCAM. It's some kind of camera. Promised he would have it back before noon. Seems the station only owns one of these things and Mildred Dunlop needs it for this afternoon's crossword puzzle show."

Good grief! What's with these old men? Every time they got together there was trouble.

"Betty, call everyone back. Tell them not to worry. They've probably just lost track of the time. If they don't show up in another hour, I'll send someone out to look."

The switchboard buzzed again. Betty took another call. Seconds later, she was back on the intercom.

Now what? How was he supposed to get anything done?

"That was Ethel Johnson," she informed him. "She said she saw a strange man hanging around the Hawkins place when she went to pick up Mrs. Yokohama for bingo. She spoke with Mr. Yokohama, but he's too busy with the lunch crowd to go home and take a look. She thought you should know."

The Japanese place was busy? Who would have thought?

"Oh, and looks like we found Sam and the others," Betty added. "Ethel said she saw them outside the Hawkins barn. Ben was taking some pictures. You want me to call everyone back and tell them they've been found?"

"Yeah."

"We'll still need someone to ride out there and chase them home."

Bromley thought for a moment. He was needed here, and his other men were busy: one was directing traffic near the new gas lines being installed along Route 7, another had gone home early with a toothache. That left only Hill.

"Call Hill. Tell him to get back to the station. I'll have him run over to the Hawkins place and hustle the old men along. While he's over there, he can also check out Ethel's mysterious stranger."

"Hill?" Betty asked. She felt it prudent always to get confirmation whenever the sheriff evoked Hill's name.

"Yes, woman, I said Hill!"

"Don't take my head off. I was just making sure."

"And no more interruptions," he said, getting up and slamming his office door.

Harley looked up as though asking what all the ruckus was about, then shifted slightly, letting off a burst of gas. Lord, that was foul! Bromley rushed to open the window. Darn his wife Barbara. He had told her not to feed the dog breakfast sausage. He should probably take him out for a walk. But the new FBI report had just come in and he wanted to read it. It seemed that Barry Hornibrook's old partner, Hessler, was also wanted for mail fraud.

Bromley sat back at his desk and resolutely reached inside the top drawer for his new pair of prescription glasses. No use in denying it any longer: His eyesight was shot.

The sheriff slid the glasses out of their case. Bold black plastic frames and scratch-resistant lenses. Darn things had cost him nearly four hundred dollars, a fact that only irked him further. Imagine paying that much for something that made him look like an old fart. But there was no getting around it. It was either reading glasses or he had to grow longer arms.

Bromley had just commenced reading when Deputy Hill burst through the door without benefit of knocking. He had run all the way from the Country Kettle. His face was flushed and he was breathing hard. It wasn't every day that the sheriff summoned him back to the station.

"Hi, Chief. Betty said you wanted to see me. I thought I'd better race right over here. See what you needed done. Hey, are those new glasses? My grandfather has the same pair. His eyes went at about your age, too."

Bromley removed the glasses. "I need you to do something for me."

"I'm your man," Hill said, hitching his fingers through his belt loops and arching his back. He had practiced this stance in front of his bedroom mirror, certain that it exuded confidence. "What do you need?"

"I want you to go over to the Hawkins place. Find Sam, Ben, Timothy and Father Keene. Tell them that they're wanted back in town. And while you're out there, check out a complaint from Ethel Johnson. She saw a strange guy hanging around the property."

"Check out the Hawkins place?"

"Is there an echo in here, Hill?"

"An echo?"

"Hill!"

"Yes, Chief."

"Don't call me 'Chief'!"

"Yes, Chief."

The sheriff's blood pressure began to rise.

"Do you think there's a burglar on the loose in Dorsetville?" Hill asked hopefully.

"Let's hope not. I've got enough things going on in this town right now." Bromley pulled out a bottle of Tums.

Hill watched the sheriff pop four tablets into his mouth. Poor guy, he thought. The stress was really getting to him. The sheriff was right about there being a lot of strange things happening in Dorsetville. The mysterious explosion at Barry Hornibrook's place. The church fire. Then there were the two guys downstairs who had run over Father James. Yep, the sheriff sure did have a lot of things to worry about. But lucky for the chief, he was here to take up the slack.

He told the sheriff, "I'll get right on it, Chief. Can I have the keys to the cruiser?"

Bromley poured himself a glass of water and took a long drink. He felt as though he had just eaten a handful of chalk. "You're kidding, right?" he asked, wiping his mouth with the back of his hand.

"Oh . . . yeah." Hill's record with department vehicles was not good. The first week on the job, he had landed the police cruiser in Platt's pond. There was a dense fog that morning and he hadn't seen the curve in the road until it was too late. It had cost the department a tidy sum. The cruiser had to have the seats and electrical system replaced.

Then, a few months ago, he had been issued the 1991 Ford to transport a prisoner down to Cheshire. The car used a full quart of oil every couple of hundred miles, and he had forgotten to fill it before leaving the station. Halfway to the prison, the engine seized up. To make matters worse, while he was waiting for a tow truck, the prisoner asked to take a dump in the woods. Hill started to go along, but the guy insisted that he needed privacy. Hill had complied. The prisoner had escaped. Two weeks later they found him in Louisiana.

Hill ventured a query. "Ah . . . how do I get over to the Hawkins place without a car?"

"You walk."

"It's about three miles from here."

"Three and a half," Bromley amended. Hill didn't move. "You need directions?"

"No, I know how to get out there," Hill replied, oblivious to the sarcasm. "It's just that I was thinking, you know, Chief, my walking over there could be a good thing."

Bromley had returned to his paperwork without the benefit of his reading glasses. He couldn't see a thing. "What's good about it?"

"I've been thinking over what the Town Council said at the last meeting. About how Dorsetville needs to find some new sources of revenue."

"Yeah?" Bromley said tentatively.

"What if I were to bring a garbage bag and collect trash along the way."

"You plan to supplement the town budget with turning in bottles and cans for deposits?"

Hill smiled broadly, exposing two newly capped teeth, courtesy of the police dental plan. "No, I'll bring the trash back here and fingerprint all the bottles and cans. Then I'll track down the perpetrators. There's a hundred-dollar fine for littering. Just think of all the money we'll take in."

"So, let me get this straight. You want to start a new unit in charge of garbage control?"

"But we wouldn't call it 'garbage control.'"

"This is getting better and better." He folded his hands behind his head. "All right, Hill, what would you call it?"

Hill's smile brightened like a hundred-watt bulb. "Debris Reclamation Assessments," he announced proudly. He waited for the sheriff to be duly impressed.

The sheriff leaned forward and picked up his pen. "Hill . . . take a walk."

"Sure, Chief," Hill said. It was obvious that the sheriff was too impressed to speak. He'd give him some time to think it over, sort out the particulars. Hill was confident that when he had, the sheriff would realize it had enormous potential.

"Don't call me 'Chief.' And Hill?"

Hill turned expectantly.

"Take Harley with you. He could use a walk."

The Galligan twins were in their room when Doc Hammon arrived, sitting on the edge of their beds wearing only their underwear. They were quite a sorry sight. Nearly every square inch of their bodies was covered with flaming red blotches.

"Hello, boys," Doc said plaintively, setting his bag atop a nearby desk. "Looks like you've been busy."

"We didn't do nothing," they said in unison. It was their standard reply.

Doc reached inside his bag for a pair of latex gloves while Mrs. Galligan hovered nervously nearby. "I don't know what they've gotten into this time," she lamented. "But whatever it is, the rash keeps spreading. Last night it was only on their arms, but by this morning it had spread all over their chests and backs. Do you think it's something . . . treatable?"

She was near tears from worry and concern. Mrs. Galligan, who had given birth to the twins late in life, feared every ailment possessed catastrophic possibilities.

"I'm sure it's nothing that we can't handle," he assured her. "Why don't you go downstairs and make yourself a nice cup of tea while I examine the boys?"

She hesitated.

"I think they're of an age that being examined in front of their mother might cause them a little bit of embarrassment," he suggested, rolling up his sleeves.

She blushed. "Oh . . . yes. I never thought of that. I suppose they are getting older. All right, then I'll be right downstairs, darlings, if you need me." She reluctantly began to back out of the room. "Can Mommy bring her boys something up from the kitchen?"

"I'd like some butterscotch pudding with whipped cream," Dexter said, hopefully. He had just polished off the last Popsicle.

"Oh, dear, I'm afraid that we're out of butterscotch," his mother lamented. "I have vanilla or pistachio,"

"Rodney likes vanilla and pistachio, not me," Dexter reminded her. "But it's all right, Mom. I don't really need it, although . . . it does take my mind off the itch."

Mrs. Galligan's eyes flooded with tears. "Why of course it does, dear. I tell you what. I'll call Daddy and have him pick some up on his way home from work. I can have it cooked and chilled in time for tonight's dessert. Would you like that?"

"That would be great, Mom," Dexter said, pretending to smile bravely through the pain.

Doc Hammon watched all this with amusement. Poor Florence,

she was the only one in town who didn't see through these junior con artists.

He waited until their mother had closed the door. "All right, you two. Let's see what you've gotten yourselves into this time."

He examined Dexter's leg, Rodney's chest. Just as he had suspected: poison sumac. The stuff spread like wildfire and itched to beat the band. It almost made him feel sorry for these two troublemakers.

"All right, I won't torture you anymore." He took off his latex gloves and threw them into the wastebasket.

"*Please* stop it from itching," Dexter pleaded, pounding the bed.

"We'll see what we can do," Doc Hammon said, walking into the adjoining bathroom to wash up. As he was drying his hands, he remembered Father James's request.

He smiled into the bathroom mirror. Help motivate the twins? Why, he'd love to. There wasn't anyone left in town, including himself, who these two hellions hadn't tortured with one or more of their pranks.

Several years ago, the twins had been inadvertently left alone in one of his examining rooms. Later it was discovered that they had sprayed all the tongue depressors with the photo mount he had brought in to fix a Norman Rockwell print that had begun to slip inside its frame. Poor Mildred Dunlop had come in later that day with a simple sore throat and ended up having to have the tongue depressor removed under local anesthetic.

He stepped back inside the room and pretended to be very distressed. God, he was really going to enjoy this!

"I'm afraid, boys, this is *very* serious," he said.

The twins paused midscratch and looked up with anxious eyes. "Serious?" Rodney echoed.

"Now, I may be wrong about the diagnosis. I mean, I'll have to go back to the office and look it up in one of my medical books to be absolutely sure, but I'd be surprised if I were wrong. And if I *am* right, this would be the first reported case in nearly ten, fifteen centuries. It's very rare."

"What do we have, Doctor Hammon?" Rodney asked, his eyes growing bigger.

The doctor pulled up a chair, flipped it around and straddled the seat. Leaning his arms across the back, he said, "It looks like a case of Icki-o-i-tus."

"Icki-o-o??" they repeated.

"Better known as 'the Egyptian Curse.'" He slowly rolled down his shirt sleeves, watching the twins' faces fill with horror.

Rodney spoke first. "What *exactly* is 'the Egyp . . .'"

"Egyptian Curse?" The doctor shook his head sadly. "It's a very nasty disease. Very prevalent in Moses' time. You two do know who Moses was, don't you?

Neither boy was certain but they nodded anyway.

"Well," the doctor said, throwing up his hands expansively, "then you know about the diseases God brought upon the people who sinned and refused to repent. You know, refused to tell the truth. This was one of them."

Dexter swallowed hard, then asked, "So what happens to the people who get this disease?"

"Oh, you don't want to know," the doctor assured them. "Besides, there's no reason to believe that God would curse you two with a disease like this, now, is there?"

"Us? The Egyptian Curse? No way," Rodney laughed. "Why would He do that?" He grew quiet, then thought for a moment before asking, "But . . . these people who got it. Well, what happened to them? Did they die from it?"

"Worse."

"Worse?" Dexter asked incredulously. "What could be *worse* than dying?"

"A long, painful death," Doc said trying to keep a straight face. "Now, like I said before, I'm not one hundred percent sure that you even have the Egyptian Curse. You two didn't commit any sins that you haven't owned up to, now, did you? No, of course not. Why do I ask? I mean, you guys are altar boys and everything, right?"

"Er . . . right."

"But, if you *did* have the Egyptian Curse, well, let's just say a quick death would be easy compared to what you would have to go through."

The boys swallowed hard, their eyes riveted on the doctor.

"Like what?" Rodney asked.

"Well, I wouldn't want to scare you boys."

"No, it's all right," Rodney insisted. "We won't scare easy, right, Dex?"

Dexter shook his head no.

"Okay, if you think you can handle it." The doctor paused for effect. "You see, it's like this. First it starts with a bunch of red blotches. Like you two have now."

The boys looked down at their blister-covered arms.

"Then the blotches begin to itch. They get so bad, it's near impossible to stop from scratching."

The twins began to scratch.

"The itch grows worse and worse. Some people with the curse scratch so hard they open up the blisters and bleed to death."

The two stopped midscratch and examined themselves. As far as they could tell, there was no blood. Then, after a moment's thought, they sat on their hands.

"Next, you get so cold that your teeth chatter so hard they break off at the root. Unless, of course, you stuff your mouth with rags."

Dexter grabbed for a pillow and stuffed a corner in his mouth.

"And then the *final* torture begins."

"'The final torture'?" the boys whispered.

Doc Hammon leaned over the back of his chair, also whispering. "Let's just say that *certain* body parts start to fall off."

Doc Hammon threw his medical bag in the backseat of his Toyota Avalon, loosened his tie and slipped in behind the wheel. He was smiling from ear to ear. He couldn't remember ever having so much fun. The clincher was when he had told the boys' mother to keep the air-conditioning on.

"It will help stop the itching," he said, which was half true. "Keep it around fifty degrees or so. Even if they complain, don't let on it's cold. In fact, why don't you and your husband act as though the temperature is just right. Pretend it's just them who are cold."

He started the engine, hit the button to slide open the moon roof, backed out of the Galligans' driveway and gave in to a belly laugh that brought tears to his eyes. He was halfway down Meadow Street before he could catch his breath. He punched in Father James's number on his car phone and hit SPEAKER.

"St. Cecilia's Rectory," Mrs. Norris intoned.

"Margaret, this is Doc Hammon. Jim around?"

"He's right here, Doc. It's Doc Hammon," she told the priest, handing him the phone.

"What's up, Doc?" Father James said, laughing at his own joke.

"That little talk you suggested I have with the twins?"

"Yes?"

"Well, let's just say that it went better than we had hoped. I don't know what they've done, but I can bet that you'll be hearing from them shortly."

Doc Hammon hung up the phone, feeling absolutely no remorse about what he had done.

Chapter 17

The women hadn't stopped screaming at Ernie and Larry since they'd left the police station; and the only reason they had stopped now was because their mouths were stuffed with Harry's famous home fries.

Neither Ernie nor Larry was hungry. They sat nursing their cups of coffee: Larry held a bunny mug; Ernie's heralded in the year 1983. Both men were thinking that it had been less stressful in jail. At least there they didn't suffer this public humiliation. A nearby table of elderly ladies blushed so hard after Marlene's last outbreak that they packed up and left. One even tied a napkin around her dog's ears. "You needn't hear these types of things, dearest," she told the golden retriever as she pulled him out the front door.

"Pass me the cream, Jailbird," Marlene taunted Larry.

He slid the creamer toward his wife, wishing he could dunk her head in it but quickly concluding that fitting her big mouth in might be a problem.

"Geez, I always heard that country air gives you a big appetite, but I didn't believe it," Denise said, scarfing down the last of the Country Kettle's infamous breakfast special, "The Kitchen Sink": four sausages, four strips of bacon, three eggs, home fries, six pancakes, two pieces of Texas French toast and a Belgian waffle.

In the Kettle's long history, Denise was only the twelfth person who had ever finished it. The other eleven were all blue-collar men under the age of twenty-five.

Wendy arrived with a Polaroid camera, along with the bill and a free T-shirt that read I ATE THE KITCHEN SINK AT THE COUNTRY KETTLE.

"The owner wants me to take your picture."

"Really?" Denise said, smiling as though she had been chosen by *Vogue*.

"It'll go over there." Wendy pointed to a wall dotted with other Kitchen Sink luminaries. She aimed the camera. "Say 'I can't believe I ate the whole thing.'"

"Wait." Denise pulled a mirror the size of a tennis racket from her purse. "Let me freshen up my lipstick."

Wendy waited impatiently. Her order of poached eggs was up.

Ernie watched his wife strike a pose. "Where did she put all of that food?" he asked the others seated around the table. Denise stood five foot six and weighed less than a hundred and twenty pounds, ate like a horse and never gained an ounce.

"I'm ready now," Denise said, also striking a pose.

"She burns it off. It's just nerves," offered Marlene, who, by comparison, had stoically adhered to her latest diet craze, which allowed unlimited calorie consumption if she drank four glasses of water before eating and after, meaning she could never be far from a bathroom. Marlene was five foot two and weighed a hundred and ninety-six pounds, no matter how much she dieted.

"Isn't this a hoot?" Denise asked, inspecting her new T-shirt.

"Great accomplishment, Denise." Ernie scoffed.

Denise made a face, then turned to Marlene. "After we're through, let's go visit the nuns. I think we should before we leave. After all, it was their prayers that helped to spring these jailbirds." She slipped her new shirt over her head but kept on talking. "Maybe we could rent the nuns again. You know, kind of keep them on retainer. With idiots for husbands, you never know when we could use a few extra prayers." She modeled the shirt. "So, what do you think?"

"It needs a little something," Marlene said. "Maybe some silver hoop earrings . . ."

"Let me get this straight," Larry interrupted. "You two 'rented' nuns to pray for us?"

"So???" Marlene said.

"Just asking." Larry held up his hands, warding off any further verbal abuse. He turned to Ernie. "You'd think a guy's wife would care enough about her husband to at least say a couple of prayers."

"We tried," Denise said, still flushed with her moment of fame. "It's just that we couldn't get in the mood."

"Yeah, I know about those moods," Ernie mumbled.

"Never mind. I think it's a great idea," Marlene said. "And while we're at it, I wanted to ask Sister Claire where she got that medal of the Immaculate Blessed Mary she wears. Did you see it? It had malachite around the edges. It would go great with that new black jersey shirt I bought at TJ Maxx. I wonder if she got it around here? Then, I want to go check out that cute little outfit I saw in the consignment shop window next door."

"Secondhand Rose? I saw it, too!" Denise exclaimed, adrenaline pumping. She loved the rush of a shopping high. "And did you see that adorable little hat?"

"You hate hats," Ernie reminded her.

"Well, I might wear one if I could find the 'right' one for the shape of my face," she said.

"Whatever."

"And what are we supposed to be doing while you two shop?" Larry asked.

The sixty-four ounces of water Marlene just drunk were kicking in. She edged herself away from the table. "I suppose you two could stay here and finish your coffee, or grab a newspaper and find a bench somewhere."

"Marlene," Larry whined, "I just want to go home and forget this place."

Marlene shook her head, which had a sort of ripple effect on her multiple chins. "What makes you think I care about what *you* want? It's because of *you* that I was forced to travel up here in the first place. *And*, because of *you*, I will forever be known as the wife of a common criminal."

"Why don't you say it louder, Marlene?" Larry hissed, "Maybe there's someone within forty miles that didn't hear you. And, for your information, I am *not* a criminal. Father James came to the jail. We talked things over and he forgave us, unlike some people I know. He's not pressing charges."

"All we have to do is pay for his medical bills," Ernie added. "End of story."

" 'End of story'?" Denise asked, rising to stand next to Marlene in a show of solidarity. "How can you two look us in the face and say that? In case you've forgotten, a couple of cops showed up on our doorsteps at one in the morning the other night, handcuffed you guys and hauled you off to another state to answer a hit-and-run charge. And we're sup-posed to do, what?! Forget it?

"All the neighbors saw it. I bet the phones are still ringing off the hook. People love to kick you when you're down. Why, even our deli business is bound to suffer."

"Denise, don't exaggerate," Ernie said.

"Exaggerate? Exaggerate?" Denise's voice rose an octave with the second question mark. "You putz!"

Ernie sat farther back in his chair. He didn't like the nasty red flush of his wife's cheeks.

"Besides the fact that *we're* Catholic . . . that is, if we haven't been excommunicated already for your part in trying to kill a priest. Have you forgotten that most of our business is 'Catholic'? Like the Knights of Columbus? We cater their St. Patrick's Day dinner every year, re-member? And then there's Infant Jesus Church's CCD's annual meat-ball hero fund-raiser. We make the sandwiches. Or at least we *used* to. I wouldn't be a bit surprised if they gave their business to Rube Stein-man down the street. He may be Jewish but at least he's never tried to take out a priest."

Marlene had no intention of leaving Larry unscathed in this ha-rangue. She grabbed a white paper napkin for the tears she was about to manufacture for effect.

"You two have humiliated us," she began. "All of our friends know, mostly because of that big mouth Sissy Lambert. She called just before

Denise and I came up here. You know how she loves to lord things over. She's always been jealous of me marrying an orthodontist. Well, she called to say her husband—that loser Warren—just saw a photo in *Newsday* showing you being hauled out of our house by the cops." She paused. "I still can't understand how the reporters got there so quick."

"They listen to the police scanner," Denise offered. "I saw it on one of those cop shows."

"Well, I guess it doesn't matter how they found out, the thing is they did—and now all our friends know. I'll bet that by the time we get back to the Island our social life will be dead." She dabbed at imaginary tears. "Can you blame them? I've got a husband who's a priest killer. Who wants to have people like that over for coffee?"

"How could you have done this to me?" Marlene smacked Larry on the back of the head.

"Ouch!"

The restaurant was dead quiet. Everybody was riveted on this real-life soap opera. Harry had come out from the kitchen, where he had been peeling potatoes. Lori stood next to Wendy and the other waitresses behind the counter. They were sipping coffee and passing around a plate of apricot scones hot from the oven.

Denise threw a comforting arm around Marlene's shoulders. "There, there, don't cry. Tell you what we're going to do. I've got it all worked out."

"What?" Marlene looked at her expectantly.

"We're going to move down to Marco Island now instead of waiting until next year. We'll put our homes up for sale as soon as we get back."

"Maybe that's best," Marlene sighed.

"Sure it is. No one knows us in Florida, or the two goons we're married to." She glared at Ernie. He slid down deeper into his chair.

"You're absolutely right. It's a chance to start over again," Marlene said with great drama.

The two men shifted uncomfortably. This didn't seem like an appropriate time to enlighten the wives about the retirement funds they had lost to Clyde Hessler.

Marlene pointed a three-inch fake nail lacquered in Morning Glory

Red at Larry. "As soon as we get home, I want the hundred thousand from our retirement fund for a down payment. Denise and I have already decided on this new development on Tiger Tail Beach. The realtor said there are only four homes left, so we'd better hurry if we don't want to miss out. And we don't intend to. Do I make myself perfectly clear?"

"Yeah, yeah," Larry said. "I hear you."

The sudden thought of accessorizing her new home, and the pleasure she would derive from spending all that money, helped to derail Denise's anger.

"Ernie, you should see the brochures. Real imitation Italian marble entryway floors, and I know just the perfect vase that would look great by the front door. Did I tell you that the kitchen has a Jenn-Air stove with barbecue attachment . . ."

Ernie remained quiet, although normally he would have burst out laughing. The only thing Denise ever made foodwise was reservations. Even at the deli, he did all the cooking.

". . . And there's even a screened-in swimming pool outside the family room. We can buy some wicker furniture for there. What do you think?"

Ernie put his head in his hands. "Whatever."

Marlene leaned over the table, her 42DD breasts falling forward like cannon balls. She pointed her finger just inches from Larry's nose. "No more stalling, do you hear? I want this house NOW. Besides, it's the least you can do after what you've put me through."

"Yeah, it's the least you can do." Denise repeated, facing Ernie.

Both men looked away.

"Come on, Denise. Let's find the bathroom and powder our noses." The two women tottered toward the back of the restaurant, their sharp stiletto heals clicking on the linoleum, their legs tightly encased in spandex like sausage links.

"Now what?" Ernie asked Larry.

"I don't know," Larry said, rubbing his eyes with the palms of his hands. He felt like crap. "Maybe we should tell them about the money on the way home. You know, when they're traveling about ninety on the expressway. Let them throw us out while the car is moving. That way, at least, our deaths will be quick and painless."

Ernie looked out the window and took a sip of coffee. It was ice cold. The waitress hadn't been around in a while to refill it. Probably afraid of the wives. Smart.

Ernie was digging in his pants for a tip when he spied a white Chevy Cavalier pulling up in front of Stone's Hardware across the street. He watched as a man got out dressed in jeans and a gray sweat-shirt with the hood pulled up. He looked like one of those thugs back home who fashioned careers out of holding up 7-Elevens. Suddenly, something about the man's swagger caught his attention.

"Larry, look at that."

"Look at what?"

"That guy. There's something about the way he walks. Clyde Hessler walked like that, remember? We used to joke about it. You said he looked like he needed a realignment."

Larry inched closer to the window. "It could be. But, nah, why would he come back here? He'd be an idiot. You heard the sheriff. Everyone's looking for him. Clyde Hessler is probably on vacation in the Cayman Islands right about now, sipping a margarita by the pool courtesy of our money."

"Look! Look! I'm telling you it's him!" Ernie punched Larry in the arm.

"Ouch!"

"Look, the guy with the shovel coming out of the hardware store. See? Watch the way he walks."

"Holy crap! I think you're right," Larry jumped to his feet, nearly knocking over the table. Coffee and milk spilled out of the cups and creamer. "What should we do?"

Ernie was already headed toward the door. "We follow him, that's what we do, and we make him give us back our money or we feed him to the wives."

When Nellie entered St. Cecilia's, she was disappointed to discover that she wasn't alone. She had hoped to pray in silence. Two women with heavy New York accents were speaking with Sister Claire as she tried to change the altar linen. Nellie had less than thirty minutes before she was due back in class. Her students were now in the art room being taught how to make papier-mâché pumpkins. She hoped these women wouldn't be long.

"When we get home, we're going to tell our friends all about your order and about your direct link to God," said Marlene. "Maybe they can rent you, too."

"Rent us?" Sister Claire asked.

Denise chimed in. "Marlene and I were talking it over and we decided we want to keep you and the other nuns on retainer."

Sister Claire noticed Nellie enter the sanctuary and motioned the two women outside.

"This really isn't the place to discuss this. Why don't you come over to the retirement home? I'm certain that the other sisters would like to hear how well their prayers have been received."

Sister Claire herded the women down the center aisle. Nellie mouthed "Thank you" as she passed.

Nellie genuflected by the pew, facing the tabernacle. It held the hosts, or Communion wafers, that had been consecrated, lifted up to the Lord during Mass. It was at that moment, Catholics believed, they were transformed into the physical body of the Lord Jesus Christ.

As Nellie knelt in the pew, she pulled the rosary beads out of her sweater pocket. She made the sign of the cross, and, gazing up at the statue of the Blessed Virgin Mary, asked for her intercession.

Dear Mother of God, I need your prayers.

You once interceded on behalf of the bridegroom in Cana, and Jesus suspended natural law to turn water into wine. I humbly ask you to intercede once again on my behalf.

My new agent, Jonathan Seymour, is meeting with Panda Publishers this morning about my book, The Christmas Tree Who Wished for a Star. *If they decide to take it today, there's still time* to get the bank to cancel the foreclosure. I spoke with Mr. Hennings yesterday. He said I have until twelve o'clock this afternoon before they finalize the papers. He's willing to stop the proceedings if I can prove I have a book contract.

I know that to the practical, rationalist mind, my prayers don't stand a chance. Even Jonathan says that the wheels of publishing grind slowly and that it might take months before I get a formal offer. But I need it now to stop the bank.

I believe in your son, Jesus. I trust Him. He has never let me down. She smiled. He even gave me a boyfriend after all of these years. Harry has been such a darling since my mother died. I don't know what I would have done without him. I just pray that he can find it in his heart to forgive my deception.

The Bible says that God is able to do exceedingly, abundantly more than we can ever think or imagine, and, because of that, I know that there is no miracle too big for God if it is in His plan to answer a request. Ah, therein's the rub, right? How do I know if it's God plans to answer my request? Father James seems to think that saving my family's home comes under His provisions. I hope so. But, to be honest, I really don't know.

Heavenly Mother, please pray with me that I will be given the grace, and the peace, to know that all things work together for the good for those who are called according to His purpose.

Then Nellie looked up at the crucifix. Into your hands, dear Jesus, I commend my needs and trust all into your care.

Nellie sat quietly for several minutes, almost hating the fact that she must soon leave. Finally, she made the sign of the cross, put the rosary in her purse, then slid out of the pew. Her footsteps echoed off the marble floor as she headed toward the back of the church.

Halfway down the aisle, her cell phone rang. How strange, she thought as she reached inside her purse. She had tried to make a call earlier and couldn't get it to work. She assumed that there was something wrong with the battery.

"Hello," she whispered, now rushing toward the back. Cell phones in church were one of her pet peeves and here she was an offender. She paused at the door, relieved that there was no one else in the sanctuary.

"Nellie? It's Jonathan."

"Is your meeting over already?" she asked. According to her watch, he had spent less than thirty minutes with the publisher. This couldn't be good.

"No, in fact, I'm still in the meeting, with Doug Tracy, the senior editor. He was so excited about your book that he wanted me to call you right away. He loves it, Nellie, and wants to publish it!"

"He does?"

"There's more."

"More?"

"Normally it takes eighteen months to three years to publish a book. But the people here at Panda are so excited about *The Christmas Tree Who Wished for a Star* that they want to publish it immediately. They are convinced that it's going to be the next Christmas classic!"

She needed to sit down again.

"I hope you don't mind, but I told Doug about your problem with the bank and he's going to call to assure them that you'll be able to meet your obligation."

"I will?" Now she really did have to sit down.

"Yes, you will," Jonathan said, laughing. "Panda Publishing wants to sign you up for four more books and is offering a six-figure advance! Isn't that wonderful? Nellie? Nellie, are you still there?"

Nellie stumbled out of the church and across the town green in a daze. God had done it. She didn't know how, but He had managed to overturn the policies of one of the world's largest children's publishing houses to fit her needs. Even Jonathan, an agent for over fifteen years, was flabbergasted.

"I've never seen anything like it," he kept saying.

And they were going to give her, a mere nobody, a six-figure advance! It was unbelievable. Not only would it save her home, now she could realize her lifelong philanthropic dream. There were so many causes she always wanted to support—the Dorsetville Library, Meals-on-Wheels, the Humane Society, soup kitchens—and now she could.

"Nellie! Nellie, wait up!" Harry called, racing across the green. "I've been trying to get you all morning but your cell isn't working."

"Oh, Harry, I have the most wonderful news!" She ran to meet him. They both started talking at once.

"You first," he said, laughing.

"No, you go ahead," she insisted.

Harry scooped her into his arms. "First, I want to say that I've missed this." He rested his chin on the top of her head, taking in the scent of her lavender shampoo. "I came to tell you something I should have told you a long time ago." He held her at arm's length and looked deep into her eyes. "Nellie Anderson, I love you. I've been a fool to wait so long to tell you."

"Oh, Harry . . ."

He reached into the pocket of his flannel work shirt and pulled out his mother's antique engagement ring. Taking her hand into his, he slipped the ring on her finger and knelt on the grass.

"Nellie, I don't know how I've lived all of these years without you, but, now that I've found you, I don't ever want to be without you again. Will you marry me?"

"Marry you? Oh, Harry . . ." Her head was spinning.

"I won't take no for an answer," he said. "I don't care what this other guy thinks he can offer you . . ."

"Other guy???"

"The one that you've been dating on the side."

"Harry, there isn't . . ."

"It doesn't matter. You don't have to deny it. I've thought it over and I have decided to fight for you. I won't give you up."

Nellie smiled down at his face. She loved him so dearly she wondered if she might burst with happiness.

"Harry, there isn't anyone else. There never has been."

"There isn't? Then why do you keep breaking our dates, or saying that you're too busy? And then the other night, I saw you come home after eleven."

"It's a long story. In fact, maybe you should wait until we can find Father James. He can verify what I've really been up to."

"I saw him a few minutes ago at the rectory," Harry said, struggling to get up without falling on his face: his knees weren't what they used to be. "Let's go right now. I'm through with waiting."

"I can't. I have to get back to class."

"Isn't the student teacher there?"

"Yes."

"Do you have your cell phone? Give her a call. Tell her you're going to be a few minutes late."

It would be fun to see the look on Father James's face when she told him about the book deal. And he could also help alleviate Harry's fears.

"All right," she said, feeling like a schoolgirl skipping class. She pulled out her phone and tried to use it. The strand of rosary beads fell, unnoticed, onto the grass. "Strange, it was working a few minutes ago."

"Here, let me have a look." Harry took it in his large hands. He switched it on and off a few times. Tried to punch in a number and make a call. Nothing. He banged it on the palm of his hand and gave it a good shake. It was dead. Finally, he flipped it over and scrutinized the display.

"Well, here's the problem, Nellie," he said. "You forgot to recharge the battery."

Chapter 18

"Well, we'd better be getting you back, Father Keene," Sam said. "It's eleven o'clock. You have a doctor's appointment at twelve, and I have meals to deliver."

"I'm ready to go," Ben said, taking one last look around the barn to make certain that he'd packed up all his equipment. The shoot had gone well. Mother cat and her kittens had cooperated nicely. Ben hoped that it would bring in several adoption offers.

"I've just begun a tale. The telling won't take but a few minutes," Father Keene said, perched on an old milking stool in the shadows of a rear stall.

"We really should be going back," Timothy reminded him. "Mother Superior will be worried. We promised to get you back a half hour ago."

"Did I ever tell you boys about the story of the O'Shannistys' barn in County Cork?" Father Keene continued as though he hadn't heard a word. "It was haunted, you know."

"You can tell us the story in the car," Sam offered.

"The O'Shannistys owned a farm, just like this one. Lovely place, it was. They had a peck of children, twelve in all. Good Catholics. But one day a relative came to visit and found that the entire family had gone. Just disappeared."

"What happened to them?" Ben asked, walking over to where Father Keene was seated.

"No one knows." The priest motioned for the other two to join them.

Sam and Timothy looked at each other and shrugged. What the heck. So, they'd be a little late. They dragged a pair of wooden crates over the dirt floor, stirring up some dust, then positioned themselves along the wall of the stall.

"Now, as strange as this might seem, something even more strange was about to happen." Father Keene paused for effect. He was a masterful storyteller. "Things really got interesting a few years later when a young couple bought the place and began to hear strange noises at night coming from the barn."

"For Pete's sake, Hill, open the window. That dog is stinking up my van!"

George wasn't sure what was worse: the smell coming from the dog in the back or the odor of rancid garbage coming from the plastic bag at the deputy's feet. Hill said he was collecting trash as part of some anticrime program.

Hill rolled down the window and stuck out his arm. "I appreciate you giving me a ride to the Hawkins place."

"I was heading out there anyway," he said, switching on the back defroster. The dog had fogged up the rear window. "Henderson sisters' sink is backed up again. It's those darn wildflowers. I keep telling them to wash them outside or in a bucket. Do they listen? No."

But George wasn't really upset; in fact, he had planned his day around this visit, knowing that if he finished up around noon the sisters would offer him lunch. He, however, would prudently refuse any cake.

Something rattled in the back of the van. "Hey, tell that dog to sit down. I just picked up that toilet for the Dwyerses' downstairs bathroom. If he knocks it over, I'm out some serious dough."

"Harley, sit," Hill called out. Harley continued to wander.

George reached for a cigar behind the visor and then punched in the cigarette lighter. "The sheriff have any new leads on the church fire?"

"It's still under investigation. But we're pretty sure we know who the perpetrator is," Hill said confidently though he knew even less than George.

"That bag lady, right?" George lit his cigar; gray smoke sucked through the van and out the open back window. Harley sneezed.

"I'm not at liberty to say," Hill replied.

"What about the explosion? Does the sheriff have a lead on that?"

"I'm not at liberty to say."

George chomped down on his cigar and glared at Hill. "Well, what in blazes *are* you at liberty to say?"

"Now, George, you don't want me giving away departmental secrets, do you?"

"Since when is anything a secret in Dorsetville? Besides, if you don't tell me, someone else will."

"Hey, look at that."

"What?"

"The cans on the side of the road. Somebody dumped a whole load of beer and soda cans." Hill grabbed the plastic bag. "Pull over, George. I'll walk the rest of the way. I want to pick them up."

"You sure? The Hawkins place is still about a quarter of a mile up the road."

"It's a nice day. I don't mind walking."

"It's your feet." George pulled off. "What are you going to do with those cans, anyway?" They were his cans.

Hill slid out of the van and closed the door. "I'm not at liberty to say."

Clyde Hessler wasn't taking any chances. He figured he had maybe an hour to trek down to the barn, dig up the cash and make his getaway before the old woman came back. Some lady with a golden retriever had come earlier to pick up old Mrs. Yokohama. Maybe his luck was changing.

He parked his Cavalier safely out of sight behind a clump of mountain laurel, then took the path that wove in and out of the woods at the back of the Hawkins place. Clyde was growing nervous. Minutes ago, he'd heard a report over his police radio that state troopers were out looking for him. That Jersey bookie must have turned him in, like he threatened to. Said if Clyde tried to squeeze him for the dough he owed him, he'd make an anonymous call to the police. Apparently, the guy was as good as his word. The Feds were also on his tail, although he wasn't certain what for. Maybe it was that check-cashing scam.

The dirt path to the barn was overgrown from lack of use. Button-like clusters of yellow-green mugwort, prickly purple heads of burdock and lance-leaved goldenrod made the going slow. The Hawkins place hadn't been farmed in nearly fourteen years, ever since the old grandfather had died. A hundred acres of fields that once had supplied most of the cows in the county with hay had quickly been reclaimed by Mother Nature. Farther on, briars, jute, walls of blackberry bushes made the walk even slower going. He grew anxious. The sooner he was out of here, the better.

It hadn't helped that he had lost nearly an hour this morning. The shovel that he kept in the back of his car was missing. Probably left by the side of the road when he took it out to fix a flat. Luckily, most of Main Street was deserted and the town's idiot deputy was busy talking someone's ear off. Clyde was able to pull up right in front of the hardware store and run in. He wore a pair of dark glasses and a sweatshirt with the hood tied tightly around his face so no one would recognize him. He had grabbed a shovel off the back wall, dropped a fifty on the counter and hightailed it out of there without waiting for change.

The trek to the barn would have gone much quicker if his balance hadn't gone haywire again. He'd had the problem since he was a kid. No one could seem to fix it. Something to do with his inner ear deteriorating, which, in turn, released small particles into the ear canal that short-circuited the electrical impulses that controlled equilibrium. Dramamine helped with the nausea, but nothing could alleviate the maddening dizziness when these attacks struck. It felt as though he were walking on the deck of a ship on a storm-tossed sea.

Driving was the worst during these episodes. The lines on the road got wavy, and keeping the car on its proper side became quite a challenge. Twice in the past he had been stopped by cops and given a

Breathalyzer test. This was the reason he had elected to take his time on the way back from town, keeping his full attention on the road. That's why he didn't noticed the Cadillac Seville tailing him.

Finally, he cleared the last portion of brush. The barn was just up ahead. He tried to pick up speed but caught his foot in a tangle of wild grapes, falling headfirst into a patch of wood nettles. The shovel flew up in the air, catching the corner of a rock wall with a loud clang. Clyde swore under his breath and yanked his arm out of the bush, yelping in pain as the nettles' stinging hairs raked across the bare flesh on his arm.

He scrambled to his feet, the worst thing he could have done. The sudden movement increased the vertigo. Stay calm, stay calm, he told himself. Just be still. It will pass. He anchored his vision to a nearby elm tree. Slowly, things came back into focus.

While he searched for his shovel hidden somewhere in the thick brush, he cheered himself by thinking Bahamas, white sunny beaches, sexy young chicks. Just a few minutes more and he'd be on his way to paradise.

Twigs snapped behind him. He pulled out the Beretta tucked in his waistband and aimed in that direction. He waited, scanning the landscape, watching for something to move, but everything was still. He exhaled and slowly lowered the gun. Probably just a deer. They aren't just nocturnal anymore. He had nearly clipped one that morning turning off the interstate.

He found the shovel and resumed his walk, carefully sidestepping the horse plops. The barn was now less than a couple of hundred yards away. He was almost home free. In just a little while he would be watching Dorsetville fade from his rear view mirror.

If only he hadn't buried the money here he could have avoided all of this. But at the moment, he hadn't many choices.

Clyde had planned his last day in Dorsetville for nearly three weeks. He had gotten up at eight o'clock, showered, towel-dried his hair, shaved and by nine o'clock was standing in front of the Webster's Bank with a withdrawal slip in hand cosigned by his partner, Barry Hornibrook, for seventy-five thousand dollars. (With a little expert tampering, Clyde had added another zero, making it seven hundred and fifty thousand.)

Clyde took his time at the bank. Talked to all the tellers and the girl behind the front desk. Had to pay off the subcontractors, he said. Yeah, it was a lot of money, but, heck, the Old Mill Hotel and Conference Center was going to be a first-rate facility. You get what you pay for, right? Everyone smiled and said they couldn't wait for the place to open.

Clyde had told Barry he was taking the rest of the week off. He was moving to a smaller house over in Woodstock. That way, Barry wouldn't question his absence, putting a few extra days between Clyde and detection.

He drove back to the farm with the construction money stuffed in a large envelope in the front pocket of his sports jacket. He had been so psyched about withdrawing the seven hundred fifty thousand that he had completely forgotten about the two hundred fifty thousand that was buried inside the barn, the money he milked from those Long Island jokers.

Clyde had opened the strongbox he had just dug out of the dirt floor when he heard a car pull into the driveway. He raced to a window. It was his former landlord, Bob Hawkins, in his Ford Taurus. A Volkswagen camper was following close behind.

Clyde's car was parked in the driveway, so Hawkins knew he was there. He heard people getting out of their cars, snippets of conversation. Clyde had only minutes before they would make their way into the barn. What could he do with all these bundles of money? Before he had time to think it through, he crammed them in the box along with the rest of the money and covered it with dirt. He had just moved a bale of hay over the spot when the first of a dozen men and women clad in traditional Japanese robes spilled into the barn. Several were carrying boxes of restaurant supplies.

Hawkins was initially surprised that Clyde was still hanging around. (He had returned the house key the night before.) So Clyde was forced to turn on the charm, quickly disarm any suspicions.

He told Hawkins that he wanted to take one last look around, just for nostalgia's sake. He'd really grown attached to the place even though, as previously agreed, it was much too big for just one bachelor.

Finally, there was no reason for him to linger. Clyde said his good-byes and drove back down the driveway. Now what was he going to do? Sneak back some night while they were sleeping and dig up the box? Maybe, but wouldn't it be better to let the new tenants settle in first? Establish some kind of routine. That way he could return without getting caught.

Meanwhile, he figured he'd take a drive to Jersey. A bookie there owed him some money.

Clyde came to a marshy spot right behind the barn that was overgrown with tall swamp grass. Parting the grass, he took a look around. Darn! A gold-colored Plymouth Duster was parked in the driveway. It must have pulled in while he was making his way down the back field. No one was around outside. That probably meant whoever owned the car was in the barn.

Clyde reached for his gun and released the safety. Time was running out. If he waited much longer, the law was sure to nail him. It was now or never.

"Shush . . . what's that?" Timothy asked. It sounded like it came from the woods out back.

"I didn't hear anything," Sam said.

"Me neither," Ben said.

Timothy made his way over to a window. "Dear Blessed Mother of God . . ."

"What is it?" Ben asked.

Timothy raced back to the stall and in a harsh whisper said, "Get down and hide. There's a man outside and he has a gun."

The men had moved deeper into the shadows to watch through the wide spaces between the boards partitioning off the back stall as Clyde entered the barn. He held a gun in one hand and a shovel in the other.

Clyde moved slowly, letting his eyes adjust to the dark interior as he inched forward, methodically scanning for the owner of the car parked outside.

"Anybody in here?" he called.

He waited. Seemed like whoever owned the car wasn't in here. Probably just parked it and took a walk somewhere. People around here were always taking walks, which mystified Clyde. Why walk when you could drive?

The spot where he had buried the cash was slightly to the right, over by some milking machines. He tucked the gun back in his waistband and walked in that general direction. He stopped by a bale of hay, where the mother cat lay sleeping.

"You're going to have to move it," Clyde said, and heaved it over. The cat landed safely on her feet, arched her back and hissed.

"Get out of here, you mangy beast."

From the back stall, the others watched quietly. Timothy, who was the farthest away, had to stretch to see more clearly. The movement brought the all-too-familiar tightening of calf muscles. He eased back a little. He didn't need a cramp now.

Although bending accelerated feelings of dizziness, Clyde worked on, plunging the shovel deep into the earth floor. Spadesful of dirt flew over his shoulder, one right after the other, until the air was filled with tiny particles of grit backlit by sunlight streaming in through the window, making a hazy brown mist.

Finally, the top of a strongbox was exposed. Clyde tossed the shovel aside and fell to his knees, digging around the box with both hands until it was free. He stood, placing the strongbox on the bale, as the cat circled him warily, intrigued by the newly dug soil.

Clyde tore open the box, relieved that the money was still there. Seventy-five bundles of ten thousand each. The Long Island money, rolled up with a wide rubber band around it, was stuffed in on the side.

"I think some of that belongs to us," said a voice just inside the doorway.

Clyde looked up slowly as his hand reached for his revolver. "Who are you?"

Ernie and Larry stepped out from the shadows.

"Well, well, well . . . if it ain't the guys from Long Island," Clyde said casually, his eyes taking in the doorway behind them. They appeared to be alone.

"So, what brings you two up to this neck of the woods?"

"Like you don't know," Larry said hotly. "We want our money back and we want it back now."

"Oh, really?" Clyde pulled out the gun. Both men stepped back.

"Oh, geez . . ." Ernie moaned. "I told you to let the cops handle this, but *no,* you had to act like John Wayne." Why did he listen to Larry?

Clyde waved the pistol. "Put your hands up and move over there."

The men did as they were told.

"How did you two find me?"

"We saw you leave the hardware store," Ernie offered, "and we just followed you here."

"Anyone else outside?"

"We're alo—"

Larry elbowed him hard in the ribs, then, with as much bravado as he could muster, considering the circumstances, said, "Our wives know we were headed here. In fact, we told them that if we weren't back in thirty minutes they were to call the cops." For effect, he looked at his Rolex. "They're probably making that call right about now."

"Really?"

"Yep, I'd say the cops should be out this way shortly."

"Well, in that case, I'd better make a fast getaway. Oh, there is one more thing." He leveled the gun at Larry's face. "I don't want to leave any witnesses behind."

"Please . . . please . . . no . . . wait a minute." Larry whimpered.

"Look, we were wrong. You can keep the money. All of it. Keep it as our gift, right, Ernie?"

"Right," Ernie said. "And as far as being able to identify you, we've already forgotten what you look like."

"You guys are such idiots that it seems a shame to waste a perfectly good bullet on either of you." He drew back the hammer. "Say good-bye, fellows."

Larry fainted.

"Larry! Larry get up!" Ernie shouted. He kicked him hard. "Wake up, you hear me? I'm not dying alone."

In the back stall, Timothy began to feel the first inklings of a cramp. *Please, dear Mother of God,* he prayed, *don't let it seize up.* He tried to slowly move his leg, carefully stretching, elongating the calf muscle in hope of releasing the spasm. But just when he thought he had caught it in time, the muscle clamped down like a vise. The pain coursed though his leg like an electrical charge. He screamed, then shot up and began to hop around.

Clyde swung around. The movement caused the room to start spinning. He could make out a figure of a man in the stall . . . at least, he thought it was a man. Clyde brought up the Beretta, tried to take aim and pulled the trigger. The bullet lodged in a beam overhead.

The noise made Ernie jump. The gunshot also frightened the cat, who now tried to dart across the floor in search of refuge. Ernie landed on her tail as she flew by. The startled feline spun around, savagely digging her front claws deep into Ernie's leg. He screamed out in shock and pain as his hands flew up in surprise. The sudden movement knocked the gun out of Clyde's hand. It landed with a thump in the dusty mistiness several yards away.

While Clyde was busy with Ernie, Ben and Sam tackled Timothy.

"We really do have to do something about your potassium levels," Sam said, sitting on top of Timothy to keep him out of harm's way.

"I've had enough of this circus," Clyde yelled and lunged for his gun just as something large and hairy flung itself through the open window. It hit him with the speed of a torpedo, ramming him against the shoulder, smashing him flat against the ground like a bug on a windshield.

Clyde lay on his back with his face just inches away from a set of lethal white fangs. They were attached to the meanest-looking dog he had ever seen.

"Get him off me," he screamed, grabbing hold of the dog's fur and trying to yank him away. It was the wrong move. The dog grabbed his arm and dug in. Clyde could feel the bones in his arm begin to crack.

"Stop, in the name of the law!" Deputy Hill shouted as he charged through the barn door, gun drawn.

"Get this beast off of me," Clyde yelled.

"Deputy Hill," Sam called, coming forward. "Are we glad to see you!"

"You men all right?" Hill asked, completely ignoring Clyde still struggling beneath a hundred pounds of German shepherd.

"Yeah, just a little shaken up," Sam said. "It's a good thing you got here when you did. This man was going to shoot us."

"That's Clyde Hessler," Ernie broke in, slowly recovering from his near-death experience. "He's the one who stole Barry Hornibrook's construction money and our two hundred and fifty thousand dollars. The money's over there."

Hill glanced down at Clyde still pinned under Harley. "So you're Clyde Hessler? A lot of folks are looking for you."

"Yeah, well now you've found me," Clyde spat angrily. "You want to get this dog off of me before he breaks my arm?"

Larry moaned and blinked open an eye. "Am I dead?"

"I only wish," Ernie said, kicking straw in his face.

"Okay, Harley, let him go," Hill said.

The dog released Clyde's arm but continued to stand guard, growling whenever he tried to move.

Hill reached around for his handcuffs as the elderly foursome came forward for a closer look. They had never seen a real criminal up close before. Timothy was still rubbing his leg.

"Wait until the sheriff sees that I nailed this guy," Hill said. "It's going to really make his day. Might even earn me a raise."

"I'm happy for you," Clyde said as Hill cuffed him.

Hill pulled Clyde to his feet. "Sam, can we use your car to transport the prisoner?"

"Sure, Deputy Hill. As long as you don't mind if I stop off by the senior center first. I need to explain to Mrs. Hopkins why I'm late picking up the noon meals."

"I can't wait to see her face as you explain," Timothy said.

Ben and Father Keene laughed.

Ernie helped Larry to his feet while Hill gathered up the metal box and the cash.

"I suppose there's no way we can take the money that belongs to us," Ernie asked.

"I'm afraid not. This is state's evidence now."

"I guess that means we still have to tell our wives about the money," Larry said, picking the straw out of his hair.

"I guess so."

"Maybe it would have been better if Hessler had just shot us," Ernie lamented.

Hill stepped outside with Clyde in tow.

"If I remember correctly, there's a fifty-thousand-dollar bounty on your head," he said, leading the prisoner toward Sam's car. "Like I was telling the sheriff earlier this morning, there's a lot of money to be made in garbage collection."

Chapter 19

Sheriff Bromley stared at Hill's police report detailing the capture of Clyde Hessler and scratched his head. Hill had actually managed to capture a wanted criminal and, in the process, saved several men from possibly being killed. Could this be the same deputy who only yesterday had helped a woman at Grand Union—a known shoplifter—carry her groceries to her car and never thought to question the cans that kept falling out of her coat lining? If the store manager hadn't raced after them and demanded Hill do a search, the woman would have gotten away with over forty dollars' worth of stolen goods. Go figure.

"Sheriff? Father James is here," Betty's voice came over the intercom.

"Tell him to come on in." Bromley threw the report to one side. Maybe he should frame it and hang it on the wall. That way when someone called complaining about another one of Hill's screwups, he'd have a reason to hope.

Father James peeked in his head. "You got a minute, Al?"

"Sure, Jim. Come on in."

Father James stepped aside as the Galligan twins spilled into the room then rocketed into two empty chairs. Bromley looked to him for an explanation.

"The twins have a confession to make," Father James offered, closing the door.

"A confession, huh?" The sheriff leaned back heavily in his chair, the springs groaning under his weight. "Isn't that more in *your* line of work?"

The priest leaned against the door. "I'm afraid that this confession is one *you* need to hear."

"Oh? What have you two done this time?"

The sheriff knew all about their recent magazine subscription prank. Rochelle Phillips, over at the Congregational church, had finally put two and two together, and none too soon. Members on her church board had received an anonymous tip that Reverend Curtis was receiving *Hustler* in the mail.

"You tell him." Dexter elbowed Rodney in the ribs.

"No, you tell him." Rodney poked Dexter in the arm.

"Now, cut that out," the sheriff barked. He raised an eyebrow and glared at Dexter. "You first."

The boy shifted uncomfortably in his chair. "We sort of . . . well . . . we kind of . . . started the fire."

"What fire?"

"The one in the church."

The sheriff looked over at Father James. The priest nodded soberly.

"It was you two?!!"

"We didn't mean it," Rodney whined.

"Why, you little . . ."

"It was an accident," Father James broke in, hoping to dampen the sheriff's infamous temper before it raged out of control.

"Yeah, an accident," Dexter repeated.

"Did you know that I arrested the bag lady because we thought she did it?" Bromley asked.

The boys studied the floor.

"So, you *did* know and yet neither of you came forward with the truth! Do you have any idea how much suffering you've caused this poor, innocent woman?"

"We didn't mean to start the fire," they cried.

"I don't care whether you meant it or not. I'm assuming that you *did* know it was wrong to let someone else take the blame for something you did?"

The twins were silent.

"Well, did you?!!" Bromley yelled.

They nodded their heads yes.

"You know what I should do? I should haul your little behinds down to Bridgeport, to the county juvenile detention center, and let them put you away."

"Please, Sheriff Bromley, we promise never to do anything like this ever again. Cross my heart," Dexter pleaded. He wasn't quite certain what a detention center was, exactly, but it sounded ominous.

"We'll do chores around town to make up for it," Rodney bargained. "Like Matthew Metcalf had to do after that mess he got into last year with the computers."

"Community service?" the sheriff asked. "Yes, you will. In fact, after this mess, you're probably be doing community service until you're both old men."

He pulled out a desk drawer and began to search for a blank police report. It was underneath a pile of rap sheets on Clyde Hessler. "Let's start from the beginning. Tell me *exactly* what happened the night of the fire."

"You tell him," Rodney said. "It was all your fault anyway."

"It was not!"

"Yes, it was. I told you not to light those candles."

"Stop it or I'll drive you straight to Bridgeport myself," the sheriff barked. The boys stopped. "You," he pointed at Rodney, "begin. And you," he pointed at Dexter, "shut up until he's finished."

"It all started because my dumb brother put a snake in Mother Superior's desk . . ." Rodney began.

Within thirty minutes, the boys had finished.

"All right, then. I guess that does it for now." Bromley stood up and stretched. "I'll call Reverend Curtis and tell him we found out who burned down his church. You boys had better tell your parents to expect a call."

"Thanks, Sheriff," Father James said, rising to go. "Does this mean that Molly is free?"

"As soon as I can get Betty to open her cell."

"Then I think I'll hang around and see if she needs a lift. Besides, I also feel the boys should give her a personal apology. Right, boys?"

"Yes, Father James."

Bromley walked out into the hallway and bellowed, "Betty, tell Molly to collect her things. She's free to go."

"She is?" Betty yelled back. Why in heaven's name had this office installed an intercom?

"Why am I constantly repeating myself around here?" Bromley hollered. The glass panel in his office door rattled. "I said she was free, so release her."

"I'm going."

Keys jangled, followed by the sound of shoes pounding heavily down the stairs.

Bromley stepped back into the room. Rodney's and Dexter's heads were bent together and they seemed to be in the midst of a heated debate.

"We've *got* to tell him or the curse won't go away," Rodney insisted.

"We told him about the fire," Dexter insisted. "That should be good enough."

"Tell me what?" the sheriff asked suspiciously.

"That there's . . . er . . . one more thing we have to confess," Rodney answered.

"Oh, geez . . ." the sheriff moaned.

"Well, it's kinda like this," Rodney began, hesitantly. "We . . . sort of . . . *accidentally* . . . blew up Mr. Hornibrook's boat."

Sam stood on the porch of the Sister Regina Francis Retirement Home, uttering a quick prayer of thanksgiving that he and his friends were safe. Father Keene was inside regaling the nuns and residents with a lively account of their ordeal at the hands of a wanted criminal. And Ben and Timothy were at the television station working on a news special with the station manager. The sheriff had allowed Ben to film Clyde Hessler being led to the police cruiser in handcuffs. He was to be transported to the state facility in Cheshire. The segment would certainly add some spice to this evening's *About Town* program. Ben glowed when Carl Pipson, the station manager, said it was the best piece of footage he's seen since leaving *Channel 8 News*.

Sam walked down the flagstone pathway and through the wrought-iron gate. A soft breeze rustled through the trees, releasing a shower of autumn leaves that blanketed the ground in a patchwork design. They crunched underneath Sam's rubber-soled shoes.

He crossed the street with a new bounce to his step, heading toward the town green. It was wonderful to be alive and, taking in the beauty of his fair town, he felt as rich as Solomon.

Where else could a man walk among such grandeur, all free for the taking? All of New England was now canopied with bejeweled trees, each one, it seemed, more magnificent than the next. No museum held as rich a cache of treasures as an autumn countryside painted by God's own hand.

The invigorating current of the clean country air, the smell of wet leaves and chimney smoke, spoke to him of the richness of life. Amazing how these ordinary things took on deeper meaning when one was confronted with one's own mortality. He could have been killed today. They all could have been killed.

A horn beeped twice just as he stepped up on the curb. It was Father James heading toward the rectory with Molly seated beside him. Sam waved. News had already circulated around town that the twins had confessed to starting the church fire. Sam sure would have liked to be a fly on the wall when Mike Galligan got home from work tonight.

"Who parked here?" George Benson shouted, his voice ripping across the town green like a sonic boom. He stood in front of the Congregational church, a cigar hanging out of the side of his mouth.

"I told you guys that I wanted this section kept clear. There's a new furnace being delivered today. Is this your Bronco, Pete?"

George's new assistant, Ted Holloway, climbed out of the passenger side of the van. "You want me to get his keys? I can move it for him."

"I'm not paying you to move someone else's truck. Start unloading the pipe and I'll go straighten out these guys. Hey, Pete! Get the lead out. I want that truck moved sometime today."

Ted was twenty-six years old, an eager young man, clean-shaven and mild-mannered, who helped with the youth group at his church over in Woodstock. The patrons at Kelly's Bar were taking bets on how long it would take George to corrupt him.

More shouting ensued, making Sam smile. The Congregational church's restoration was heavily under way. The church council had hired an art historian/architect who insisted that, once completed, no one would ever be able to discern between the new and the old. And, based on the excellent job that Chester Platt's construction company had done on St. Cecilia's and the retirement home, Reverend Curtis and the council had hired Chester as the contractor.

It had taken Chester's crews several weeks to haul away the debris and clear the site, but now the framing was nearly completed, looking like the skeleton of some prehistoric beast. And knowing how fast Chester's men worked, Sam was confident that it would more closely resemble a church within a few weeks.

He had just started to cross the lawn, heading toward the gazebo at the back of the green, when he spied rosary beads lying in the grass. He bent down to retrieve them.

The beads were made of glass the color of the sky on a clear summer morning, and the delicately proportioned silver crucifix felt surprising heavy in his hand. Funny, it reminded him of another rosary he once held, a long, long time ago. He slipped it in his pocket. Maybe Father James might know who owned it.

Just as he reached the gazebo, a minivan pulled up in front of the green. He got comfortably seated, then leaned back to watch Myrtle Bromley and several other women unload the van, their arms soon laden with baskets and shopping bags filled to overflowing. A small discussion ensued before they descended on the park bench, now referred to by most people in town as "Molly's Bench." Within minutes, it had been outfitted in a coordinated assortment of linens, pillows and quilts. The ladies stepped back to inspect their handiwork.

"Wait a moment," Myrtle cried, rushing back to the van, then returning with a sign that read WELCOME HOME. The women hung it on the back of the bench.

Sam watch with even more delight as Judge Peale's wife and Mrs. Norris arrived in a Chevy Suburban and lifted out a Grand Union shopping cart heavily decorated with ribbons and silk flowers. They wheeled it over alongside the bench. It was filled with a wide array of foodstuffs—boxes of crackers, small bottles of juice, individual servings of cereals and other nonperishables. Mrs. Norris had added a packet of salted soybeans and several energy bars. Then, as quickly as the women had come, they all disappeared. It was getting late. Suppers needed to be started. Wash pulled in off the clothesline.

Sam sat enjoying the magnificence of the autumn day. The way the sun slanted down the mountains, casting the valley in a golden glow; the sound of saws and hammers and men's shouts coming from the church next door, with an occasional round of raucous laughter. A sense of peace and safety stole over him, knowing that he was a part of this town and these people.

From the corner of his eye, he caught sight of Molly leaving the rectory by the side door, heading toward her park bench. Sam watched with amusement as the bag lady drew closer, her eyes shining with delight. The quilts caught her attention first. She gently ran her hands along the soft cotton fabric, her eyes closed as though in prayer. As with the rosary now in his pocket, once again he was plagued by something familiar, but the memory remained just out of reach.

He studied her face more closely, oval shaped with a nose slightly off center. Her gray hair was cut short and combed straight back. But it was her eyes that drew his attention. They were filled with a gentle sense of peace. At that moment she looked up and stared in his direction. God of Abraham! he nearly shouted as the memory jarred him to full recognition. Molly looked just like the old woman who had helped to rescue him out of Germany more than sixty years ago. In fact, she could be her twin sister.

He reached inside his pocket and pulled out the rosary beads, to run them between his fingers. Strange, they, too, were connected to that memory.

As Molly shook out the quilts and settled down for a nap, Sam traveled back to that day when he stood shivering on the stone pavement as his family readied to board a train to Buchenwald.

Sam had just turned eleven that January when the Nazis marched into their small village. Within weeks, hundreds of his family's friends and relatives had been sent to work camps, from which no letters ever came, no word to assure those left behind that one day, when the madness ceased, they would be reunited. No one dared voice what they knew in their hearts.

The few Jews who had been allowed to stay worked at jobs pivotal to the Nazis' cause or which no one else wanted to do. His father, a university professor, had been assigned to the group responsible for cleaning the city's disease-infested cisterns. All health precautions were abandoned. The men weren't even allowed to wash their hands when given their rations of stale bread. One man after another fell victim to disease—dysentery, tuberculosis, pneumonia—but this was of no concern to the Nazis. Jews were expendable, easily replaced.

Sam's father had never been a strong man. He died early on in the war, leaving a widow with three children. The family joined others in sharing what they could scavenge either from the countryside or the few merchants left in town. Then one night the soldiers burst into their small apartment and rounded up his mother, his four-year-old sister, Rachel, and his older brother, Enoch, and forced them out into the street. There had been no time to change out of their bedclothes; minutes later, they stood shivering in the icy cold of predawn darkness.

"Where do you live?" one of the soldiers taunted, leisurely rolling a cigarette, his rifle leaning against his leg.

Sam's mother, who had always been such an elegant lady, stood in her nightdress and bare feet, shivering in the snow-crusted ground as she tried to cover herself with a thin shawl. She looked up toward their apartment and pointed towards the front windows.

"We live up there," she said softly. Sam clung to her nightdress. "Your men ordered us out into the streets."

"So now you are a streetwalker," the soldier said, then turned to his comrades and whispered something. The men began to laugh. Sam's mother blushed, but kept silent. Finally, the officer walked over and blew smoke in her face.

Sam's teeth began to chatter so hard that he had to strain to hear what the soldier said next.

"As of this moment, you are now classified as a vagrant, and, since the Reich prohibits vagrants from cluttering up our streets, you and your litter of brats will be moved to a more suitable location."

Sam didn't understand the threat that underlay the soldier's words. He was far too young. But he did feel the terror those words evoked in his mother. Her body stiffened. Sam began to cry.

"Hush, hush, my beloved," she whispered. "All will be well. We are in God's charge now."

"March!" the soldier ordered, prodding them along with something sharp. Sam turned to see what had poked him in the back and came face-to-face with the barrel of a rifle. He recoiled in horror.

"Come along, Samuel," his mother urged him. "Hurry." The bedraggled family stumbled forward.

"Why do they want to send us away, Mother?" he whispered, clutching tightly to her nightdress. "What have we done?"

"Nothing," she assured him. "We are mirrors of God's light that reflect their evilness. And, like all evil men, they think if they destroy us, they will destroy God and not have to suffer hell."

"And will they, Mother?" Sam asked, grasping her hand tighter.

His mother squeezed his hand reassuringly. "You must always remember God's light will always prevail."

Their family was quickly joined by other Jews who also had been rousted out of bed. Many were naked, including an old woman whose face was filled with unimaginable shame. Sam's mother walked over and wrapped her shawl around the woman's shoulders. The woman looked up with tears of gratitude in her eyes.

The march took them to the train station by the town square, where neighbors had gathered to watch. A pall of silence covered the crowd.

"Move back," the guards ordered, rushing the crowd. "Stay behind the barriers or you will suffer their fate."

It seemed to Sam they had stood for hours, shivering on the cold stones that made up the city streets, as they waited for the train to arrive. Whispers of "Buchenwald," "death house" spread like a virus. Aside from murmurings, however, all was quiet, even though the soldiers had collected nearly a hundred Jews that morning, dozens of whom were infants and small children. It was as if the young sensed their parents' terror and were to afraid to cry.

It was nearly dawn before the faint sound of a train whistle could be heard in the distance, heading toward the city. Within a few minutes, the frightened Jews would be herded into boxcars like so many head of cattle. Many would become ill from lack of food, the endless, bone-shattering rocking of the cars, the heavy smell of perspiration. Vomit and feces would soon add to the noxious odor of fear.

The Jews moved in unison several steps toward the train at the north end of the square as though anesthetized. Most knew that to board the train meant certain death, yet they walked as if already resigned to their fate.

They found themselves near the edge of the onlookers, many of whom were neighbors. They seemed just as dazed as the Jews. What had happened to their beautiful country? the neighbors wondered. These people were their merchants, their doctors, their teachers and friends. But what could they do? To speak out would only bring a similar fate to their own families, so they remained silent—a silence that would haunt them the rest of their lives.

A hand reached out from the crowd behind Sam; a voice whispered, "Take these. Put them in your pocket." A rosary of blue beads was placed in his hand. Sam turned, but the people were packed much too close for him to see who had given it to him.

"Look, Mother," he said, "someone just gave me this and said to put it in my pocket."

"Who?" his mother asked, searching the crowd until her eyes fell on an elderly woman, her gray hair wrapped in an old shawl, her clothes patched and tattered.

The woman spoke in an urgent whisper. "Tell the boy to hold on to it. It will protect him."

His mother sensed something in the woman's eyes. "Do as she says," she told Sam.

It had taken the soldiers nearly four hours to process their prisoners. Finally, Sam and his family were next in line. His mother stood in front of an officer seated behind a beautifully appointed burled-wood desk that had been taken from the shop of a Jewish woodcarver across the street.

"Name?" he called out indifferently. He was hungry and in a hurry to finish.

"Oh, thank you, Lord Jesus!" a woman's voice exclaimed as she pushed her way forward.

"Halt!" a young officer said, pointing a rifle in her direction.

It was the woman who had given Sam the rosary.

"Please, sir, there's been a great mistake," the woman pleaded. Pointing toward Samuel, she said, "That's my grandson, Christian. He was staying at the Rosenbergs' house because I had to visit my sick sister in Berlin. I went to pick him up this morning and the neighbors told me he had been taken along with the rest of the Jews."

The officer behind the desk studied Samuel more closely.

"So you are Christian, are you?" he asked.

Samuel's mother quickly broke in. "I tried to tell the men who came to our apartment that he wasn't mine, but they wouldn't listen." His mother stood defiantly gazing at the officer, daring him to contradict her.

"Here." The old woman reached into Sam's pocket and pulled out the beads. "What Jewish child would carry this?"

The officer was tired and hungry. He didn't wish to argue. Waving his hand, he said, "Take him, old woman. And may this be a warning to you. Don't let your grandson stay at the homes of Jews. Next time he might not be so lucky."

Sam's mother looked deep into her son's eyes, silently urging him to say nothing and to go with the stranger. "Don't look back," the old woman cautioned. Although it was the hardest thing he had ever had to do, Samuel obeyed. He never saw his mother's face again.

Later, he would learn that his mother and sister were killed in the gas chambers as soon as they arrived at Buchenwald. His brother, Enoch, lived for another year, but then had contracted one of the myriad sicknesses that plagued the rat-infested barracks and had died.

Memories of this last meeting lingered as Sam got up to leave. The sun had dipped behind a cloud. The temperature began to drop. Sam studied the rosary more closely. It looked exactly like the one the old woman had given him that morning in Germany.

Sam walked down the gazebo steps and headed toward the park bench where Molly lay sleeping peacefully, her mouth open, snoring lightly. He studied her profile. Time could not dull the memory of those horrific years or the face of the woman who had risked her life to save him from certain death. Molly looked exactly like the old woman, although Sam knew that was impossible.

He took the rosary from his pocket and placed it on Molly's lap.

May God protect you and bless you, Sam prayed. Then he tiptoed away.

Chapter 20

Father James sat in the kitchen of the Sister Regina Francis Retirement Home savoring a bowl of New England clam chowder while the season's first snow drifted aimlessly outside. A small fire hissed and popped softly in the fireplace to the rear of the kitchen in concert to the rhythms of Anonymous Seven wafting in from somewhere deep within the house.

The priest bowed his head and gave a heartfelt blessing for what he was about to receive, and the fact that what had just been ladled into his bowl he was able to recognize. Mrs. Norris's health kick continued unabated, and no amount of insistence on his part or Father Dennis's could get her to revert to the meals they had grown to love. The only upside to this new health regimen was that each man had lost fifteen pounds.

"I'm sorry that Father Dennis couldn't join us," Mother Superior said.

Father James dabbed at the chowder that had dripped down the front of his shirt. "He sends his regrets, but he had another invitation."

"With the Curtises?"

"Yes, how did you know?"

"News travels quickly in Dorsetville. My sources tell me that Father Dennis is taking cooking lessons."

"Then your sources are right. We do what we have to do to survive."

"How is the chowder?"

He took another spoonful, closed his eyes and allowed the sweet, rich cream base, chockful of large chunks of clams and laced with butter and sherry, roll over his tongue.

"You may tell Sister Theresa I don't believe I will find a better-tasting chowder anywhere this side of heaven."

The nun laughed. "Perhaps I won't repeat those exact words. We wouldn't want Sister Theresa getting a swelled head."

"May I have another of those rolls?"

"Help yourself," she smiled, and for just a moment Father James glimpsed a younger girl, the girl who once had held Chester Platt's heart. She passed him the butter.

"So, how are Father Dennis's cooking lessons with Mrs. Curtis coming along?"

"He's a natural-born chef," Father James said. He tore open the roll, buttered it lavishly, then dunked it into his soup. "Last week, when Mrs. Norris went to visit her sister over in Gaylord, Father Dennis made us veal medallions, garlic potatoes and pecan pie. It rivaled anything Wolfgang Puck could have created."

"He has a great teacher. Invitations to Mrs. Curtis's dinner parties are highly coveted." Mother Superior removed the priest's empty bowl.

"More?"

"As tempting as that offer is, I had better say no. I've already had three."

"Coffee?"

Doc Hammon had discovered that he had been drinking coffee again and strictly forbade it. "Caffeine is the worst thing for an intestinal condition like yours," the doctor had said.

"Yes, I'd love some." Father James got up, took an apron from a peg alongside the pantry door and tied it around his waist. He always did the dishes when invited to anyone's house to dinner. Plunging his hands into the hot soapy water in search of the sponge, he said, "I wish things would get back to normal over at the rectory. I certainly can't expect you and the rest of the village to go on feeding Father Dennis and me indefinitely. I'm beginning to feel like George Benson, always showing up at mealtimes hoping for a handout."

"You could always fire Mrs. Norris," she reminded him, pouring water into the coffeemaker.

Father James lathered a soup bowl. "I don't see how. She's ruled over the rectory for nearly forty years. It would be like firing the Pope."

Always the pragmatist, she rebutted: "Then you'll have to settle on your friends taking pity on you and inviting you to dinner more often."

"I suppose."

"Now, leave those for later," she said, moving back to the kitchen table where she had placed a freshly baked pumpkin pie. "I want to ask your advice about something."

Father James dried his hands on his apron and walked over as the nun took out an envelope from a sideboard drawer and placed it on the table. "I'd like you to read this through and tell me what you think."

"What is it?"

"Sister Ruth, over in Granby, wants to start up a soup kitchen. She's sent these cost projections over. I told her I'd look them over."

"I hope she succeeds," he said, pulling out his chair again. "Granby could use all the help it can get. The folks over there have had a rough time since the pharmaceutical plant went bankrupt. I read that more than half the people in town had worked there."

"There was more about it on the five o'clock news tonight," she said. "They have a secret star witness who has been placed in protective custody. Apparently, whoever it is can testify that the board of directors has been diverting research money from government grants for months and channeling it into private accounts in the Bahamas."

The nun handed the priest a manila envelope. "I'm afraid that there will be many people in Granby left homeless this winter because of a few people's greed."

"I've already offered Father Stephen over at Our Lady of Sorrows our support. I brought the matter up at our parish council meeting last night. Ethel Johnson plans to start a clothing drive, and my old friend Jeff Hayden will gather together a team of people who will help with job placement, economic development, things like that."

"But in the interim, someone has to see that these people are fed and sheltered. That's why this soup kitchen is so important," the nun reminded him.

"Has Sister Ruth found a suitable location?" He opened the envelope and pulled out several forms.

"Yes, as a matter of fact, she has. A large building on Main Street that used to be a restaurant. There's a good-size kitchen with a wall abutting an interior room that she plans to take down to make a serving area. Lots of room for dozens of tables and chairs. All she needs is another fifty thousand dollars to help with the purchase of new appliances and she could be opened within the month. She's asked for our prayers."

"Fifty thousand, you say?" Father James asked smiling, feeling a rush of excitement. He pushed the papers aside and reached into his coat pocket.

"What are you grinning about?"

"The mysterious ways of our Lord."

"What . . . ?"

He handed her a check. "Apparently, this is for you."

"For me? What is it?"

He sat back in his chair and watched Mother Superior's face as she read the amount.

"I can't believe it! It's a check for fifty thousand dollars. But how . . . ??? Who . . . ???

"Nellie Anderson." He laughed. "She gave it to me just a few hours ago and said that I was to give it away when I saw a need." Lord, how he loved being a priest!

"But how would Nellie get fifty thousand dollars to give away?"

"Panda Publishers has just bought her first children's book and given her an advance for several more. This is her way of sharing the Lord's blessing with others."

"I don't know what to say, but I need to call her right away."

"You might want to put that call off until tomorrow."

"Oh?"

"Nellie should be the one telling you this, but . . . she's accepted

Harry Clifford's proposal of marriage. They're with Barry Hornibrook right now, planning their wedding reception."

"The hotel is finally going to be finished?"

"Yes, now that the money has been returned." Father James took a quick sip from his coffee cup. "The subcontractors have been paid in full and are already back on the job. Barry says that, with any luck, the hotel will be up and running by Christmas. In fact, he's already planning a big Christmas party for the whole town, complete with fireworks." That reminded him, he had better make certain the Galligan twins were well monitored that night.

"I'm so happy for him."

"Yes, I am, too. He's a good man." Father drained his cup, then got up and poured himself another. Hang his intestines, some things in life were worth suffering for.

Mother Superior stared at the check, her blue eyes filling with tears. "I'm still so flabbergasted. It's the exact amount Sister Ruth needs."

Father James's smile widened. "It's just a coincidence," he teased.

"There are no coincidences where God is concerned," she said, sounding just like Sister Regina Francis.

"I agree. Won't this make a great story for one of my sermons? It's just another example of the power of prayer." Father James never ceased to marvel at the miracles that flowed forth into people's lives once they handed their problems over to God.

The nun gazed around the room. "Like the creation of this home."

"You and the sisters should be very proud of what you've accomplished. This home is just that . . . a home. It's warm and inviting and filled with God's love. You have given your residents quite a wonderful gift."

"God provided the idea and the capital," she insisted, "we simply put everything into place."

"I wish you had more openings, though." He grew reflective. "Yesterday, I got a call from my old mentor, Monsignor Casio, in New York City. He's thinking of retiring soon and is looking for a place to live. It would be nice to have him nearby."

"God works in mysterious ways. You never know what He might do," Mother Superior said with a twinkle in her eye. "Who knows, by then we just might have an opening."

"Is someone moving out?"

"No, but we are thinking about expanding. The third floor is still unfinished and could easily accommodate four or five more bedrooms. Of course, we would have to redesign the fire escape and the elevator shaft would have to be reconstructed. Then, we're thinking about buying the house next door . . ."

He threw up a hand. "Wait a minute. I thought you told me that you're already overextended and that expansion was impossible. Where will you get the money?"

Now it was her turn to smile. "I want to tell you about a rather unorthodox fund-raising plan the sisters have devised. They are calling it Rent-a-Nun. Sister Joanna has put it up on our Web page and it's already gotten quite a lot of interest. In fact, a television crew is coming here tomorrow to do an interview with Sister Claire. Here's how it works . . ."

It was dark before Father James left Mother Superior and the nuns to place a call to Sister Ruth. Their silhouettes were visible from the sidewalk as they alighted around the front rooms with large notepads and pens, talking eagerly about the project in Granby and the renovations upstairs. He could almost guarantee there would be little sleep tonight.

The soft dusting of snow covered the road, which sparkled like glitter under the light of the streetlamps—Victorian-style, black wrought-iron fixtures that curved gracefully overhead. The scene stole him away to the carefree winters of his childhood, and suddenly he was overwhelmed with the urge to run and slide on the snow-covered street. Why not? Checking to make certain no one was watching, he backed up several paces, then ran as fast as he could, locked his feet and slid across the snow.

It was pure magic as he sailed past lit-up houses, riding the magic carpet of snow. Only once did he start to flail and, for a fleeting second, feared that he might break another bone. But he quickly regained his balance and, with the grace of a figure skater, glided neatly all the way to the entrance of the town green without further incident. He jumped up on the curb and tipped an imaginary hat to the impromptu skating rink, then turned and began the short walk home.

The kitchen lights were on in the rectory, which meant that Father Dennis had returned from dinner and was experimenting again with another of Mrs. Curtis's dishes. His stomach still had room for a sampling. Maybe Father Dennis was baking another pie. Father James loved pie.

Chimney smoke drifted from the home a few doors down. It had recently been sold to a young single mother of twin daughters, Valerie Kilbourne. Father James had met them last Sunday after Mass. Nice family . . . but a hard job for any single mother, and the twins seemed like quite a handful. He wondered if Dorsetville could possibly handle another riotous set of twins.

A few houses down, another home had been purchased and newly painted. A single middle-aged man had bought it. Now, what was his name? Reminded him of a piece of clothing. Cummerbund? Oh, well, he'd ask Mrs. Norris.

The snow began to thicken and his eyes searched the town green for Molly's bench. This was no night for her to be out in the cold. But Molly's bench was empty, her bags gone. Only her newly decorated shopping cart remained, parked to one side. Knowing the kind people in this town, Father James was certain that someone had come along earlier and taken her home. More than likely, Molly was now safe and warm in someone's guest room, sipping hot chocolate. He'd make inquiries tomorrow.

He turned back just as the wind increased and the temperature began to drop. It was a good night to be inside by a roaring fire. He looked up. Smoke was coming from the chimney at the rectory. Apparently, Father Dennis had read his mind.

He stood in the center of the green and let his eyes scan the homes across the street, now softly dusted with snow: the retirement home, whose lower windows were ablaze with warm light; the Congregational church, now swathed in blue plastic tarps, the outside sheathing to be installed tomorrow. At St. Cecilia's, all the scaffolding had been removed. The church still looked as misshapen and out of place as it had since its inception, but at least now it looked tidy.

Father James let out a sigh of relief. Finally, the restoration was complete, although he didn't know if he would ever get used to the raspberry-painted walls in the church's basement. It made him feel as though he were standing in the middle of a rather large ice-cream milkshake. Oh, well, at least Mrs. Norris and Arlene Campbell had finally managed to agree on a color. He figured their choice was a small price to pay to have peace reestablished between the two women.

Father James paused to watch the lights from Main Street brighten the sky, a fitting backdrop for the snowflakes that danced and whirled, carefree and gay, unconcerned for where they landed. It seemed that they trusted that wherever God placed them, they would find welcome in Dorsetville.

The midnight bus pulled up to the curb. Not many people were traveling on a night like tonight, so the bus was empty when Molly stepped in and handed the driver her ticket. She wore an old pair of elastic-waisted, polyester pants and three oversize sweaters. Her other outfits had been left near the clothing box in front of the Salvation Army. Molly always traveled light.

"Looks like you're my only passenger," the driver said cheerfully, stamping her ticket.

Molly nodded and just smiled.

The driver turned off the interior lights and adjusted the rearview mirror as he headed out of the parking lot and toward the interstate. The windshield wipers swiped back and forth with a soft rhythm.

He caught Molly's eyes reflected in a mirror overhead and offered, "We won't run into much traffic on a night like tonight. I expect we should get into Manchester around two o'clock. Essex by three, three-thirty."

Molly didn't reply.

"Is that where you're going, ma'am?"

Molly took the rosary out of her sweater pocket and placed it neatly on her lap. The blue glass beads glowed softly in the darkness as though lit from within by some inner light. It gave off a soft hum.

"No, I'm going to the end of the line," she said. "To Granby."